JOURNEY OF THE LOST AND DAMNED

LILIAN HORN

Text copyright © 2024 by Lilian Horn

Cover Illustration © Jon Stubbington
Distributed by Blackstone Publishing

ISBN: 978-1-998076-07-9
Ebook: 978-1-998076-08-6

FIC009100 FICTION / Fantasy / Action & Adventure
FIC009030 FICTION / Fantasy / Historical
FIC009120 FICTION / Fantasy / Dragons & Mythical Creatures

#JourneyoftheLostandDamned

Follow Rising Action on our socials!
Twitter: @RAPubCollective
Instagram: @risingactionpublishingco
Tiktok: @risingactionpublishingco

JOURNEY OF THE LOST AND DAMNED

CHAPTER ONE

THE TRADE

A dispirited clang from the clocktower echoed over Kvenchester's damp cobblestone streets. A cat chased a rat that disappeared into the dark corner, sandwiched between sagging two-story buildings with crumbling brick mortar. The streets were lit only by the scant rays of the cloud-covered full moon.

Captain Rosanne Drackenheart flicked open her pocket watch; the hands pointed to one o'clock, as the clock tower had announced. Eyes low beneath a wide-brimmed cavalier hat adorned with a broken feather, she swept her gaze up and down the deserted street. This was the meeting place, wasn't it? Rosanne bit her lower lip and tapped her foot.

A distant hollow clang of metal captured her attention. Pushing off the brick wall against which she had been leaning, she scanned the road, searching for the noise source. From behind her, the sound of quick shuffling feet and rustling coats arose.

"Of course, it's a trap," Rosanne sighed. She pressed her lips together, aware of her shallow breath, and fought for calm. Blinking, she allowed her inner turmoil to dissolve as her hand swept over the cold steel concealed within her vest.

Half a dozen men, armed with batons, knives, and one-handed flint-locks, grinned at her with cruel smiles as they converged on her from both sides of the street, trapping her between them and an alley blocked off by a pile of garbage. Rosanne drew her dagger, displaying it at her side.

"Come now, sweetheart." the man in the lead, clothed in a worn leather jacket, gestured towards her weapon. "Join us quietly, and you won't get hurt."

Rosanne let her gaze drift from him to a red-cheeked man reeking of spirits, standing by his side. A third man flashed a grin, revealing two rows of brown teeth.

Rosanne wrinkled her nose. "Have you boys lost your way? The near-est tavern is by the docks." She placed a hand on her hip, nodding in the direction from which they had come. Leather-Jacket and Red-Cheeks' hands twitched, seemingly itching for the opportunity to land the first strike.

"Gunny wants to see ye," Brown-Teeth growled, spitting a sizeable droplet onto the ground.

"Gentlemen, please." She placed a hand over her chest and tilted her head to one side. "Your employer was supposed to meet me here. He should have sent a note if there were changes to the location. I'm hardly prepared to meet him elsewhere. For my safety, you understand."

A crow-haired young man smacked his baton into his open palm, fixing her with an unquestionably intimidating leer. The prominence of her cheeks grew as her smile widened, but it was devoid of any pleas-antries. She couldn't shake the stiffness in her face as she realised how monumentally screwed she was against six armed men. Closing her eyes, she offered a silent prayer to whoever would allow her to beat the crap out of these bastards.

"Tell Gunny his *request* has been denied." She hardened her mild-mannered tone and sharpened her gaze.

The men stared at the unimpressive length of her chosen weapon. Uncontrollable chuckles escaped their breaths. Leather-Jacket wasn't smiling. "Boss said we have to deliver."

"Oh, for Terra's sake," she muttered under her breath as the men closed in. Red-Cheeks motioned towards the dagger, indicating that she should surrender it. With the hilt of her sheathed dagger, Rosanne whacked his wrist. He clutched his hand with a gasp and stepped back while the others advanced. Rosanne evaded a swinging pipe from Brown-Teeth and deftly slapped her palm against his ear. Dazed, he clutched at his ear, but Rosanne quickly seized his jacket and gave a forceful shove, sending him tumbling into two of his colleagues. Crow brought his baton down hard on her thigh. An explosion of pain blossomed in her side, forcing a cry from Rosanne. As she fell, she grabbed the baton with one hand, pulling Red-Cheeks down with her, and slammed the hilt of her dagger into his forehead. He crumpled to the ground in a pile of writhing movements, blood spurting from his nose. Leather-Jacket seized her by the vest, hoisting her to her feet as if she weighed no more than air. Rosanne kicked out between his legs, and Leather-Jacket squealed as he toppled over.

A brief flash of light sparked behind her eyes, quickly replaced by encroaching darkness. As her vision swam with dizzying movements, she threw out her hands, only to slam onto the ground. Their coarse laughter echoed around her. Rosanne tried to stand, but confusion and pain sapped her strength, leaving her powerless. The men threw a musty hemp sack over her head and dragged her between two heavyset men. Head spinning, suffocating from inhaling the hemp's dust, Rosanne ceased her struggle.

She realised that she should've brought backup despite the meeting terms stipulating privacy. Her lieutenant, Farand, had always warned her about the lack of honour among people. Once again, he had been proven right at the worst possible time.

While feigning unconsciousness, she listened in on their evening plans. Her head throbbed, reminding her of when she had downed shots in Georgetown after a dare on her thirtieth birthday. "Never again," she had vowed. That was until her spring trip into the Grey Veil. After that, she was plagued with a persistent headache, as frequently as she glimpsed the bottom of the whiskey bottles. But the current pain stemmed from different reasons, and she wasn't even inebriated. She had been sober for quite some time, amassing her wits and courage, all trampled by six twitchy bastards with a major in fist-fights. She would rather be at the inn or the bathhouse than deal with whatever came next. Yet, here she was, being dragged, on the tips of her shoes, into what sounded like the echoing cavern of a warehouse.

They shoved her into a wooden chair, their hands firm on her shoulders. With the hood yanked off, Rosanne coughed and stared, bleary-eyed, at the blue-white glare of an alchemical lamp. She blinked, clearing the dancing dust from her vision, and spat out a stray lock of hair.

A man sat in a high-backed chair, the light behind him, hands folded on an oak office table sparsely adorned save for a knife and a solitary, untouched red apple. Rosanne raised an eyebrow, questioning the implications of the scene—a snack or torture, which would it be? Squinting against the faint light, she discerned a pale-faced man in his early forties, his features concealed within the deep shadows.

"The famous Demon of the Sky, Captain Rosanne Drackenheart," he announced, his voice thrumming through the words like a harsh river. Rosanne could tell his gaze roamed from the broken feather that adorned her wide-brimmed cavalier lying on the floor to the skin-tight trousers tailored specifically for her. Leather-Jacket swiped the hat off the floor and placed it on her head with a reassuring pat.

Ignoring the throbbing pain in her head, she straightened her back and crossed one leg in front of the other. "My reputation precedes me. I'd have you know I prefer flowers and sugared fruits to your brutish thugs. Brandy, perhaps in front of a cozy fire."

His blue eyes crinkled at her obvious stalling. "The lady desires gifts in a transaction," he said, giving half a laugh.

"It sets the mood."

His eyes immediately hardened at Rosanne's stiff-faced, polite smile, the kind she wore whenever she had to deal with men who looked down on her. Regardless of which colony she frequented, men would invariably belittle her achievements, title notwithstanding. Might as well look like she's humouring them, even when she was a prisoner. However, the man's lips were as rigid as a stylus, and his scrutinising gaze resembled that of a buyer inspecting a racing horse before purchase. She let the falseness melt away, but the drumming in her head was still present. Screw this charade.

"I didn't come here to be inspected like merchandise. I am here to negotiate," she finally declared.

"Information pertaining to the southern colonies, I was told?" His tone remained businesslike.

"Trade routes of the southern Grey Veil, to be more precise, but you didn't hear that from me," Rosanne smiled with scarlet-painted lips. Was the effort even worth it after the beating she'd received?

"And then you show up to carry out said transaction without backup, muscle, or thought..."

Rosanne let go of an audible sigh. "I try to conduct my business honourably, but I'm not averse to violence should the situation necessitate it." She cast a glance at Red-Cheeks, who was nursing his broken nose. "Why you deemed it necessary to send half a legion to transact with a single woman is beyond me. Frankly, I feel you've overestimated me."

"Clearly, I expected something different. Yet, here you are, conducting business as usual, as if the head wound is the least of your concerns." The man turned his hand, palm-side up, in her direction—a gesture clearly indicative of her condition.

Rosanne fought the urge to touch the tender spot and remained silent. A sheen of sweat had formed on her face due to the creeping nausea. He was perceptive, or he was too familiar with his men's style of delivery.

The man, illuminated by a mysterious rim light, chuckled and leaned forward again, elbows on the table, hands loosely folded. "You may call me Gunny, Captain Drackenheart."

The man beside Gunny—bald and built like a fortress—relocated the alchemical lamp to the desk, presumably for effect, Rosanne surmised. She had envisioned a hooked nose or narrow, suspicious eyes, but Gunny proved to be so bland and unremarkable that she would forget his face the moment she looked away. Ashen hair, blue eyes, and composed features weren't what she had anticipated of the infamous gang boss of Kvenchester. The bodyguard gave him away, though.

Gunny swiped the apple from the table and sliced it with a knife, creating long strips of peeled red skin.

"I'm honoured to finally meet you, Gunny," Rosanne exclaimed, pushing aside the snack-based torture happening before her. A wave from Gunny had his men take a step back, and Rosanne rolled her shoulders. "Now, why did your thugs drag me here instead of honouring the appointed place? Is my word not good enough?"

He splayed his hands innocently. "You'll have to forgive my precaution, Captain. I only know your reputation for breaking things."

Rosanne flicked her eyes toward the man in the leather jacket. He returned her glance with a surly grimace.

"You are forgiven," Rosanne said and returned her attention to Gunny. "Now, that particular information that I seek, do you have it?"

Gunny let out a laugh. "Nothing bristles your fur, does it? You're on my turf, surrounded by my men, your crew nowhere in sight, and you have the balls to make demands?"

"Ovaries," she corrected, drawing a pause. When Gunny lifted an eyebrow, Rosanne let out an audible sigh. "They can take quite a beating, you know. But yes, I've weathered stormy days before. Your man gave me his word, which I under no circumstances thought of as naive, given your *reputation* as a businessman who honours his agreements. But it seems my trust was misplaced." Wrestling with the throbbing pain in her skull, she clicked her tongue in disappointment.

"Touché, Captain. You talk a good game. I like you." Gunny said, signalling his men to leave the warehouse. Only the tall, stone-faced guard remained at his side. How different would this meeting have been had she brought Farand along to match bulk with Gunny's henchman?

"Talk." Gunny sliced off a piece of the apple and popped it into his mouth.

Rosanne adjusted her hat, leaning forward to let her arms rest on her thighs. "I know a shortcut through the Grey Veil," she announced. A name that would give any sailor pause—a haunted, foggy hellscape plaguing the colonies since their inception. Nestled in the ocean between the east and the west, the Grey Veil acted as a barrier, permitting no one passage. Rosanne had ventured into its depths, and her discoveries left her craving more. No one had ever escaped its depths alive—except for her ship, the *MTS Red Queen*.

Gunny halted his peeling, his eyes revealing not surprise but intrigue, then suspicion.

"Lies," he scoffed.

"I arrived from Orvel across the Veil nigh two days ago. The trip took five days."

"Orvel is at *least* seventeen days travel around the Veil. You're telling me your ship has survived without means of navigation, inside the Veil, and escaped? Your tales are tall, Captain, but your wits have been lost with it."

The gleam in Rosanne's eyes was impossible to contain, capturing Gunny's attention. "Ever heard of the hangman's fruit native to Orvel? Hardy little thing, but it doesn't grow anywhere else. The fruit rots before it even grazes the first wisp of the southern Veil," she let her voice slow, almost thoughtfully, as she was delivering a point. Gunny's eyebrow shot up at this, yet he remained quiet. "That's why northerners favour potatoes." Unfastening the pouch from her belt, Rosanne tossed it onto the table. Gunny untied the leather string, upending the pouch into his hand. A single, plump hangman's fruit tumbled out, its skin still a vibrant purple. Having guarded the pouch as if her life depended on it, Rosanne nearly wept with joy at the sight of the fruit's unblemished, pristine skin. Gunny's questioning gaze shifted to Rosanne.

"Taste it," she prompted.

With a great deal of reservation, Gunny narrowed his eyes to thin slits. He didn't break eye contact as he brought the fruit to his lips and bit into it. Purple juice burst from the bite mark, staining the table. He chewed on the fruity meat, nodding his head.

"This side of the Veil has never seen a hangman's fruit. I haven't tasted one in years, yet its unique flavour remains unchanged," he said thoughtfully. He turned the fruit from side to side in his hand as though he couldn't quite believe it.

Silence stretched between them while Gunny's eyes scrutinised her face for any hint of a lie. Rosanne's smile held firm, extending to the corners of her eyes. She was confident she had him.

"Why such interest in my southern trade routes, Captain Drackenheart?" Gunny asked at length.

Rosanne straightened. "They skirt the Grey Veil. I heard one of your ships discovered a cluster of islands."

The leather cushion creaked as Gunny relaxed into it once again. "What of it? There's nothing there."

"I hear you've dubbed it the 'Wandering Isles,' and they haven't been spotted since," she pressed.

"Drunken tales picked up from the tavern, undoubtedly," he waved it off with a dramatic flick of his wrist.

Unfazed by his dismissal, she leaned in. "I want to hear all about it."

The barest twitch flashed across his brows. "What's it to you?"

"A secret route through the Veil in exchange for a location. I stay out of your business, and you stay out of mine."

Gunny licked his lips, then gestured to his aide at his side. The shadow-clad figure, moving like a living statue, slipped into an adjoining room, reappearing with a tube containing maps. Uncorking the tube, Gunny spread the map out on the desk. It detailed the southern central colonies, the arid deserts of eastern Ovrack, and the tropical islands along its coast in the Emerald Sea. About a day's travel west of Ovrack, three small islands were circled in black ink with a question mark.

"They were rich in anti-gravity minerals, hovering about two hundred metres above sea level." He pointed to a cluster of broken shorelines. "It would be a viable mining operation; however, like everything else coming from the Grey Veil, they vanished without a trace. You won't find them there."

"Perhaps not, but I'd like to try." She pulled out a thick stack of papers from within her vest, sliding them towards Gunny, who unfolded them with a keen eye. A look of scorn crossed his face, and he flicked dismissively through the papers spread on the table.

"Is this a joke?" They were covered with intricate drawings of a box-shaped mechanical device and a list of notes.

"Ah, I see your confusion." She turned the papers around and flattened them with her palms. "This device will help you navigate the Grey Veil. If you build it and follow these coordinates, you can enjoy all the hangman's fruit on this side of the Veil."

Gunny exhaled incredulously, his coiffed hair tumbling. He quickly slicked it back with his hand. "Do you realise what this means? If you provide me access across the Veil, there's no telling how the market will react. What if words get out that the *Red Queen* knows of safe crossing?"

Rosanne's eyes hardened. "The Grey Veil is never safe to cross, not even there. The risk might be lower, yet it persists. I simply provided you with a way to cut through the inconvenient routes."

"This information you're spreading, Captain, is dangerous. If a whisper reached the crown or the inquisition, you'll be in grave danger."

"And now you're in the know as well," she countered, unbothered by the indirect threats the crown had held over her head since the dawn of marine trade. Gunny's jaw danced with tension, and Rosanne knew he understood he had been trapped— and that anyone who had overheard was trapped, too.

"How do I know you're not conning me?" His fingers dug into the paper.

Throwing out her hands in resignation, Rosanne feigned shock. "And what have you given me in return? Some floating islands that no one cares for?"

Gunny's accusatory tone softened. "The costs greatly outweigh the benefits. What, Captain Drackenheart, would be so valuable that you're willing to share such secrets with me?"

Her mirth-filled gaze withered to unfaltering calm. "I find transoceanic trade of little value, yet I possess the means and opportunity. Your islands are of little value to you, yet you know of their whereabouts. It's a straightforward trade, Gunny. Are you interested in the secrets to crossing the Veil or not?"

His tongue flicked over his teeth, no doubt considering the benefits of this trade.

"We don't shoot our own," he concluded, extending his hand.

"We share the spoils from afar," Rosanne replied, shaking it.

"This secret will be well kept," he reassured. However, Rosanne's gaze flickered to his bodyguard. "Oh, him?" Gunny chuckled. The bodyguard opened his mouth and wiggled the stump of his tongue. "There aren't many who can speak here, Captain. Uphold your end of the deal, and I'll duly fulfil mine."

As she turned to leave, she gave Gunny a slight nod. "Don't forget to send me a gift in Valo when you return from Orvel. I am a whisky person," she winked, exiting the warehouse without hindrance.

Expectant eyes turned her way as Rosanne burst through the double doors of the trader's inn, where the crew of the *Red Queen* resided. With a thick folded paper between her fingers, she waved a hand and smirked. The tall figure of Lieutenant Farand Duplànte positioned himself next to her, awaiting news. His curls were cropped short and tight to his skull, and his sharp eyes were softened by the neutrality of his expression. He must have visited a barber during her absence. There wouldn't be any decent ones where they were going.

"We set sail," she announced to the room, her hand patting her vest as confusion crossed her face. "Dammit, I've lost my handkerchief. Farand, could I—"

Farand promptly retrieved a plain linen kerchief from his jacket and handed it to her. Rosanne wiped off the lipstick she had applied for the sole occasion of meeting Gunny. Realising it was a waste on a man as astute as him, she almost felt foolish, thinking he'd be as easily swayed by her charms as the rest. She knew she wouldn't need to do this again for a while and settled comfortably into that thought.

"And the trade?" Farand inquired.

"Not as smooth as I'd hoped, but I escaped with minor injuries," she said, massaging a bruised knuckle. Despite the discomfort, she flashed Farand a triumphant grin. "We'll be sharing the Devil's passage in the Veil."

Farand grunted, seemingly unable to keep his deeper undertone of displeasure to himself. "I hope this information is worth it," he remarked.

"We'll find out soon enough. How fast is our allotted route to Kantor from here?"

"Roughly three days if we cut through the Aster mountains. Nearly five if we opt for safer routes."

"The Aster mountains it is." She nodded, pleased with the plan. "Mr. Lyle!" she summoned.

A tall man, hair of salt and pepper and with a neatly trimmed moustache, stepped forward with an informal salute. His glasses glinted in the hearth's ember. "Ready to take off at any time," he replied promptly.

"Excellent," Rosanne blew an excited breath and searched the faces around her. "Pack your bags and get to the ship. We're leaving immediately."

With that, the crew scattered, each attempting to reach the door before the others. Once they'd left, Rosanne's enthusiasm wilted into a grim frown, and she turned to her lieutenant.

Observing this change, Farand folded his arms. "Anything amiss?"

"Where are our watch captains? They were both staying here, weren't they?" Rosanne questioned more than she inquired.

"I suspect they made their way to the tavern while your meeting dragged on."

Rosanne closed her eyes, her lips forming a thin line. "With emphasis on dragged, I assure you. Round up our crew and get them back to the ship. I've got maps to study before we leave." As she turned towards the door, Farand placed a firm hand on her shoulder. Rosanne's glare held a stern warning to not hold her too long, even if the man was twice her size and could stop her with both hands tied behind his back.

"Are you certain you want to go through with this?"

Rosanne sidestepped and brushed off a stray curl that fell across her face. "I got the last piece of the puzzle, Farand. I'm not letting this slip by like a ghost ship at night."

The man nodded, albeit a faint sigh of resignation escaped him. "I am only making sure we are ready to pursue this. Expanding our horizon isn't always a good thing."

"Come now, Farand. We stopped believing we'd sail off the edge of the world ages ago. We haven't spent all summer mapping wind currents to give up now. With this," Rosanne said, waving the map, "we can delve deeper into the secrets of the Grey Veil. It might even lead us to the origin of whatever takes our ships." Her lieutenant appeared uncertain but remained silent. "Do you know why Thompson excluded coordinates or measurements in his work?" Rosanne prompted.

Farand shook his head.

"Because the island is too massive to simply be nothing. That or my father ordered Thompson to skimp on the details. Hard to tell which."

The lieutenant's expression was replaced with that of resignation. Despite her lack of foresight concerning unexpected obstacles, Farand never lost faith. However, Rosanne knew her words didn't convince him this time. Instead of questioning her endlessly, he simply said: "I will take your word for it."

"Come on, Farand." She elbowed him. "Have I ever let you down?"

"One too many times, I fear." He flashed her a smile that softened his sharp jawline. "What about your better half then?"

Rosanne stuffed the map back in her vest. "Antony won't ask questions."

"Still. For him to look the other way whenever we conduct our usual business seems..."

"Naive?" she reflected, hoping that wasn't the answer, although her decisions had been less than mindful recently. Embarking into the Grey Veil, especially after her recent experience, was certainly one of them.

"Dangerous or perhaps shortsighted," he concluded, his tone firm but considerate of her current mindset. Farand truly knew how to read a room, and Rosanne was grateful.

"He won't betray our trust merely because he's on leave from the Royal Defense of Aerospace. Besides, he's not here for the ship but for me. I owe him that trust, especially after he saved our backsides."

"I'd say," Farand chuckled, "this might be the ballsiest move you've ever made, Captain. And I say that with reservation."

"Ah!" Rosanne lifted a finger, her face alight with humour. "This is the second time tonight I've had to remind people that I have ovaries of steel." Farand's polite smile didn't give way to laughter as he looked positively confused and out of the loop as to what had transpired in the warehouse earlier.

The brief silence ushered in an intrusion of doubt once more as a solemn look swept across her face. "I want this to work, Farand—for him and for me. I can't afford to lose him like I lost my head last spring. Antony is my lifeline, and I'd appreciate your support in this. Perhaps after this journey, I can finally leave that bloody island behind."

His warm brown eyes landed on her, sympathetic in their study of her vulnerability. "A word of warning then, as a friend to another: Guard your heart closer than your career."

Rosanne feigned a dramatic gasp, clasping a hand over her chest. "Is that a hint of doubt I hear, Farand?"

"Just a smidgen." He echoed her mirth with a rumbling chuckle. "I'd better fetch our watch captains before they find the bottom of their bottles."

"Good shout."

The crew had made a beeline for the tethered galleon at the docks, leaving the streets deserted. Ships weren't permitted to depart from the towering skyports post-midnight due to low visibility and other arbitrary regulations enforced under the queen's skytrade monopoly. Consequently, Rosanne had done the next best thing – landing her ship in the water. Once Farand had left the inn, she retrieved her bag filled with modest belongings and proceeded towards her ship. After Gunny's men had ambushed her, she kept a vigilant eye for potential threats, wary of the gang boss reneging on his word. Yet the alleys were empty, the buildings dark, presenting no threats—apart from her mounting anxiety.

Two city guards stood at attention on either side of the gangplank leading to the *Red Queen*. Clutching muskets and swords at their sides, they had safeguarded the ship from street urchins and drunkards that night. Rosanne passed the men a small pouch of coins, after which they resumed patrolling around the docks.

In the distance, the bell tolled thrice. Lingering by the gangplank, Rosanne searched for the mountain of a man who would be invisible in the darkness if not for his two pale companions. Where was Farand?

Antony DiCroce, the Captain of the *Arctic Pride*, emerged from below deck, dressed in civilian splendour—a leather jacket and neutral cotton. He rested his elbows on the rail next to her. "Is Mr. Duplànte late?" His accent gave her no hint of worry, yet his eyes were as riveted to the streets as hers.

"I'm sure it's nothing." Rosanne drew in the chill air, letting calm permeate her being before exhaling a smoky wisp that quickly twirled out of existence.

"Yet, your unease is palpable," Antony observed, nodding to her foot tapping rhythmically against the deck. Despite herself, Rosanne offered a smile and moved closer, examining him. He had trimmed his shoulder-length black hair for the southern journey, and his olive skin had taken on a tanned hue during the summer. She felt a fleeting pang of envy, considering how quickly she tended to burn, a trait inherited from her ancestors hailing from the central colonies where the sun was piercing and relentless for five months a year. His amber eyes met hers, a silent interaction that soothed the anxious rhythm in her chest.

"I would like to leave this town before anything happens. Everything has gone well so far. A little too well, suspiciously so, and the silence is unnerving," Rosanne eventually expressed.

Antony's hand gently covered hers. "You are never one to accept the blessings of calm," he remarked.

His thumb glided over her knuckles, a warm and comforting gesture. Contrary to her previous experiences, it wasn't suffocating or sweaty as she had always imagined it.

Lifting their entwined hands, he placed a soft kiss on the back of hers. "You used to look at me with such scorn whenever I did this," he whispered.

A grimace formed on Rosanne's face as a blush tinted her cheeks. "I used to at many things," she admitted, "but circumstances have changed, and I believe I've grown to favour such gestures."

He appeared to contemplate her words, turning them over in his mind.

Rosanne licked her lips. "We're so close, Antony. I know this journey will uncover some secrets of the Grey Veil. I just..."

Antony turned to Rosanne and drew her in, leaving only a small breathing room between them. She flitted her gaze down, anchoring it to the buttons of his open leather jacket, finding it easier to look at than his eyes.

"Is this too much still?" He chuckled despite the evident disappointment in his voice. Rosanne shook her head, but not in denial. "No..." She squeezed his hands, grappling with her thoughts. Taking a shaky breath, she lifted her hazel eyes to meet his amber ones. "I must be out of my damn mind looking for another island after what happened last spring." Though not technically a lie, they weren't the honest words she wanted to share.

"You were ill-prepared back then. Your fates will be turned from the redundant precautions you've taken. You haven't spent the entire summer planning this expedition to doubt yourself now." Drawing her into a comforting embrace, he planted a gentle kiss atop her head.

Exhaling a sigh, Rosanne buried herself against his chest.

A clamour of voices by the dock caught their attention. Rounding a warehouse came Farand dragging a bladdered Creedy by the upper arm with the assistance of a slightly less intoxicated Dalia on Creedy's left. The senior watch captain turned to Farand, his voice resonating powerfully enough to carry across to the ship where Rosanne and Antony stood observing them.

"I tell ya, Mister Duplànte, no one heard me talk about yer mission. I swear!" Creedy slurred, his thinning hair flopping as he stumbled. Dalia promptly clasped a hand over his mouth, her gaze sifting between the streets like a vigilant crane.

"Keep talking, and there won't be a mission," she hissed.

Creedy let out a gormish laugh and waved a hand in front of Farand. "Didya know Dalia is the best ropemaker in the Central United Colonies?"

"I am aware, Mr. Creedy. She's part of our crew, remember?"

Creedy recoiled in surprise. "She is? Betcha I could tie that knot quicker than she can say 'I do.' Ah, you're right here."

The tall woman rolled her eyes.

They reached the gangplank. Creedy, having surrendered to his drunkenness, let himself be hauled aboard, a scene reminiscent of when Gunny's goons had dragged Rosanne to the warehouse.

"He talked?" Rosanne questioned with alarm.

"Nothing important, Captain. He shuts up easily as long as there's ale in his mug," Dalia replied in passing, helping Creedy down the stairs to the hammocks. Rosanne turned to Antony, a relieved smile on her face.

"That is everyone accounted for. Rouse the night shift. I don't want to risk using the bell."

Antony acknowledged with a nod and vanished below deck. Within a minute, the yawning skeleton crew filed to their posts, ready for orders. She stalked up the stairs to the quarterdeck as quickly as her heeled boots allowed her to without running, eager to be gone from this town. She lifted the intercom from the instrument panel, pushing the side button to open a line to the engine room.

"We're ready to leave, Mr. Higgs. Fire up the anti-grav."

Static interference crackled from the intercom. Rosanne rapped it hard a few times in her hand before redoing the call. A young woman's voice sparked at the other end.

"Higgs has turned in for the night, ma'am. Gavin and I are on duty." Second engineer Ida responded.

"Copy that, Miss Simonsen. Fire her up."

The street adjacent to the tavern—where Farand had unearthed Creedy and Dalia— erupted in activity. A group of men swivelled their heads around, searching until they pointed towards the moored *Red Queen*.

"Shit." Rosanne hurriedly toggled switches on the instrument panel's navigation board, rushing through the pre-flight checks.

"We've got company, Simonsen. Light a fire under your asses and get us in the air," she urged into the intercom, letting the device slap back against the panel. Dalia staggered up the stairs to the quarterdeck.

"Evening, Captain. Hwang's in charge of the night shift and ... oh fuck." Her half-drunk stare sobered at the sight of the men hurrying toward them.

"Friends of yours?" Rosanne asked.

Dalia offered a wry smile. "Creedy might've let slip that we were on to something big and that he lost a hundred and fifty pieces to the cards."

Rosanne opened the channel for the aethersails to conduct power to the offline thruster engine despite being in the water. Time was pressing, and the mob was drawing closer. Safety be damned if it got them out of there. "I warned you all to be careful. Money draws attention!"

"I didn't think Creedy brought that much! I am just as surprised as you are, Captain," Dalia exclaimed, turning to the skeleton crew. "Skip the pre-flight checks! Loosen the ropes, secure the plank, and let's get the hell out of here!"

The men cheerfully chimed, "Aye!" and scattered to their posts.

Water sloshed aside as the circular ports of anti-gravity tech lining the *Red Queen*'s hull activated, creating a protective buffer separating the ship from the gravity's tether. Deckhands released the ropes anchoring the ship to Dock 18 and hurried aboard, plank in tow.

A surge of people leapt from the dock, attempting to grasp the *Red Queen's* railing, bobbing in the low tide. Rosanne yanked a lever and tilted the wheel towards her, lifting the massive galleon free from sea level. A pair of thugs clung stubbornly to the railing, shouting their protests. Senior able seaman Hwang clobbered one man over the head with a bat just as he came aboard. The man staggered, flipped over the railing, and splashed into the waters with a dramatic cry. Dalia kicked fingers encircling the peg, and the second man disappeared with a panicked yelp.

"Cleared!" Hwang called from the main deck.

Rosanne let out a puff of air, relieved to have avoided that confrontation.

The whir of the thruster port covers uncoupling from the panels and sliding into their compartments at the ship's sides reached her ears. Moments later, the instrument board's lights flickered green, and the sails, in their hexagonal beauty, shimmered white in the moonlight.

Rosanne spun the wheel, the hiss of the *Red Queen's* fine thrusters humming as the ship pivoted.

21

With the sky clear and the two-disk skyport closed for the night, Rosanne didn't have to request take-off clearance, or deal with the following confusion when a ship needed to be airborne from the marina, a feature unique to the *Red Queen*.

A fog bank loomed over the surrounding forests and hills—the perfect cover to slip out of the city unnoticed. Operating on low power, the *Red Queen's* rear-mounted thruster panels emitted faint blue flames—easily lost against the backdrop of a star-filled sky. With the moon in its waning phase, they vanished in the blink of an eye.

CHAPTER TWO

VETTING THE PLAN

Mid-autumn in Bunnsboroux was a sweltering affair. Despite being merely a hop, skip, and a turn across the bay south of Noval, the woodlands remained untouched by human intervention. Rosanne swatted a mosquito into oblivion, one that had been buzzing around her with its lamenting cello piece.

Farand handed her a list of names alongside a stack of resumés, which she perused at leisure. Names, experience, education, nationality, language proficiency—her lieutenant's meticulous notes filled the papers to their edges. With a significant secret at stake, Rosanne had to be selective about the number of positions. With the promise of work, food, and shelter, the silence of desperate men was easily bought. While the rest of the crew revelled in their sizable cut from last spring's escapades in the Baltansea, Rosanne had invested her share into upgrading equipment. Even after cashing in the insurance policy—claimed due to piracy—the damage to the *Red Queen* and the loss of goods had the ship's treasury scraping the bottom. To exacerbate their problems, they had lost Iban Vasilyev, a landman in his first year aboard the *Red Queen*, to the storms of the Grey Veil; it was a loss and persistent guilt she felt. One would always be too many. His brother, Kristoff, remained under her command. Surprisingly, despite the tragedy, he chose not to return home after losing Iban. Instead, the young man had told her he felt closer to his brother when working on the *Red Queen*, a bittersweet sentiment Rosanne understood. Plus, he needed the money. A point she didn't argue against.

"This man," Rosanne handed Farand the paper. "Able seaman in the Navy despite four years' experience. Why?"

He flipped the page over and read his notes on the back. "If memory serves, they passed him up for promotion because of paternity leave, and then the economic crisis hit Bunnsboroux last season."

Her gaze narrowed. "Did he wear a wedding band?"

"None that I could see."

"Sounds like a bullshit then. Plus, he has assault and battery to his name. We have enough of those already What about this one?" She showed him.

"Fifteen years serving aboard *S.S. Queen Mary*—"

"We're *not* hiring anyone who served the crown's flagship, no matter how desperate they may seem."

Farand promptly crossed out the name from his notebook with an audible scratch of his pencil.

Rosanne continued. "How about this one?" She brought out another piece of paper and read from it. "Five years working on a Cintechan schooner, but no qualification papers and not a dime to his name. How did he seem to you?"

"Mr. Isaac Kavanaugh? Mid-thirties, in decent health, but a tad on the lean side. Found him at the docs with the other ragged sailors, holding a sign that read 'boat-work." He illustrated with air quotes.

She snorted a laugh. "He literally held a sign reading, 'Will sail for money?'"

Farand pinched his lips together in a poor attempt to suppress his chuckle. "He seems earnest and desperate enough. Speaks Angelsk and Cintech well, understandable in poor Beufranc and a few words of Novalian. Well-mannered, too."

"Drinker?"

"More sober than when Creedy was born."

Rosanne snickered. "Did you ask him about the Veil?"

"Asked, grilled, and vetted. He served a ship notorious for sailing outside the regular trade routes in the Central United Colonies, or so he claims. Couldn't find work due to his ship being sacked by the RDA and no formal papers of servitude outside of his work permit."

Nodding, Rosanne gave the paper one more glance. "Place him under Dalia. Creedy's too temperamental, and I won't have any of his nonsense on this voyage." Her steely gaze met his tranquil brown ones. "No squabbles, not even a frown. The first sign of trouble lands you in the brig. I'm done finding creative ways to punish the crew, at least for this voyage."

"What about childish name-calling?" Farand's teasing tone was barely concealed under his breath, which drew a smile from her.

"I'll allow it."

"I'll let the crew know." Farand nodded, seemingly pleased with the new policy, although Rosanne could tell he was relieved to escape detention duty.

"Before we roll out this wonderful no-tolerance policy to the crew, what did you offer the candidates during the interview?"

Unfazed by this, Farand replied without missing a beat. "I played it by ear and asked for their preference: cheap beer to those who asked for alcohol and coffee to those who couldn't 'possibly' impose on my wallet."

"What did you buy, Mr. Kavanaugh?"

"Coffee."

"How did he react?"

"As if he'd tasted the elixir of the gods."

Rosanne nodded, looking satisfied. "Give the man new clothes if needed. Wait, can we even budget for that?" She searched for the budget ledger kept in a locked drawer, but Farand beat her to it.

"I believe we've got some spare uniforms from last spring's shopping spree," he said.

Stretching from her chair, Rosanne let out a satisfied sigh along with the pops and cracks of her elbow joints. "What would I do without you? You always seem to beat me at my own game these days. I'd say the Grey Veil trips have done you good."

Farand remained quiet as a guilty smile crept over his lips. The brief silence prompted reflection of doubt creeping into Rosanne's mind, and she said: "Do you think following the southern wind current will guide us to the wandering isles?"

Farand's thoughtful expression revealed his doubts. The man was known to question his doubts at times, but he was never known to hold fast to them, sometimes even doubting his own indecision. And considering the missions and the treasures they'd garnered from their successful stint in the Veil, it was wise to heed both. "Considering what we've learned from the Grey Veil, the unchanging wind currents, and that hidden equipment you've got." He nodded towards the carpet in the middle of her office, indicating the Geographical Positioning Tracker they'd snagged from *The Retribution*. That little piece of technology was the only reason they could navigate the Grey Veil; without it, this would all be for naught. "The logic is sound. Higgs' instruments have reinforced what we know and have learned. But if I am honest ..." Farand paused with a deep, thoughtful frown. "I do not know."

"Your faith in me is truly commendable," she said, her voice dripping with sarcasm.

"It's as much about faith as it is about logic. Your ideas may seem mad, but you always deliver. The crew's hungering for more."

"We haven't wasted our summer for nothing then." Rosanne rubbed her face, then sat up suddenly, thinking. "Where do the wind currents flow at the coast of Ovrack?"

Farand marched over to the shelves, home to hundreds of map tubes, and fished out a specific one. The map was marked as featuring a Novalian coastal town. Yet, as Farand unfurled the paper, instead of meandering coastal lines, the tremendous undefined blob penned in as the Grey Veil was in its place. He traced a finger over the location of Captain Drackenheart's request and let out a sound of affirmation. "The wind blows counterclockwise northbound. It veers west, just south of the passage we crossed to Orwell. As for the southern wind currents, they're mere guesswork."

Rosanne scanned the map and nodded. "We're off to Ovrack then. We dive into the Eastern wind current and let's see where the winds blow."

Farand nodded in agreement.

Unable to hide her excitement, Rosanne burst into a small hop-skip and a fist-clenching dance. Once she regained her semi-calm demeanour, she turned to Farand, who chuckled at her infectious enthusiasm. "Let's inform the watch captains and engineers."

As he rolled up the Thompson map, Farand paused and looked at her. "You should tell Captain DiCroce first. I'm sure he's eager to know where this unofficial romantic getaway of yours is headed."

Lingering in the doorway, Rosanne nodded with a sheepish smile. "You're right. He rarely crosses my mind when we're on the job. It's so hard to keep track of folks who aren't part of the crew."

"All part and parcel of the domesticated captain's wife handbook, isn't it?"

A smile spread across Rosanne's face at Farand's joviality. "Me or Antony?"

"I'll let you two figure that out."

Rosanne left behind a trail of laughter as she departed.

Rosanne found Antony on the quarterdeck, deep in fervent conversation with Watch Captain Creedy. Alarm bells rang in her mind, suspecting another tussle between men, their primal instinct pushing them to assert dominance. Yet, when she saw Creedy's vigorous pointing, she found herself relaxing. The man only waved fists and bared teeth when he itched for a fight.

"Apologies for the interruption, gentlemen. Might I borrow Captain DiCroce, Mr. Creedy?"

"All yours, Captain." Creedy waved them off and resumed his duties.

"Aren't you shining like the Eastern star in the summer night," Antony noted. As she pulled him aside, Rosanne found it impossible to contain her grin.

"We've got a promising lead on the islands, but we'll need the right wind currents to get there. I'm so excited I can't stand still!"

"That's fantastic news!"

Rosanne shushed him and dropped her voice to a whisper. "We're holding a meeting later, but until then, don't tell a single soul. If words get out, we could attract unwanted attention or company. Again." She watched Creedy and Dalia exchanging friendly banter on the main deck; the two watch captains as thick as thieves, as usual. She hadn't forgotten Creedy's loose lips in Queensland.

Antony assured her with a not-so-subtle wink.

"Now you've got to tell me what had Creedy so excited."

"Fascinating fellow!" he exclaimed. "I asked about the new sails, and the man gushed about the improved technology and energy output of the design. Frankly, I'm a bit envious, but the sails wouldn't fit the engine model of the *Arctic Pride* anyway, so I'll savour it here while I have the chance."

Rosanne practically glowed with pride. "Given what our last voyage did to our sails, a double trim was the least I could do."

"And costly, I imagine. Where did you find it?"

"The RDA's scrapyard in Kvenchester has an impressive array of cutting-edge aero-technology We caught ourselves a bargain."

"A leftover sail sale, was it?" Antony mused.

Rosanne let out a chuckle.

She watched his gaze drift towards the skies, a light of realisation drawing on his face. "So, that's why I keep seeing ships with mismatched parts stranded on top of the mountains in Noval," he mused. Rosanne had come across quite a few of those, especially in Noval. Aethersail technology performed poorly in the cold.

"It's important to check the maintenance log and have top-notch engineers who know their stuff. If you're planning to skimp on the equipment, at least hire folk who can build steam engines out of barrels and a straw."

"I've always wondered how you did it, Rosanne. You come back from a near-death voyage, somehow have funds to overhaul your ship, spend months out of work, and then rally the crew for another round of insanity." If this query had come from anyone outside the ship's crew, Rosanne would have questioned their motives, but Antony, with a shake of his head, appeared resigned to being kept in the dark.

"These economic times call for drastic measures," she said.

Antony allowed his gaze to drift over the sailors' new clothes and fresh shoes. "I'm sure that's what it is."

"Listen," Rosanne said gently, tucking a stray curl behind her ear. "I've got a bit of free time. Fancy coming along to my private quarters?"

Antony let out a thoughtful hum. "Private quarters. Those quarters we have shared for the last two weeks. The quarters especially made for captains. Your quarters?"

"My quarters," Rosanne echoed, her smile sweet at Antony's wit.

Hooking his arm, he extended it for her to take. "Lead on, my lady. Take my love and affection."

The crew let out wolf-whistles at their half-hearted flirtation as they retreated to Rosanne's private quarters.

CHAPTER THREE

St. Emmanuel

The grassy plateau that stretched between Bunnsboroux and St. Emmanuel swayed in the wind, resembling an ocean of gold. To the west and east, green forests dotted with yellow and red hinted at an early autumn following a dry spell, but the even-spaced trees of the neighbouring vineyards retained their viridian hue in the heat. The port city of St. Emmanuel was nestled snugly in a cove between the shoreline and the eastern river. The two-disk spire skyport, standing at about half the size of Valo's, saw significantly less hustle and bustle from incoming traffic. Given their limited space, the disks catered to military, trade, and commercial travel and were strewn with cranes and docks, unlike larger skyports, which often accommodated housing options.

"Tower, this is *MTS Red Queen* requesting docking," Captain Rosanne Drackenheart called over the intercom to the skyport's central communications unit, which was responsible for directing traffic.

"Business or pleasure?" a nasal voice enquired.

"Resupply," she responded succinctly.

"We're swamped, *MTS Red Queen*. You'll need to wait a few hours. You can join the queue west of the city with the others."

Rosanne flicked open her spyglass, spotting numerous dots of aero-ships drifting in the high winds above the city. She grimaced, picking up the intercom again. "What about the marina?" she tried.

A stretch of silence followed before the man returned the call. "Dock 18 is available."

"Copy that, tower. *MTS Red Queen* is heading for dock 18."

Another pause in the intercom, and Rosanne knew what was about to happen. "The *Red Queen* is a marine ship?"

"Both. We're equipped for water and air docking."

"Copy that, *MTS Red Queen*. Dock 18 is yours."

Rosanne managed to quell her surprise at how easy the docking pro-cedure went this time around. Explaining the general workings of her hybrid ship to the tower was typically an arduous task. The *Red Queen* never failed to turn heads, no matter which city they visited. She could imagine half the tower staff, binoculars pressed against the glass, eager to glimpse the incoming hybrid galleon.

Farand marched with a straight back up the stairs to the helm, his face a mask of neutrality.

"How're the recruit looking?" Rosanne asked, nodding towards the crew assisting Dalia on the quarterdeck. The woman's focus was ab-solute as she enthusiastically explained the technology of the *Red Queen*, and the cap-wearing sailor mirrored her every move.

"Diligent. Hard-working. He seems happy to have a place to sleep and eat," Farand replied.

"Good. I don't have time to find any replacements. Once we dock, let's trade our surplus grain and potatoes for supplies better suited for the southern climate and for the long haul." Rosanne's gaze lingered on St. Emmanuel, taking in the quaint splendour of its thatched-roof housing district and the ornate sewer grates dotting the winding streets. The most prominent structure, aside from the skyport, was the university. It hadn't seen any renovations since the days of Queen Mary, when she transformed the city into the trading hub of the central colonies. The school's Gothic architecture was crumbling, the stones marred with soot stains from the chimneys of neighbouring buildings.

"We've never been further south than Grace's Point, and now we're pushing well beyond that." Tapping the wheel, Farand allowed Rosanne a moment to gather her thoughts, then cleared his throat. "After our near-death experience on the northern island, this doesn't seem as daunting. No matter where we go, the gold we brought back is enough to soothe whatever troubles the crew might have about our adventures. They may not realise it, but their savings outweigh our own." His tone carried a hint of bitterness, causing Rosanne to bite her lip to stifle her laughter. He shook his head as though banishing thoughts of the ship's expenses. "Perhaps the Grey Veil makes the rest of the world seem benign in comparison, turning us into battle-hardened souls, ever greedy for more."

Rosanne gave a soft snort. "Gold is like an infectious disease. Once caught, it spreads and never lets go until you've been sucked dry."

"We all feel it, captain. It seems we got a better deal out of the journey than our enemies."

"Certainly a better outcome than what befell the hulder clan you mentioned. I wonder if anyone knows what happened to them after you killed their queen?"

Farand looked up, squinting slightly as he recalled the volcanic battle Captain Drackenheart had completely missed while ensnared in the alluring grasp of the Forest Devil. "They functioned as a unified entity, much like a beehive. The tribe likely fell apart now that she's gone."

"Do you ever regret it?"

Shaking his head, Farand exhaled deeply. "Only in moments of deep contemplation and self-doubt. It was a matter of kill or be killed, and that hulder witch was hellbent on trapping us all. My only regret is that it was us who had to do the deed."

"Never the one to dirty his hands."

At this, Farand folded his arms, his face hardening with deep lines, jaded even. "It was a question of moral direction. While it brought us out of danger, that we survived meant that they didn't. I don't ever wish to find myself in a similar predicament. They weren't ... people like us. Deadly, yes. Capable of empathy, sure. But they weren't like us."

Patting his shoulder, Rosanne offered a weak smile. "Hopefully, this journey will be different. We're prepared for anything the Grey Veil will throw at us, and we know there are creatures out there, thinking, breathing, living, organised. Maybe this time, we can avoid unnecessary bloodshed."

Rosanne could only imagine what how the ordeal had affected Farand. Despite his honesty, she couldn't help but question if this experience had broadened his moral obligation to encompass other sapient creatures. Not that she doubted his judgement; Lieutenant Duplànte was more than capable of holding his own. Yet, she couldn't help but wonder if she could make the right choices under similar circumstances. Every entity she'd encountered had been bent on ending her life.

Except for Yerrik, she realised.

A tightness spread across her chest, a lump rising in her throat, inducing nausea. She thrust aside the memory of the man who had been her saviour, of the creature he was, and suppressed it beneath the lengthening checklist of flight preparations.

Her profound silence prompted Farand to glance around, and seeing no one nearby, he leaned slightly over. "The nightmares are worsening, aren't they?" His words pierced her like a blade, and she found herself gripping the wheel until her leather gloves creaked. The pressure in her chest constricted her breathing. She yearned to retreat to her private quarters, but her momentary paralysis only accentuated her reluctance to confront this ordeal Especially now of all times.

"They are," she admitted, averting her gaze.

"Have you talked to anyone about it?"

Farand's unwavering friendship had always been a voice of reason and a rock in stormy weather. Rosanne knew she had put things off for far too long. Farand had been patient, assuming command when she faltered or appeared uncertain, supporting her in this mad quest they had embarked upon. However, she wondered if she truly wished to explore the intrusive thoughts that plagued her undistracted mind. Rosanne drew a deep breath.

"I remember it all so vividly, as though it happened merely an hour ago. Yet the memory feels like a distant dream. It wasn't torture, and it wasn't brainwashing," she said, feeling her insides coil in protest of the thoughts she pulled from memory. After she had been poisoned by Nikor, the humanoid ghoul in the swamp, Yerrik had brought her back from the brink of death. She remembered the shadow-creatures in his hut, fighting yet embroiled in passion, one begging for survival, the other for peace. Rosanne wasn't sure any of it had happened or if it was another one of Yerrik's planted dreams. There had been summer meadows as well, with the sun gentle on her face, the air crisp and calming, and laughter she had shared with the forest devil himself. "I can't even describe it," she said. "So no, Farand. I am not ready to face it." Her lips formed a thin, tight line as she scanned the horizon, seeking distractions.

Farand exhaled, resting against the instrument panel. "I sincerely hope for your well-being, as well as ours, that we never cross paths with such entities again." Farand's eyes glided over her stern expression. "Are you going to tell Captain DiCroce about it?"

She knew her pause lasted too long. Every challenge Farand presented today was difficult to process or answer, but she swallowed the lump in her throat and regained her composure. "I will when the time is right. For now, I need answers from that island. It will change everything. I am certain of that." The ensuing silence between them served both as a respite from the topic and a silent warning to Farand not to pry. He left it at that.

The marine docks formed a labyrinth of wooden overhangs and aero-vessel canopies anchored to modest-sized towers—perhaps for commercial travel. Before aeroships were the standard, St. Emmanuel was the heart of sailship trade in central Einsbor, and its glory days remained as ghosts of a long-forgotten era. Next to the shipyard, a repurposed beach—riddled with trams and railway tracks emerging from the sea itself —extended into numerous repair facilities dotting the sloping coast. Next to the long-term mooring, the processing docks held their positions at the heart of the waters. Their star-shaped berths, reserved for sizeable shipments, were teeming with cranes and conveyor belts running to the mainland, ensuring more efficient distribution of cargo. Rosanne guided the still-airborne galleon towards the waters in search of Dock 18. She listened to Olivier's inputs in the intercom as the youth deciphered the waving flags from the lower tower guiding them on to the right path. Sailors and dockworkers paused their activities, their attention drawn to the galleon approaching the modest gangways typically reserved for smaller vessels guided in by rope. Rosanne followed the standard maritime route, with topmen and seamen on either side of the ship vigilantly monitoring for any obstacles that might cause an insurance claim they couldn't afford.

A dock prowler garbed in blue, his head topped with a flat, round hat, hailed them with a golden whistle, fervently waving his arms to halt their progress.

"Another whistler, Captain," Dalia called from the stern, amusement in her tone. She gave a small wave to the man, whose red-faced, confused expression made the noise of his whistle chime in stuttering blusters. He sprinted after the ship but was quickly blocked by a crowd of people amassing by the edge of the water to view the spectacle.

Rosanne guided the ship down with gentle inclinations of the wheel and foot paddles, allowing the small thruster ports at the keel to adjust the ship's position with a hiss. With the flip of a switch and locking of a lever, the hum from the thruster engine receded, its echo lost among the bustling dockworkers and the rhythmic clacking of cogwheels from cranes. From concealed compartments at the *Red Queen*'s stern, a pair of whirring side panels folded over the now-cooled thruster panels.

A bulb flickered to green above the engine switch, showing the protective covers had effectively sealed the panels into a watertight compartment. Rosanne dipped the ship sufficiently for the anti-gravity to peel away the surface of the water.

"Contact!" Creedy announced, his limber form hanging precariously over the side of the main deck from the rigging.

"Disable the anti-grav," Rosanne commanded over the intercom. The ship shuddered with the shift in external gravity, and the *Red Queen* gently lowered herself into the water as the anti-grav technology lining her hull receded. Water surged around the vessel, and the *Red Queen* settled alongside the dock with a bowing halt.

The whistle slipped from the dock prowler's agape mouth, left to dangle from the cord around his neck. Dockworkers scrambled to seize the ropes, securing the ship, while the crew busied themselves preparing the gangplank and cargo covers.

Switching the power relay controls to disconnect the sails from the engine, Rosanne adjusted her wide-brimmed cavalier and disembarked from the ship. She tipped her hat to the dock inspector, who was awestruck by the hybrid ship, then strode off to flag down a cab, ledger in hand. The horse pulling the cab clopped on towards the trade centre, a weather-beaten, poorly maintained three-story angular wooden house. Despite its peeling paint and missing roof tiles, people still flocked to this unassuming building to trade their goods. To the sailors, this place was a veritable goldmine.

Stale air, laced with smoke, brine, and the less-than-fresh scent of fish, assaulted the captain as she entered through the open front door. The interior was sweltering and damp, thronged with people queuing at the counter to register their shipment, trade for a different type of goods bound for other cities, or cash out. Rosanne joined the back of the line, craning her neck to count the number of people ahead of her. Were she not a seasonal professional, she might have been driven to tears. This would be a long wait.

On the docks, Farand spotted the *Red Queen's* cook, Hammond, accompanied by newly promoted Able Seaman Norman, Landman Kristoff, and the recruit, Kavanaugh. They were just returning from their resupply spree, trailing two donkey-pulled carts stuffed with crates and barrels. Farand counted his blessings that they didn't need to resupply water. His sacred duty was to keep the *Red Queen* level, and the tedious task of cracking open the ballast to rearrange the water supply was his least favourite pastime.

"Open the cargo door and hoist the crane!" Farand called out. Deckhands swiftly removed the detachable cargo grate, setting it aside. Beside the main mast, the crane stood firm. Creedy unfastened the safety straps that immobilised it when not in use. Manipulating a small wheel by its base to swivelled the arm, then depressed a lever to extend it.

From the docks towered another, much larger crane—easily operated by anyone with basic wit and skills. Hwang, seizing the task, prepared the chains to attach to the palls in the cart.

Farand greeted the wagons at the dock, his eyes meticulously scanning the crates and barrels, their contents, and weights etched in smoke-smelling burns.

"Move those barrels to the other cart before you secure them with safety nets."

"Aye, sir," Norman responded and hopped on the wagon. Meanwhile, Kristoff and Kavanaugh braced themselves, ready to receive the barrels. Despite the sweltering heat, new hire Kavanaugh kept his hat pulled low over his eyes. A sheen of sweat covered his pale skin in the blistering heat, yet he stubbornly wore his cotton sleeves rolled down. The man would have a heat stroke if he persisted, but a man had his prerogative as long as the job came first. Unlike Kristoff, whose habitual drinking often led him to the wrong hammock, or Creedy, who frequently found himself too hungover to tend to the ropes. Farand's eyes followed the watch captain, whose steady stride and snappy words rang throughout the docks. A sober day, it seemed.

Once the supplies were secured, Hwang arrived, dragging chains hooked to the crane, which he then secured around the pallets. The crew then attached guide ropes, preparing to hoist the supplies aboard while skillfully directing the pallets to avoid mishaps. The team then had to switch to using the ship's crane, which could lower the pallets to the cargo deck. The operation involved ten men from start to finish. Their task was to keep the supplies steady to avoid them knocking into the deck rims covered by the cargo doors, averting any potential disaster of tumbling crates and barrels. Supplies were costly, and human lives were even more so.

Hammond lumbered aboard, his limp pronounced after his excursion. His hand flew to his side from the short hop from the gangplank to the deck, pressing on the scars from the hulder attack he had suffered months ago, Farand assumed.

"Are you alright, Mr. Hammond?" he asked.

"Aye, sir. The scar pulls a bit when I move too much. Pay it no mind." He surveyed the food supplies. "This should last us a fair bit when it rains." Hammond stretched his back and grunted; the popping of his joints was audible even from that distance.

"Nothing too perishable, I hope," Farand said, crossing his arms.

Hammond handed over the requisition documents. "Just the usual—dried fish, cured meats, ship's biscuits, beer, flour and so on. My thoughts be since we're headed to the tropics, we could use salt from the distiller in the storage rooms to absorb moisture."

Not the worst idea Farand had heard today. He nodded. "I'll leave you to it." Farand flipped through the supply manifest, scanning the items listed. "Hold on, Mr. Hammond. Why have we purchased dried chilli peppers, carrots, and white-stemmed cabbages?

Hammond rubbed his hands together, his eyes twinkling eagerly beneath hooded wrinkles. "Hwang told me about a side dish that uses fermented cabbages! Potatoes won't keep forever, and the ice storage melts too swiftly in this heat."

Farand's closed his eyes in a moment of silent exasperation at Hammond's continual tendency to turn the crew into guinea pigs. "Perishable?"

"He claims it can be stored for a year."

"As long as it keeps us healthy, as the captain says, I will allow it."

"Gracious captain that she is, I am sure." Hammond snickered. "I've restocked us with chickens, so we'll have plenty of eggs." The cook hobbled as he made his way down to the cargo deck with Kristoff, Kavanaugh, and Norman. The recruit briefly looked up from under his cap at the lieutenant as he passed by but quickly cast his eyes down again. Farand dismissed it as nervousness and carried the manifest to the captain's quarters. Longer voyages always came with their own set of challenges, such as the crew's health because of their limited diet, but Farand couldn't deny Hammond's intent to improve that situation. Farand wasn't sure how long the journey would last. He knew that anything past a month would stretch their budget thin, but with

Hammond's dietary intervention, there was hope that no one would fall ill this time around. A man could only hope.

Evening descended in indigo waves across the sky, unfurling veils of stars and a sliver of the waning moon. Captain Rosanne Drackenheart exited the trade building, her eyes lined with dark bags and her hair damp, limp and lifeless from sweat. She inhaled the cooler air, allowing the crisp feeling to surge through her like a wave of euphoria. Nights in the south felt colder than those in the north, given the stark contrast between the day's sweltering temperatures and the cool night air. Rosanne welcomed it despite the shivers racking her body from being thoroughly soaked.

She hailed a cab back to Dock 18, which was quiet save for a few stragglers leaving a nearby pub. All pubs seemed to reside near the docks—a potential health hazard should anyone fall into the ocean.

A group of seamen huddled on the forecastle, gathered around lamplight and a couple of card decks.

"Welcome back, Captain," Norman greeted her, starting a chain of welcomes from Dalia, Creedy, and Kristoff, who were engrossed in a game of King of the Hill. Rosanne approached, returning the greeting with a fatigue-tinged vigour.

"Lieutenant Duplànte has retired for the night, but we've resupplied, and storages are now full," Dalia informed, laying a card on the pile amidst collective groans of disappointment.

With a nod, Rosanne Drackenheart left the crew for their game and retreated to her private quarters. Antony lay in bed, engrossed in a hefty tome, squinting in the dim lamplight from her nightstand. His face brightened at her arrival.

Rosanne mustered a weary smile. "I'm sorry it took so long."

"You could use a bath," he remarked, neither frowning nor reprimanding her for the scent.

"If only I had one aboard, I certainly would," Rosanne replied, locking the door behind her. She shed her clothes, crossing the wooden floorboards in her nudity to join him on the bed. Despite the open windows, the room remained swelteringly hot. "I'm off for a quick rinse, then I'll be right back here," she stated, trailing two fingers up Antony's exposed chest. He was clad merely in his trousers; the heat forbade anything more, and decency demanded nothing less.

He drew in a breath, his eyes narrowing even as his lips curved upward.

"A rag and a bucket of water can still pass for a bath, right?"

Leaning in closer, Rosanne whispered, "The bathing corner can't fit two."

"We'll just have to squeeze in and draw the curtain then. The door's locked. I can wash your back while you fill me in on the trade house's travails, at least till the hot water lasts."

"I'm afraid we might be out of hot water," she said, her disappointment feigned.

"Cold water then," he proposed.

"In this heat? It'll be lukewarm at best."

"Water," he persisted. Rosanne leaned on his chest, her hands gliding over him. Antony set the book aside, gently pushing back a loose strand of hair that had fallen over her face.

"That sounds wonderful," she murmured softly.

He then sat up, head tilting as he studied her. "You're doing it again," he said. She knew he had caught on, understanding that something was weighing on her heart, something she wasn't sharing. "Rosanne, I feel like I'm not there enough for you," he confessed, his tone sounding absent-minded but carrying a hint of disappointment.

An alarm flickered in her eyes. He raised a hand, continuing, "What I'm trying to say is, you've got a ship to run, a journey to plan, and all the secrecy that entails. I may not be of much help," he said, his hand caressing her cheek, "but you'll always find me right here when you need me. I'm currently not working for the RDA, and I have no interest in ruining what we have by prying into your secrets. I simply want our time and experience to extend beyond these four walls."

Exhaling her worries, Rosanne traced a hand down his cheek. She leaned in, pressing her lips to his and closing her eyes, allowing the room's silence to form a shield against the woes of the outside world. Antony's shoulder relaxed beneath her touch. She was the first to break the contact, tucking a stray lock of hair behind her ear. She nestled into his chest, his arms wrapping around her in response.

"Having you by my side, it's like a lighthouse when I'm lost in a storm. You're the ray of sunlight piercing through the storm clouds, the blue sky I search for on lengthy voyages... as cliché as that may sound." She grimaced slightly. "I wanted you here because this journey will be the toughest one I've ever had to face." Sitting upright, she folded her hands in her lap, idly picking at the dirt under her nails. "I've told you about my father, haven't I?"

He propped himself up to an almost upright position, setting aside their moment In favour of her need to talk. "In few words, but I understood the implications."

Rosanne stooped to pick up her hat from the floor, twirling it in her hands. She traced its cavalier shape, a relic by today's fashion norms, the worn red-brown felt, and the stains and blemishes it had accumulated over the years.

"By trade, my father was a marine investigator, but at heart, an explorer. He led a skyship, commanding a crew of kindred spirits, equally adventurous. His passion was charting the Grey Veil and uncovering its mysteries. Soon after the official ban on traversing the Veil was imposed, a series of inexpiable phenomena began wreaking havoc across the Baltansea. Ships would vanish without a trace, only to resurface abandoned months later. This was nothing new, but the increase in disappearing ships prompted the RDA to investigate, and they chose my father to lead the task." She stared down at her hands folded in her lap. "Days turned to weeks. Weeks to months. Still, nothing. Expecting the worst, we dispatched a private search party; unsurprisingly, the RDA flatly refused to lift their arses high enough to even sign the search order. They discovered the *Saint Christopher* with broken masts, ripped sails, but not a single soul aboard. The ship seemed to have been drifting along the northern coast, likely for weeks, perhaps even months."

Her eyes fixated on the fabric as she stroked the worn patches. "This hat was one of the few things recovered from the ship. My mother wanted to burn it, but I took it when no one was looking. He'd always worn this dingy old thing ever since I was a little girl. A piece of my father that always came back to me." After staring into the bullet hole from her battle with the pirate ship, *Blue Dragon*, she poked a finger through it. They had sacked the ship and thrown their captain and crew in the Bunnsboroux prison, but it was ultimately their clash that stranded them in the Grey Veil. Without that, she would never have discovered the map Thompson left behind—a hint of her father's adventures in his final months. Her eyes stung as the press of memories resurfaced. "This journey we're undertaking into the Veil was my father's last destination before he disappeared. I want to understand why he mapped out that island and what he discovered. This is the first time I've pursued any leads regarding my father's fate, and I'm not ..." Rosanne hitched a breath and wiped away falling tears.

"I need this, Antony." Her voice trembled. "And I need you with me. For eighteen years, I brushed aside that depressing part of my history, thinking there was nothing I could do. But then, on the most perilous voyage I've ever undertaken, where we all nearly lost our lives, I discovered a clue that might be linked to my father's disappearance and every victim of the Grey Veil. Now that I have a chance, I'm seizing it, and this continent that Thompson charted—it's the key."

Antony pulled her into his embrace. "No matter what happens or what we find, I'll be there with you. All the way," he murmured into her hair.

Rosanne sniffed and buried her face in his neck. "Not so sexy now with all this snot, tears, and teabags under my eyes." She chuckled and pulled back.

"I quite like tea and emotional baggage. It's like cargo. You trade it in for something better," Antony said, and after a moment added, "after standing in line for five hours in a smelly, damp warehouse by the fishing docks."

Rosanne laughed. "As long as the cargo isn't infested with mice."

"There are always mousetraps and cats. But first, a bath." Rolling out of bed, he scooped Rosanne up in his arms. Her face scowled in embarrassment, but she couldn't hold back giggles as he carried them both to the corner of her quarters where a single bucket, a faucet of water, and the washing rags awaited them.

CHAPTER FOUR
ON PERILOUS WINDS

T he *Red Queen* broke away from Grace's Point, between Queensland and Northern Ovrack, continuing southwest towards the
open sea. They veered outside of official trade routes and ventured into
potential pirate territory.

Rosanne scanned the horizon, her lips thin with anticipation. Ribbons of mist clung to the ocean, casting a muted glare on the sun. A
warm southern breeze accompanied a light, cloud-dotted sky and drew
a veil of darkness over the waters.

"I've never appreciated the calm before the storm," she admitted.

Farand leaned against the navigational panel beside her, closing his
eyes as he drew a deep breath. "It feels like a lifetime ago when we first
entered the thick of the Veil and feared for our lives. Our futures and
livelihoods were all at the mercy of a paper-pusher half my size."

"Those were good times," Rosanne jested. "We've since shed that
noose. We can only become victims of our shortcomings and whatever
fate has in store for us. Hopefully, nothing too outlandish."

"Nothing *too* far from the ordinary," Farand corrected, a point
Rosanne didn't dispute.

The intercom buzzed to life. Rosanne picked it up and pressed the button in an attempt to ask the caller to repeat. No matter how insistently she pressed, however, only static filled the speaker. She cast her eyes over the topographical map. Its display remained as blank as the calm sea, showing only interference lines dancing across the screen.

Farand furrowed his brows. "It's too soon for the panels to act up. We can't even see the Veil yet."

"Olivier!" Rosanne barked towards the crow's nest.

The youth, sporting a burgeoning afro, peered from the bucket of his snug perch. "Report!" she ordered.

Olivier scrambled for the spyglass, sweeping the horizon for threats.

"Nothing, Captain!"

Her gaze returned to the horizon, her mind rifling for answers.

"Could another ship be sending out interference signals?" Farand suggested.

"You mean like the tactics pirates employ?" Rosanne pulled the thruster lever back to neutral, letting the *Red Queen* sail on momentum alone. With their eyes trained on the sky and the distant horizon, the crew reached for their weapons, knives ready at hand in a flash. Master Gunner Lyle activated the loading mechanism of his plasma rifle, the weapon humming with latent energy. He pushed his spectacles up his nose, focusing his sharp gaze on the horizon. The topmen remained silent, their eyes darting around the ship.

A chorus of alarmed shouts came from the staircase leading below deck, trailed by the thudding of numerous feet. With a trembling hand on the flintlock pistol at her side, Rosanne's heart pounded in her chest. Why now, of all times? Why such a visceral reaction to the mere clamour of feet? She clenched her teeth, and gathering herself, drew her pistol.

Second engineer Ida Simonsen stumbled up the stairs, her arms flailing as she pursued a small, airborne metal sphere.

"Catch it!" the petite blonde screamed, tumbling face-first onto the deck. Third Engineer Gavin stumbled past her, his legs tangling as he lunged for the whirring mechanical orb and crashed onto the deck with a thud. The topmen scattered, giving a wide berth to the advancing piece of tech as commotion spread like wildfire. Creedy leapt, stretched out his hand, and closed his fist around the sphere, landing both feet firmly on the floorboards.

"What are you techies up to?" Creedy's tone shifted from annoyance to amusement as Ida reached for his hand. He deftly evaded her grip, hoisting the sphere well above her head.

"Knock it off, Creedy! It's a prototype for tracking wind currents, and I ... need ... it!"

"You trying to rob me of my job?" His grin broadened as he continued to wave the sphere around.

Her petulant frown only stoked his amusement. "It's for the journey. If we can chart the wind currents ahead of time, we'll detect any changes before they even hit us. Now cut it out and give it back!"

The sudden fright brought flashes of their fight against the *Blue Dragon* from months prior, but today, the only disruption to their activities was a small metal sphere from a science experiment. "Stand down, Mr. Creedy. Let the engineers do their job."

Creedy opened his palm, and the small gadget took flight. Ida let out a shriek and chased after it. It drifted towards the port railing, and Ida sprang into the air, catching it just before it left the ship. She keeled over, gasping for breath.

Gavin frowned at the torn fabric on his knee. "What Ida was trying to explain, Captain, is that she's come up with a better way to measure wind currents. Mapping winds manually has been a pain in the ass, so we got to thinking."

"How so?" Rosanne inquired.

Brushing off his pants, Gavin straightened up. "With a fixed position using the ship as an anchor, we can accurately chart the course of the wind."

Ida made her way back to the group. "Knucklehead Gavin here opened the door while it was airborne, and out it flew. It followed the aerodynamics of the decks from the ventilation in the engine room. The device worked perfectly; I couldn't keep up with it, though." She rubbed her nose and grinned, a tick she always exhibited when she felt she had outdone herself.

"What about the signal interference?" Rosanne folded her arms, to which Ida's face turned to a sheepish grin.

"I'll have to find a way around it. I still can't get a proper connection despite the sphere sending out short-wave radio signals, much like the spear that the *Blue Dragon* used to cripple our engines."

"That explains the static in the intercom and the topographical map interference." Rosanne exhaled, feeling a touch foolish for her overreaction. Still, she had never heard of anything like this weather sphere. Their 18th-century technophobia only heightened the crew's reservation toward any such innovations. The world moved too fast.

"False alarm, everyone. My apologies!" Ida called out. The crew snickered or shook their heads before scattering to their idle posts.

Rosanne drew a breath again. This far from the Veil, as captain of the *Red Queen,* she couldn't believe her overreaction. Yet, considering the dangers they've encountered before, everyone remained on edge, expecting another electrical storm that would have them stranded on the northern island. All she could do was pray it never happened again.

Farand could see the captain's unrest as clearly as hail in midsummer. She didn't say much about her general thoughts or inner turmoil. She had yet to speak in detail about the events following their disastrous trip to the monster-ridden island just a few months prior. However, she had picked up tells that were hard to dismiss.

Farand watched as Rosanne descended cautiously to the main deck. She walked slower than usual, and the pressure on her heels lessened as if she wanted to soften her steps. The straight-backed captain, chest always puffed out, chin held high, and a gaze that could pick you apart. But now, even when attempting this faux bravado, she appeared to slump.

Out of respect, Farand reserved his thoughts to those occasions that might affect them all. He had humoured Rosanne's mad plan to chart the Veil's wind currents the moment the *Red Queen* was airborne again. Even if they didn't coin a profit from the work, it served as a welcome distraction. The crew bounced back from their ordeal, but it had changed their captain. For once in her life, she'd encountered a foe she couldn't overcome. And that opponent had appeared human. Now that they were teetering on the brink of a discovery, and Rosanne appeared more self-assured, he felt brave enough to bring up the topic of her captivity and how it affected her, or so he hoped.

"She's less on edge now," Antony said to him, having noted Rosanne's demeanour on deck. "After the ship's repairs, she barely had the nerve to step aboard. I never saw her unease until then. If it weren't for that day, I wouldn't have known anything was amiss."

"She's a tough woman," Farand replied, turning the wheel to hold their course steady. The clear sky above was shading into darker blues, with faint specks of stars dotting the horizon. "When you're out there chasing pirates, what's it like to know each journey could be your last?"

Antony's face twisted into a wry smile. "I don't dare entertain the thought. Maintaining the trade routes to Noval pirate-free is challenging enough, and we've met heavy resistance on a few occasions. When it comes to that, home's the last thing on my mind. I think of her instead." He nodded toward the red-headed captain, who was basking in the breeze on the forecastle. "When I imagine a world where I can't stand by her side, the job turns into second nature, and staying alive becomes top priority. Death will always linger in the back of my mind. Even aboard the *Red Queen*, I know safety is but an illusion. Especially when we're headed straight into *that*." The distant wall of the fog marked the beginning of the Grey Veil, and the start of their journey.

That wasn't the answer Farand had expected, but it was a welcome one for sure. "You're a good man, Captain DiCroce. But I can't help but wonder how you're able to separate business from pleasure. Or should I say, Rosanne from her trade?"

Antony threw out both of his arms towards her like he was showcasing a priced possession. "Have you met the woman? She's a dime in a million! I'm not going to jeopardise what we have because of moral obligations to the law, which, I might add, is unfair."

A deep laughter rumbled up from Farand's chest as he threw his head back. Heads turned in their direction at this unusual sight, but no one raised an eyebrow. "I might not worry so much then. We should have you on our side."

"Meanwhile, I'll be hunting pirates, not those who take certain freedoms to sail through the Veil." He wiggled his eyebrows, which drew a chuckle from Farand. "Although I'm still curious how you're navigating the Grey Veil. Perhaps some advanced technology fell into your laps?"

"Ah, the mysteries of life are many. Navigating the Grey Veil's just one of them." Farand's lips stretched into a secretive smile.

As the evening sky drew a cloak of darkness across the heavens, cannon fire resounded in the distance. The mirth fell from their faces, eyes now locked towards the noise permeating the air from a few kilometres away. Farand spun the wheel, steering them away from the noise but closer to the mystical world shrouded in the fog.

Come noon, the *Red Queen* pulled up before the towering wall of fog that was the Grey Veil. Unlike up north, here, the fog danced with invisible wind currents.

Rosanne tightened her leather gloves, the material stretching over her fingers as she took hold of the wheel. She ran her eyes over the instrument panel to her left, taking in their altitude, the topographical map sweeping the expanse below them for any landmasses—blank as always—and the green lights indicating the electrical input to the aether sails and, subsequently, the current feeding the engine. Every indicator glowed a reassuring green.

Rosanne had ventured into the Grey Veil countless times in the past two months, but today, they entered with a specific goal in mind. Today, they dove in, hunting for adventure and answers.

Antony, clad in fog-repelling, breathable wool—just like the rest of the crew now that they could afford it—watched from behind her. Though the south was hotter, the humidity was hell. Given the rampant diseases and pesky parasites, keeping dry was crucial—especially when the Atmos couldn't repel the Veil's forces that negated their standard navigational instruments and ignored the laws of physics.

"All clear," Olivier's voice rang through the intercom, the device clicking audibly in the surrounding silence. The watch captains across the decks responded, raising their hands to signify their readiness. The topmen stood by their designated post, set to crawl up the ratlines at a moment's notice. The silence bore into Rosanne, making her acutely aware of her shallow breaths.

She snatched up the intercom, clicking the side button. "Higgs, are you ready for entry into the Veil?" Rosanne asked.

"One second, ma'am. Ida's keen on testing her new device."

Rosanne arched an eyebrow, but before she could respond, Ida and Lyle emerged onto the main deck and advanced to the front. Lyle carried a wide-barrelled blunderbuss and prepped it with gunpowder and a charge. Ida stuffed a spherical container inside the bore. She gestured towards the swirling fog, and Lyle fired. The singular shot cracked once around them before fading into silence. Rosanne hoped nothing else had heard it, but she couldn't help but watch as the ball made a slow arch and vanished into the thick mist. Ida clapped her hands and let out a squeal, pulling out a tablet with long antennas and a screen from her pack. She sprinted to the quarterdeck, drawing up alongside Rosanne and Antony.

"I have refined my invention, Captain!" Her bumbling joy was infectious, making Antony pull on his polite smile, reaching even his eyes. Rosanne examined the tablet; the clunky block displayed green lines swirling with activity.

"And what improvements might those be?"

"I've isolated the frequency the sphere can tap into, pinpointed by this receiver right here." Waving the tablet excitedly, she proclaimed, "It doesn't interfere with the nav-panel. Triple-checked that! And we should see ..." She let the words hang and adjusted the dials on the side of the box. The screen flickered to life in static, jumbled lines. As Ida adjusted another dial, the static died down. The central dot, which the radar circled, and further off, a smaller dot was caught in what appeared to be a shroud of wind.

"Colour me impressed, Miss Simonsen." Rosanne marked the dark circles around Ida's blue eyes. The engineer had been pulling many all-nighters lately, and Rosanne could see why. An invention like this would revolutionize how they sailed in the Grey Veil even further.

"I don't have its exact range yet, but I have encased it with an anti-Veil-field, AVF for short. It should penetrate the worst interferences. Again, it might only be effective up to about three hundred metres, but it does give us a rough idea of the weather—electrical storms or those cyclones. Short-range scoping, so to speak."

Antony studied the screen, his eyes large and wondering. "That is impressive engineering. If you're interested, I could recommend you for the Royal Navy's Engineering Initiative."

Ida pulled a face of discontent. "Thanks, but I already took the exams, and I didn't like how they run things."

Her blunt response had Antony blinking in surprise, momentarily robbing him of the persuasive charm that usually left promising cadets drooling. Rosanne couldn't help but snigger at Antony's slack-jawed confusion, although he recovered quickly with a nod of his head.

"Permission to sail then, Miss Simonsen?" Rosanne prompted.

"Let's fly, Captain!"

Rosanne released the lever that locked the *Red Queen's* thruster engine in idle, nudging it forward. The ship glided towards the cloudy wall, gaining speed. Within moments of touching the Veil, the *Red Queen* was swallowed by the dense fog, her decks thrust once again into an ethereal world painted with muted colours. The grim expressions on the crew's faces were replaced by the glint of adventure and the prospect of profit. Kavanaugh stood wide-eyed on the forecastle, gesturing expansively, before Dalia ushered him back to his post. What they discussed remained a mystery to Rosanne, but she had bigger concerns to focus on, keeping her eyes peeled for shadows in the fog and her ears sharp to any warning sounds. Anything at all.

Ida sat down on the forecastle. She tinkered with her tablet, delicately adjusting the dials as the signal wavered. Creedy stared at the screen, absorbing the sight of the green cloud formations gathering around the ship. Armed with this new information, Creedy consulted with Rosanne, subtly adjusting their course. Due to a lack of sunlight powering the aethersail technology, they had to reduce their power consumption. They rode the centre of these wind tunnels, which, thanks to Ida's invention, they could pinpoint with high accuracy. Yet, despite all the ship's gadgets, the GPT tracking their route on a semi-global scale, Ida's little marvel predicting shifts in wind currents, and their comprehensive plan and maps of the Grey Veil, Rosanne felt unprepared for what they might find. She had dedicated countless hours to planning the trip to increase their chances of success. The Grey Veil, with its multitude of mysteries and horrors, called to her. Much like Yerrik, the Forest Devil of the northern island, who had seduced her with otherworldly abilities, they wrapped her in a false sense of safety and dependence. "I won't be fooled again," she vowed. She wouldn't let her emotional vulnerabilities

57

lead to her downfall in her quest for answers about her father's fate. Not again.

CHAPTER FIVE
YOU HAD ONE JOB!

Immersed in the hushed world of eternal fog, the crew signalled the shift change with hand signs and whispers instead of the bell. Rosanne preferred to maintain their element of surprise rather than find themselves greeted by a face full of plasma shot.

"We're catching a different wind current," Farand noted, pointing to the angular tilt of the sails.

Rosanne picked up the intercom and flicked a switch to the designated department. "Hwang, what is our position?" She had reassigned him from deck duty to safeguard the GPT, Global Positioning Tracker, and its secrets in case of another pirate attack. That invaluable piece of technology stored all the raw data tracking their position through the Grey Veil—a region they had meticulously mapped throughout the summer. The only difference was they hadn't visited the northern island again. The outer rock belt of hovering anti-grav stones clearly marked its position, and Rosanne felt no urge to revisit the island—for many reasons. Once again, she pushed the thought away—its persistent intrusion, a distraction at a time when she needed focus. Seconds ticked by as she awaited the senior able seaman's response. "We've just entered the southern circular current," replied Hwang. Holding the intercom to her lips, Rosanne scanned the instrument panels. Static danced across the topographical map while the compass spun, only interrupted by the neutralising field that Higgs had engineered into the electronics—dubbed the AVF by Ida—to enhance their navigation. She paused, realising that the technology aboard the *Red Queen* was unprecedented. With the military-grade GPT they'd swiped from the *Retribution*, combined with Ida's and Higgs' genius, they had the ability to navigate anywhere within the Grey Veil. Nothing could stop them—except for monsters.

"You know, Farand, with all this knowledge we possess about the Grey Veil, the wind currents, and this navigational technology, we've become the most knowledgeable sailors in the northern hemisphere."

His brown eyes drifted to the fluttering admiral's pendant Rosanne had claimed as her own. The axe carried by the flag's golden dragon seemed to slice through the fog, its red dye a stark contrast to the monochrome world.

"And the most coveted should our secrets be spilled. As unnerving as that is, I'd rather we have science on our side. We're unravelling more about the Grey Veil and its puzzling physics."

"You a man of science, Farand?"

"I have my moments. For instance, I always found it strange that the fog never extends beyond the mapped areas we're aware of or further south than the tropics. How the Veil maintains its integrity—is a mystery as old as mankind itself." He punctuated his tangent with a grand sweep of his hand over the horizon—a dramatic flair that was unusual for him.

Nodding, Rosanne drew a deep breath and let her eyes glide across the horizon in search of Farand's unwavering focus she sorely lacked at present. "Gravity, magnetism, and whatever force that makes the Grey

Veil untraversable," Rosanne mumbled, chewing on her lips. "At least Higgs' and Ida's AVF seems to take care of the interference."

Leaning against the instrument panel, Farand looked lost in thought. "Sitting on this knowledge makes me question whether we're too mistrustful. If we lose key personnel, or if one of us gets incapacitated, what do *they* do?" Their attention turned to the crew on deck.

Farand had a point, but Rosanne knew their freedom to explore the Veil hinged on maintaining their secrecy. "Given Creedy's flapping lips at the tavern, I'd disagree. Besides, we've got new blood we should keep an eye on." Rosanne gestured towards Kavanaugh. "I am always wary of the quiet ones."

"Shall I let the watch captains know?"

"No. We wouldn't want to arouse any suspicion in case we're wrong. The crew's sharp. They'll catch on."

Farand nodded.

During their downtime, the crew engaged in various games on the main deck. Creedy was introducing Kavanaugh to the traditional game of hacky sack. Men and women cheered joyously as one of them made a daring dive for the beanbag just before it could hit the deck, kicking it to Kavanaugh, who tripped and ended up rolling onto his back. His cap fell off, which he quickly snatched from the deck and pulled down low over his thinning eyebrows. Brushing off the embarrassment with a grin, the surrounding crew laughed.

Rosanne's heart wrenched in her chest, thinking her eyes had betrayed her. The crooked grin on Isaac's face was familiar somehow, although she couldn't say why. His nervous laughter reached her, and Rosanne's insides coiled as though she's been punched. Unwanted images flooded her mind, memories of an event that had never happened, but had been in the audience of the Forest Devil.

The bonfire blazed in front of an oak tree, its orange flames licking at a form suspended above, screams piercing the meadow's quiet night outside the timber hut. *It didn't happen*, she told herself, wrestling with the gut punch that left her breathless.

It never happened, she repeated to herself, again and again. *It was just a dream!*

Despite her vehement denial, Rosanne released the wheel in a daze. Her eyes peeled as she stomped over and stood before Isaac Kavanaugh with eyes aflame. She heard Farand call out after her but it drowned under the barrage of thoughts.

"My office immediately," she commanded. The pale-faced man hesitated briefly before trailing after her. She gave a curt wave for Farand to follow, who signalled Dalia to take over the wheel. People around them voiced their confusion, but Rosanne ignored them.

Once inside her office, she slammed the door behind her, facing her lieutenant.

"Is this some kind of joke, Farand?"

His suspicious gaze darted between Rosanne and Kavanaugh. Picking up on his confusion, she gestured towards Isaac, who was standing off to the side with his head bowed and a stiff smile on his face. With a huff, Rosanne marched over and tore off his cap, revealing the clumsy sailor with his shaved head, pale skin, and thick stubble. Despite the disguise, it was unmistakably Aros Bernhart, the former pirate captain of the *Blue Dragon*. "The man who got us stranded in the Grey Veil ... *Why* is he here?!" She gestured sharply towards the pirate, who shrunk under her rage. "One man, Farand! I tasked you with recruiting a single deckhand,

and out of all candidates, you chose the biggest cutthroat bastard in the Baltansea!"

Farand's features darkened, yet he took a deep breath to regain his composure.

"I can wait outside if you, sirs, would like." Aros piped up, his voice high, drawing their attention. He stood off to the side, hand half-raised like an uncertain child seeking permission.

"Out!" Rosanne barked, tossing his cap back to him. Aros snatched it up before it hit the floor and made for the door. "Actually, wait. Go sit on the balcony or something," Rosanne grumbled after him.

Aros turned on his heel and whisked past them to the side door leading to the sterncastle balcony. The door clicked audibly behind him.

Farand rubbed his temples as he moved to the chair across the desk, his stiff shoulders relaxing. "In my defence, his documents are genuine. His work papers were in use at the time of Captain Bernhart's imprisonment. I checked them thoroughly at the RDA," he assured.

Rosanne exhaled sharply through her nose, her hands firmly planted on her hips as she paced the confines of her office. She closed her eyes, stealing a moment of composure and quelling the rage inside of her. She wanted to tear the desk from its bolts and throw it at Aros twiddling his thumbs by her balcony, but instead dedicated a minute to silence the accusatory voices clamouring in her mind. She drew a deep breath.

"I apologise, Farand. You're right. He bears no resemblance to the pirate captain we fought in the Veil." Rosanne said, collapsing into her chair with a deep sigh. "At first glance, he was unrecognisable. To everyone, I sensed something was off, but I thought it was all in my head." She shivered, relieved that her instincts were still intact. "You didn't see him up close either! Only Lyle and I have. How in the hell is he here? I thought he was in prison?"

"What do we do with him?" Farand inquired, his hands folded in his lap as he leaned back, his eyes on her face.

Rosanne wrinkled her nose. "I'd like to toss him overboard and rule it an accident, but we need all the hands we have, and it's far too late to turn around. Tell me everything about the interview. How did you even find him?"

Farand let his hand glide over his chin, and his brows furrowed in thought. "I saw him by the docks in Bunnsboroux amongst the unemployed veterans looking for work. He was younger than most, had all his limbs and bore no visible ailments or signs of ill health besides looking gaunt. I chose a couple of people to interview, vetted their papers, and he seemed like what we would need."

"A pirate and a con man?" Rosanne asked sourly but quickly shook off the bitterness. "You said you checked his papers with the RDA?"

"Genuine, if you can believe it. Frequent runs between Kvenchester and Bunnsboroux on *St. Row*. Let go due to bankruptcy. The *St. Row* is beached in Saint Emmanuel."

"Undoubtedly a stolen identity," Rosanne stated, standing to look out the window. She tapped her foot against the floorboard, nodding her head. "I'd like a private word with him."

"What are you going to do?" Farand's question wasn't about the severity of her intended actions but a concern to ensure she didn't kill him and land the ship in trouble with the authorities. The last thing they needed was an inspection.

However, the malicious gleam in her eye when she turned to Farand drew a chuckle from her lieutenant.

With Farand out of the way, the deep frown on Rosanne's face promised violence. Aros wrung his cap, his gaze wandering around the office, seemingly admiring the room. He opened his mouth to speak, only to be quelled by her flame-touched gaze. A minute passed, and Rosanne, tightly wound with fury, didn't interrupt him when he finally mustered his courage.

"I like what you've got going on here. Nice trimmings. Solid, dark wood." He knocked a fist on her desk; the firm thumps against the woodwork indicated no hollowness. "And you have a pleasant view wherever you go." His half-hearted smile withered under her intense stare.

"Why are you here?" Her question was authoritative, demanding, and imposing.

"I needed work."

"You were locked up. I made sure of that."

"They let me out for good behaviour."

His reedy attempt to lighten the situation only served to infuriate her. How dare he crack jokes in a situation like this? Rosanne cocked her head to the side, eyes a soulless reflection. "Less than four months with your record? Didn't our island trip teach you anything about my wit and ability to detect bullshit?"

"You let a monster seduce you," he muttered under his breath. Overhearing this, Rosanne's hand twitched towards a paperweight, which, in a blind fury, she raised above her head.

Aros shot his hands up in panic. "I needed work after getting out of jail!" he blurted out. Rosanne froze, her hand raised, the paperweight heavy in her grip. She drew a deep breath, her expression turned into an ice-cold mask, and she slid the paperweight back to its original position with the back of her hand. He continued. "I spilt secrets. That's how they let me out. I gave them our routes," came his breathy reply.

"You betrayed your own people?" Her eyebrows arched dramatically.

Aros huffed. "It's more complicated than that, lady. I may have had a crew, but they weren't mine to begin with, and someone else oversaw the territory we covered. I'm just a captain, *was* a captain of a larger fleet," he corrected.

"In exchange for valuable information, you were let out? Just like that?"

His jaw danced with tension. "Something like that."

"And then?" she prompted.

"I heard rumours you were in town, so I did what I had to do to get out of there—which was to get hired by you."

Rosanne snorted. "Why on Terra would you think that was a good idea? You don't know the *Red Queen*. You don't know me or my crew. Do you even have a clue where we're headed?"

Aros straightened his back, raising his chin with confidence. "I knew you were going into the Veil. I saw the gold you picked up on the Island of Doom! Only someone stricken with the fever would be mad enough to dive back into the Grey Veil." He placed a hand on his chest. "I figured you must be after a bigger haul. Naturally, I wanted a piece of the action after rotting away for months in that shithole. I noticed you even brought your fiancée along! How's that working out? I mean, you lot seem rather occupied during the wee hours. I mean, you really," he exhaled audibly, "I could hear it all."

Rosanne merely blinked at him. "And?"

Aros paused, taken aback by her blank stare. "And," he gestured vaguely in the air as he sought the right words, "most folks would be embarrassed knowing how exposed they've been during noisy, intimate moments." He crossed his arms, thinning his lips defiantly.

Rosanne let out a snort of laughter. "This is a ship, Aros. Not much room for privacy here. I was under the impression you'd captained a much smaller vessel with far fewer hidey-holes."

"I didn't have any women on board for that very reason."

At that, Rosanne held back a laugh, threatening to diffuse the tension. "That doesn't stop anyone from seeking pleasures where it may find them, does it?"

Aros shuddered theatrically.

"Oh, come on! You can't possibly be that averse to the intimate affairs of people."

Aros crossed his arms and stuck out his chin, his voice suddenly quiet. "No, it's just that I prefer to be in the company of a beautiful lady without the entire crew chewing corncobs behind a white canvas."

Rosanne pinched the bridge of her nose. "Corncobs aside, you being aboard the *Red Queen* is a colossal conflict of interest, *Aros*. Or whatever name you go by these days."

"Actually, my name is Isaac," he said, his tone flat.

"Lies. You've stolen this identity from someone under the perfect guise you were employed up till recently."

Aros huffed, unbothered by how childish it might appear. The nerve of this man. "You know how hard it is to get a trade license these days? I rented mine out so I could have a cover should I find myself in deep waters. And deep it got after you sacked us outside of Noval. A good pirate always has a backup plan."

There was a pause. Then she folded her hands on the table. "You're truly Isaac Kavanaugh?"

"The one and only," he declared, straightening his posture and radiating self-satisfaction.

Rosanne licked her lips and drew a hand over her changing expression. "Your real name is Isaac Kavanaugh? You're baptised, then? Born and raised in Cintecha?" The incredulity dripped off her tongue thick as tar.

"Can't tell by looking at me, eh?" He wiggled his eyebrows.

Rosanne scowled. "So, Aros Bernhart is your false name?"

"There's a funny story in there. This easterner—"

"Not interested."

"Yes, ma'am," he agreed, his enthusiasm deflating like a dead pufferfish.

Rosanne stood and moved around the desk to confront him. Aros rose his chin, standing a head taller than her, yet his eyes wavered beneath her icy glare. She could see he was doing his best not to appear intimidated by someone two-thirds his size, but the faux bravado the former Captain Bernhart carried was gone with the wind.

"Besides needing a job, what are you playing at?" she asked, crossing her arms.

His throat bobbed as he swallowed. "I needed to escape the colonies, and your ship was nearby. You operate under the cover of darkness, as one does when you trade on the side and you frequent the Veil. It fits my needs perfectly."

Her eyes narrowed. "There are other ships you could've hailed out of Bunnsboroux. You aren't making a strong case."

"But I know *you*, Captain." His gaze became firm suddenly. "I know you wouldn't stop after your last encounter with the devils of the Veil, being the Demon of the Sky yourself. You're drawn to the thrill the Grey Veil offers."

An amused snort escaped her lips. "Do people believe in that rumour? Ever thought it was something I made up?"

"It certainly adds to your impressive resume, for sure. But more importantly," Aros lifted a finger, gesturing in the air as if encompassing the whole ship, "all your crew are of dubious origin or without papers. You barely have ties with the RNAA or the RDA, suggesting you have something to hide. If you were to report Aros Bernhart to the authorities, you'd have to tell them about your connection to that island."

"Or I could just toss you into the ocean. No one would know," she said, her tone flat.

"Aha! But that would open up an investigation and a mountain of paperwork."

Rosanne closed her eyes briefly, the all-familiar bitterness of blackmail spreading through her like rot. "You're at my mercy here, *Isaac*. Mine. Do anything that could jeopardise this journey, any attempt at a coup. If I so much as see another ship bearing your name and your crew, I won't hesitate to tie the noose around your neck and kick you off my ship. Laws be damned." She ran a hand over the table, circling the letter opener. Aros stole a glance at her hand. For a second, the briefest moment, she spotted a nervous twitch in the tough exterior she knew he fought hard to maintain. She had expected a flippant reply, a joke, something to divert her attention from the fact that he was putting on a brave front, as he had done so many times during their journeys. It didn't come. Had she finally frightened him into silence?

She jabbed a firm finger into his chest. "Betray me, and I'll make you regret even setting foot on my ship. If you stick to your job and stay out of trouble, you'll live. But everyone on board will know who you are and what you've done. You're on your own."

An amused crinkle returned to his eyes. *There it was,* Rosanne thought.

"That's almost kind of you. I wouldn't mind a quick death if it comes to that. So, I get to stay and learn the inner workings of the ship? Share meals, cheat at cards with your crew, have a drink with the Katshov—"

Her finger paused sternly in front of his face, silencing Aros.

"I don't want to hear any complaints. Not even a whisper. May the skies have mercy if I ever hear what goes on in that twisted head of yours. Understood?" Rosanne asked.

Aros gave a stiff nod.

CHAPTER SIX

ISAAC KAVANAUGH

Captain Drackenheart remained the spitfire dragon Aros had met during his expedition into the Grey Veil—an ordeal that had claimed half his crew, ship, and entire pirate career.

Even towering a head taller in her presence, the captain's icy stare could bring a man down to his knees, and the faintest scoff from her lips could sting like a whip. Caught red-handed aboard her ship after a daring prison escape and cloaking his white lies with truth, Captain Drackenheart had demonstrated mercy, as he had expected. She was not a woman who would sentence him to an early grave due to personal whims, but she was damn close this time. Passionate about her work and tightly guarded with her secrets, sure, she was not as cold and indignant as many assumed. She always put on a good show, that one.

Aros recalled his ill-conceived sacking and how disastrous his first journey into the Grey Veil ended, shackled and entertaining the Majesty's inquisitors. The company was poor, the food was questionable, and the security was tight and merciless. His cellmates were loud and stark, raving mad. Years of confinement in a damp cellar, with but a slit of light shining through the ceiling, could reduce any man from sophistication to rambling lunacy.

The dungeons of Her Majesty are distinctive in their approach to torture; simple confinement and starvation often fall short for their inquisitors. They had propped one of his cellmates full of anti-gravity dust, a more refined variant of anti-gravity minerals; immediate side effects comprised of a burning sensation, nausea, headaches, and a prevailing sense of doom, given the knowledge that the dust would gradually dissolve one's internal organs. Prolonged short-term consequences of anti-gravity dust mineral poisoning include levitation, panic, and impending death. A snickering inquisitor would force the dust, stored in a watertight oilcloth sack, down one's throat, savouring the macabre taste. They channelled a specific current from one finger to another, neutralising the effects of the anti-gravity minerals, lest one remains silent on the secrets they were keen to extract.

A wild-eyed inquisitor had shoved a small leather pouch of the fine dust down Aros' throat, and he had prayed to the high heavens his stomach acid wouldn't dissolve the bag. Only spilt secrets would grant him mercy.

Aros spilled them all. Every detail of his ill-fated journey aboard the fucking *Blue Dragon*: how their raids originated north of Cintecha, how their business had spread to the Baltansea, and how they'd looted commercial aeroships and their wealthy guests. Yet, regarding his final journey into the Grey Veil, he'd played the fool, allowing them to draw their own conclusions. Given Captain Drackenheart's testimony at the time of his imprisonment, he didn't need to go into details, for both of them wished for their shared history to remain a secret. Somehow, they had collaborated on each other's stories, with their final showdown marking the end of his pirating days and sending him with a one-way ticket aboard the *Colossus*, destined for the prison cells of Bunnsboroux.

They had tossed him in a dark cell for the whole sweltering summer, his skin almost transparent when he saw daylight once more. He could hardly believe that he was a free man, but the cost of this freedom was higher than he could pay, and his identity, his name, and his pirating ways had long since sailed off. Remaining in Bunnsboroux with the local inquisition was out of the question, even after they had bled him dry about Aros' routes through Noval and Einsbor. Before long, the inquisition filled the prisons with disgruntled members of the Central Einsbor Pirate Association, and Aros desperately needed a plan to get the hell out of town. He had his birth name to fall back on, a name reinstated upon his release. He'd spent years in the skies as a pirate, and he wasn't about to let his original identity eclipse that persona.

In a glaring call from the celestial heavens themselves, he spotted the red tar hull and golden sails of the *Red Queen* flying into town. Aros had never been much of a religious man (*sorry, Mum*, he thought guiltily), but at that moment, blessed bells rang in his mind. He'd shaved his head and thinned his eyebrows to a patchy state, and ignored food and drink to maintain his image. As he stood by the docks clutching a sign asking for work, he was just another unemployed sailor suffering from cutbacks. Then, Lieutenant Farand Duplànte, a man capable of wringing him like a rag, lumbered about town interviewing sailors. As the saying goes, the rest is history.

Now that Rosanne had caught him, the crew viewed him differently. They slunked away from him in the galley, leaving him to solitary meals. Nevertheless, he received wages, he could eat and sleep, and he lacked nothing but social interactions. The crew, despite their biases, didn't toss him overboard. But Creedy, now there was a man whose knife-sharp looks promised a world of pain. The deep-rooted sense of mistrust emanating from his sunken, tea-bag-like eyes reminded Aros of his standing aboard the ship. The watch captain glanced at him in his periphery, twinning the rope around his shoulder and bringing it with him to a chest secured on deck where they kept their reserves. Aros remained silent, continuing to practice his sail knots, just as Dalia had taught him, hoping that they could somehow put the sour history between him and the *Red Queen* to the past.

Though no stranger to deck work, having spent his teens through his mid-thirties aboard various ships, he needed the refresher. It was a *Red Queen* policy for every recruit to undergo the same training. Months in prison and little food left him weak, but he was regaining his strength day by day. He felt gratitude for being employed again, invigorated by the perils of the seas and sky. Being a part of something again was nice.

"Oi, pirate," a voice called out in a thick northern Queensland accent behind him. Aros frowned, dreading what would come next. Turning, three sets of folded arms, three stern condemning faces and a simple question greeted him.

"Who didya run with?" a pale, stocky man piped up.

The question was so unexpected and without a shred of hostility that Aros' jaw fell open with a gormless, "Ha?"

"Go on, then. Tell us. Who didya run with?" the man repeated.

"And how in the blooming fields did you slip past Duplànte?" the second man queried, his nasal Angelsk accent suggesting he might be Gerneran. His icy blue eyes sized Aros up and down, making him uncomfortable. The third, a man with a dark tan and sun-wrinkled face, pushed the bushes of his black eyebrows together.

Aros considered the three men, each fully capable of breaking every bone in his skinny body. He raised his hands as if summoning courage from behind a protective shield of weak digits. "Gentlemen, please. My previous employer was a bastard who left me for dead. Allow a man to lick his wounds before having them poked."

The three men shared inscrutable glances, their expressions softening. When they said nothing, Aros realised he hadn't even answered their second question, as if his defiance were meaningless. He licked his lips. "I have a trade license with the RDA. Duplànte is a reasonable man. My wide range of experience must have impressed him."

"Listen to this bastard lie." The pale man snorted while the third man wagged a finger.

"No no, Denny. I did the same. Lent mine out to my brother."

"You never told us that!" Denny exclaimed.

Aros blinked at the trio of mismatched individuals, who, despite not working on the same teams, unmistakably ran together socially. They were similar in age, perhaps no older than forty-five, making him younger than the lot.

"Isaac Kavanaugh. Deckhand in re-training. A pleasure to meet you, gents." He extended his hand, which remained unshaken. After a pause, he withdrew it.

The blue-eyed man waved a dismissive hand. "We know that, but who were ye before ye came aboard the *Red Queen*?"

Aros folded his arms and thrust his chin up. "You gents first."

The pale sheet of paper of a man straightened and thrust a thumb into his chest, entirely on board with the idea. "I'm Denny Nicholson, able seaman. Seven years aboard the *Red Queen*."

"Quinn Saros, topman. Been 'ere three years." The Gerneran shifted his ice-blue gaze around, checking for potential eavesdroppers.

"Vincent Carman. Two years seaman and a year as a gunner under Lyle." The third man, with slick black hair, nodded in greeting.

Aros returned the look. "Former Aros Bernhart. Ran my crew in the north, but you can say it went ... south."

His joke drew amused snickers.

Vincent sized up Aros, raising a pointing finger. "I recognise the shifty eyes. The Bunnsboroux dungeon has left him paler than you, Denny."

"Not my fault. I ain't got much sunshine below deck!" Denny complained. Aros longed to slink away from their scrutinising gazes, but his escape routes were either overboard or amidst a less-than-enthusiastic captain or lieutenant. Or worse, the trigger-happy old-timer who kept his hawkish eyes fixed on him. He stood on the forecastle, his rifle in front of his foot. He nodded when Aros spotted him, his glasses glinting in the lamplight hanging from the mast. A shiver coursed through Aros' spine. Seeing Lyle, especially after what had transpired in the swamp, surprised him—saved by the devil himself, who would have guessed?

"Listen, guys. I ain't lying to you all." Aros' pitch changed, swapping his broken Georgetown accent for his native Cintechan. "The northern passage is the best hiding spot in Baltansea. You guys should know. My ship got wrecked in a freak electrical storm, and my crew is sleeping with the fishes. I just want to get back on my feet and sweep the rest of this bullshit overboard."

Quinn's gaze swept over him. "You say you had a ship and a crew. A two-spire mayfly with dragon sails, no?"

"It's clearly the captain from that *Blue Dragon*," Vincent interjected.

Aros felt the blood drain from his face. "What can I say? I had a change of career."

"More like a change of sanity after being imprisoned, I reckon," said Quinn, drawing laughter from the others.

"Listen, fellas. All I want is food and a bunk. I accept the work here. This captain you met doesn't exist anymore. The man carrying that name is dead and buried."

"How did you convince the captain to keep you on?" Denny's eyes sparkled with curiosity.

"Let me spill some beans about my involvement with our dear Captain Drackenheart." Aros slung his arms over the shoulders of Quinn and Vincent, pulling them all into a tight huddle of shared secrets. "She's got a mean fist, a sharp tongue, but a soft heart. Make no mistake, she wants me off her ship, but here's the deal." He quickly glanced around, then dropped his voice to a whisper. "I know what happened to her on that island inside the Grey Veil."

"Lies." Vincent protested but didn't pull away.

"I know she was occupied with her own demons when you reclaimed the ship from those hulder bitches, but since you don't believe me, I ain't telling you." Aros patted Quinn and Vincent's shoulders, standing tall again.

At this, three pairs of eyes narrowed.

"I still wanna know who ye ran with," Dennis said.

"Pass," Aros responded.

"A secret for a secret, then?" Vincent suggested. They were all clearly buying into Aros' bullshit, but life hadn't handed him a shovel and told him to dig for nothing. He knew when to call it quits now.

Aros shook his head.

"How about a hint for a hint?" Quinn interjected. "We can guess who ran with who, and you can hint at what you know of the captain. Trade?"

Aros pursed his lips. He was familiar with a fair few from the Einsbor Pirate Association on both sides of the Veil, but he'd never mingled with crews outside of his own. "Alright then. I'm game." He gave in pathetically, suppressing that tiny voice in his head, cautioning him to stop digging.

Quinn nodded. "Me first. Trochack Mountains in the '80s."

Aros hadn't come across that name in ages. "You're a Wilkrow's man? Never met him, but I heard he enjoyed executing defectors by setting them on fire and planking 'em from up high."

"Oh, he did. Until someone turned him into the wicker man." A shadow passed over Quinn's face. Aros studied his expression and nodded in morbid fascination.

"Cintecha. 1697," Denny announced.

Aros racked his brains. "Hey, your thicker-than-glue Queenie accent tells me you ain't local to the west side of the Veil. What did you do to end up there, join the colonisation?" "I had to get out of service by hook or crook," Denny laughed. Aros bit back his sneer and quickly returned to the topic at hand. His grievances with the colonisers could rest another day. "I'd wager it was either Harkman or Chryler, then. They picked up quite a few deserters," he surmised, given Denny clearly hadn't sailed with him and the options weren't plentiful.

The pale sailor offered no further hints, leaving Aros to ponder over which captain he might have served under.

The trio turned to Vincent, his lips tightly pursed, his brown eyes narrowed into thin slits.

"One served, one exception. Once alive, now departed. Forever, I will remain loyal."

"That's a touch poetic, mate. Can't you tell us who it is? You never did, same as your brother using your trade license." Quinn grumbled. Vincent's lips twitched, but he offered no response.

"Lucky bastard had a good crew and captain," Denny muttered, and all nodded in agreement.

Aros had no clue to whom Denny referred, though competent pirate captains were a rare breed. It must have been before his time, then. He licked his lips as he thought about how to deliver his line. "Their reach is law, and wrath is mean. Even jailed, you are not free."

The trio crossed their arms, their expressions morphing into thoughtful frowns accompanied by contemplative murmurs.

"Sounds like a legend," Quinn remarked.

"Sounds like bullshit, if ye ask me," Denny pronounced, passing his judgment.

"I'm thinking of a lass. Perhaps Eihras?"

"She's been retired for years!" argued Vincent.

Finding the men unable to reach a consensus, Aros clapped his hands together.

"As promised, a hint for a hint," he began and was arrested by the mental image of Rosanne's promise to keelhaul him marine-style upon hearing how he had opened his mouth about something that was personal. He chose his next words very carefully. "A creature that can burrow under your skin, leaving nothing but dreams." The men let out disappointed huffs.

"The hell is that?" Denny's words erupted in a flurry of protest.

"That is not fair! We have not got a clue what else was on that island. That's cheap. Very cheap, mate." Quinn's eyes narrowed in discontent.

Aros shrugged. "Anything more, and the captain will keelhaul me," he admitted. At least he spoke the truth this time.

Vincent's eyebrows arched, a finger-wagging in amusement. "False respect of the captain's privacy. *That* is cheating."

"Nothing but the best for the captain," Aros smirked. "Now, tell me, gentlemen. What do you know about this journey? What lurks in the Grey Veil that has you lusting so in your trousers?"

The men fell quiet as Kristoff strolled past, though the young Katshovan appeared to be embroiled in his own thoughts, counting on his fingers. When he was out of earshot, Denny leaned forward. "We're on the hunt for new land. Methinks there are treasures, but no one's confirmed it yet. The captain says we don't know what to expect, but I reckon she's full of shit after the last stunt she pulled. You're not a solicitor perchance?"

"I believe there are monsters," Vincent stated with unwavering conviction.

"I think we're all gonna die." Quinn declared his tone void of any jest.

Aros shook his head. "That's dark, mate. But what if there's treasure? The haul from the other island must have given you blood on your teeth." The men shot him a questioning look. "Blood on your teeth? Hungry for more? You don't know it? Has no one here heard of famous Novalian proverbs? For fuck's sake ... Anyway! *Who* gets to keep a pocket of the newfound riches? You guys understand how the pecking order works. The little man finds the loot, and the captain and the lieutenant get the bigger cut. Now that ain't fair, is it?"

Quinn bobbed his head. "Our last cut was good, but he isn't lying. Fixing the ship didn't give us on the bottom rung much to write home about."

Denny wrinkled his nose. "I've heard Creedy's already squandered his money on booze and gambling. And what do we get? A fresh set of clothes and an allowance lasting us two months. Now, we're back here to earn our wages and crossing our toes for gold."

"I propose a plan," said Aros, lowering himself and prompting the wide-eyed men — excluding the already squinting Quinn—to offer him their full attention. "If we stumble upon riches, we hide a substantial stash only we can access and hand over the remainder to the captain."

"Deal," the three men agreed.

"Woah, now! Your hasty acceptance makes me question your loyalty to this ship. The captain ain't skimping on the pay, is she?"

The three men simultaneously shook their heads. Denny motioned around them. "Fixing the ship cost us a fortune, and we haven't seen any income all summer. We're down to scraping the barrel of our cut from last spring."

"Then what *have* you been doing all summer?" Aros questioned, blinking in confusion. He had assumed that with the riches they'd secured, they would all be enjoying extended siestas on some tropical paradise or, at the very least, invested in their futures.

Denny nodded towards the sky. "Charting the bloody wind currents of the Grey Veil. In and out all fucking summer and nothing to show for it."

A bell rang in Aros' mind. If the ship possessed the technology to chart the Grey Veil, such information was priceless. Could this be what the inquisitors were after? "How'd you manage that without getting lost?"

Denny shrugged. "Haven't the foggiest. The watch captains know something we don't, and the captain hasn't feared the Grey Veil since we visited that island. Something's up." Aros could feel a plan form in his mind. If Captain Drackenheart knew how to navigate the Grey Veil, that could change the future of the trade. People would kill for such information. His former employer would have his head if they got wind of his involvement with the *Red Queen*.

Should've gone home. The thought left a bitter taste in Aros's mouth.

His simple days of working the deck had become significantly more complex, a complication he didn't much appreciate. He harboured a secret, one he needed to unravel to survive should they come across anyone who saw no value in their lives. The difference was that he had found men who, like him, had a thirst for gold and sought to improve their lives. Aros had to be careful.

It wasn't all that surprising that Captain Drackenheart kept secrets from the crew, considering her role. The pressing question was, how could Aros find more information without putting himself at risk? If they were on the hunt for treasure, he was all for it. But if their journey was skinny-dipping with nymphs in shark-infested waters, he needed an exit strategy.

Aros pondered over who among the crew might have the crucial information he needed: the watch captains Creedy and Dalia, Hwang—the head of the seamen, the engineers, and Duplànte—obviously, but he wouldn't even spill his coffee in stormy weather. The sole person on that list likely to open up was Creedy, but only after he'd sunk three bottles of rum. The scornful looks Creedy shot the able-seaman-in-training didn't give Aros much hope. But their voyage could span weeks, and the crew might warm up to him. He hadn't endured months of torture only to be stepped on by blue-collar seamen who thought they were superior to pirates. Especially not when Aros knew which people would be interested in the *Red Queen's* navigational technology of the Grey Veil.

CHAPTER SEVEN

IDA SIMONSEN

I da sat on the forecastle with her tablet, turning the dials on the sides to adjust the signal received as static lines and electronic snow obscuring the scan. With the central dot pinpointing the *Red Queen*, a second dot to the north sent sweeping, rippling waves of new information across the screen, the expanding rings fading at the edges. Hunched over the tablet, Ida brushed a loose strand of blonde hair behind her ear.

The *Red Queen* flew in the southern wind corridor arching north. The passage was wider than what Ida's device could read—more than half a kilometre she gauged—but the wind was weaker and sporadic on one side, often twirling into wisps.

Despite being this far south, the weather remained chill, like the coast of Noval. Ida wore a snowflake-patterned wool sweater, her many-pocketed trousers and leather boots. Her tool belt rested next to her, filled with screwdrivers, electrical measuring equipment, pliers, and everything she needed on a day-to-day basis for maintaining the many kinds of technology the *Red Queen* employed.

Creedy and Olivier squatted beside her, staring at the screen over her shoulder.

"Nice sweater," Olivier marvelled.

"Thanks. My mom knit it for me. Said to bring it for when it gets cold."

Olivier rubbed his arms as he wore only a cotton, long-sleeved shirt, and he was barefoot, as he enjoyed treading the decks and ratlines that way. The temperatures had dropped in the last hour, and most sensible sailors had changed into warmer wool and caps. Creedy donned a plain grey sweater dotted with cigarette burns and stains. He smelled just as dodgy, too; Ida noticed and wrinkled her nose.

"Do you even have free time to be tinkering with that?" Creedy asked. Without tearing her eyes away from the screen, Ida adjusted another dial and wrote the numbers on the bottom of the screen in a notebook beside her.

"We got ambushed badly by wind funnels, pirates, and that electrical storm. With this, if I can get it working properly, we can predict the weather before it hits us. It's crude, but I think I might expand on it, if I can only get these damn calibrations correct." She let out a frustrated huff, making Olivier and Creedy shrink back to give her space.

"How are you getting the sphere back?" Olivier tried, his pronounced lisp muddling the words, but Ida understood him anyway.

Ida pointed to a net to her right. "I can make it stationary, so when we get close enough, we can catch it."

Olivier took the net in his hands. "Just with this? Can't you put a fishing line on it and reel it in?"

Ida laughed.

"What about a manual recall button?" Creedy offered.

She blinked at him. "You think I installed mini-thrusters into a ball the size of my fist? I'm not that good. An electrical field around it prevents it from going too slow, but if I disable it as long as it is within reach," she pushed a button, and on display, the ball started getting closer to the central mass that was the ship, "it negates the surrounding air, thanks to anti-gravity technology."

"Sounds more complicated than mini-thrusters," Creedy commented with a wry expression.

"Says the man who knows the ins and outs of aether sail technology and can fix it with needlework and a strip of glue."

Creedy ruffled her hair and strolled back below the main deck.

Fixing her locks, Ida stared at the screen. "It should arrive in a few moments. Get ready."

Olivier shifted his weight to the balls of his feet. "Why didn't you stay in Valo with Nelson?"

Uncertainty crossed her face. Bobbing her head, she struggled to form a proper reply. "He had stuff to do, and I'm not done apprenticing with Higgs yet."

"But you're okay, though?"

"Yeah. Yeah, I think we are okay. It's not like he asked me to marry him, although that is implied, considering he met my parents." She let out a nervous chuckle but shook her head. "Ship life isn't Nelson's style, and I want more experience before I set up shop somewhere. We're making it work in the meantime."

Nodding, Olivier placed a hand on her shoulder and looked her dead in the eyes. "If things don't work out with Blackwood, you can give Isaac a chance." He grinned.

It was only yesterday they were all pressed against the captain's door, listening to Rosanne's infuriated holler. After that, word spread like wildfire throughout the ship. The pirate who had stranded them in the Grey Veil was among their ranks.

"That is disgusting." Ida shuddered.

"I heard that." Isaac, less commonly known as former Captain Bernhart of the *Blue Dragon*, walked up to them on the forecastle, feigning hurt. "What is so disgusting about me?"

"You're old," Ida retorted, but it wasn't the excuse she really wanted to use. She simply didn't like him.

Isaac slapped a hand over his breast. "Little lady, I am in my thirties and still quite the looker. It's all about taste."

"I guess you haven't looked at yourself in a mirror then."

Olivier barked a laugh as Isaac retorted, "Just wait until your boy toy reaches thirty, and he'll go bald and have a beard."

Screwing up her face at the thought, Ida refocused on the tablet screen.

"Be ready, Olivier. The device is almost within reach."

The little metal ball emerged from the fog like a slow moving projectile, throwing Olivier, Ida, and Isaac into a frantic chase down the forecastle, across the main deck, and to the sterncastle stairs. Olivier swung the net. It grazed the metal ball, knocked it aside where it remained to hover just above the deck, the floorboards flying past at high speed.

"We're flying too fast!" Ida sprinted after it. Olivier tripped on the topmost step and face-planted on the deck. Ida snatched the net from his flailing hands. She swung it once, twice, but missed both times. Isaac swiped his cap over the ball, securing it in his hands.

"What's this wonderful technology you've got here?" He turned the sphere around in his hand, taking in the intricate details of the metal sphere. The tiny antennas and holes created the null field that countered the Grey Veil's electrical field.

"Give it back, please." Ida's typically bubbly voice and smiling eyes were replaced with suspicion, reservation, and deep contempt. Isaac stared at her for a moment, then shrugged.

"All yours, little lady." He clapped the sphere into her hands and proceeded downstairs. Ida spent a moment regaining her breath. Olivier dusted himself off and came up to her.

"I don't like him," she said, letting her scornful eyes follow him to the main deck.

Olivier did the same. "Me neither. He does not belong here."

"It's not just that. He works well and knows the basics, but everything about him makes me question his motives. The way he carries himself around the ship makes my skin crawl."

"Fake as the doc's hair." Olivier quipped.

After a pause, she asked, "What does Dalia say about him?"

Olivier scratched his stubbled chin. "He's charming with her. Dalia don't care for it but plays along. Says that we all came from similar places and not to judge."

"Well, she isn't wrong. But I'm not so sure his intentions are that simple. He may work hard, but he's far too comfortable on a ship to come right from the streets. We should spread the word, at least to those in our inner circle. I don't like how much he's chatting up the other crew with his jokes and easy smiles. And I don't like him calling me 'little lady' either." Ida patted down her arms as if shaking off the pet name Isaac had given her.

"You don't feel safe without Nelson here to protect you? Ye of little faith." Olivier commented.

"It's not that! You're all great, but it's him I don't trust." She nodded towards Isaac, who was chatting with a couple of deckhands, saying something that made them all burst out in laughter. "Few people give me the willies, but he's one of them."

Olivier nodded and patted her shoulder. "He might be just trying too hard."

"I'm sure you're right. But with us inside the Veil again ..." she let words hang but couldn't avert her eyes from the man who had almost killed them all.

Ida returned to engineering on the cargo deck. Squeezed into the outer hulls, the crew quarters contained a sparsely furnished sleeping cot with a single desk and working lamp. Ida shared quarters with Gavin. Their modest room consisted of a bunk bed stacked against the wall and boxes of mechanical parts on and under the desk. They didn't have windows on this deck like traditional aero-ships, but Ida was used to alchemical lamps, which were stronger, clearer, and lasted longer than oil lamps. It had been the best investment for the department after their last cut.

She placed the sphere into a depression carved into the table. Nuts, bolts, and other instruments of the trade occupied the other depressions. The hardwood stool was merciless on the buttocks without a cushion, but she sat down anyway and stared at her handiwork strewn across the table, all in varying states of completion. She had buried herself in work all summer, and the few precious days when they resupplied in Valo, she spent with Nelson. It had already been two weeks since they left, but it felt like months.

Twirling a finger around a mass of pistons and bolts jutting from a different spherical invention, Ida let her head and thoughts rest on the table for a melancholic yet lonely moment of contemplation. Olivier's question revived feelings she had suppressed for weeks. Perhaps she should have stayed in Valo? She had the money, and she could bunk with her aunt on the farm outside of the city or even with her parents if she was desperate. So why hadn't she?

Ida let her hand glide across the beaten surface, feeling the grooves and depressions caused by her soldering tools and dropping heavy objects. She knew the table like the back of her own hand, knew every nook and cranny of this room she had bunked in for many years. The only life she knew was with Higgs before he lost his shop and their life aboard the *Red Queen*. Ida had never been without her found family, Higgs and Gavin. It was the best home she had ever known. The thought of living somewhere else settled like a tight knot in her stomach. Apathy overtook her reasoning, leaving her immobile and staring.

Nelson might have come along on the voyage, like Antony. A curious choice, Ida thought. Captain DiCroce cracked down on piracy and smuggling at the RDA's behest, while the *Red Queen* ... Ida let the thought disintegrate in its infancy. Letting Captain DiCroce aboard was a bad idea, he being the exact opposite of what the *Red Queen* stood for. But seeing how Rosanne was with the man—infatuated, that being the emotional limit of her ability to display affection—and with him saving their butts after the Veil broke their ship, Ida accepted their temporary alliance. Even if he was a guest aboard the ship, he helped where he could and showed interest in their inner workings and technology, although that might be professional curiosity rather than gathering intel.

He did an excellent job of hiding his intentions if he was out to arrest them. But the captain kept their business confidential, and the only law they were breaking was the Grey Veil travel ban, which no one enforced. If anyone pursued the lawbreakers, they would have a hard time surviving.

She picked up the sphere and turned it in her hand. Crude instruments and excessively low temperatures during the shaping process had left the metal surface uneven, but the bevelled depressions acted like dishes that could pick up the signals it emitted from tiny holes around the sphere. She gave it a firm squeeze with both hands and twisted. The protective lid came apart, revealing the chaotic interior of wires around a central glass chamber with swirling anti-gravity minerals.

She disconnected the chamber and held it before the lamplight, where the dense particles drowned out any light in black. Without the electrical current to disable its properties, the chamber floated on its own. The reused dust was impure and filled with trace particles found in the air, but it could still hold the weight of the object it connected with.

The mysterious properties of these invaluable minerals, which the Queen's Colonies discovered less than a century ago, had always fascinated Ida. She wanted to learn more, but such knowledge was confidential, and processing raw anti-gravity minerals was under the Queen's domain. Everything went through their processing plants in Queensland, including their mining operations around the world. The minerals were unique to the Grey Veil, originating from somewhere inside. That would mean the Veil would eventually dry up, right?

A hard rap on the door startled her, and Ida dropped the anti-gravity chamber. It drifted on by itself. The door opened, and Higgs popped his head inside.

"There you are, girl. Didn't you hear the dinner bell?" His gruff voice was laced with a curious softness at her startled expression.

Ida blinked. "No, sorry. My head's not quite here." She shook the thoughts away and plastered on a smile. Higgs snatched the floating piece of glass.

"Still working hard on your inventions, eh? You getting anywhere?"

"I still need to adjust the wiring and signal amplifications. Make a ball with a bigger surface area the signals can bounce back on."

"It's a nifty little gadget if you get it working." He returned the glass to her. "Remember to rest and not just drown yourself in work."

"Am I that obvious?" Her tired complexion prompted a sympathetic crinkle in his eyes, and Higgs ruffled her hair. "Why does everyone have to do that?" She swatted at his hand.

"Like sizzling bacon. Now, come on. Get some tucker in that body of yours." Higgs tapped the doorframe before he left, but Ida didn't have the mental strength to follow. Loud voices and ignorant words would press on her insecurities, causing her to destabilise and lose what little cool she had, and she didn't know why she felt so at a loss with herself lately. Perhaps it was missing Nelson or the underlying fear of what they might discover inside the Veil. She lingered for a few more minutes until the thought seemed less daunting and mustered her courage to leave the safety of her room.

CHAPTER EIGHT

WE'RE NOT IN NOVAL ANYMORE

The captain's quarters were wreathed in impenetrable darkness, brought on by lightproof curtains drawn in front of stained-glass windows. Rosanne kept an oil lamp lit for her convenience and flipped the carpet spread over the midsection aside. At first glance, the dark wooden floor appeared bare and untampered, but along a pattern of dark knots in the wood, if one lowered the light, one could perceive the faint outline of a hidden compartment. Rosanne dug her thumb into a knot in the wood, and a button clicked, followed by a soft whirring of a mechanism sprung to life. An uneven panel of floorboards popped open. Setting the lamp down, she moved the lid aside, revealing a depression in the floor where the very illegal but exceedingly handy Geographical Positioning Tracker rested.

Reaching into the depression in the floor, she clicked another button on the side that raised the GPT to above floor level and displayed the four rods, which unfolded like a blooming flower. Light flickered as the rods sent out blue beams through a complicated light-refracting process that Higgs had explained to her—during which Rosanne's eyes had started to glaze over—and the light converged to create a holographic representation of the planet's surface, at least in part. Rosanne hadn't yet sailed all over the world to verify if the machine was capable of recording everything, but so far, it showed promise. With the tracking active, Rosanne could trace their route from the southern colonies of Ovrack straight west into the Grey Veil and see how they now followed a northern current circulating the southern tail of the Veil. Thanks to Farand's meticulous wind charts and Ida's weather sphere, they could collaborate to create an accurate picture of their travel route, where the nightmares of finding longitude were just that.

Rosanne fetched the map made by R.S. Thompson, unrolled it on the floor next to the GPT, and secured it with paperweights. She fetched another set of maps showing wind currents inside a massive pencil blob representing the Grey Veil, using the southern colonies of Ovrack and Queensland to the northeast as a reference.

The GPT tracked their position in terms of travel distance, but the maps of the wind currents assisted Rosanne with keeping them on a course of least resistance and conserving their power. Overlaying Farand's wind-currents in combination with Ida's invention and the travel time in the wind tunnels could be halved. The GPT mapped places they went to, but it didn't have a topographical visual. She could trace their route north, which eased her worries. But there was no telling if the mapped southern wind currents connected or if they changed due to electrical storms or coiled, like the vortex the *Retribution* circulated for six months. She refused to let her ship suffer the same fate.

Rosanne studied the two islands on the outskirts of the Thompson map. If the islands followed the same laws of physics as the floating rock belt surrounding the northern island, another large continent might draw the isles to it through a central force. They should be able to find it along their current route.

Rosanne jotted down their elapsed path in her notebook and drew a line inside the wind charts. Now that she understood more of the inner workings of the weather patterns within the Veil, Rosanne's confidence increased, along with their chances of finding the isles. The *Retribution* had almost claimed them all, but her inexperience and lack of knowledge were to blame.

"Curse you, Blackwood," Rosanne muttered, recalling the lawyer Nelson, blackmailing her into undertaking that search-and-confirm mission. But it was also thanks to him that they had found Thompson's map and clues to her father's last voyage in the Grey Veil before he perished.

While Rosanne recollected that disastrous journey with a bitter taste, she reassured herself that they were better prepared than any ship before them. The technology to navigate the Veil was before her father's days, and as far as she knew, no one else possessed it either.

"You've done everything right," Rosanne reassured herself, refolding the maps and hiding the GPT. Her attempt at self-reassurance failed to ease her discomfort. She flicked open her pocket watch, which was still in working condition thanks to Higgs installing an anti-veil field in the room. The technology worked long enough to allow her to keep track of time, but its flaws required her to let the device rest every few hours. It was like wading through an ocean of tall grass, only finding vantage points tall enough to look around now and then. Fumbling around, but with a purpose.

There was a knock on her door. Rosanne parted the curtains, flooding the room with soft grey daylight. "Come in," she called, setting herself to clear the rest of the maps. Antony popped his head inside, positively beaming.

"How were the games?" she asked.

Antony grabbed a chair by the desk, turning it so he sat facing her as she went about rolling maps into tubes and locking them in the cabinet. "Hammond makes a mean mutton stew, but Vasilyev is a pro at sleight-of-hand, and I'm not sure which I distrust more in King of the Hill: Hammond's food bribery or Kristoff's card cheating." His infectious mirth served as its own confirmation that he had enjoyed his break with the crew in the galley. He conversed well with her crew, or it could simply be that Antony was an easy person to be around.

"They'll steal a lot more than your money if you let them," Rosanne chuckled. "But on to a more serious question. It's your first time in the Veil. How are you finding it?"

Antony folded his hands in his lap, his eyes locked on a specific spot on the floor, and sucked in a breath. "It's quieter than I thought it would be. There is always noise in the ocean and sky: a seagull, the splashing of whales, and other ships. Out here, there's nothing but fog. At first, I was nervous, but seeing as nothing has happened so far, it feels more like bad weather. I think our preconceived notion that dangers are lurking in every part of the Veil makes us paranoid."

"You won't be saying that if we get ambushed by an electrical storm or a cyclone," she said, wiggling her eyebrows.

"You don't say? So far, you seem to know what you're doing."

Rosanne tucked a strand of hair behind her ear. "It's not my first time, but the fog can play tricks on your mind. Sometimes, we hear things that aren't there. That's why I don't leave anyone alone."

He folded his arms and thrust up his chin, smirking. "I see. So, I am your emotional anchor, then?"

"Of course. Every ship needs a handsome mascot strutting about," Rosanne said, and they shared a laugh. Rosanne sat down by the desk, rolling her shoulders to chase away the stiffness in them. A rumbling, deep wail resonated from outside, penetrating the hum of the thruster engine. Turning towards the window and seeing nothing but the grey fog, Rosanne's breath hitched; her eyes were wide and alert.

"Please tell me you also heard that," she said, stiffening in her seat.

Antony nodded, his focus on the outside as well. "Maybe it was a whale."

"At this altitude?"

Rosanne noted the steady pace of the *Red Queen*, feeling no change in direction or altitude. After a minute of silence, they exchanged glances, Antony shaking his head in confusion. Rosanne let out her breath.

"Whatever it was, maybe it's gone," she said, interlacing her fingers to try to stem the tremor in them. Antony placed his hand over hers, drawing her attention.

"Nothing happened, Ros,"

"Nothing *yet*," she said, her thin-lipped mouth accompanying worried eyes, the memories of last spring flooding her like a broken dam.

A shadow swept over the *Red Queen*, throwing her quarters into the dark gloom.

"It's too early for sundown," Antony said, frowning and releasing Rosanne's hands. She fought against the thumping in her chest.

"Let's go outside. This isn't helping me at all," she said. The chair screeched against the floorboards as she stood.

Nodding, Antony joined Rosanne as she exited to the quarterdeck. Lieutenant Farand Duplànte's chiselled features were stiff and focused as if expecting an attack. Creedy and Dalia exchanged words, their eyes searching their surroundings. Lyle's men were seen scurrying around the decks, weapons at hand.

"Update," she softly asked as she came up to Farand. Before the man could reply, a crack resounded against the floorboards on the main deck, making Rosanne jump and reach for her plasma pistol. Before she could see what it was, Kristoff cried out from the forecastle, and another crack broke the air. A small but firm object crashed onto the sterncastle, throwing everyone into a pre-emptive state of panic and causing them to duck for cover from the aerial assault.

Antony and Rosanne both squeezed next to Farand as if the large man could shield them from the invisible attack. Before Rosanne could investigate, a head splitting scraping sound issued from above—the main mast was caught on something. The sudden lurch of the ship threw them both off their feet, tumbling them back into the wall of her quarters. Crew members slid down the decks, grasping for handrails or secured crates. Surprised yells called all over the ship.

Farand snatched the lever back, feeding power into the forecastle thruster ports. As they continued to rise, the bowsprit pointed towards the dark skies, going, going. The ports hissed to life, and the ship slowed in an upward arch. Chips of wood and rock showered down on the deck. Farand wrapped his arms over his head, still clutching the wheel, unable to steer the ship's nose down. Rosanne rolled onto all fours, bracing herself against the steep incline of the quarterdeck. She hooked onto the mizzenmast and swung herself towards the helm. Farand fumbled for the engine buttons, but amid the hail of debris and struggling to keep the wheel from pulling back, he couldn't find the panel. Protected by her hat, Rosanne swiped her hand over the switches, heard the clicks of contact, and silenced the hum of the thruster engine.

The momentum slowed until the ship came to a bowing halt, and the hull thrusters forced the vessel back. Rosanne leaned against the mast before shifting her stance to stand firmly on the floor.

Wide-eyed and huffing, she glanced at Farand, who mouthed a curse as he wrestled with the wheel, managing to move off it just enough to level the ship. They all stood for a breathless moment, stunned and confused, trying to comprehend what had just happened. Seconds later, Olivier emerged from the crow's nest, scuttled along the mast, and nosedived for a rope before sliding down.

"Are you alright, Olivier?" Farand called out, having rushed to meet his brother.

"I'm fine!" He replied, his voice shaky. "Something attacked me." His panic accentuated his lips, and he shook out his wool sweater.

"Do you hear that? Over the engine?" Dalia asked, pointing to the source. Rosanne listened, sharpening her senses until she picked up faint but distinct pulsating echoes. Another sharp thunk resounded from the forecastle. The crew threw their hands above their heads, scanning the skies. Fat drops of water rained from above, but they were too scattered to be rain.

Rosanne jerked to attention when something crackled in her boot. She looked down to see a crab wiggling with pointy legs, its body broken from the fall. Its spotted shell glowed with red rings, pulsating as if in a futile attempt to ward off enemies.

The commotion on the deck grew, fuelled by quick whispers and pointing fingers toward the main mast–the source of their sudden halt.

The fog cleared around the mast's broken tip, which poked against a rocky surface teeming with thousands of creatures. The reverberating echo of their wet scuttling resonated, bouncing off the rocks they clambered on.

Rosanne gaped in astonishment at the shadowed underside of the massive rocky formation that was anything but bare. Twigs of coral jutted from the surface, tended to by milling crabs. Floating fish darted around them, biting at the hard shells or outright swallowing smaller ones whole. Broad-winged manta rays swooped over the ship's deck and beelined for the crabs, scurrying for cover in rocky nooks.

The commotion had drawn everyone to the main deck. They stared wide-eyed, pointing in horrified excitement at what appeared to be a reef. Rosanne and Farand were too stunned to give orders. Olivier fished out a tiny crab still caught in his sweater, holding it by its shell before his colleagues. Hammond locked his eyes on the crab and snapped it from Olivier.

"Someone yelled for me?" Hammond let out a chortle at this sudden feast raining from the sky, where most people sought shelter under the overhang of the forecastle.

"Anything you recognise, Mr. Hammond?" Rosanne called from the helm, her hands stacked atop her head.

"No, ma'am! Never seen shell shapes or colours like these."

The little creature flared with colour, snapping at Hammond's beard.

Unable to avert her gaze from the creepy crawlies scuttling on the rocks, Rosanne leaned closer to her lieutenant. "You think we should backtrack and climb to higher altitudes?"

Farand nodded, still stupefied.

Antony's open-mouthed wonder turned into a grin of excitement. "I understand now why you sail the Grey Veil, Ros. The things you see make the ordinary of the known world seem bland."

"I'd rather face ordinary than extraordinary. These are the least strange things I've seen." Rosanne said, taking the wheel and punting the crab at her feet overboard. More crabs, in varying shapes and sizes, rained down from above in a steady, almost rhythmic clunking. The crew brushed off the dead ones and chased the live ones.

Re-firing the thruster engine, Rosanne turned the ship around, following the underside of the reef formation and climbing in altitude at a gentle slope for the better part of the next half an hour.

"Are you thinking the same as me, Farand?" she confided to the large man. Nodding, he fixed his eyes on the uneven surface.

"This might be one of the isles we're looking for."

Rosanne stared at the altitude metre, which passed the two-kilometre mark. The fog along the roof was thinner here, mere wisps in comparison. She wiped a sheen of sweat forming on her forehead. "Is it getting warmer?" she asked.

"You're not wrong, Captain," Farand said, fanning himself with his hat. The moisture left pearls of water droplets on his tight curls and darkened his twin-buttoned jacket. The vast shadow above them disappeared as if someone had withdrawn a curtain and replaced it with white clouds. Rosanne kept a steady pace for a few more minutes, steering clear of any potential obstructions in the uneven rocks.

"Sky!" Creedy called from the forecastle.

Subtle traces of blue peeked through the layers of mist, breaking the monotony of the Veil. The light hit them like hot daggers. Rosanne shielded her eyes but embraced the sun on her skin. Cumulus clouds lay thick about them in pillows of white. The wall of the Grey Veil loomed at its outskirts a few hundred metres away, warded, it seemed, by an invisible force. She steered the *Red Queen* around a cloud, pulled the ship's nose skywards, and flipped in the direction.

The sultry air was a welcome change from the chill underside, replaced by a sky spreading out like a blue blanket embroidered with feathery clouds and, before them, land. Mist-shrouded viridian forests of towering trees dotted the landmass, with sharp, white-crested mountains cutting through the island like an elevated scar. At the island's periphery, lakes were encased in the hollowed crust with boulder-lined edges. It was an island, but not the isles they were looking for. This was much, much bigger.

Rosanne let herself catch a breath as she took it all in. The view stung her eyes with its mystified beauty and the realisation that she might have found the land her father had traversed all those years ago. She pushed back the tears, reminding herself that this was the first step of their journey. The isles were nowhere in sight, and they were vital to this whole operation.

"Listen up!" she announced to the crew, who lined up before her with excited expressions. "You all remember the island in the north. We can expect other nasty surprises in this place. I want no one to venture off on their own. You go in teams or not at all. We find a safe spot, set up camp, and get our bearings. No ambushes this time!"

"Aye, Captain!" they called in unison, scattering back to their teams.

She let a shaky breath escape and turned to her lieutenant. "I can feel it, Farand. This is the land the map told us about. We need to find corresponding locations, and maybe, just maybe, we'll get answers. My father was here for a reason, and he left it alive. I want to know how and why." She shook, barely able to contain her excitement.

"Beyond the clouds—" Farand began.

"The sky is always blue," Rosanne finished with a grin.

Farand lumbered down the stairs to the gun deck, where Lyle and his men performed their weapons check. The door to the gunroom stood ajar, and the men swapped rifle heads and ammunition or armed themselves with daggers for close combat. A couple sported sabres, while others preferred the bayonet-tipped rifles, a modification carried over when gunpowder was replaced by plasma created from superheated anti-gravity crystals. The Grey Veil provides, Farand mused.

"Mr. Duplànte, sir," Lyle greeted, straight-backed and attentive. His men followed suit, but Farand dismissed the notion with a wave of his hand.

"Why the change?" Farand nodded to the guns. He'd never cared much for firearms, not even during his cadet days with the Royal Navy in mock sea battles against the Einsbor fleet. He much preferred to shout orders and coordinate teams, but this time, he would have to stick to managing the decks in silence. Who knew what monsters he would attract if he were to open his mouth?

"Gunpowder ammunition will be difficult in this tropical heat and moisture, and I'm not taking any chances of another pirate attack," Lyle said. "Plasma will be more efficient and quieter. I wouldn't want anyone or anything to hear us before we even set foot in the jungle." A sound reasoning Farand shared. Plasma was a logical first choice being this far away from civilisation and with a limited ammunition supply.

"Vigilance is key," Farand said suddenly, the rustle and clacks of changing magazines dimming to silence at this change in tone, the men giving him their utmost attention. "This will be your sacred duty as long as we are here. Keep an eye out for anything unusual that doesn't look normal. You report to me or the captain and always have a skeleton team circling our camp or wherever we might venture."

"Yes, sir. I've had enough of feet-grabbing monsters and trolls with excellent aim." Lyle agreed, and absent-mindedly rubbed at his shin.

Farand had heard the tales from Lyle and his men about how trolls had ambushed them in the forest during their confrontation with the pirate crew. The last thing he wanted was to be hauled into darkened caves to be sliced and served as dinner. The captain had more tales of creatures than Farand would hopefully never have the chance of meeting, but if this place was anything like that island, they could never rest easy. However, if Captain Drackenheart Senior could escape this island alive, so could they.

"I want all gunports closed tight. All quarter doors are locked. If anything gets aboard the ship, they will have a tough time getting around," Farand said.

"Yes, sir," Lyle replied and tested the reload mechanism on top of the plasma rifle, letting the charge reach the chamber in a whirring crescendo, he pulled the locking mechanism back, and cut off the charge before it could be released. He handed it off to one of his men.

Farand made his rounds through the ship, checking the food supply storage, now riddled with pots of salt to suck the moisture out of the air and to kill the unusual aroma coming from Hammond's food experimentations. The orlop deck remained organised as he went over the straps securing the crates and barrels. The water storage in the ballast chamber hadn't run off or shifted, but he gave the straps another tug just in case. They were prepared this time. He knew that.

He peered out of one of the open gunports, his eyes gliding over the lush forest below them. He spotted an enclosed beach, a perfect place for a camp. He closed the lid and secured the peg, locking it.

He jumped in response to a faint scuttling of tiny claws on wood. His eyes flew to the floor, but the source of the noise was already gone.

"Must have been a rat," he muttered and briefly wondered where Senior Ratcatcher Fuzzypaws had skulked off to. Snoozing in one of the storage rooms, undoubtedly. Ida and Gavin strolled up the stairs, so embroiled in their conversation they passed by him without a greeting.

"I am not on call this evening. You are," Ida's voice rang in an annoyed pitch.

"Please swap with me. I am so tired!" Gavin whined.

"Absolutely not. I wasn't the one who drank with Kristoff until dawn," Ida replied.

"Higgs will tan my hide," Gavin added.

"Take it up with Mr. Duplànte while we're here then," Ida motioned towards Farand, who crossed his arms at the junior engineers.

Gavin's panic-stricken face quickly turned neutral as he feigned calm. "I'm fine with the night shift. Good day to you, sir," he nodded as they passed the lieutenant. Farand shook his head.

"A moment, you two," he called. They paused.

"Sir?" Ida asked.

"We briefed you on the lockdown protocols, right?"

"Grilled like Hammond's dingo barbie," Gavin replied. Farand nodded and waved them on. His underlying nervousness didn't help the situation they were getting themselves into. The closer they came to land, the more Farand feared they would repeat their last disastrous voyage. His shoulder throbbed with his growing unease, and he massaged the three-clawed scar, a memento of his fight against the hulder. Farand never wanted to relive those moments when his confidence wavered. Yet, as prepared and drilled as they were, the oncoming beach reminded Farand he needed to get his act together. He needed to be the lieutenant this ship needed, the support Captain Drackenheart required, and he needed to stop being so hard on himself.

CHAPTER NINE
WELCOME TO THE JUNGLE

A thick fog hung low over the jungle at midday. The *Red Queen* glided over the crystal-blue shallows at a snail's pace, heading towards a small cove surrounded by bare rock and a sandy beach. Lyle and his men stood stationed around the deck, their plasma rifles ready and keen eyes watching. Below them, schools of fish swam in great blobs of darkness, interrupted by a hungry shark cutting through for a meal. Belts of corals lined the shallows, meandering towards the deeper blue waters, and then stopped by the rocky ledge of the island, keeping its ocean in place.

Lyle came up to Rosanne as she slowed the ship to a crawl. "All is clear, Captain. Nothing of note so far."

Rosanne didn't know what she expected, but she was relieved to hear it. "Scout the beach, but leave someone in the nest. If we're being ambushed from anywhere, they would see it from there first."

Lyle nodded and sent a wave of hand signals to his men.

Rosanne lowered the ship until it hovered a few metres above the ground. The jungle of tall trees and lush vegetation would make it difficult for anyone to spot the camp from the ground, and limit access.

They used rope ladders and longboats to disembark. That way, no one could abscond with the vessel and stuff it into a volcano, unlike what the hulder did.

As the engine powered down and the sails disconnected, Norman dropped the anchor with a pull of a lever. The mechanism whirred to life in a series of rhythmic clangs from the gun deck. The anchor hit the rocky outcrop, and the flukes locked the ship in place.

Rosanne removed her gloves to brush the hair off her face. The surrounding air was clean, gentle, and warm, a stark contrast to the biting northern winds or the smog-filled docks at the skyports. Rosanne closed her eyes as the breeze brushed against her skin. The shuffle of boots against the wooden decks resonated through her, the voices of the crew a mixed murmur in the background as they went about their tasks.

When Rosanne opened her eyes again, the sky was the clearest blue she had ever seen. Her expression hardened as she knew that the beauty of this island could be deceiving. This was the last known location where her father and his crew were still alive. Now, they needed to find the mapped coastline and its secrets.

"Captain!" Farand called from the main deck, standing next to the hovering longboats filling with people and supplies, disembarking to the beach. "We're ready to leave."

A third, much smaller boat seated Olivier and Hwang. "We're off to scout, Captain," Hwang informed.

Rosanne gave them an approving nod, and the two men set off in the tiny boat, leaving a trail of blazing blue flame as they zipped around the ridge, heading west.

Approaching the longboats, Rosanne adjusted her hat and turned to the remaining crew. "We set up camp. No one wanders off, and if anyone sees or hears anything strange, you inform your watch captains or Duplànte the first chance you get."

The men and women nodded, filling the air with a cheerful "aye!"

Lyle and his men established a perimeter on the outskirts of the jungle while the crew set up their tents. A small group went to fetch firewood, and another team prepared supplies and gear to scout the nearby ridge.

Hammond caught the lower-ranking seamen and put them on kitchen duty; Norman threw the fishing net around with no clue what he was doing while Kristoff moved crates at the cook's whim. They sent Kavanaugh with a basket to gather crabs, and the sight reminded Rosanne of watching the manor servants chase the chickens her family would have for dinner- a lifetime ago. She revelled a little too much at him fumbling around the sand but shook the glee aside as she had more pressing matters to attend to.

The tall main tent was suitable for hosting meetings if the firepit didn't suffice. Rosanne shifted the crates to build a makeshift table with Antony lending a hand. Despite not being on duty or even a part of the crew, Antony pulled his own weight wherever he could. He kept himself busy, giving Rosanne breathing room when she didn't have time to play the good host.

Lyle appeared in the tent opening with four men. "We're ready to scout the area, ma'am."

"If you're not back before dark, I'm not sending anyone to look for you." She flashed them a mischievous smirk.

Lyle let out a dejected moan, feigning hurt.

"Before you go, Mr. Lyle," Rosanne halted them with a simple gesture of her pointed finger trained at the recruit with the awful buzz-cut, "bring him with you."

Lyle's eyebrows shot up. "I'm surprised you would even allow the former Captain Bernhart a firearm."

"He'll do with a sabre. You are the best person to make him squirm when I'm too busy to figure out what he's up to. If he's as cowardly as I remember, this test will be easy."

"With pleasure, Captain." Lyle nodded to his men, and they marched over to Aros, who paused his chore and stared at them in confusion before they hauled him away by each arm. Rosanne enjoyed the half-panicked negotiation Aros threw at them, and when his eyes caught hers, she smiled and waved.

Aros wasn't enjoying any of it. Trekking through the sweltering jungle accompanied by the *Red Queen*'s sharpshooter—who had been responsible for decommissioning the expensive plasma cannon on *The Blue Dragon*—was the last thing he wanted in terms of grunt work.

With sabre in hand, Aros hacked a path for the group, spearheading the trek as the rest kept watch, much like how he had led the way through the swamp before that ghoul sleeping in the waters attacked them. The forest was alive with movement from the leafy undergrowth to the canopies. Insects as large as Aros' hand scuttled across tree trunks and over their shoes, making the men jump in terror and punt the critters into the afterlife. The flying bugs nipped on their skin and drank their sweat, coming in large clusters and sticking to them like the plague. This felt like a punishment, but with the Queen's long, lawful arm out of reach, Aros almost felt safe. Almost.

"Let's head for that ridge and get our bearings." Lyle pointed to a rocky face on the nearby hill. Captain Drackenheart had chosen her landing point well, as this island's personal sea, and the gnarly terrain—which would make a land-based attack difficult—surrounded the beach.

Aros chose his steps carefully, leading the men around a giant tree with tall roots snaking over the ground. Thick sap ran from the crevices of its layered bark, encasing a broad-shelled beetle glinting in the sunlight.

The trees thinned the closer they got to the ridge, replaced by low-growing bushes and, after that, rocky slabs. Sparse foliage with tufts of grass and crawler vines jutted through the ground. From this vantage point, the ship stood out like a sore thumb, but the jungle concealed the beach. Intruders would still have a hard time reaching camp without alerting everyone in the vicinity, and the wildlife was vocal about their passing. Primates jumped across branches, howling at them and moving in clusters, probably to scare off the intruders. *Us*, Aros thought.

On the top of the ridge, the five men paused to catch their breaths. They hunched down next to a cluster of leafy bushes, staying low so as not to draw attention to themselves. The landscape before them was a dense and tall woodland with the occasional rolling hill as sparse decoration, before transitioning to the jagged mountains cutting west like the edge of a crude knife. The ribbons of mist cleared with the growing heat of the day.

Aros wiped his sweaty forehead and squinted against the sun. The woodlands appeared undisturbed by human hands, with no signs of flying ships having wound up here of their own accord or by accident. A small cluster of grey smoke, almost completely obscured by the white clouds, nestled around one of the tallest mountaintops where the jagged face had been worn down.

Aros stuck out a finger in the direction, drawing the team's attention. "There's smoke coming from that mountaintop."

The master gunner stared through the rifle scope towards the mountain, a grim expression replacing his calm demeanour.

"You think it's people?" Aros pressed.

Lyle shook his head. "Odd place to live, wouldn't you say? We're far above the water level, and at that mountaintop's elevation, breathing would be difficult."

"Could be locals, like those things we saw last spring. We did meet a ghoul living in a bog once," Aros mused.

"A fair point," Lyle responded, twitching his moustache as he often did when thinking, Aros noticed.

"Sir, there's another vantage point due east. It looks like we can make it there and back to camp before nightfall," one man suggested. Carlos, Aros recalled.

"Break's over. Let's not waste any precious daytime," Lyle told the men.

Aros groaned, knowing his feet would suffer gnaw-blistering pain because he hadn't worn the right pair of shoes. Again.

The sweltering heat and high humidity left Aros's breath laboured and watery, and the gnawing pain from his blistering feet was no less helpful. Images of the northern, monster-infested island flashed in his mind, and he considered adopting the natural shoe approach if not for the scouting team's incessant push into the jungle.

"Timeout. For the love of Terra, I need to sit." He found the nearest fallen log and limped with each step. His teammates groaned in frustration.

"You were clearly not prepared for this," Lyle pointed out, with only the barest hint of animosity. He sat at the end of the same log.

Aros huffed. "You guys dragged me off against my wishes and shift schedule. Besides, it's my shoes that are killing me."

The barest of smiles snaked up the sides of Lyle's lips, almost hidden under his moustache. "Boots fit for piloting but not for hiking. How do you work the deck in those?"

Aros paused. "You and the captain are two peas in a pod. Do you know that, old timer? I expected sand and crabs, not mist and friction. Gimme a moment to fix this awful pain." Aros picked at the leaves by the trunk and yanked free a pile of grass. If his shoe problem was this similar to his last journey, what else had this island in store for him? Trolls? Shape-shifting monsters? Athlete's foot?

Lyle nodded to the men, who shook their heads in resignation at this unforeseen break. As Aros aired his feet and stuffed the insoles with leaves, Lyle cleared his throat.

"Now that we're far away from camp, I think this is a splendid opportunity for you to tell me exactly what I want to know." Lyle's hawkish stare glinted. "Tell me, whatever your name is, why are you even here?"

Aros looked up from his task. "Your interrogative tone tells me the captain's concerns about my intentions haven't eased at all." He huffed. "My real name is, as I told the captain, Isaac Kavanaugh, but I prefer

Aros. I'm here for the food and accommodations, and I'm eager to put a million miles between me and the colonies."

The master gunner's icy orbs scrutinised him. "I find it curious that you, a pirate captain, somehow sprang from prison, reclaimed your working permit while avoiding the city police, and then landed an interview with Mr. Duplànte. Why you and not all your little friends?"

"I find it curious that an old-timer like you survived a bog monster." Lyle's eyes drilled into him.

Aros ran his tongue over his teeth. "I did my time, and the Crown saw no use for me. Plus, the prisons were full, so I got an early release. I rented my work permit to someone who needed it more than I did."

Aros caught Lyle's critical gaze roaming over his hands, which he tried to conceal in a curled, awkward manner.

"Since we picked you up in Bunnsboroux, I assume you spent time in Her Majesty's dungeon. I find it far more believable you're being used by the crown." His eyes were piercing and merciless. Sweet Terra! Are all the people aboard the *Red Queen* able to intimidate him? Aros realised he should have known better; they were all cut from the same cloth, after all. They weren't people to be trifled with. While the crew had each other, Aros had no one but himself, his wits, and his tortured fingertips. He had to get on the good side of at least one of the upper echelons on the ship. People wouldn't let him be otherwise.

Lyle's hand suddenly gripped his leg, massaging his calf with a groan. Was this the same leg the ghoul had raked when it pulled Lyle into the marshes? He didn't know what had happened to the old-timer after the shape-shifting devil tossed Aros like a ragdoll to the hereafter. While it piqued his curiosity, he made a mental note of Lyle's discomfort. He coughed to change the subject.

"See, here's the thing. Most people think we turn to piracy because we're former sailors rebelling against the Crown and thus formed a cut-throat and lawless band of brothers to sail the skies in search of riches." He gave a brief pause, eyeing how the men's attention drew from their surroundings to him. "It might have started out that way, but it turned into a lucrative business for land-based gangs who wanted to expand their business. These gangs are powerful, and they will employ people as they see fit, create fleets, and invest in weaponry to boost their haul. Very few pirate ships work independently."

Lyle huffed a humourless laugh. "You're saying you were a victim of one such gang and served them up to the Crown?" He crossed his arms, and his moustache wiggled when he frowned.

Aros licked his lips and sighed. "I joined because I was desperate like everyone else. And just like after landing in prison, I spilt whatever information they wanted on my employer, who didn't do shit for me and my men. The inquisitors baited us with early release if we talked about our Cintechan routes, which we gave. I don't know why I was released, and the others weren't. I didn't stay to figure it out. The point is, I did what I had to do to survive because no one stuck their neck out to help us, not when we were all in prison, and even less after the Crown sacked Cintecha. After our economy collapsed and we became dependent on exporting our resources, the Crown had the gall to crash the market value. Everything we had became worthless." Aros let his gaze wander over the listening men. He recognised their looks, that dejected and hopeless shift of eyes that couldn't meet his. Anger, disappointment, un-derstanding—even. "You all know what I'm talking about. The Crown has been doing it to every country rich in resources. Gangs formed fleets of pirates to steal shipments, destroy the Crown's trade ships, and thus can sell the goods for a higher profit because those royal bastards lose money that way."

"Ah, so it's for a higher cause," Lyle interjected, albeit his tone was less than impressed. Aros couldn't tell if the man was cautious or just skeptical because the *Red Queen* operated differently.

Undeterred by the suspicion, Aros raised a finger. "Illegal, yes, but morally right in my eyes. Queen Bitchface the III spilt blood since she was old enough to say 'daddy', and I'm not sorry for what I did to survive. The Queen's trade ships are innocent by law, but considering who they work for, I don't regret my actions. I don't expect a central colony citizen like you to understand how absolutely shitty things got in Cintecha after our sacking or what we had to do to survive. That bitch with the Crown? The biggest criminal of them all. Noval was lucky in that it's too fucking cold and has too much mountain range for the Crown to care about it."

Lyle flicked his eyebrows and gave a slow nod. "I can't say I know the full tale of Cintecha, and I probably never will. The central colonies economically depend on Queensland, which is blackmail of the highest order. The only slack the Crown gives us is a rope long enough to hang us all."

"You do understand!" Aros threw up a hand and gave an elated grin. "But isn't the *Red Queen's* reasoning the same? Your hands aren't as clean as you want me to think." The men scowled, but Aros relented, softening his tone. "My point is, I get it. You're careful; you must uphold a reputation and keep secrets, and my being here is a threat to you all."

The surrounding men shifted, exchanging nervous glances. Aros caught Carlos' hand tightening on his rifle.

"There's no going back for me," Aros added quickly. "I'm literally in the same boat as you are. Economically fucked, cast out by society, and homeless. I don't want any trouble. For now, I just wanna survive."

"Then this is the last place you should be." Lyle softly laughed while the others snickered. Bobbing his head, Aros thought it was a better choice than remaining in the colonies where the Inquisition hunted ex-pirates for sport. They let him out once, but they would capture him again, and he had nothing to spill but his guts.

"I ain't believing a shite of what ye say," Abernathy, a tall black-haired man in his forties, argued.

"I'm sorry my sob story doesn't entertain you," Aros said, exasperated. Looking up, he caught Carlos's brown irises boring into his. He didn't know the man, but with his darker skin and tight-set eyes, he could pass for someone from Ovrack or the mountainous region of south Cintecha. Carlos hunched down in front of him, his brows furrowed.

"Why did you attack us last spring?"

Aros raised an eyebrow at the unexpected question. The others fell silent, observing the two.

"It wasn't obvious? We spotted a trade ship coming out of the Grey Veil unscathed. Do you know how rare it is to find ships crossing the Northern Veil going from Georgetown? Like a virgin in the red-light district! Your ship is unique. I have never seen a hybrid ship, so I thought the Crown had created a prototype that could navigate the Veil."

Carlos flicked his eyebrows, stood, and appeared pleased with the answer.

"Ye picked the wrong ship to attack, *pirate*." Abernathy's intense stare didn't relent, and he spat on the ground. That was rich, coming from a man whose employer broke laws regularly.

"I still have no clue how you guys escaped the Grey Veil. We were just lucky to follow the trail you left behind. I don't even understand how we landed on this island in one piece! Imagine what the Crown would do if they could travel unhindered through the Veil? We would all be victims of that bitch's bastardised fantasy of a unified world under a single monarch. If they do, we're all turned into CUC-suckers. You can't aurally appreciate what I just did, but the joke is the current grim reality of the Central United Colonies."

Abernathy screwed up his face as he stared into the distance, his hand before him as if he were trying to pluck out the joke.

"Indeed, we are..." Lyle nodded and stood. "Enough dallying. We're burning daylight."

CHAPTER TEN

THE SEARCH

Rosanne chewed on her thumbnail while watching the waning daylight turn the distant clouds orange. The forest was alive with unfamiliar screeches, accompanied by something primal howling in the distance. For once, she enjoyed the ambience, meaning no large force of creatures stood ready to attack the scouting party or her ship at the camp. It also suggested a lack of foreign activity, something she wished to know existed here. "They're late," she said, unable to tear her eyes away from the edge of the forest.

"Sun's still up." Antony reminded her, flipping through a volume of star charts, useful for navigation now that they had clear skies again.

"Barely," she frowned and folded her arms.

"Come sit. The air is thinner here, and I'll wager you're exhausted like everyone else." Antony patted the carpet on the sandy floor. Chairs were a luxury during camping, but they had no shortage of carpets and pillows.

Rosanne nodded but didn't admit she had been out of breath all day. She let the tent flap drop and flopped down onto the pillows.

"Please tell me I'm not making you feel useless by joining us here?" she asked hopefully.

Antony leaning close enough to tickle her face with his breath, a secretive smile painted on his lips. "You're not making me feel useless," he whispered, then leaned back. "I haven't been this excited since running into you in Valo past the midnight bell."

"You had to remind me!" She threw a pillow over her face and groaned. Antony's hand slid over her white-knuckled grip, clutching the pillow. She slid the pillow down and stared into his hazel eyes.

"I am glad you asked me to join. I feel like I get to see a whole different side of you. And I would still fall for you, even if we had met under professional circumstances."

"Maybe not if you had caught us under wildly different circumstances."

He bobbed his head with a wry smile. "Maybe? You stole my breath the first moment I laid eyes on you. That's a crime in itself," Antony laughed at her doubtful expression. "How about we visit your family when we're done here? I'd love to meet them."

"I doubt you would say the same if you knew them."

At this, he lowered his gaze to the floormat. "That's the thing; you've never talked about them. I would love to know more about you, but you have kept things so close since your return." There was no judgement in his tone, only observation. Yet it cut her to her core how much she had kept from Antony.

She waved her hand through the air as if it helped her find the right words. "It's not much of a tale. I haven't kept in touch with them for a while now. But I reckon I should once I'm done here, if I find answers, that is."

He laid beside her on his side, propping himself up with a single elbow. "How does a multi-million riksdaler salt corporation heir set an alternate course in life when you could manage books from the comforts of your office?"

She mimicked his pose and stuck out her chin. "The kind that involves being an heir to a multi-million riksdaler salt corporation and an overly controlling mother."

"I'm sorry to hear that."

"Don't be. My mother and I don't see eye to eye. I wanted to sail the open seas, while she claimed, 'We have seas at home.' Her ships never sailed further than to the mountain islands across the bay." They both laughed at the irony. "What about me meeting your parents? You've never talked about where you grew up, either." They had never talked much about their private lives or families in the two years they had shared a bed. It was a refreshing change.

Antony flicked his eyebrows knowingly. "Ah. That is because my childhood was bliss. My parents aren't poor, but they don't harvest riches running their vineyard in Einsbor. Everyone there earns their living from grapes and wine. When the Navy drafted people, I signed up. The pay was good, it's a respectable career opportunity, but most of all, I got to travel, and my parents had one less mouth to feed."

Rosanne's eyes were thin as slits. "You're the middle child, aren't you?"

"Always so perceptive, my love."

A resonating cheer broke out in the camp, and Rosanne sprang to her feet. "They're back!" She exited the tent in a flurry. Outside, Lyle with his men and Aros stood conversing with Farand.

"What news do you bring?" Rosanne shouted before she even reached them.

"We saw smoke coming from the topmost mountain," Aros butted in, receiving a stern look from Lyle, as if he had spoken out of turn.

"Captain," Lyle greeted, offering a straight-backed salute.

"People?" Rosanne asked, voicing her concern.

"It's unlikely," Lyle continued. "The forest around appears undisturbed."

"That's comforting, at least. Let's reconvene and plan tomorrow's schedule after supper. You look like you could use the break."

The men saluted and returned to their tents or changed shifts with the perimeter crew. Rosanne saw Aros limping away from them and called after him: "Did you wear the wrong shoes again?"

"Bite me!" He hobbled off.

Antony crossed his arms. "He's far more malleable than I thought he would be, considering your history and all."

She couldn't deny the sadistic pleasure she felt seeing Aros in pain, but his compliance was comforting. "I'm surprised he's cooperating at all. I guess he truly wanted to escape the colonies. Who would have thought?" Rosanne paused, watching Aros retreat into his tent, wearing an expression of exaggerated agony. "You saw his hands, right?"

"It's hard to miss that they are always bleeding, and he flinches every time he lifts a fork. Remind me never to have my fingernails pulled." Antony grimaced and shook his head.

"The Inquisition reduces people to squealing meat sacks with secrets to spill. I almost pity him. Almost."

"By the seas, that's dark even for you," he said, giving a nervous chuckle.

"It's the truth, though. But let's hope our dear Isaac Kavanaugh has changed after his summer endeavours and no longer adheres to his pirate name." In her mind, Aros would always be Aros. Nothing he said could change that.

Crossing her arms, Rosanne thought back to their battle last spring. She had never asked why he attacked the *Red Queen* or even what he hoped to achieve from it. His bold approach might have stemmed from assuming the galleon carried goods—a safe bet, considering where they were at the time of the attack. Now, seeing his mellow mannerisms and willingness to work for his wages with his head down, perhaps he longed for something familiar with a chance of escape. The skies knew Rosanne wouldn't want to live through a second of what Aros had experienced in prison. She shuddered.

She turned to the tent but caught Denny Nickolson, Quinn Saros, and Vincent Carman making their way to Aros's tent. The three men wrestled through the open flap and squeezed into the small space built for two. Within seconds, Aros had their undivided attention, his wide gesticulation drawing the men into his narrative. Saros, despite being the skeptic among them, nodded in agreement. The little voice in her head didn't enjoy seeing four ex-pirates conversing. She had no reason to distrust any of the men, except for Aros, but she couldn't help her uncertainty playing tricks on her.

She forced herself to look away and focus on the task at hand.

The camp was sombre that first night on the island. Not a single cloud broke from the world's edge to travel over the island, leaving the sky clear and lit with stars. The jungle calls drowned out the usual busy conglomeration of conversations or games. Prey and predator sounded the same, and what could be a panther might as well be a bird.

Rosanne sipped a cup of hot tea by the central firepit, almost lost in an apathetic stare as she processed their journey thus far. Around the glow sat Farand, Watch Captains Dalia and Creedy, Able Bodied Seaman Hwang, Master Gunner Lyle, Captain Antony DiCroce and First Engineer Higgs.

Rosanne studied the faces of the department heads of the *Red Queen*. "We have survived our first day on a new land, neck deep in the Grey Veil. What are your thoughts, gentlepeople?" she asked, gnawing on a piece of dried meat.

"No monsters so far," Lyle quipped, sucking on his pipe and blowing a ring of smoke.

"Engine's golden, and hardly any electrical disturbances after we calibrated the thing," Higgs remarked, downing medicinal tea and making a wry face at the taste. Rosanne could smell the foul brew from over the smoke and wiggled her nose.

"Provisions haven't run off," Farand said, flicking his eyebrows.

"No mind-reading hulder," Dalia breathed out, followed by nods and muttered agreements.

Rosanne, having missed that event during their last voyage, didn't want to delve deeper into it. "Praise Terra for that," she agreed. "At the crack of dawn, I want everyone ready to depart. Leave a skeleton crew for the ship and main camp. Their sole task is to keep an eye out for anything that might jeopardise our stay here and keep our livelihood safe. Recommendations?"

"The landmen ain't experienced enough for that. They can go with the scouting team," Creedy said.

"I can stay behind with Nickolson, Saros, and Carman," Hwang put in.

Rosanne shook her head. "Send them instead. Norman can stay behind with Swanson and Manning."

Hwang nodded.

Rosanne hadn't meant to single the trio out, but a gnawing sensation told her they were up to something. As long as said plans didn't involve the *Red Queen*, she wouldn't care too much, but having them on the scouting team instead would be a better use of their time and experience, anyway.

"Gavin and I stay behind. This blasted heat is making my bones ache." Higgs massaged his knee.

Rosanne accepted the idea, counting how many more they needed for the skeleton crew. "That's six people. We need four more."

"Hammond always stays behind, so that's seven," Farand interjected.

Dalia and Creedy exchanged competitive glances, shook their fists in the air three times, and splayed them out in different fashions. Creedy frowned as Dalia's scissors trumped his paper.

"Eight with me," the Watch Captain beamed. Rosanne looked to Farand, whose eyebrows were so close together they could have shaken hairs.

"Farand. Are you up for managing the *Queen*?"

The man froze, his cup still against his lips.

"I know that if there are hulder here, I can count on you to keep the *Red Queen* safe," she said as she drank from her mug.

"You're taking Kavanaugh with you then." Farand said pointedly, his expression caught between betrayal and determination. Keeping Aros away from the ship would remove a million worries by themselves.

Snickering, Rosanne couldn't recall seeing Farand this fired up over such a small matter. "Deal. One of yours, Lyle?"

"I'm sure I can find a volunteer after they've duked it out. You'll have a man by the morrow."

"Excellent. I'll see you all at dawn then." She poured the rest of her tea into the fire, throwing sparks that danced through the air.

At first light, after packing supplies and consuming Hammond's morning gruel, the scouting team set off in two longboats, leaving the mini-scouter and skeleton crew behind on the *Red Queen*. They glided over the foggy forest, keeping the blue energy issued from the thruster engines low to conceal their presence. They followed the coastline west, with the mountains towering to their north.

Rosanne trained her spyglass on the mountains, scanning for the smoke Aros had mentioned the day before. It rose from the tallest mountain in a steady stream; the top, unlike its jagged neighbour, was flat and bereft of snow.

"If I didn't know better, I'd say that's a volcano," Antony commented, lowering his spyglass.

Rosanne shared similar thoughts. "It's eerie. We've seen dead volcanoes inside the Veil before, but this land is two kilometres up in the air. Should have brought a geologist."

Antony folded the spyglass and pursed his lips in thought. "Perhaps it has a central anchor point, which gives us the illusion that the land is floating."

Rosanne chewed on her lips. "Anti-gravity minerals coated the underside. It's not impossible. But for now, let's steer clear of *that* mountain in particular. I heard the hulder lived in the last volcano we visited."

"What do we do about spooky cabins in the woods?" A pause.

"Not funny." Rosanne couldn't help but snort at Antony's flippant gesture, although she made a mental note to steer clear of buildings that looked like something was still occupying them.

Rosanne consulted the compass. The needle pointed toward the central mountain chain, just as it had further east when they landed here. Perhaps the isles were attracted to the magnetic pull as well, not revolving the island along the coastline. The next step was finding the piece of land that matched Thompson's map. But whichever came first, Rosanne was certain something hid among the grooves of the jagged coastline, underneath the shaded forests, resting somewhere at the foot of the mountain. With no directions on the map or a scale to abide by, they could search for days, weeks even, and find nothing.

If they found nothing by the month's end, she would return to the colonies and continue her by-the-books trade, or maybe doing runs through the Devil's Passage to Cintecha if she was desperate. The good thing was that a certain paper-pusher stationed in Valo was excellent at straightening the *Red Queen*'s books, and with him dallying with second Engineer Simonsen, Rosanne was certain it was something she could extort should it be necessary. She could turn the tables around, too.

Ida sat occupied with her weather-scanner machine, tinkering with the dials. She held up the sphere, consulting the tablet and glancing at the small ensign swaying from the rear. Rosanne wondered how Ida managed to be here without Nelson. Shifting her gaze to Antony, Rosanne let it dawn on her she had brought him along, not just out of her own need for emotional support and to deepen their relationship, but also out of cowardice as her last brush with death was also one in disguise of love. Or was it? Ida had grown close to Nelson in the few weeks they spent in the Veil, while Rosanne was still half a world away from Antony. She enjoyed his company, of course, although she rarely thought of him when he wasn't close by, and whenever she did, she pushed it aside, filling her mind with work. She sought change, needed the change, a desperate reprieve from the anxiety haunting her. It scratched into the back of her mind when she didn't occupy or guard her thoughts. This jungle brought it out like a hissing serpent. Always nearby, always hissing its warnings, never fully in view. When had it become this bad? Was Antony simply not enough? She banished the thoughts as quickly as they came.

They travelled west for three hours before their first stop: a rocky outcrop surveying the vast forest. Fog rose in wisps from the trees, as tall as four-storey buildings. The hushed silence of the forest reverted to that of activity, with trees creaking, distant clacking, singing, howls, and the tack-tacking of unfamiliar animals and birds. Flashes of colour zipped past branches. Other times, only rustles of leaves showed moving life forms, gone from sight before anyone could react.

Rosanne studied the coastline to the south and then the mountains to the north. Neither matched up with Thompson's map, but she didn't expect them to this early in their voyage. They were never that lucky. She jotted down a crude outline of the lakes and mountains they had passed, giving herself a few extra minutes to add details.

"I took notes." Antony showed her his leather journal covered with neat, curly lettering and shaded drawings. She frowned, a sense of betrayal coming over her.

"You didn't tell me you knew cartography, and *this* well at that!" she exclaimed.

Antony leaned close. "I'm not that good."

She held up her indecipherable chicken scrawls, and Antony bit his lips shut to prevent himself from laughing. Her crew wasn't as subtle, snickering behind their hands or lowering their heads, but Rosanne was used to her shortcomings being taken advantage of in such a humorous manner. "You're our mapmaker from now on," she announced to Antony. Rifling through his journal, she compared it to the map she pulled from her vest's inner pocket and unfolded it. "What scale is this?"

"About one to one thousand," he replied.

Rosanne studied Thompson's map again.

"What are you thinking?" Antony leaned over her shoulder to peer at the map as if it would help him understand her thought process.

A disappointed murmur came from her throat. "Why this area? Why not map the entire island while they were here?"

"Maybe they didn't have time?" Antony suggested.

"And somehow their ship escaped and ended up floating in the Baltansea," Rosanne said, doubtful. "We should get moving. We'll cover another two hours west before nightfall and get our bearings wherever we end up camping. If we need to continue even further east, I suggest we move camp."

"Solid plan," he agreed.

Rosanne roused the crew from their break, and within minutes, they embarked west in the longboats. A couple of hours later, when they still couldn't find any sign of the Thompson shoreline, they set up camp in a clearing by the shore, surrounded by dense forest.

Rosanne considered the bizarre geology of the island, a piece of land somehow afloat above sea level with its own ecosystem and populated lakes, corals growing out of water that in turn housed extraordinary wildlife. It even had its own coastline, cupping the lakes around the mountains like the hands of the creator. While Rosanne and Antony updated their sketchy maps, others whipped out their fishing gear and went to the lagoon. The waters teemed with life and colourful reefs. The surrounding forest had fallen quiet at their noisy approach, but the lookouts reported nothing out of the ordinary.

"I swear it gets warmer the further west we travel." Rosanne fanned herself with the hat. Antony's white cotton tunic was stained dark with sweat, a look she didn't mind at all.

"Twiddling my thumbs at home didn't sound nearly as exciting as joining you and sweating through my clothes," Antony remarked, noting her wandering gaze and wiggling his eyebrows, making her pull at her lips.

That night, Lyle's men patrolled the camp in shifts. They sat out of sight in the shadows, alert and awake. The forest was quiet here, mere whispers compared to their landing point on the beach. Fog danced over the treetops, and small animals hunting or foraging skittered about the forest edge. Crawling bugs lit up the darkened woods, blinking in and out of existence. A small frog called out from somewhere in patterns of *breee breee breee*. Over and over again.

Rosanne snuggled up against Antony in their tent. He slung an arm over her and let out a puff of breath, the only sign she had disturbed him. He was far more relaxed than she was, but Rosanne could, for a moment, breathe easily, knowing she had done everything to ensure the camp's safety. Yet, what might lurk outside didn't ease her fears as much as it kept her hyper-vigilance reeling. She noted the shuffles of boots trudging through the sand, knowing they were the patrols from Lyle's team. Rosanne closed her eyes. Her dream pulled her through the tent canvas and into the twilight sky in hues of blue.

Carried by a mysterious wind over the misty jungle, she floated high above the trees, clad in her tunic and trousers, feet bare against the elements. She scanned the landscape and its deep pools of black dotting the clearings. Mystified, she let the dream unfold despite being aware of it, a feeling she couldn't recall having felt before.

The cold wind bit at her cheeks, and she blinked away the tears in her eyes. Ghostly whispers called to her. She couldn't make out the voices teetering at the very edge of her perception, but she knew they followed her.

The wind guided Rosanne down into the jungle. Her naked feet touched the moist ground, toes digging into the dirt as the force that carried her there disappeared.

A black pond rested undisturbed in a small clearing. She gazed at the pristine, mirror-like surface, a dark, endless pool reflecting the stars in the heavens despite none being visible above. The reflection stared back at her with wonder. Her hair framed her sun-kissed face in a curly mess. Sensing that something was off Rosanne studied the reflection's eyes. When she turned her head from side to side, the reflection mimicked her. Rosanne touched her face, and her lips parted in wonder, drawing her eyebrows together. She couldn't put her finger on it, but an eerie detachment came to her as if the reflection weren't hers. The reflection drew her lips into an empty smile.

"Dragonheart," a voice whispered loud and clear in her ear.

Rosanne jerked awake. With wide eyes, she searched the white canvas of her tent, not recognising it. A presence stirred behind her, and she picked up a familiar scent. Breathing out, she rubbed her face as she realised she was in the tent next to Antony. The sky was bright, but the sunrise was still far off.

"What is it?" Antony stirred with a complaining yawn.

"I had a strange dream." She drew another breath and shook her head to collect herself. "Of ponds, voices, and reflections. I can't make sense of it, though. It must be the altitude that's messing with me. I'll get the pot going." Rosanne stripped out of her sweaty tunic and dressed in passable undergarments, which were not up to society's standards but did the job well enough for practical reasons. Besides, she was too exhausted to care. For the climate, Rosanne had chosen cotton-spun trousers, loose and breezy, along with thinner leather boots with wider soles to accommodate her hiking needs, and lastly, a dark cotton tunic. So far, the greatest enemy was the sweltering daytime heat accompanied by humidity, but nothing she couldn't handle. She could stave off sleep deprivation with a pot of strong coffee.

Cool morning air greeted her outside; the tent was a sauna in comparison. She nodded to the sentries popping into view to check on the noise.

"Anyone else awake?" she asked in a low tone, to which the men shook their heads. In the central firepit, she stacked logs and stuffed them with kindling. The firesteel remained in a secure tin in case the weather wetted the flint. She struck it twice, producing sparks which turned into fragile embers, consuming the kindling.

An exhausted sentry who couldn't stay awake had probably used the coffee pot earlier that night. Rosanne poured the cold brew of coffee into a cup, tasted it, and contorted her face from bitter disappointment. She tossed the gruel into the sand and found water in the supply crates they had brought. Reaching over for the bag of ground coffee, she noticed a single set of footprints passing next to it. She traced them to a tent on the far side of the camp, and from there leading down to the beach. She saw her own footsteps and the shuffled sand from erased prints. One tactic the sentries had employed since coming to this island was to erase their footprints before nightfall or at least make it appear no one had wandered through when they should have.

She gave a low whistle in a distinct pattern, and three men popped into view. She pointed to her eyes and then to the footprints leading away.

"Whose are those?" she whispered.

The sentries looked at each other. "Jeffs, I think."

"Has he returned?"

"We checked the camp an hour ago. The sand was clear," another answered. Abandoning the thought of coffee, Rosanne marched over to Jeffs' tent and yanked the flap aside. The sleeping mat was empty, and the blanket rumpled in a pile. Jeffs' footwear remained by the opening. Alarm bells rang in her mind.

"Wake the camp," she ordered and jogged to her tent. The men hollered the rousting call, opening tents and kicked feet. Protests erupted all around her, demanding answers to why the hell they were called at this ungodly hour, while some stumbled out of their tents scantily clad before getting their pants on, wide-eyed and alert. Rosanne burst into the tent she shared with Antony. He jolted, sat up, and rubbed his eyes.

"Someone's missing," she said, reaching for her remaining clothes and belt with the sabre.

"How long?" Antony tugged at his trousers and dressed at great speed.

"Maybe an hour. We don't know where he went, but we have a trail. Stay here with the rest. I'll take Lyle and search for him." Rosanne unclipped the battery to the plasma gun, checked the metallic connection for any corrosion, and the light showing how many charges it had. She packed extra ammunition into her vest pocket and stormed out of the tent. Her eyes darted between the scurrying people in search of her master gunner. She spotted him straightening his vest coming out of his tent.

"Lyle!" she hollered. His normally coiffed hair was reduced to a sleepy mess, which he combed aside with his hand. He joined her marching out of the camp, following the footprints down towards the waters before meandering west. She readied the plasma gun in one hand.

"Why would he leave the camp?" Lyle's brows furrowed. The waves lapped against the shore, erasing the prints. They veered into the forest. Rosanne spotted muddy prints on the soft earth, discerning places where Jeffs had slid as he followed a hidden path. She hacked at the dense plant life standing between her and her missing crew member. Lyle was ready with his rifle behind her, keeping an eye out for any unwanted attention.

The morning grew brighter with the passing minutes. Lyle approached her, leaning close to keep his voice down. "Captain, we should turn around. We're getting too far away from the camp."

"We still have his prints to follow. I see a clearing up ahead. Maybe he's there." Desperation lined her voice, and a deep unease had settled into the pit of her stomach.

"And if it's a trap?"

"Ready a sound flare."

Lyle flicked his eyebrows as if unsurprised by her answer and pushed a button on the side of the battery. A sound flare was a high-velocity plasmic bullet that made more noise than harm, and anyone within a certain radius could hear it. Everyone and anything.

Inside, Rosanne was panicking. She prayed it wasn't hulder or trolls. However, neither seemed plausible because of the lack of prints and activity. They had been ordered never to go alone. So why did Jeffs?

CHAPTER ELEVEN

RAIN

Aros sat outside his tent and stared down at the beach. He subconsciously picked at his scabby nails, plucking the dried skin away, flaking off patches of blood that had formed without his knowledge. He winced from a sharp pain, looked down to view the destruction he had performed to his fingers, and knit them together to prevent further damage. He was ready to lose his marbles after half an hour had passed, and there was no news from the captain and the master gunner. The crew sat bleary-eyed, scanning their surroundings, expecting a fight. When sunlight hit the top of the trees, the master gunner and captain came marching, but there was no sign of Jeffs.

Shit.

Everyone gathered around her, Rosanne standing with her hands on her hips and a troubled look on her face. "We're officially announcing Jeffs as missing," she said, almost hesitantly.

A panicked buzz spread among the crew, all turning to each other for answers when they were equally clueless.

The captain raised her hands to stave off the growing discord. "We can't see that anyone or anything lured or took him. His trail simply vanished."

The crew's ease did not come.

"Who was he bunking with?" she followed up.

"He had the only single's tent, ma'am," Creedy informed her, crossing his arms.

"Did he drink on the job?"

Creedy shook his head. "Never. Steady as a mast, that man."

Aros noticed how intently the crew paid attention to Rosanne's every move, their eyes like lost souls searching for guidance.

"There isn't much we can do at this point. Let's have breakfast and become human again. We'll leave for scouting as scheduled, but we'll return here by nightfall should Jeffs return."

The crew nodded in agreement. Rosanne dismissed everyone and returned to her tent, where her lover boy waited. They exchanged words. Antony doubtlessly said something reassuring, which made her nod, and when he snuck his hand to encircle hers, her face relaxed. Aros scowled. *She loses one of her crew to the wilderness of the Grey Veil and immediately seeks comfort in lover boy's arms?* He spat on the ground. *Where was the wandering ice maiden who had punched him in the jaw as a polite greeting after he had taken her crew captive? The island truly had changed her,* he thought.

Turning, Aros paused at the sight of Denny, Quinn, and Vincent standing cross-armed beside a tree, away from the rest. He approached them, interrupting their exchange of worries over Jeffs' disappearance.

"This changes things," he said. "Anything you have encountered before?"

Denny shook his head. "This is new. No one's seen or 'eard anything, and Jeffs wasn't the kind of person to break protocol."

Quinn leaned forward. "This raises the stakes."

"Jeffs could have been a test of our camp's defences. I'll bet more of us will disappear after nightfall," Vincent said, a worried look crossing his features.

"Gentlemen, it'll be fine," Aros assured, with faux bravado that he fished out of the dark hole in his backside. He slung his arms around Quinn and Denny, with Vincent between those two. "Listen, no piss on Jeffs, right? It's the perfect distraction for us to do what we want—look for treasure. No way the captain dragged us all out here willy-nilly for the sandy beaches."

"If we find anything," Quinn said with a scowl.

"Come now. Would our dear Captain Drackenheart pursue a map that wouldn't lead to riches? I think not. We need a copy, and you three are perfect for it."

Vincent's gaze narrowed while Denny and Quinn exchanged uncertain but bobbing nods.

"He'll turn up soon enough. He must've gone for a leak and got lost. The captain herself said there was no suspicion of foul play, right?"

The three men muttered their agreements after a pause, and Aros applauded himself for turning the situation around.

"I have a better idea," Vincent interrupted, his heavy accent spilling through. "You steal the map while we create a distraction."

Aros frowned; this would put the blame on him should they get caught, but it was an excellent opportunity to build trust.

"Fine. We can strike while we pack before returning to base camp. She won't need it until we head in a new direction."

The three men nodded.

"Coffee's ready!" Kristoff announced by the fire, where people queued up to get a sip.

"Come on. Business as usual." Aros patted Quinn and Denny's shoulders and sent the three men on their merry way. He watched them as they joined the rest, catching fragments of conversations and hearing people who had spoken with Jeffs before going to bed last night. A certain blonde outside her tent caught his attention as she rummaged through bags as if searching for something. An idea popped into his head.

"Morning, little lady," he greeted with a toothy grin.

"What do you want?" Ida scowled.

"I was thinking ..." He squatted down next to her. Ida deliberately turned to the side and continued to ignore him in favour of whatever caught her attention in her satchel. He understood Ida wanted nothing to do with him, but she didn't have to make it so goddamn obvious! Rolling his eyes, he let Ida have the extra space.

"If your fancy device can map shifts in the wind and in the fog, and this is just a thought, could you do something similar for this area?"

"Could you be a little more specific?" she asked, her tone dripping with disinterest.

Oh boy, engineering talk. Aros's favourite subject to leave to qualified personnel. "What if there's energy in the surrounding air that we can't see, and that device of yours can scan it?"

She paused as her inner clockwork turned, and she leaned back with a suspicious squint. "Why should I waste my time on something like that?"

Aros expected worse, but her hands hadn't moved during the last three spoken sentences. An intrigued glimmer in her eyes told him she'd taken the bait. Now was his chance. "No one saw or heard anything when Jeffs disappeared. I was thinking, this being the Grey Veil and all, maybe there's something here. Something we can't see or hear."

Distrust mixed with curiosity flashed across her face. "What do you base that on?"

Aros scratched his chin to hide the fact he wanted to grin at how easily she was baited. "Everyone's on edge, but it's not just from Jeffs' disappearance. Look at their faces." He pointed to the saggy-faced crew in the coffee line. "Doesn't look like anyone slept well last night, and judging by your sour expression, you didn't either. I know I didn't, although there's no reason we shouldn't have. I think there's something in the air, but we can't see it."

Ida stared at the wet sand, her silence a transition to thought. She always appeared worlds away whenever she had an idea.

"I'll give it a shot," she said at length, rummaging through the bag again for no reason he could see. Aros accepted her answer with a nod and left to get coffee, hoping to stave off the terrible headache and the dreams which had haunted him—the same dreams he had heard others speak of in the sombre mood following Jeffs' disappearance.

Watching Aros saunter for the coffee queue, Ida got to thinking. She had used the weather sphere for charting changes in the winds during their travels, but Aros' words made her believe she could do more. She had the tablet and the tools to take the sphere apart and the extra vials of anti-gravity dust Higgs had given her, but she had left behind all the instruments needed for fine adjusting the sphere.

In one of her bags, Ida excavated a small wooden box that, when released, floated on its own. She made sure the tent flap was closed to ensure that no stray wind might run off with the box. The sphere rested lifelessly on the makeshift table among her tools. With a simple twist of the outer shell, she removed the lid, exposing tangled wires and the glass core filled with swirling black anti-gravity dust. Plucking it from the clasp that kept it in place, she held it up before the table lamp. Scrutinising the vial, Ida spotted a small portion of the dust settling on the bottom—a sign that its anti-gravity properties had degraded.

She couldn't have used the sphere longer than a couple of hours. What could have made the dust degrade so quickly? It wasn't the battery, or the ship's ports would have failed years ago.

Pursing her lips, she studied the open ports surrounding the core inside the sphere. What if the gap between the ports and the shell allowed light scattering, which degraded the dust? The spare anti-gravity dust was left aboard the *Red Queen*, and Ida didn't have the tools to seal the gaps, anyway. It would have to do for now.

No one had taught her this, but studying the inner workings of a topographical scanner, she had the idea to scan their surroundings for shifts in the weather. She had watched Higgs as he studied echo sounding and sonars when they hit the market a decade ago and drew from what she remembered then, though, in hindsight, she should have just looked at his notes. If they could use light to map out their surroundings, she could amplify the signal by narrowing the beams, adding more reflective mirrors to amplify the signal, and using more prominent grooves in the sphere itself. The sensors would pick up any particles that pass the light and give her a colour output on the tablet. It worked well for rain and wind inside the Grey Veil, where the fog was thick, but could she amplify the signal to pick up other things invisible to the naked eye? She didn't have the parts to make a large-scale version of it, nor the room to work on it.

After replacing the core, she switched on the tablet and deactivated the containment field, preventing the sphere from floating away. There was no wind outside, but that didn't mean she couldn't deploy it and let it hang.

Ida left the tent, positioned herself almost dead centre in the camp next to the bonfire, and deployed the sphere. Denny and Quinn looked at her with pale-faced misery, chewing their breakfasts with little vigour, then returned to their inane conversations. Ignoring them, Ida studied the tablet as the sphere did its job. On the display, several dark and complex shapes popped up, shifting with each revolution as the sensors scanned the surrounding air. A constant shadow stood right next to the central space on the display; something Ida knew was the marble picking up her presence. Besides that, it didn't show anything else. Not even a breeze within one hundred metres.

She knew the ins and outs of how the sphere functioned, but she still didn't fully understand how it picked up all the subtle changes while inside the fog. It was a glorified signal disruptor that could show the sudden whims of the weather, but it gave far better readings inside the fog as if amplified by the mysterious forces haunting the Grey Veil. Yet on the island, the winds appeared more clear on the screen despite often being mere wisps in comparison. As much as Ida disliked the idea, Aros pointed out something she had refused to consider. There was something invisible at large. The hulder used songs to enchant their victims.

How was this any different? Maybe if she amplified the sphere's signal, she could see even smaller particles appear on the screen.

The sky above had turned a darker grey with the promise of rain. If she was going to test out her new theory, she had to hurry. Ida snatched up the sphere and returned to her tent, where she laid out all the tools and parts she had brought along on her sleeping mat. The prototype had a shell with deeper grooves and more expansive dishes, which didn't work the way she thought it would, partly due to her ignorance about how calibrating the thing worked. Everything she had done was experimental at best.

Without the lid, she switched it on. Small chambers lit up with tiny beams of concentrated red light. The width of the beam worked well for wind charting, but not much else. Each light emitted from a cap could be adjusted for thickness. Lucky for her, she had brought along smaller caps in case she needed to change something.

"Thank you, past me," she muttered and swapped the caps and shell before hooking them to the inside of the larger sphere. Perhaps she could made even further changes with this modification. She blew in front of the sphere, but nothing showed on the tablet. She twisted the dials, bringing the resolution far higher than usual, and then tried again. This time, it picked up a dense green blob.

A head popped into her tent with a brusque "Hey." Ida gave a startled yelp, then rolled her eyes over her jumpiness.

"Sorry," Creedy said, stretching his lips to a thin, apologetic line. "Just checking up on you. I saw that Isaac bastard chatting with you earlier, and you didn't look too happy."

Ida leaned back to look at him. "And you care?"

He frowned.

"Pardon my lip, Watch Captain, but you are the biggest ass on the ship, and you caring is disturbing."

He chuckled at her honesty. "I get that. But since we have a rat in the pantry, I'm keeping an eye on things so we don't get bit in our sleep." The marble in her hands caught his attention. "Still working on your little invention that will steal my job, eh?"

"While you're here, can I ask you a favour?"

"Sure?" Creedy regarded her doubtfully.

Swaying from the top branch of a tall, dead tree bereft of all its leaves, Creedy clambered on with his hands and bare feet. "Is this high enough?" he called to Ida, who stood at the foot of the trunk with her tablet.

"Yeah! Deploy it, but don't let it fly off!" she replied.

"De-what now?" he called.

"Let it go once it floats!"

Creedy shifted his weight and held so that he had the branch secure between his knees, his feet interlocked, and arms free. He dug the marble from his pocket and held it out on the flat of his hand.

"It's on!" Ida called, and Creedy lowered his hand; the sphere floated by itself. It didn't do anything special. In the distance, he spotted a white haze creeping closer to camp.

"It's gonna rain soon," he muttered, but he knew that this wasn't why Ida decided to test her little invention. Whatever plans she had, she wasn't telling him. She always sought to please Higgs or the captain with her little inventions, like a good girl, and he wondered why she bothered. They were doing just fine before the tech.

Well, "fine" might be an overstatement, as Creedy had experienced the worst sleep of his life. His head was a foggy mess, and his eyes stung, but the stubborn man folded his arms and waited. He could see half the forest towards the mountain from here, dotted with black bodies of water, eerily similar to his dream.

On the ground, Ida turned the knobs on the tablet. "Come on, you bastard," she muttered as the display remained blank. If she furrowed her brows any harder, she might develop a thinking crease.

She expanded the scale on the screen to cover a larger area. Then she adjusted another dial to strengthen the signal, though, under other circumstances, she knew this hadn't worked. The screen sparked to life with movements. A dark shape covered a portion of the screen, which Ida assumed was the tree behind Creedy, but on the other side, there was constant movement in two layers of shaded blobs. The outer layer was light green and moved slowly with little change to its shape, while the inner, denser particles morphed with sharply rounded extremities reaching the edge of the outer field. Judging by the movements, the outer ring depicted rain gliding over the screen.

"What the hell is that?" she said, nearly pressing her face against the screen. The inner blob burst with activity, throwing spikes outwards, but never made it past the outer line. The hairs on Ida's neck stood up. Was this her technical ignorance throwing her into emotional turmoil? The forest loomed like a dark, menacing shadow in muted greens, and Ida almost expected to see a physical manifestation of what the tablet showed her. "Creedy! How far away is the rain?" she called to the topman.

"Five hundred metres!" he shouted.

"You see anything else?"

"Not a damn thing. Are you done? I can't feel my arse."

Ida considered the readings on the tablet and decided it must be a calibration error or a system malfunction. The denser, jagged formations shot through the outer layer of rain again as it moved south towards their position, but hastily retreated into the rain.

As they wrapped up their field trip, the rain fell in fat droplets. Ida decided she didn't want to stay out any longer, fearing what she didn't understand. She glanced back into the forest, expecting to see the dark embrace of a shadow, even though she knew it was impossible.

CHAPTER TWELVE

HER FATHER'S HAT

The drizzle continued as morning progressed to noon. Rosanne spent her time charting the coastal area around the camp, waiting for the rain to dissipate enough so she could take the longboat and search for Jeffs.

Antony came through the tent flap with two wooden bowls of stew made from dried meat and overcooked vegetables. The smell was all wrong for Hammond's stew, and she immediately regretted having let him stay on the *Red Queen*. They could all use a good meal now.

"We can take a longboat and search from over the forest," she said absentmindedly, as if his presence couldn't break her concentration. "The problem is, if we make noise, it might attract company, whatever that might be." She chewed on the pencil, the saliva-drenched wood sour in her mouth.

Antony slid a bowl over the map right under her nose.

"You're right. Sorry." She grabbed the spoon and dug in. Outside, the sky thundered. The rumble resonated loud and close. "You were saying?" Rosanne finally met his amused, if worried, eyes.

Antony spent a moment formulating his thoughts by swirling his spoon around the gruel.

"I'm not saying you shouldn't worry, but I'm noticing that you take your sorrows with a shovel instead of a pinch."

It was a humorous statement, she recognised, but she couldn't find it in herself to smile.

"The sky is looking pretty bleak," she said between the portions of stew she shoved into her mouth. He didn't argue.

When she was done, she grabbed her hat and the empty bowl, refocused, and searched the camp for Lyle. She spotted the older gentleman with the off-perimeter-duty team sitting on crates under a canvas stretched between the trees, and she handed the bowl to Kristoff, who was on dishwasher duty. "You're with me, Mr. Vasilyev," she ordered, and the man dropped the dishes like hot coal and followed.

Lyle nodded to her in greeting.

"I need the two of you with me," she said.

Lyle paused his movement, the spoon hovering over the bowl while he studied her. "We're searching in this weather?"

"Yeah. I don't want to leave him out there for too long. This place is depressing enough."

Abandoning their lunch, the men gathered their rifles, and within minutes, they set out. Rosanne steered the longboat until it hovered just above the forest while Lyle, Kristoff, and Carlos kept watch for the missing man on the ground below them. So far, only animal tracks and mud greeted them. The sky above turned darker, and the drizzle cloaked the forest in muted greens. A flash of lightning shot through the sky, illuminating the treetops. Thunder rolled across the forest like boulders seconds later.

"That is too fucking close," Rosanne said and shielded her eyes from the torrent of rain. The water puddled in the longboat, rising to cover her shoes. Kristoff took the small bucket floating in the puddle and began to bail. The rain persisted, soaking them through to their unmentionables, leaving them shivering. Due to the hole in her hat, Rosanne felt the cold invasion running down her neck.

God damn you, Aros. She grimaced at the memory of where a bullet had knocked the hat off her head during their battle with the *Blue Dragon*. Lightning struck again and again.

Lyle turned to her and hollered through the rumbling noise. "We should head back. We can't see anything in this blasted weather!"

Rosanne slowed the longboat before making a U-turn. Another loud crack shot over them, and, in a flash, the thruster engine's case blackened with branching lines. Rosanne jumped from her seat and tumbled over the bench in front of her, ears ringing, vision blinded by the light. The boat lurched in mid-air and then swayed as it lost its anti-gravity properties, the engine giving a pathetic static sputter before dropping stern-first towards the trees. Rosanne felt herself lifting from the seat she clambered onto, the world rushing past them as they fell. Branches snapped and cracked against the hull, the wind a howl in their ears, penetrated only by their panicked screams. The boat crashed onto a thick branch, balancing precariously. Not two thoughts passed through Rosanne's mind before she gave a choking scream as the longboat slipped right out of the canopy. Vines and branches snapped all around them, the fall seeming endless, turning the boat on its side. Rosanne clambered to her seat, and the violent impact on the ground threw her from the craft. Half sunken in the mud, she gasped for breath, reeling from the adrenaline-infused terror of falling out of the sky. She slipped through the mud, propping herself up to scan her surroundings, eyes wild.

"Anyone?!" Rosanne called out. No response. Groaning, she turned herself over, beaten by the brutality of the fall. Her ears were still ringing, and a great ball of light danced in her vision. A few metres from her lay the master gunner on his stomach with his arms spread out. His hair flopped over his unconscious face. "Lyle!" She turned him over and patted him on his cheek. The man didn't respond.

She examined the other two, both unconscious. The rain drowned out all signs of life in the dark forest. Dense foliage obscured any view of the mountain chain they had seen only seconds earlier. Rosanne rubbed her cold arms. Her teeth chattered uncontrollably. In her confusion, she stared blank-faced at the men without understanding how to help them.

A whisper brushed her ears, and she spun around. A small pond greeted her in deep blackness, its surface beaten by the rain. Was that always there? The rush of the rain faded around her, her eyes locked on her wobbly reflection in the waters, steadily growing clearer. The noise of her own beating heart dissolved to calm echoes, and Rosanne subconsciously stepped closer. Staring into the black pool, its hidden depths reflected only her own insecurities. But there it was again, that uncertain feeling as she stared at the mirror image of herself. She turned her head to the side without breaking eye contact. "Dragonheart," she whispered as if recalling a dream.

"Captain," Lyle groaned. Rosanne snapped out of her daze and rushed to his side.

"Are you alright?" She helped the man to his feet. He shook his head, one hand hovering over the side where he must have banged himself in the fall. The rain poured around them in deafening waves, the skies flashing. She leaned him against the overturned longboat and rushed for her pack, lying next to a tree. It was soaked through with rain and mud, but as Rosanne brushed off the fabric with her hand, her skin stained crimson. She froze, staring at her quivering hand. Was that blood? A trickle of red drew her gaze to the tree, its gnarled bark running with rivers of red-coloured liquid. She felt it between her fingers, its dense, sticky consistency reminding her of the very life force which flowed through their veins. What the hell was this place?

"*Dragonheart*," a voice whispered, evident through the rain and thunder, as if spoken right into her ear. Rosanne turned. She shielded her eyes against the rain, searching between the trees and the bushes.

A man with a beard, hat, and dark brown coat stood as still as a statue a stone's throw away. He stared at her with a pale, blank face.

"Jeffs, is that you?" she called out. Smoky wisps left her stiff lips and chattering teeth. The man didn't respond despite looking directly at her. Rosanne shivered and went closer.

"*Dragonheart*," the whispers warned. The man hadn't said a word. The cold encircled her throat, snaking its way into her, growing like pressure in her chest. The face appeared familiar. Dark, hooded eyes locked with hers, his pose rigid as if caught moving when he shouldn't, and the hat that was identical to the one on her head.

Her mind screamed for her to run, but Rosanne was too stunned to move, too scared that the apparition would disappear if she looked away. But there it was again, that familiar voice she couldn't place, the soothing security of her name spoken over and over in her mind, suddenly turned to a rumbling warning. Rosanne stepped back and slipped in the mud, and that was enough for her to flee to the overturned longboat. "Lyle!" she called to the man. "We need to go!" Carlos stirred by the boat, raising his face just enough for Rosanne to spot the trickle of blood running from a gash on his shaved head.

"We're not alone. Get the longboat around!" she urged. The men, in their daze, stumbled to their feet while Kristoff remained unconscious but breathing. Rosanne, Lyle, and Carlos lined up on the side of the longboat and reached under to the lip.

"Heave!" Rosanne called, and they flipped it the right way up with a loud splash. Lyle and Carlos grabbed Kristoff by the legs and arms and hauled him into the boat.

Either paranoid from the encounter or feeling the presence drawing closer, Rosanne scanned the forest for the man. All that met her was the violent patter of rain and swirling mists.

"Captain!" Lyle called from the driver's seat of the longboat. Drawing her attention from the jungle, she turned to Lyle's alarmed face. "The engine's dead," he said, his voice low.

Swearing, she climbed aboard. It wobbled with each movement, and she made her way over to the metal-plated engine. "Keep an eye out. There's something out there." At this, Lyle and Carlos grabbed their rifles.

Rosanne removed the metal plating, spotting the blackened battery fastened with clamps on the side of the thruster engine. She reached into it, wiggling her fingers between a crevice in the metal and the engine. Her fingers encircled a familiar shape, and drawing her hand out, she discovered with trembling elation that the spare battery had survived.

Her shaking hands worsened the longer she fumbled with the battery. The slick metal slipped from her grasp, and Rosanne let out a panicked yelp. The rain fell in torrents around them, a constant drone intruding as it crept closer. Rosanne clicked the battery in place and closed the lid.

The button lamp glowed blue, a sign that the firing mechanism was now working.

She pressed the button far harder than necessary. The boat swayed and levelled itself as it hovered just above the ground.

With gentle spurts of the thruster engine, Rosanne guided the boat away from the trees and pushed them upwards, past the reaching branches and vine-infested canopies. She steered them away from the flashes of lightning, the barrage fading in the distance.

She had to prevent herself from reaching for her hat for the hundredth time to still her shaking hands. Searching the forest floor, she, in a twisted sense of curiosity, hoped to spot the man who bore the face of her long-departed father.

Vigorous cries woke Aros from his nap. He pulled on his boots with little regard to the blisters still hurting his feet and burst through the tent flap. The misty sky, accompanied by the deluge, turned the camp into a slippery mudhole. Aros skidded across to the spectacle at the beach. The longboat approached from the sea and settled next to the other boat. The captain, Lyle, and Carlos hopped out, pale-faced and looking like they wrestled with the cook's livestock. Rosanne remained by the longboat, and watched the men haul Kristoff to a nearby tent. Her expression bore witness to something which had shaken her to her core, a face Aros had never seen her wear. Not that he knew her well, but her appearance said she had faced something she couldn't process—as he had after his encounter with that creature living in the cabin. Aros shuddered.

Captain Drackenheart clapped her hands, summoning the rest of the crew. "I hoped to come back with answers that would ease our worries about Jeffs. Instead, I come with grave news. We are not alone."

The crew's hopeful faces turned to those of disbelief and disappointment. Aros folded his arms, as defensive as the rest.

"The storm cut us off, and we couldn't find any trace of Jeffs. Whoever is out there knows of us, and considering our previous dalliance with the Veil, I'm sure you can imagine why I am calling this off. It's too dangerous to stay here. We're returning to base camp."

A wave of protest swept through the camp, followed by shaking heads and clenched fists.

Captain Drackenheart raised her hands to quiet the murmur. "I understand you are angry. Jeffs is one of ours, and we don't abandon our own. We'll leave supplies and directions for him should he find his way back, but right now, we need to get the hell out of here."

Aros caught a couple of men hanging their heads, another stomping off in protest—friends of Jeffs, he guessed. A thunderclap made people jump and scurry for their tents, seeking safety under the jungle's trees.

"What about the storm?" Creedy called out, shivering.

Aros recognised Rosanne's crestfallen look. Shaking her head, she steeled her expression and summoned the radiant authority she bore when shit hit the fan. "We leave as soon as it clears. Until then, stay vigilant and stay armed!"

Creedy scoffed and stalked back to his tent. People dispersed, but before Aros could return to his rainproof tent and dry off, a kick to his boot made him jump. He stared at the sour expression of the second engineer, wearing a wide-brimmed hat far too big for her head but which kept the rain clear off her shoulders. Practical *and* fashionable. Aros pressed his lips together to prevent himself from laughing.

"Can I help you, little lady?"

"What made you think that there's something tangible messing with us? What do you know?" Her quick-as-a-master-gunner interrogative tone prompted a sly grin from Aros.

"Let's talk in my tent."

Ida folded her arms. "I'd rather not."

"And I don't want to stand out in the rain and feel my shoes get soggy around my toes, so if you'll excuse me, I'd like to talk inside."

Rolling her eyes, Ida followed Aros to the tent, and they ducked inside.

Shaking off the rainwater from their hats, Aros moved the blanket aside from the supply crates he used as a bed so Ida could sit without shuddering in disgust from whatever she thought he was doing in there besides sleeping.

"Talk," she ordered. Her stern expression drilled into his eyes, but Aros couldn't take her freckled face seriously. She reminded him of a murderous bunny with her white, rounded front teeth, a small twitchy nose, and her incessant glances at the tent flap like a cornered animal seeking escape.

"Word is, we all had nightmares. People here talk a lot when something's up, and I bet you we all dreamed the same thing. If that doesn't sound like manipulative mystical forces, I don't know what does." He watched her straighten her back, suddenly more attentive, but kept quiet. "I've heard tales about the monsters you encountered on the last island, hulder that can plant illusions in their victims' heads and make them obey their commands. I met a fiddle-playing creature who could change his shape. Maybe there are more here."

Ida's eyes flitted around the tent. "Makes sense. What were your dreams of?"

Aros's conspiratorial smirk drew a questioning look from her. "You don't believe me, do you?"

She folded her arms. "I don't have a reason to."

"Yet here you are." He gestured with his arms, half-wide, from the cramped tent. When she scowled, he licked his lips and reformulated his strategy. "Alright then. How about a body of water that reflects a night sky when it's morning? And when you look into it, you feel this complete sense of disconnection from the reflection, like it's a ghost that only looks like you."

Ida's face blanched.

"Told ya." Aros sniffed and rubbed his nose.

"I was field-testing some new calibrations on the sphere earlier before it rained," she began, leaning forward as she turned the words around in her head. "At first, it didn't look like there were any readings, but then the rain came. There was something inside it."

"It wasn't just more rain?"

She shook her head. "Rain has a certain density and appears more or less uniform. This thing, this shadow, moved erratically. It couldn't extend beyond the rain, at least not far."

Aros scratched at his stubble. "You told the captain about this?"

"I won't until I know for sure. I don't have all the tools I need to double-check my calibrations. It could be a technical error. I'll know more after we return to the *Queen*."

"Tell you what. Why don't you take your little machine and have it up and running throughout the night? We ain't going anywhere with this storm, and if this thing lives in the rain, we need all the heads-up we can get."

"I'm already way ahead of you." She huffed like a cute little student who thought she was far cleverer than her peers. Compared to Aros, she most likely was, but he wouldn't fight her over it. "Let me know what you find, yeah?"

She crawled over to the tent flap but looked back at him. "Don't take this as a weird way to feel connected to us. You're an outsider, and no one here wants you around."

"Harsh, but true. I'm used to it." Aros shrugged. Ida snorted and left. "Sweet dreams, little lady," he called after her.

Two hasty splashing stomps returned to the tent flap that was flung aside. "Stop with the nicknames, you creep!" she shouted and stalked off.

Rumbles and flashes of lightning hung above them like an ill omen. The camp remained quiet and sombre; most have retreated to their tents or to stretched canvas, sipping their coffee to stave off their miseries.

Rosanne stared through the flap of her tent, noting the growing puddles from rain excavating the ground. "We can't stay here," she mumbled. "There are people in the forest, and I don't know what they want."

"You didn't stop to ask?" Antony's humour-laced question made her scowl. Rosanne caught herself before she said anything and sat down in front of him.

"If I told you I saw a familiar face in the forest, would you believe me?"

Antony cocked his head at the question but gave a slow nod. "Of course, I would. Unless you saw something that made you question your sanity."

"That's the thing. Our longboat crashed, and while we all took a beating, I was awake and conscious the whole time. I didn't hit my head, didn't even break as much as a finger, and yet," Rosanne's eyes fell to the floor, her voice barely a whisper, "I saw my father."

Antony studied her for a quiet moment before saying, "But that's…" He faltered, his face screwing into expressions of confusion, doubt, searching for logic.

"Impossible, I know. He's been dead for eighteen years. We found his ship in the Baltansea, for fuck's sake! Ever since it started raining, I've had this uncanny feeling that someone is watching me. And then I see that thing that resembles my father, dressed in the linen and hat he disappeared in. The same hat I am wearing right now!" Rosanne licked her lips, calming herself with each breath. "I didn't think much of the strange dreams, but now I'm questioning everything."

Antony looked uncertain, but he appeared to believe her.

"What did you dream about?" he asked.

Rosanne shook her head, battling with her denial. "It was bizarre. I was in a clearing in the jungle. The woods were the same as here. I was standing in front of a pond with waters so dark you couldn't see the bottom. When I looked at it, I saw my reflection except …" She studied her hands. "It looked like me, but …"

"It didn't feel like you?" Antony tried. Rosanne nodded. Folding his hands, he flicked his eyebrows as if he had difficulty accepting her explanation at face value. Still, this uncertainty about him made her feel as if he doubted himself more than her. "I believe we shared the same dream, but it's hazy." The silence that they shared affirmed Rosanne's worry for their safety.

"There's something wrong with this place, Antony. And I think it wants us. This isn't something we have encountered before, yet somehow it's worse. Could stress be a part of it? Absolutely. But first, the dreams, then Jeffs disappears, the whispers I heard, and my father's presence. I don't know what to make of it."

They fell silent, listening to the pattering rain. Even through the noise, Rosanne could hear the whispers, the words so close she could feel their breath on her ear. "This damn rain is messing with me!" She dug her face into her hands.

"You're not alone, Rosanne." Antony placed a hand on her shoulder, pulling her in. "I feel it, too, but I haven't seen or met what you witnessed on that last island. But I am here now. I'll stay with you no matter what." Somehow, she believed him more than she believed herself. And yet she doubted everything.

That night, Rosanne slept in fits. The white-misted marshes spread out around her, along with crooked birch trees and grassy tufts bubbling along the murky surface. Traversing the semi-solid tufts, she wandered aimlessly. In the waters rested the bones of an elk, its carcass stripped of fur, flesh, and muscle.

Fiddle music played somewhere in the fog, a soft melody that soothed her. She still remembered it, could recall the subtle shift in the melody for each verse, and pick out the moments of sorrow woven into the song as if she held the instrument herself. She remembered her first night in the Forest Devil's company, the heated conversation between the two shadow creatures, and how the menacing shadow had accused the woman of losing their child. Rosanne wondered if perhaps Nikor, the creature that lives in the bog, had played a part in that tragedy.

Hearing Yerrik's music again brought her back to the days she had spent in his cabin, doted on and cared for by the man who could read her mind and give her everything she ever wanted. It had made her happy and content but ultimately scared. She had always taken care of herself, and this was different. That alien feeling settled in her like a nightmare, and she didn't understand why. Yerrik wasn't human. Desperate to push the memories of him aside, she had drowned herself in work and impossible journeys through the Veil, never once stopping to rest or process.

The world shifted around her. The bog is filled with grass and dirt. Crooked acacia trees grew around her, maturing fully in seconds. Rain misted from the hot air and rose in wispy clouds. She saw a man sitting in front of a pond.

"Antony?" Rosanne reached out a hand, touching his shoulder.

"It looks like me, doesn't it?" he said without lifting his gaze. Leaning forwards, Rosanne stared into the black waters. Both reflections mimicked their owners, and yet she felt detached from it. What did it mean?

"Come now. We're returning to camp," she uttered, but Antony remained captivated by the alluring pull of his reflection. Rosanne considered why they were here. The pond was beautiful in a haunting way with its inky black surface depicting stars that didn't exist in the heavens above. The eyes of her reflection gleamed like an invitation into the waters. She leaned forward. Closer, closer.

"Dragonheart!" A hand on her shoulder yanked her back from the waters, and the world swirled before her eyes. Rosanne sat up, screaming, in her tent. She threw the covers off and stood, heaving for breath. Tears streamed down her face, and she twitched in nervous fright, unable to stand still to calm herself. She clutched her shirt, pressing her fist hard against her chest, fighting for calm.

She recognised the voice now.

"Yerrik," she uttered, the nauseating pit in her stomach grew. Why was he in her dream? She touched her shoulder where she had felt Yerrik's hand. It felt so real, so tangible, as if his hand lingered. Why here and why now? It had been months!

It was only when Rosanne had calmed herself that she noticed the sleeping mat next to her was empty. Antony's shoes stood by the flap of the tent. Another wave of nausea swept through her at the implication.

She dressed hurriedly and stormed outside, her shoes half-laced. The rain had stopped, though the sky remained cloudy and grey right before dawn. The rain had washed away all the footprints in the mud, except for a single set of naked feet leading away from camp.

Antony! Rosanne ran. She followed the footprints leading west into the jungle, cursing as she slapped aside foliage and branches. "Antony!" she called, disregarding twigs snagging at her hair and scraping against her face and arms.

She fell into the clearing, slipping on the mud. "Antony!" she called to the man sitting on his knees in front of the pond, his eyes locked on the surface. Scrambling, Rosanne made her way over to him and grabbed him by the shoulders, forcing him away from the water's edge. "Antony!" She shook him, confusion crossing his blank features.

"Ros? What are you doing here?"

"Why are you here?" she returned, her face a red-hot mess from her mad dash. Antony's face scrunched into a frown, and he looked around as if searching for his memory.

"When ... when did we get here?"

"Something called to you. We need to go!" she huffed, relieved he was coming to his senses and alarmed at the realisation. "The rain has let up. We're returning to the ship immediately."

Antony nodded and stood on wobbly legs.

"How long was I out of it?"

"I don't know, love. But we're not staying a second longer."

CHAPTER THIRTEEN
BEACH STORIES

O n the morning of the third day, the sky cleared from a cloud-dotted airscape to brilliant blue, bringing with it scorching temperatures and not a breath of wind. Albeit sweating like a sinner in church, Lieutenant Farand felt invigorated. Most of his northern colleagues hid in the shade, half-passed out from the heat or sunburned, while he and Olivier soaked up the sun before they were forced into the darkened hull of the ship and the perpetual overcast sky plaguing Noval. Not to mention all the health issues accompanying a lack of sunlight. He was tired of feeling tired.

Farand forewent the shirt but kept his trousers, enjoying a book on star charts while lounging on a blanket in the sand. He crossed his legs and brushed off the sand that had made it into the black curls on his chest. Meanwhile, his brother, Olivier, napped in partial shade, dressed in his undergarments with a cloth over his eyes.

Being a part of the skeleton crew was the sailor's equivalent of a holiday. Except for those maintaining the perimeter and the person staffing the crow's nest, the rest were sitting on their hands or assisting Hammond in cooking whatever oddities he caught by the beach. Crab stew was on today's menu, just as it was yesterday. At least their budget was well within limits, Farand thought with relief.

The bell rang on the ship's bowsprit. Farand jumped to his feet, letting the book drop into the sand. Swanson, by the bell, pointed west. Farand squinted against the sunlight; two dark shapes approached from the lakeside. Or was it the seaside? He couldn't decide what to call the shoreline to the floating island.

A minute later, he could make out the longboats and the blue flame they trailed. He rushed to the tent and got dressed before meeting them. The rest of the idle skeleton crew filed out from the shade to observe the surprise.

The scouting teams were two days early.

Landing at their designated spot, the crew disembarked from the longboats before Rosanne and Creedy set them down and switched off the engine. She came marching up to Farand; her face had a grim shade of uncertainty.

"Fetch the team leaders. We need to talk," she said in a low voice as she passed by. The plain, simple order threw Farand's mind into chaos, and he summoned his wits about him before any theories came to mind.

She brought her bag and rugs to where she would pitch her tent and dumped them in a pile.

Farand gathered the team leaders—Dalia, Creedy, Higgs, Lyle, and Hwang—in his large tent. Rosanne was already there, pacing around the table, unable to stand still.

"I take it that something happened since you're all here far earlier than planned?" Farand had grown accustomed to the captain's news of concern and challenge, but this time, her expression carried an uncertainty as if she couldn't openly talk about it. Tense-jawed, her gaze flitted from one spot on the ground to another.

"The hulder you met last spring, they could sing and have you obey their commands, correct?" She looked at him now, determined and searching.

Farand gave a slow, thoughtful nod, picking up where this was going. "They're here as well?" The one piece of news he didn't want to deal with was monsters, or rather, the hulder. While not malevolent by nature, Farand wasn't confident his moral compass could withstand more bloodshed. Even if they stole the *Red Queen* and imprisoned the crew, the lieutenant would rather not repeat that bloody history.

Farand scanned Creedy, who had accompanied Rosanne. He stood high strung, with arms folded and hunched shoulders, not wanting to be there. Dark rings lined his eyes, and while the man wasn't cheery by nature, he rarely looked this foul. Antony appeared less concerned than Rosanne, but he still carried the air that something he had witnessed disturbed him.

Drawing a breath, Rosanne straightened. "It spoke to us."

Farand had to withhold his alarm at whatever this meant and let her continue.

"It started subtly with dreams. Everyone I talked to dreamed the same thing about the jungle and a dark pond. We neither heard any songs nor saw any strange creatures. After the first night, Jeffs disappeared."

"He's gone? What happened?" Farand blurted, studying Rosanne's disappointed expression. She shook her head.

"We traced his path to the jungle, but he was just gone. Then the rain came, and with it, the nightmares got worse." She nodded towards

Antony. He cleared his throat and took a step forward, signifying he had the floor. Everyone's attention turned to him.

"Something called me to that pond. I don't remember getting there or how it made me leave the camp without being consciously aware of it."

"My team guarded the camp all night, yet people slipped out without our knowledge," Lyle interjected.

Farand considered their brief but disturbing statements. "It doesn't sound like the hulder, but neither does it sound like anything we know of. All has been quiet here. No rain either."

"That's some good news, at least," Rosanne breathed out. "I'm not optimistic about Jeffs returning. If we can't see our enemy, I'm not chancing another encounter."

A red flag waved in Farand's mind. The captain usually wouldn't be this nervous about people disappearing or wandering off. Creedy was such a person to disappear, before stumbling drunk as a Bunnboroux sailor back to the ship. Even if Jeffs was unaccounted for, no one had died. Yet something spooked Rosanne enough to cancel their scouting mission. There was something she wasn't telling him, but Farand knew this place, with all these people, was not the time for it.

"It came with the rain, you say?" Higgs stroked his beard.

"It struck at night, but the nightmares grew stronger when it rained," Antony said.

"And everyone dreamed the same thing? Calling you to this ... pond?" Rosanne shook her head. "Do you know something?"

The older man let out a gruff puff of air. "Sounds like another trick of the Veil. Maybe my team can whip something up to heighten the security of the camp, like a perimeter detector. Or perhaps the AVF can work on some miracles. I'll have the kids on it immediately."

"I appreciate it, Higgs," Rosanne said and rubbed her face, eyes still downcast. "If you don't mind, Farand, we should let the scouting team rest for today, and we can head north in the morning. As long as the base camp is untouched, I think you should remain here."

Farand nodded. "We were prepared for a physical enemy, but this changes things."

"We need more security and defences against the Veil and its ... bloody creatures!" Rosanne threw out a huff but quickly settled, her tone sombre. "Let us hope those lost to us find their way home."

Farand knew she was withholding information from him; anyone could see that, but he couldn't call her out on it in front of the team leaders. He would have to ask her in confidence later.

Ida squatted outside the main tent with her ear pressed up against the thick canvas. She caught bits and pieces of the captain's conversation with the department heads, but it was hard to hear through the treated fabric.

"What are you doing?" Gavin hunched down next to her, mimicking her eavesdropping.

"I'm trying to hear how much they know."

"What the hell happened over there? Don't think I've seen you this grim since Kavanaugh talked to you on the ship the other day," Gavin said in jest, but when Ida didn't relent in her hardened expression, he deflated.

"Later. I don't want to say anything in case I sound crazy. Isaac had similar theories, but we're keeping it on the down low."

Gavin's frown drew her attention from the canvas. "Why the hell have you been fraternising with that bastard?"

"I haven't!" she hissed. "He told me about stuff only I should have known, and it gave me an idea how to protect us all."

"You're not making much sense."

"I'll fill you in later. I promise."

The tent flap opened, and people filed outside. Ida and Gavin ran up to Higgs and flanked him on either side.

"What are you trouble-making wallabies up to?" he grumbled and hobbled to the central firepit, which was currently a pile of ashes.

Gavin threw his hands up in defence. "Don't look at me. Ida's the one bursting with conspiracies."

Ida let Higgs get seated. He wiggled to get comfortable, brought out his pipe, lit it, and sucked in a deep breath.

"Well?" he prompted in a puff of smoke.

She sat down next to him, Gavin on the other side, both slightly too close. Higgs arched an eyebrow at this, and Ida took the word. "You know the weather sphere I made?"

"Hard to forget. You've been working on it for weeks without sleep."

"That's right, but what if it picked up not only wind or electrical storms but even rain?"

Higgs leaned back and studied her. Ida dug the sphere out of her sack and held up the modified version for Higgs to inspect.

"I thought that model was useless," he said, turning it over in his calloused hands, stained with grime and scratches. Rough, just like his personality, Ida thought.

"Useless for wind, yes. But when word got around that there was some invisible creature calling to us, I got creative," Ida said.

Higgs cocked his head towards her, eyes wide open. "Drag me into the well, girl. You didn't," he said in disbelief.

"You got the electromagic sphere working?" Gavin's wide-eyed enthusiasm earned him a whack over the back of his head by Ida.

"It's not magic, you dingus!" she huffed. "But yes, I think so. I can't tell what it was or how it affected us. The sphere needs fine-tuning, and I need a new batch of minerals. I don't know why they've degraded already. Please, Uncle. I could really use your help on this, because I don't want to present it to the captain only for it to be bogus."

Higgs nodded. "Minerals don't come cheap, girl, but at least it burns nicely. Tell me what changes you've made, and I'll look at it."

Ida kissed the older man on his bearded cheek. "I knew you would understand!"

"By the way," Gavin interjected. "Did the captain seem a bit ... off?"

"You mean more than usual? We lost Jeffs. By Terra, boy, that would rattle anyone's pepper shakers," Higgs swiped Gavin over the back of his head.

The third engineer fixed his hair. "I know, but from what they told you and how paranoid she seemed, it doesn't add up."

Higgs sighed. "She's been through a lot, and she did the right thing, hightailing out of there."

"Gavin's right, though," Ida said. "When Jeffs first disappeared from the camp, the captain, albeit shaken, stayed calm as usual. She seemed different after the thunderstorm like she had seen a ghost. The longboat she took with Lyle, Kristoff, and Carlos was struck by lightning. They must have crashed in the forest, but the boys aren't saying anything about it."

Higgs stroked his beard. "I suggest you keep that in your own noggin. The captain has enough on her hands, and if she isn't telling us everything, I say we respect her wishes. Is that clear?"

Ida lowered her gaze to the ground. "Yeah."

"That's an order, kids."

"Yes, sir," Ida and Gavin replied in unison.

Higgs walked off to his makeshift workshop (commonly referred to as his tent) with the sphere and tablet in hand. Gavin shifted his gaze back to Ida, and her worried expression met him. He put a hand on her shoulder.

"If you have invented a monster detector, that's going to be a massive help."

"It's not that I made it, Gavin. What I saw made no sense in terms of physics. I can't even describe it!"

"This is the Grey Veil, after all," he noted.

"Yeah, but ... even if we see it, we have no method of stopping it."

"What about the anti-veil field?" he asked.

"I thought about it, but I'm not sure what good it would do."

Gavin shrugged. "We can test it, though. It's not like we have a lot to do here besides getting sand in our undies."

A headache replaced Ida's inner clockwork.

"I need to lie down. I haven't slept in two days, thanks to this non-sense."

"There's a nice spot on the beach," he offered.

"Lounging on the beach?" she asked.

"It's very nice."

"A nice spot on the beach?"

"We found oranges."

"You did?"

Gavin nodded.

A calm northern wind blew over the sun-baked beach. Ida and Gavin rested on mats in the sand, with round welding goggles shielding their eyes, Ida in her sleeveless undershirt and breeches and Gavin shirtless. After yesterday's dramatic return to the captain's scouting party, Rosanne had ordered a day off, which was unusual but welcome. While Ida knew little about why they fled the scouting camp, she didn't doubt the captain's decision at all. Something had spooked her, and if it spooked her, fleeing was the best plan.

Stretching, Ida sat up and took off her goggles, feeling hot and sweaty from the sun. The blue waters sparkled with large schools of fish swimming in the shallows. Geographically speaking, this island made no sense. A rock teeming with its own ecosystem and lakes drifted two kilometres above sea level, kept afloat by the gravity-mineral composition of the earth. Thick clouds swelled off the coastline and rolled out into the Grey Veil, but the sky above them was as clear as could be.

In this precious moment, things were good, as if the gods themselves smiled upon them. The jungle loomed behind the beach. Light broke through thick-leaved trees and the ever-present company of animal activity. The forest teemed with life, assuring Ida that no monster army was coming for them, but as she stared into its depths, she was left with a curious feeling of being watched. She spotted a small, brown-striped monkey on a low branch at the outskirts of the camp, munching on fruit. Its docile eyes locked on Hammond's food crates, and it hopped down with an effortless bounce. Its slender, fuzzy tail twitched as it skipped sideways over to the crate, hidden from Hammond's view as the cook sorted through a barrel of potatoes, tossing the bad ones into the bush.

Meanwhile, two other monkeys skirted the crates, drawing Hammond's attention. The cook grabbed a stick and waved it, making odd calls to chase them off. They merely stared at him and only fled when he hobbled too close. The first monkey dug into the crate of picked fruit, absconding with its arms full, and bounced back to the tree.

Ida giggled at the sight of Hammond fuming at the base of the tree with his fist raised towards the uncaring simians. While distracted, a flock of small white and black birds with large, straight beaks swooped down on the crates.

"Should we help him?" Gavin raised his goggles. The sentries patrolling the perimeter ran to Hammond's aid, waving their expensive plasma rifles to shoo the birds away. The birds, however, only let out wails of laughter and settled elsewhere.

"Not our job," Ida said. Even after that humorous commotion, she couldn't shake the feeling that the darkness in its nooks and crannies hid a sinister presence. At least she wasn't about to leave camp and wander off by herself like Jeffs had. She only hoped he found his way back.

The *Red Queen* hovered comfortably above them, a stone's throw away, her shadow splayed across the sand. Other people had joined the engineers' sunbathing, moving their mats from the shadows when the sweltering heat subsided.

Ida lowered her goggles, staring at the ship, a dark outline against the blistering sun. She focused on the masts.

"What are you doing?" Gavin's head turned to the ship, trying to spot whatever had caught her attention.

"I'm not sure ..." Ida cocked her head.

Gavin lifted a thumb and shut one eye. "The ship's crooked," he said, lowering his hand.

"Are you sure? We checked the anti-grav-ports two days ago."

"Want me to do rounds?" Gavin stood and dusted off the sand from his rolled-up pants.

"Please do. I should report to Higgs for tech duty anyway, so I don't have time. And don't just say yes so you can skulk off somewhere for a nap!" Ida called after Gavin as he trudged through the sand. Gavin raised a dismissive hand, trailing a fading "yeah, yeah," in his wake.

The skeleton crew's shift change came up by late afternoon. Denny, Quinn, and Vincent walked in single file along the outer hull of the *Red Queen's* cargo deck, bypassing the busy midsection for a quicker route to the staircase to the next deck.

In the narrowing hall, Quinn took the lead, his hands just as enthusiastic as his voice. "I tell you, man, the best tavern in Cintecha is The Wicker Man."

Vincent frowned and shook his head. "You're just saying that because it was the only place you could afford."

"And the Pig Quarry," Quinn countered.

"That backwater inn with its three-day-old, pig roast special?" Denny's face contorted in disgust.

Vincent laughed.

Denny's expression turned sombre. "Lads, what if Isaac is right about the captain hiding treasures from us? We all saw the map, right? Didn't look like any treasure map to me," he said, albeit keeping his tone low.

"That was months ago! I can't even remember the shape of the coastline. And no scale," Quinn pointed out.

Vincent wagged a finger, something he did often. "The captain is smart, keeping it to herself. That's what I would have done."

"Yes, but you never told us who this legendary captain you ran with is. Not exactly trustworthy material, mate."

"If Isaac can get his hands on that map, we'll know what we're dealing with. The captain saw something, and she was not telling us what. I don't like it," Denny said.

A loud crunch sounded from under his foot, making him stop, and his companions nearly bumped into him.

"What's that?" Quinn picked up the broken shell and turned it over in his hand.

"The hell is a crab's moult doing in here? Did one of Hammond's dinners jump the pot again?"

Bits and pieces of moulted shell were scattered all over the floor. The men huddled close, wide-eyed, as they advanced with one crunching step after another. A scuttling on wood broke the silence, followed by a wet crackling. Denny grabbed the lamplight off the wall hook and took the lead. A crab chittered down the hall and into the darkness, where the noise grew louder.

Quinn gave a nervous gulp, drowned out by the incessant clacking and chittering. The men advanced half a step at a time, not daring to avert their gazes. The light fell on large, shelled creatures hugging the side of the wall. With giant crusher claws, they clung to the trimmings of the hull and, with smaller, sharper, and more extended claws, picked at the gravity ports and stuffed their pincer mouths, rubbing them together. Eyes on stalks turned, the light tracing a sheen across their orbital organs.

"They're bloody huge!" Denny let out a terrified gasp. Vincent reached for his knife. Quinn fell into a coughing fit, covering his mouth with his hand.

"You alright?" Vincent patted him on the back. Quinn waved him off, but as he withdrew his hand, spatters of blood ran over his skin. He shook it off, but the blood formed fat droplets floating on a wobbly arch. The men stared in a frozen moment at the lazy bubbles of blood floating in the air.

"It's a grav leak!" Denny grabbed Quinn by the left arm and Vincent by the right, and both immediately arrested their breaths. The midsection door leading to the cargo deck stood agape, but Denny gave it a solid kick to close it, crushing a crab in the frame. The carcass left the door open a crack, but the men had no time to fix it. Denny and Vincent pushed past the enormous crabs snapping at their legs, the men going for the door leading to the stairs.

Vincent kicked another crustacean aside with a loud thud. It landed on its back, with feet treading air. The men stormed through the crabs lines clustering the anti-gravity ports that served to keep the ship afloat. They kicked the ones that didn't move out of their way and stepped on those too large to be avoided, leaving a trail of sickening crunches.

The door was just up ahead.

Quinn buckled over into a convulsing fit, his lungs wet with blood. Denny and Vincent hoisted him up and waved off droplets of blood hovering in the air. Another cough sprayed red dots before them, splashing into Denny's eye. The man blinked rapidly and stumbled along with Vincent.

The men burst through the door with a collective gasp and collapsed into a heap of limbs. Vincent rallied from the pile and slammed the door behind them.

"Quinn!" Denny patted his friend's face, but the sailor was unconscious; a spatter of blood lined his lips.

"Shit, this is bad!" Denny looked at Vincent.

"I'm getting Doc."

"Sound the alarm first! We don't know how bad the leak is."

Vincent nodded and sprinted up the stairs. "Grav-leak!" he shouted to the skeleton crew on his way to the forecastle. He ran to the bow, where the bell swayed in the afternoon breeze. Vincent dinged the bell once, paused, and then sounded two quick ones. The bell's resonant toll clanged throughout the ship.

Rosanne heard the bell from the beach and froze on the spot. Not once in her fifteen years as a captain aboard the *Red Queen* had she heard that call sign, apart from in demonstration. The surrounding crew exchanged fervent words in their confusion.

Antony ran up to her. "What is that?"

Rosanne snapped out of her daze. "It's the evacuation order," the incredulous words slipped out between her breaths. "The ship is dangerous." She whipped around, looking for Lyle.

"Forget the perimeter. Secure the surrounding ship!" she roared through the commotion. She spotted Vincent climbing down the rope ladder, immediately followed by the rest of the skeleton crew scrambling for escape.

"What's the danger? Why did you call it?" she interrogated Vincent, seething with rage and fear.

"We have a gravity leak! The ship's full of giant crabs that have destroyed the grav-ports!"

Rosanne didn't believe her ears for a moment. "Giant crabs? From where? How?"

"We don't know. Quinn, Denny, and I were in the hull when we saw hordes of them! The air is—" Vincent coughed. He threw a hand over his mouth and keeled over in a fit.

"Everyone back!" Rosanne ordered with an outstretched hand, backing away from the sailor. "Someone find Doc and the engineers!" Rosanne hailed Carlos, who came down the ladder. "Who's unaccounted for?"

The man searched the amassing crowd.

"Quinn and Denny."

"They're still aboard? Fuck!" Rosanne swore and rubbed her forehead.

Ida jostled through the crowd. "There's a mineral leak?" she asked, eyes wide.

"Alongside the starboard hull, at least. But it's infested with giant crabs."

Ida groaned. Vincent sat on the ground, out of breath, but had lifted his pant legs enough to show the many cuts dug into his flesh on both shins, verifying his claims.

"Gavin went in to check on the ports an hour ago," Ida said, her voice low.

Rosanne let out a frustrated hiss. "Do you have the extraction equipment here? We don't know the scale of the damage—"

The ship groaned and tilted starboard in a slow, hulking arch. People scrambled from the moving ship in wild panic. Rosanne's chest tightened painfully as she watched her ship, her livelihood and home, tip off its axis. Sails and rigging tumbled sideways, unsecured crates smashed into the railing and splintered and fell overboard, but Rosanne couldn't move.

Ida grabbed Rosanne's arm and threw them both out of the way of the tumbling barrels. Rosanne crashed into the sand, the air knocked out of her. Her eyes flew to the ship. It finally came to a standstill, tilted almost completely to one side.

Ida dusted off her pants and let out a horrified whimper. "We don't have enough capsules to fix the whole side of the *Red Queen*. We need to act now!"

Rosanne snapped out of her daze and met the engineer's worried look. "Can you go through the cargo deck?"

"Not if the side doors are open. And I gave Gavin my set of keys! All the alternative routes should be locked."

"Let's hope Gavin caught the port issues then ..." Rosanne frowned at the tilted *Red Queen*, hoping that was the last of it.

CHAPTER FOURTEEN

OH, CRAB!

Gavin awoke as he slipped off the sacks of flour on which he had napped. Having face-planted on the floor, he lay sprawled in the corner of the storage room, which was tilted on its side.

"The hell?" he muttered, pushing himself up with a painful groan, wobbling on unsteady legs.

Had the anti-gravity ports been shorted on one side of the ship? Gavin knew he should have checked them before getting distracted by Senior Petty Officer Ratcatcher, who knew the best napping spots. Ida was going to kill him for ignoring her instructions.

Massaging his neck, Gavin pawed in the darkness against the angled floor, searching for the fallen lamplight. From his pocket, he produced a matchbox, which he struck and shielded as he looked for the suspended oil lamps. He spotted one in the corner with oil puddled around the lamp canister, and the glass shattered from the fall.

"Shit!" Gavin swore as the match burnt his fingers and flickered out, plunging the room into darkness.

Supporting himself against the wall, he reached for the door, discovered the familiar metal handle, and pushed it down. The cargo deck was a pool of black with a single lamp swaying near the stairs, beyond cubicles, crates and hanging nets. Gavin flailed for purchase on a ship that was tipped at a thirty-degree angle. He leaned against the floor and tumbled his way past secured crates, bumped into a hanging net of smaller goods, and used it to swing himself to the middle of this hellish navigational nightmare.

"Why is it so quiet?" Gavin uttered between breaths. He expected thumping feet on the deck above him from panicked crew. He stretched for the lamp and struggled with the ring, keeping it locked in place. A loud series of clunks rattled down the stairs, the noise startling him with each step. He fumbled with the lamp in a moment of wild panic; he freed it from the rung and flashed the light before him, supporting himself at a steep angle against a cubicle.

Gavin heard the clacking before he spotted a shelled claw waving from the shadows, followed by needle sharp feet digging into the wood. The creature must have been a metre wide! Its snapping, crushing claw could take his hand if he got too close.

Gavin pulled out his only defence mechanism, the pointed end of one of his electricity conductors, and waved the rod in front of him. The giant, blue-shelled crab caught the rod in its claw and clamped down. Gavin pulled, but the crab wouldn't let go; instead of freeing the tool, he dragged the creature closer to him. Pincers snapped at his fingers, and he let go in a panic. The crab waved an arm as if it understood the concept of victory. Since the rod was still attached to his belt, Gavin flipped a switch on the box and jabbed the other electrical rod close to the first one. A current zipped through the shelled creature. The crab tried to flee, but when it kicked off the floor, it floated, failing with its legs, searching with its claws until it dropped the rod. He stared for an amused moment at the helpless creature spinning in the air.

"Serves you right, you little shit." Gavin snickered, pushed the crustacean aside, and headed upstairs on all fours. The lower gundeck was less dark but teeming with crabs of varying sizes. Both the side doors to the outer hull stood ajar, the crabs crawling their way up the floorboards towards the portside. Gavin's jaw fell open.

"Fuck me sideways." He drew a quick breath and shut his mouth. The crabs snapped at his legs as he navigated past them. Gavin kicked one aside, causing it to crash into smaller ones clambering on the wood. He stumbled across the deck, past cluttered chairs and tables that had broken free of their straps.

The engineering door was locked.

As he fumbled for the keys at his belt, the pounding in his head increased. Crabs nipped at his legs, making him jump and drop the keys. He wanted to swear but couldn't; his chest was so tight that he thought he might burst. A cold sensation ran through him with each heartbeat, a painful wave making his muscles burn. He swept the keyring from the floor, then smashed it against the wall, dislodging two smaller crabs that had grabbed hold.

Gavin stumbled through the door, shutting it behind him. He dove for a panel of buttons on the wall and hit the one marked "Emergency Ventilation." Air whooshed as the pump worked to clear the room while replenishing it with fresh air from the outside. Gavin gasped, then heaved for breath, kneeling over and forcing it out as hard as he could, in fear of having inhaled the anti-gravity minerals. After a couple of minutes, the black spots in his vision worsened, and he swayed, feeling as if he were about to vomit a lung. Stumbling two steps to the panel, Gavin hit the button again, silencing the room. Claws scraped against the metal door, sounding like miniature horrors begging to be let in. Luckily, the door was airtight.

Gavin had to assume he was the only one aboard the ship, having missed the evacuation thanks to his need to sleep. Hopefully the cat was safe somewhere, but he digressed, counting it as a blessing, as he now had access to the equipment needed to extract the minerals. With the cargo deck flooded with dust and crabs, neither the crew could rid the ship of the little bastards nor could Gavin remove the immediate danger of gravity poisoning.

Oh shit, gravity poisoning!

He touched his face in panic, having completely forgotten about gravity leak protocols. "Gums, lungs, hands, and arms." He examined himself for any sign of blood seeping through his pores. Breathing out in relief, Gavin counted himself lucky for having dodged the immediate danger.

Now, he needed to get rid of the crabs. But how?

His eyes wandered to the thruster engine, *Not-So-Leaky Sally*, pristine and shiny. Next to it stood the battery-driven unit that turned off the gravity ports alongside the hull. It gave the same output of electricity as it received from the backup power. If he could deactivate the ports and render the minerals inert, perhaps the crabs wouldn't feed on them. However, without the grav-engine, the ship would crash into a pile of kindling.

Gavin chewed on his lips and leaned his head back, muttering, "We're hovering twenty metres above the ground. No water below us. I have mineral extraction equipment, and all the ports and doors are locked except for the side doors. At least the minerals are contained to this level.

If I get us down, the ship will capsize, making clearing out the crab infestation and the dust a bloody nightmare. If I restart the gravity ports, there's an absurdly high chance they'll misfire and fail." He leaned his head back and mouthed a singular, 'Fuck.'

His attention drawn to the grav-port power supply unit, Gavin let out a frustrated cry. Higgs was the sole operator of it. Not even Ida, being a second engineer, knew how to turn off the grav-ports for marine docking procedures. Higgs trusted no one with his crazy inventions unless they could recreate them by heart, and Gavin had the memory of a cod.

"It's just a few buttons," he told himself. Timing and coordination with the captain was how they usually performed marine docking, but he had no visual or aural assistance. He had watched the old man do it hundreds of times. Yet his hands shook as his fingers hovered over the buttons.

"Five-second countdown to deactivate the ports after pushing the button. That's easy enough. Just wait for the delayed descent of the ship and then push the button to reactivate it before we hit the ground. Easy. Listen for the whining sound, Gavin," he muttered. Higgs had installed two metal bars on the wall to secure himself during marine docking. Wrapping his hand around one of them, Gavin gave the metal a firm tug. He steeled himself and pushed the activation button.

"One ... two ... three." He counted until he picked up the whirring electrical hum to the gravity unit. Nothing happened for two full seconds. The floor disappeared beneath Gavin, and he was left floating, clutching the bar with his hand. His feet dangled, and his fear grew to terror. He jabbed a finger at the reactivation button, screaming as he did so. The unit died out with a pathetic hum. A moment passed. The ship slowed its descent, and Gavin felt his insides drop from his chest and his feet plant on the floor again as the ship came to a standstill. All fight and courage scared out of him, an incredulous laugh escaped his lips. He shook so badly that his eyes stung with pressing tears. A minute passed.

A rhythmic metallic banging came from the rear thruster panel of the ship.

"My Morse is shite," he said. He pried himself loose from the metal bar and stumbled across the askew room to a sheet of paper with dots and lines hung on the wall.

"In case you need this one day, Gavin. With love from Ida." He frowned at the message. "You cheeky shit."

He listened again as the banging repeated.

"W. A. I. T. Wait? Oh! They need to support the ship so it doesn't fall over when I start up the anti-grav again. That makes sense." This also meant he had missed the ground by a far tighter margin than he had calculated. Gavin breathed in relief, thankful that he was still alive and that the ship was still afloat, for now.

"Move it!" Rosanne shouted at the scrambling group of seamen running past with saws and axes towards the nearby forest, attacking the smaller trees with serious abandon. A second group moved with ropes to wrap around the palm trees at the beach, a makeshift pulley in the works to bring the ship closer to the ground. The *Red Queen* still hovered three metres in the air, and a drop from that height onto any ground could do unimaginable damage to the ship's integrity. The crew hurried aboard the ship, securing ropes around the metal-plated masts, and tossed the ends to the ground below.

Farand coordinated the pulley team, having done similar work on the ship when no repair facility was available. Careening a sailing ship in the olden days involved a full crew and the forces of the ocean, but thanks to the remaining functioning gravity ports on *The Red Queen*, less brute force worked better. With the ship keeling to one side, it was susceptible to weight changes, so the portside teams took turns hauling the ropes with their accumulated strength.

"Heave!" he bellowed, and three teams of five sailors each, including himself, pulled at the ropes. The added weight and pull slowly brought the *Red Queen* down.

On the forest edge, Dalia's team rushed to fell enough trees to support the hip. "Five more! Just get them down and drag them to the beach!" She grabbed a two-person saw and waved to Antony, who ran to assist. They pulled and pushed the saw, its teeth biting into the wood. Behind them, a tree creaked as it crashed to the sand with a softened, leafy thud. Men swarmed with machetes and hacked at the branches before hauling the trunk to the beach.

"You guys experience this often?" Antony heaved his breath, an excited grin on his face despite the heat and sticky situation.

"You'd be surprised by all the shit we go through. Never a dull day." Dalia laughed. "Now put your arms into it, Captain! We've got a ship to save."

"Yes, ma'am!"

Rosanne used the railing as support as she made her way to the helm. With a single jump, she grabbed a loose-hanging rope encircling the mizzen mast and pulled herself up to the wheel. The steep angle of the *Red Queen* made this process awkward, and Rosanne clambered onto the instrument panel as she reached for the intercom.

"Mr. Diggle, are you down there?" she tried. A few seconds passed.

"Gavin?" she tried again.

"I'm here, Captain!" Gavin's voice crackled through the static. "We're overrun by giant crabs feeding on the gravity ports. There are leaks everywhere! We must get the ship to the ground before I switch off the anti-grav-ports."

Rosanne struggled to keep up with Gavin's order of business. "What good will that do? We need to contain the grav leak first!"

She heard an exasperated "ugh." The cheek of this kid.

"The crabs eat activated minerals. If I deactivate the ports, they might lose interest in those and focus on the free-floating ones instead. We can save the remaining ports."

Ah, there was the logic. "Copy that, Gavin. We're working on supports for the hull, and we're lowering the ship as quickly as we can. It shouldn't be too much longer now. We need you to come out with all the cleanup gear. You think you'll be able to do that?"

"It's heavy, but it should be fine. Get Ida and Higgs for me."

"They're already on standby, Mr. Diggle. I'll let you know when it's time."

"Copy that, Captain."

Rosanne tucked away the intercom and leaned on the console. Their careful planning was moot compared to the chaos they now had on their hands. With all doors and ports locked, navigating through the cargo deck to the engine room without suffering from anti-gravity toxicity would be near impossible. How had they missed the crab infestation? Everything had gone to hell, and they had nothing to show for it. How could she mess up this badly? Rosanne pulled at her face, the blue bags under her eyes transforming her into a ghastly representation of a walking corpse.

"We're ready to brace the ship." Norman said, peering over the side of the hull.

"Good work. Now, everyone, off the ship! Move, move!" Rosanne picked up the intercom. "Mr. Diggle, we're almost ready. We'll Morse Code you when the time is right."

"Copy!"

The rope ladder filled with people disembarking the ship and lined up next to the felled tree trunks stripped of branches. Men with shovels dug holes around the ship for the trunks while others lined them up against the hull, ready to brace.

"This is a lot harder with flying vessels than marine ones," Rosanne grumbled as she met up with Antony. His eyes swept over the airborne, careened ship.

"Wouldn't it be easier to keep her on the side?"

"It would, but we have an extermination issue inside, and with half the grav-ports still working, we need to prop her up so she doesn't fall over and destroy everything inside. Plus, there's cleanup of the mineral leak." She let out a long, drawn groan.

Antony nodded slowly as he took in her reasoning.

Farand stood on portside, having amassed most of the crew with him, ready to tip the ship.

"We're ready, Captain!" he called. Dalia, on the other side, gave a positive wave.

"Let's straighten her up, then. Mr. Creedy!" Rosanne called to the older watch captain, who turned to receive her message. "Signal Gavin."

Creedy nodded and, with a metal rod, banged against the rear thruster panel in Morse code.

Farand caught this signal, ordering the men to jump on the ropes. The *Red Queen* tipped their way in a slow arch, the same way they had used to bring the ship closer to the ground, but now the braces against the hull levelled the ship. The ship lowered itself to the trench dug under the keel, Farand's men keeping portside level with the propped starboard. Trunks creaked under the ship's weight as the anti-gravity ports deactivated. The ship gave a lurch and nestled into the ground, its entire weight seemingly sagging into the sand with groans. A support beam exploded under the weight of the starboard. Dalia threw herself to the side in reflex, a scream escaping her lips. Rosanne rushed to her side.

"Are you alright?" she asked the woman, who nodded with large splinters jutting from her arm. She cradled it with the other hand with a pained expression.

"Nothing serious, ma'am. I'll see Doc after we finish," she hissed between gritted teeth.

Rosanne helped her up, and Dalia stubbornly made her way to co-ordinate the support beams being hammered into place as the ship dug into the sand.

Farand strained against the ropes. "Tie her down!" he cried. Men rushed to secure the counterweights around a cluster of trees holding their individual ropes.

The creaking and groaning of wood stopped, and the *Red Queen* stood level. These were the longest minutes of Rosanne's life. A round of cheers resonated through the crew at the beach. She nodded to Ida and Higgs, who scurried up the ladder to board the ship.

"Creedy, Kristoff, Hwang," she called. "Assist them with the crab infestation, but do not enter the cargo hold!"

All she could do was wait. Rubbing her face, Rosanne plopped down the sand and raised her legs, letting her arms rest on her knees. Antony came up to her. Sweat and wood chips clung to his shirt, but he bore an energetic grin. His mirth was subdued by Rosanne's darkened mood in how she studied the *Red Queen* and chewed on her nails. She knew Antony noticed this about her. She had been careful with her changed habits, but right now, it was difficult to care about appearances.

"It's hard not being able to do anything to help when your own ship is in danger," he sympathised.

"It always is. That's why I have people I trust to get the job done when I can't." She stuck an elbow into his side teasingly. "And look at you running to our rescue."

Antony flicked his eyebrows and twitched his nose haughtily. "What can I say? I am more than an emotional support animal."

Rosanne slapped his arm for that, snorting a laugh.

Gavin entered the cargo hold from the machine room, his body covered in leather garb with a glass slit for his eyes to peer through. In each arm, he'd draped another set of leather coverings, and he wore a single extraction unit on his back. He waded through the horde of snapping claws from angry crabs and wrestled the door open to the next section. Just inside lay Quinn and Denny, unconscious but breathing. Droplets of blood detached from Quinn's lips and were carried by the draught weaving through the deck. Higgs and Ida lingered at the top of the stairs, both too cautious about approaching.

Gavin brought out the grav-meter from his toolbelt. The needle on the gauge hopped back and forth between low numbers. "Non-toxic levels here, but still trace amounts." He said, muffled by the head covering. "Good thing you waited upstairs."

Hwang and Creedy rushed to the two unconscious sailors and carried them upstairs, shouting for people to get them treated.

"How bad is it?" Ida asked, grabbing a leather suit and slipping into the trousers, fastening the clasps over her shoulders.

Gavin tore off the hood, his face red and sweaty from the heavy gear. "We're stranded if we don't get rid of the crabs fast. They're still eating the minerals in the air, but lucky for us, the minerals aren't flowing out of the ship, so we might salvage some."

"How hostile are they?" Higgs wiggled, the head covering in place.

"Like beach crabs on mushrooms, but they're huge and in large numbers. The suit helps against their claws, but they can still pinch your legs pretty bad if you let them."

"That's it then. Ida, girl, you're in charge of dusting. We'll get the crabs off the ship," Higgs ordered and grabbed a fallen broom, balancing awkwardly in the heavy suit and tilt of the ship.

The room inside remained dark, save for a couple of lamplights and a horde of scuttling crabs shyly retreated from them. Higgs stood dumbfounded for a second, taking in the massive shells of the crustaceans' snapping claws.

"They must be twenty to thirty kilos each! You trying to kill me?" he protested, stomping on a smaller one that tried to squeeze past the door.

Ida spotted a huge gnarled shell of another crab, its crusher claws large enough to encircle her leg. The circular patterns flushed red in pulsating beats as if warning her to stay away. "I like my limbs just as much as you do, Uncle. What do we do about them?"

Gavin pulled out his electrical conductors and held them up before him, his smirk beaming through the glass visor of his suit. Ida whacked him with a gloved hand on the back of his head.

"That'll take too long, you dingo. We need to separate them so they don't overwhelm us." Ida raised the alchemical lamp, flooding the door-way with harsh white light. The nearest crabs scuttled into dark corners, which gave Ida pause. "Gavin, look." She pointed to the empty patches of floor where the light shone. "They're photophobic?"

"That's awfully convenient. Wish I had known that earlier," Gavin muttered, dejectedly putting the rods away.

The trap door to the stairs opened, and three heads popped into view, casting shadows from above. Kristoff, Creedy, and Hwang peered down.

"Ready when you are, Chief," Hwang said.

Higgs swept a smaller crab aside with a grumble. "We'll get them to you, but keep your scrawny butts up there no matter what!"

"Yes, Chief," the three replied in unison.

Gavin grabbed a lamp and waved it ahead of him. Crabs scuttled away in panic. "We'll herd them towards the stairs. Get a lamp, Higgs."

"I'll take that." Higgs snatched the grav-metre from his hands.

The engineers wobbled inside with their heavy suits and gear. Ida guided them to the middle of the room, kicking away a stubborn foot-sized crab snapping at her while Higgs and Gavin waved the lamps to scare off the others. Higgs made a quick measure with the grav-metre, sputtering behind his mask. "The levels in here are beyond toxic! They're downright deadly! Nothing should be able to survive in here for long."

Gavin's lips pressed into a thin line. He didn't want to worry them by admitting he walked through the cargo deck without protective gear. He felt fine, honestly.

"Rod is down. Turning it on," Ida announced. The men withdrew to a corner. Purple, electric, spider-webbed lightning shot from the rod and through the air, drawn to the conductor rod a metre away. The anti-gravity minerals in the vicinity drew to each other and formed large, floating black blobs. Ida flipped a switch on the nozzle connected to the machine hanging from her back and pointed it toward the blob.

She nipped at it, unable to suck it all up in one go. "It's too dense! We need to do this in at least four passes."

"Keep the light with you, and you should be fine. I'll herd them from the front." Gavin dragged himself to the rear, shooing the smaller creatures huddled in the corners and pushing the larger ones ahead with his foot. Most scuttled aside or didn't seem to care he was there. They were passive compared to when the grav-ports were active.

They hurried past Ida in a wide arc. One of the larger crabs, brushed by the electrical field and when caught in it, became suddenly airborne. Gavin brought a broom and pushed it ahead.

"You'll float too," Gavin snickered as he passed Ida, who was doubled over from the ridiculous sight. Higgs caught the crab with gloved hands by its shell and brought it to the stairs.

"Special delivery," he announced to Creedy, whose puzzled expression matched the liveliness of the chief engineer's grin. Higgs sent the creature flying up the stairs, and Creedy fumbled to catch it without being caught by the pincers. Gavin herded as many crabs as he could into Ida's electrical field and batted them towards Higgs.

"Watch out down there!" Kristoff announced as she tossed one crab over the railing. It hovered for a few seconds before crashing into the sand with a loud crack.

Rosanne wrinkled her nose and drew a deep breath. Of all the things they had prepared for this journey, from the full line of plasma weaponry, the crew, the lockdown of hatches and doors, around-the-clock defences, and navigational instruments that surpassed any military invention in existence, they got outdone by fucking crabs. It took everything she had not to scream.

More crabs were dumped overboard, either floating down to the sand where they scuttled into the forest in a wild panic once the anti-gravity field disintegrated or they crash-landed in squalor of broken limbs. Most of them were the size of a five-litre cauldron by Hammond's measurements, while others weighed as much as a large dog. They spread around the camp, hiding in tents or going for food rations stored in barrels and crates. The once-idle crew got busy shooing them away, but the little buggers persisted.

"I don't suppose we can cook them?" Norman quipped, fighting a crab that tried to run off with a small saw.

Restricted by his bad leg, Hammond remained seated on a log, peeling potatoes as if it were business as usual. "If you want to crap blood that can hit the stratosphere, be my guest." Another crab snapped at the potato shavings on the ground. Hammond paused, pulling his ageing fishbone-bearded face into a grin. "I have a fan. Maybe I should keep him and call him Herbert. Hammond and Herbert! That has a nice ring to it, don't you think?"

"Herbert weighs twenty kilos and can sink the ship. I don't think so!" Norman nodded to the shelled creature nibbling potato peels without a care in the world. With a grin on his face, Olivier scooped up the shavings.

"What are you on about with those, lad?" Hammond squinted.

"Oh, nothing." Olivier whistled as he dropped potato shavings on a trail leading into the jungle. The nearby crabs that had survived the fall from the ship scuttled after him, stopping for snacks along the way. Only Herbert remained.

Captain Drackenheart approached them, amusement plastered on her lips. "No pets allowed, Mr. Hammond. You know the rules," her humorous tone eased what little tension was left, and Hammond let out a laugh.

***

Aros conked a shovel over a crab that had run off with his bag, the resounding clunk drawing hearty laughter from his colleagues. "Give that back, ye little shit!" He swung the shovel again, and the crab forfeited its bounty and darted into the jungle, snapping the guy line of his tent in passing. His accommodation folded in on itself in a sad pile of crumpled canvas. Aros drew his breath, letting the shovel rest by his side.

It was fine.

Laughter drifted from the campfire where Hammond peeled his potatoes. Captain Drackenheart chatted with the stocky, fair-haired youth and his friend with the afro. A seaman and the scout, Aros recalled. Whatever she said lightened their mood and made the crab infestation seem benign. Tearing his eyes from the merriment, Aros tackled the torn guy line into the tent plug. Too short to be tied together, he dug through the supply crates where he knew he had seen rope. The laughter cut through his skull like knives, and he attacked the pile of hemp in jaw-clenching frustration. How in the Terran hells were they all so calm about this?

The stark contrast brought Aros back to the days aboard the *Blue Dragon* as they fought through rain and wind, their weather-hardened faces lined with fatigue. Only the sight of the slum ports in Georgetown could turn their sullen faces to greed-stricken fools when they received their share of the bounty. The fortune would last a mere few days before they had to go back out to sea, their eyes set on the next shipment from Queensland. The crew he had sailed with during their last stint, after Aros' transfer from the Cintechan inlands, had only been together for a few weeks. Never in his life did Aros think he would sail the open seas, be surrounded by so many people, and yet be as isolated as he was at this moment.

The rope fibres grated his fingers raw, and when Aros finally found the right thickness, his still-healing nailbeds split. He stared at the blood soaking into the hemp, spreading along the threads like coloured bands.

A distant hollow scream sounded in his mind, making Aros freeze. The blood ran down his fingers, separated in fat droplets from his skin, but gravity had no hold on these as they remained suspended in the air in wobbly spheres. The prisoner in the other chair with him in the room seized in a fit of coughs. The blood detached from his lips in lazy movements. Aros hitched his breath, his muscles stiff.

"Open wide," the inquisitor said with a cruel smile.

A slap on his shoulder tore Aros away from the cell of the Bunnsboroux dungeons.

"You alright, mate?" Denny asked. Aros looked at his fingers. He shook off the memory and took the rope he needed.

"Damn, crabs ruined my tent," he said and raised the rope to indicate he would fix it. He stalked back to his tent, trying to keep his attention on the crumpled canvas. Yet, betraying himself in true envious fashion, Aros's attention drifted to the captain and the bond she shared with her crew.

Only by early evening did the engineers disembark the ship, their red and sweaty faces weary from the day and their hair clinging to their skin like leeches. They approached the bonfire with waddling steps where Rosanne and Farand were seated having supper. Rosanne waved to Hammond, who prepared three bowls and sent Norman to deliver them. Gavin grabbed his and a loaf of bread and dug in like a hungry wolf.

"How bad is it?" Farand asked.

Higgs grumbled and shook his head. "It's a disaster. The crabs destroyed three ports and damaged another six. I've got no clue if we can fix them all, but that is tomorrow's business."

"Well done, you three," the lieutenant complimented, even if the news wasn't the type anyone hoped for. He glanced towards Rosanne, who was mulling it over her own head, eyes fixed on the fire. "Your thoughts, Captain?"

Rosanne chewed on a meaty chunk from the stew, nodding as if she had formulated a plan. "We change the teams to prioritise fixing the ship and getting her airborne again. The rest of us continue scouting, but we head north instead of west and follow the coastline there."

Farand nodded. With the ship temporarily out of commission, they might as well attempt another scouting run. "Sound plan. What about the nightmare creature?"

"Perhaps it was limited to that part of the island. No one has felt anything here, so I think that is a safe assessment."

"About that ..." Higgs interfered. Farand regarded his wringing hands. "The kids and I cooked something up that might work. Don't tell Hammond. Anyway, we'll need at least a day to set it up. If you postpone your scouting for late tomorrow, I can send the kids with you."

"Are you sure that's wise, Higgs? What if you need the extra hands?" Farand asked.

"I'm positive," Higgs replied. Ida's pensive stare caught Farand's curiosity, but he said nothing. If the engineers were onto something, time was the most valuable asset he could give them. Yet, something was different with Higgs' sudden need for precautions, which made Farand wonder. The engineers had never failed, but neither had they seemed so at odds with one another.

"I'll take your word for it," Rosanne said, but she agreed to wait until they were ready with whatever they were working on.

"If we leave tomorrow, does this mean we have to work on the grav-ports today?" Gavin made a wry face.

Higgs patted him on the back. "You take the damaged ports, and I'll get stuck into the ruined ones."

"You evil cod on a beach!" Ida cried from utter exhaustion.

"Don't work them to death now, Chief. The workers union won't be happy about it." Higgs winked, promising nothing.

CHAPTER FIFTEEN

THE NIGHT SHIFT

A t dawn the next day, Rosanne's expedition crew left base camp. Bleary-eyed sailors armed with plasma rifles yawned in the longboats, but Rosanne's gaze was sharp and her mind alert. Ida and Gavin snoozed, crammed between the crew, having worked through the night to complete a perimeter defence system against invisible intrusion. Aros snored next to Vincent, who was nodding off. The older man had escaped the worst of the anti-gravity poisoning, with only bleeding gums and a sore throat. Quinn lay in the Doc's tent back at base being treated for toxic gravity mineral exposure, but other than extracting the minerals out of their lungs using painful and half-choking methods, if the lung damage was too severe, there was nothing anyone could do. Denny had been lucky, passing out from the stress rather than exposure, and could join them as usual. Rosanne prayed Quinn would recover. She couldn't bear to lose another man at this point.

She had given Antony second in command for the expedition, with him steering the other longboat and coordinating the people there. Sharing this burden with him lifted a load off her shoulders, and he understood now as well as her what potentially lurked in the jungle.

Antony had been a remarkable voice of reason ever since St. Emmanuel when uncertainty came as an unbidden guest courted by a bouquet of withering confidence and fear.

Scanning the surrounding landscape, Rosanne spotted ponds and rivers snaking through the forest. The uncanny feeling the black pools gave her returned, though she couldn't pinpoint why. It wasn't altitude sickness, as Doc had given them all a clean bill of health. Was it stress? Antony, however, couldn't remember how he ended up by the pond, so it couldn't be that. What about their shared dreams? That man who looked like her father? In fear of sounding paranoid, Rosanne hadn't disclosed this information to the crew or even to Farand. Her father was many years dead and probably a product of the nightmare creature stalking them. There could be something in the air changing their thought processes. Perhaps it was the Grey Veil itself digging its claws into them, as it always did when the outside world wanted in?

The thick jungle relented the further north they travelled, following the arching coastline of the island until they turned west. Captain Drackenheart guided them to a small peninsula, the elevated ground far enough from the shoreline and protected from the waves.

"What do you think, Mr. Lyle?" she directed.

The man adjusted his glasses in a fluid motion, his eyes scanning the narrow sandbank and the long beach. "Defensible. Should make it easier to keep us safe in case someone heeds the call of nature."

Having overheard Lyle, Aros turned to Vincent. "On the flip side, if we're attacked, we're quacked."

Vincent arched an eyebrow.

"You know, sitting ducks?"

The other man let out a delayed chuckle.

Bonfires crackled with steaming pots of coffee while the crew busied themselves with tents and supplies. The captain enjoyed her caffeine luxury far more than any other captain Aros knew of, considering their economy. Norman, the Novalian youth built like a barn, was on cooking duty along with Kristoff. Both were often stuck with grunt work or cooking duties when Hammond wasn't around. Despite Norman's shortcomings in other areas of the ship, having lost his bout with Olivier over the scouting position, again, the lad knew how to brew the perfect pot of coffee. Aros hugged his cup, letting the warmth of the metal penetrate his shivering hands. A chill wind blew from the Veil. He sipped the bitter drink until his mind felt like cooperating again.

This journey had been a proper disaster since their arrival, and Aros wondered if the captain knew what she was doing. Surely, this wasn't her first proper Grey Veil run, right? One reason he was here was that she had got her crew out alive the last time, with riches and secrets. Yet, here they'd lost Jeffs on the first expedition, and before they even left for the second, a crab infestation grounded the ship.

The captain consulted her map at the edge of the sandbank. At that distance, he couldn't make out the details, and no one besides the watch captains and a few select members of her inner circle had studied it, but Aros wasn't on speaking terms with either of them. They were searching for a specific piece of land, but for what purpose was beyond him. He needed to see the map. He needed a distraction.

Emptying his cup, he washed it in the brackish waters. A school of silvery fish flashed by, their scales catching the sun breaking through the cloud layers. He drew a deep breath, enjoying the unpolluted air. The waters lapped at the sand, the sun creating golden flutters across the surface.

Aros caught his breath. What first appeared to be a rock among the waves shone like wet, black hair. A pair of dark eyes stared at him above the surface. Pale skin peered between wet locks clinging to their pallid skin. In a flash, the figure ducked below the surface, leaving behind rings of waves. Aros leapt to his feet, dropping his cup. He found the captain in seconds, sprinting over to her.

"There are mermaids!" he said in a harsh whisper. She paused her conversation with Antony. They both served him their best incredulous stare, and Aros could only imagine they had practised it for this very occasion.

"Could you excuse us for a bit?" She looked to Antony, whose dubious scowl left Aros wondering if he understood what he had gotten himself into by making such a ludicrous statement to her.

Rosanne turned to Aros, a sympathetic smile on her lips not reflected by her dismissive stare. "Did you drink the seawater?"

Aros bristled but drew a deep breath. "Why is it that every time I cry 'wolf,' you write me off as a shroom addict desperate for attention?"

"Because you're a liar, a pirate, and nothing good ever comes out of your mouth."

Aros scoffed and crossed his arms. "You have no clue what happened to Jeffs or why lover boy wandered off in the middle of the night."

Rosanne pursed her lips, a pensive fold emerging between her eyes. "Whatever your problem is, for all our sakes, let it go. Spreading panic based on lies because you want to be in the torchlight doesn't make it alright."

"I am not pulling your leg here!" he hissed loud enough for people to turn their heads. His face contorted into a grimace as he calmed himself. "All I'm saying is that I saw a face in the water. They looked right at me and then disappeared below the surface. If legends are any indication, it sounds pretty fishy to me."

Rosanne regarded his alarmed expression. "Did they seem hostile?"

"I don't know. Curious maybe. The point is, they're out there. We should be careful."

"Oh, really? I thought we were here for the beaches and sunny weather."

"You know what I mean."

She studied his face, analysing his behaviour, no doubt. "I will take your observation under advisement. If they're mermaids, we won't have to worry about them coming to land to drown us."

"Are you at least gonna let anyone else know?"

"You know what? You can be the first watch this night. I'll inform Lyle."

Aros felt his insides boil at the sight of Rosanne's smug expression. "You distrust me that much?"

Her eyes narrowed. "Trust is earned, and you're in massive debt where that is concerned."

Aros felt his fingers twitch, but he curled them together before he made a bigger spectacle of himself. "Fine!" he said through gritted teeth.

"Fine." She crossed her arms. Aros stalked to the shore, sat, and grumbled. Crossing his legs, he closed his eyes and breathed, searching for that inner peace that had kept him level throughout the journey. "Rise above it, Aros. Rise above that woman's stubbornness—rise above!" he chanted to himself.

—◦◇◦—

After Ida and Gavin had finished setting up their dual tent, complete with a makeshift table and a whole crate's worth of tools, they circled the camp and took measurements with a knotted thread.

Ida spotted Isaac sitting cross-legged on the sand, his brows furrowed and muttering to himself. She gave him a wide berth for her sanity.

Gavin sat with a notebook and jotted down the measurements as she returned to him. "You think we have enough line?"

She shook her head. "I think we should focus on the forest face of the peninsula."

Ida waved to Lyle, who was passing by. "Hey, Lyle! Can we borrow you for something?"

The master gunner paused, hesitation crossing his features. "That depends. We're people, not guinea pigs, and I, for one, do not appreciate the uncertainty of your experiments."

"It'll be quick and painless. And non-lethal. I promise." Ida guided Lyle to a ring drawn in the sand surrounded by three poles with cables running to a medium-sized, battery-driven unit with buttons.

"This is the prototype Higgs developed for the anti-veil field that disrupts whatever signal the Veil itself created. We're thinking we can use this to at least ward off the dream-vaders."

"Dream-vaders? Might be my roots sticking out on this one, but I'm quite certain we're not fighting against dream-fathers." Lyle lifted a white-speckled eyebrow.

Ida laughed. "It's what we call the invisible monster that can invade your dreams. We haven't tested this with an actual human inside or studied its long-term effect, but so far, it's proved harmless. If you don't mind, standing inside the field for, say, five minutes? If it passes the testing stage, maybe we can set up a perimeter."

"I do not like this at all, Miss Simonsen," he said, pressing the rifle close to his chest.

"We'll stop if you feel the slightest discomfort."

"Comforting."

Ida flipped the switch on the box. The device hummed to life, and she turned the dials until they matched what they knew would disrupt the Grey Veil field. A soft humming surrounded Lyle, and the older gentleman looked around his feet as if he expected the sand to melt.

"Do you feel anything?" Ida inquired.

Lyle bobbed his head. "No pain in my leg. Curious. Ah," he studied the plasma rifle's fading battery light. "Looks like the AVF drained the plasma ammunition." His bitter reply pulled his moustache into a dance. Ida flipped the switch.

"Sorry about that. I guess we need to fine-tune it or somehow shield the rifles against it ..." Ida looked towards the horizon where the setting sun painted the cloud-dotted sky in pinks and purples.

"A valiant effort, Miss Simonsen. Now, if you'll excuse me, I need to make sure nothing else has gone wrong."

Ida waved him off with a sheepish grin.

Gavin threw his hands in the air. "We don't have enough battery to last the night, anyway."

Ida hung her head. Gavin placed a hand on her shoulder, which she found comfort in, but then he gave her his best idiotic grin, which just made her laugh.

As promised, Aros received the first watch from Lyle and his backstabbing colleagues, who thought it would be pertinent for Aros to learn what guarding the camp perimeter alone meant. While everyone snoozed in their tents, Aros ambled around the beach, kicking shells along the sand and glancing towards the dark waters with only the faintest of light illuminating his surroundings. He traced his steps for each round and removed any stray prints he left behind. The captain's paranoia paid off, and he wasn't about to question fate should the same thing happen to him as with Jeffs. With the camp perched on the peninsula, Aros' sole duty was to guard the narrow path leading to the mainland and jungle.

After completing what seemed like his hundredth round, his eyes grew heavy. He leaned against the rifle, and jerked awake when he lost his balance. Scanning the camp, he spotted nothing unusual and no splashes of activity from the saltwater lake. He sat in the sand, facing where he'd spotted the creature, feeling his head droop but powerless to stop it. The sky above traced a white shroud of dense clusters of stars and dust. He recognised the constellations: the bear with a honeycomb in its hand surrounded by bees and the mermaid perched on a rock with long, flowing hair. They had proper names, sure, but Aros could never remember them. Was the person in the water he had seen earlier a mermaid? Or was he off the rocks in a free fall to cuckoo-land?

The gentle lapping of waves against the sand lulled him. His eyelids drooped and stung with each second of this god-forsaken night watch. He envisioned himself in a fluffy bed with fresh linen. The tidy room occupied the second floor, free from annoying neighbours. The tall, narrow window with the blue shutters was open, white curtains fluttering in the summer breeze. Aros turned on his side, coming eye to eye with a pair of blue eyes, freckled pale skin, and lips painted with a hint of mischief.

"Why do I never get to see you anywhere else?" he murmured, calm and content yet disappointed. The woman with the dark brown hair stroked his cheek and said nothing. He took her hand, felt the warmth, and let his mind wander. "Just like this here, everything will disappear. You, along with everyone around me, no matter where I go." The wind wafted the scent of brine through the window. The woman pressed him to her chest in a tight embrace. She never wore perfume, not even in his dreams. Her unblemished skin felt damp and cool.

Aros scrunched his eyebrows together and tried to shake his unease by touching her hair. His hand stroked over wet tangles of scraggly locks. When he tried to pull away, she hugged him tighter. Aros stiffened. His pulse quickened, and his chest tightened the more she squeezed him in a suffocating manner. The brine made him nauseous. His dreams with her were always in this room, miles away from the coast. Then why ... Aros opened his eyes, immediately assaulted by salty waters. Through the sting and blurry mess, Aros found a pair of deep black eyes. Soft facial features grinned at him, flashing rows of sharp teeth. He kicked out, creating distance between himself and the pale face. Held fast by solid and sinewy hands, Aros couldn't draw his breath as he was dragged deep underwater. Other mermaids swam past them, beating their spined tails and gliding towards the shallows with ease.

With the plasma rifle still in hand, its blue light waning as the water seeped into its components, Aros fumbled for the safety and prayed it still worked. The light indicator blinked, but instead of aiming at the creature, he aimed towards the surface and fired. A flash of light flew from the nozzle and shot through the waters. The mermaids recoiled and threw up their hands, blinded. Aros, lightheaded and feeling the cold creep through him, couldn't resist the mermaid's hold on him as she dragged him deeper into the abyss.

CHAPTER SIXTEEN
ANTONY DiCROCE

A ntony jerked awake in his tent by a sound flare whistling into the sky. The commotion equally startled Rosanne. She reached for her plasma pistol resting under her bundled-up blanket, used as a pillow.

"Who did that?" he asked, needing a moment to recognise the danger.

"I don't know, but we have company." She pulled on her breeches and threw his to him. They burst out of the tent, weapons loaded and ready. The camp was dark and bustling with urgent shouts as people exited their tents, sleepy-headed but alert. The remnants of the blue light from the sound flare fizzled out in the sky above them.

Ida emerged from her tent with her alchemical lamp, flooding the central camp with harsh white glare. "What's going on?" she called, her tone wavering.

Antony scanned the camp, Rosanne's back pressed to his, as they searched for the threat. Her finger twitched over to the trigger of the plasma gun, but she hadn't seen anything yet.

"Singing from the beach!" Creedy shouted, immediately followed by a flash of a blue bullet zipping through the air towards the waters. Antony didn't understand why that was significant at first, but Rosanne pointed her plasma pistol in the same direction and fired. The plasmic bullet lit up the path, shooting past nocturnal eyes and the glint of slimy skin on fishlike women with sharp teeth. Discordant melodies threw the crew off, like a flashing light that dug into their skulls. Antony couldn't raise his plasma pistol any more than he could fend off the musical cries bombarding his mind with images of a faraway reality and strange faces. He couldn't make sense of it. The surrounding people passed by in a blurry smear, likely as disoriented as he was.

Some stood still with vacant, smiling faces, staring out to the horizon and the waters where the welcoming hands of mermaids awaited them with their enticing voices.

Creedy shot bullets one after another, the watch captain a howling beast of ferocity. The siren's wounded screams cut through the songs of others, breaking the binding melody and bewitched men wading into the sea. While some who regained their senses returned fire, others continued towards their watery deaths.

Antony spotted Rosanne among them, with the sea up to her torso and her gaze as empty as a doll's. Antony fired at the mermaids, but his shaking hand and clouded judgment threw off his aim, and all he could do was sprint after the red-headed captain, who was oblivious to his calls.

Behind the mermaid, a wet glint reflected by the lamps illuminated dark colossal shapes with hooded figures perched atop crab-like bodies with spindly legs. Ghoulish grey skin peeked out from behind their tatters. With spears raised, they let out guttural snarls in communication with one another. They weren't riding the crabs; Antony saw with dread, for their humanoid bodies were fused with the shells. These hybrids marched through the waters as if it were the least of their concerns, and Antony, already struggling to regain his footing from the initial shock, couldn't reach Rosanne no matter how much he struggled against the waves.

A mass of hands shot up from the waters, grabbing his legs and arms. Clawed nails crept over his chest, making Antony cry out in disgust. The mermaids encircled him with their cold, slimy bodies, locking eyes between pale blue orbs and amber—hypnotising yet terrifying.

He struggled against their weight, forcing him below the surface. The three mermaids' expressions remained soft and beckoning, almost seductive, as they sang to him. His mind exploded with images of flowery spring meadows above the vineyard by his birth home. The song carried laughter and the fresh scent of lilac.

Cool grass tickled his bare feet, but Antony knew this was a lie. It had to be. The vineyard had burned over ten years ago; the little farm on the hill was reduced to ashes. Every day since they came to this island, it reminded him of it.

The mermaids' sudden polyphonic scream shattered the illusion of green meadows and the house on the hill. Antony came to himself, half-submerged and weighed down by mermaids.

"Get off him, you wretched freaks!" Watch Captain Creedy pummelled the butt of the handgun against one mermaid's head. She gave a surprised gasp and slid off Antony, fleeing in a trail of violent splashes. He shot at another and missed, and the mermaid slipped away. The third mermaid, seeing her sisters flee, released her hold and ducked beneath the waves. Antony heaved a breath for a confused second.

"On yer feet!" Creedy called, dragging Antony to the shore. He thrust a knife into the dazed captain's hands.

"Where's Rosanne?" Antony called. Creedy fired at one of the hybrids, stabbing at Norman, who danced around it, using himself as a distraction while a group of sailors approached from behind with sabres in their hands.

"She's gone!"

Mermaids fled, leaving ribbons of scarlet behind them in the water. Antony's heart clenched, and a surge of nausea overcame him. Creedy grabbed his shoulder, giving him a firm shake. "Snap out of it! We need to kill those bastards before they take anyone else!"

Creedy was right. Antony couldn't let his personal feelings get in the way. Yet his eyes lingered on the shore briefly, where Rosanne had disappeared. No, he had to fight back if they wanted to survive. He had to live so he could save Rosanne. She couldn't be gone so easily!

Half a dozen brown-shelled hybrids swarmed the camp, attacking with spears and needle-sharp legs covered in a tough exoskeleton and barnacles. They bore down on the crew, the men screaming their determination as they attacked with makeshift spears, ducking around the creature's jabs and stomps. Gavin came running with a rope; he tossed one end to Norman, and they ran for a hybrid. The rope caught its spindly limbs, and the young men gave a powerful yank. They pulled the legs out, and the massive body collapsed into the sand, the humanoid rider hissing in protest. Carlos and Denny climbed on top of the main body and drove daggers and swords into the humanoid torso. It let out a series of complex clacking sounds before succumbing to death.

The whole beach was a clamour of men and monsters embroiled in battle. Plasma bullets zipped through the air in flashes of blue. Pincer claws knocked torches into the sand in rapid succession. Antony struggled to see anything in the scant moonlight, which barely penetrated the thick clouds.

"Ida! Get your lamp over here! We need light!" Creedy called from somewhere in the camp. Light! He could do that. Antony spotted the dying embers of the still-hot torches. A hybrid turned its attention to him and stomped over, its pointy legs leading. Antony threw himself out of the way of the sharp as hells crab legs bearing down on him. He snatched the handle of the smouldering torch as the creature launched a spear, which pierced the sand by his feet. A group of men intercepted the hybrid's attention, leading it away with screams as gunfire pinged off its exoskeleton. Antony shoved the torches into the waning embers, but they didn't catch fire. He dug around the sand for the firesteel box among the knocked-over crates. Flashes from Ida's alchemical lamp danced erratically across the camp as the girl kept her distance from the heat of the battle. She stuck close to Gavin and Norman who mobilized others to gang up on one of the hybrids. Someone screamed in the distance, but he couldn't tell who it was. The hybrids swarmed them on all sides, cloaked in darkness and armed with terror.

The cacophony of beastly shrieks and mermaid songs cut through Antony like a knife. His hands shook as he dug through the sand, the song steering his thoughts to the image of Rosanne wading into the sea. Where was that accursed fire steel?!

The moonlit outline of a hybrid marched up from the beach, its hand raised and the black glint of its obsidian-tipped weapon pointed at Antony. His hand brushed against the metal box and wrenched it open just as the monster approached him, chittering sadistically. He struck the steel against the torches, and they roared to life. The spear jabbed for him, but Antony dodged aside and grabbed a torch, which he then hurled at the monster. The flame licked at the creature's wet robe, igniting the hybrid in a hellfire torrent. Its pained shriek resonated through the camp.

Antony fell on his back with a start, the flames hot and glaring. He only wanted to distract it long enough to pass the torches around, but he couldn't comprehend how the brine-soaked garb remained flammable.

"Light!" he called, grabbed the burning heap of torches, and passed them out to the sailors who called for them. The crew of the *Red Queen* spread out around the camp, fending off the monstrosities with invigorated fervour.

The flaming pile of crustaceans writhed in the sand, its fire diminishing. The creature drew wheezing breaths, drowned out by the surrounding fighting. Armed with the last torch and a sabre, Antony drove the weapon into the creature's humanoid chest, the metal sliding between its ribs until it went no further. The creature sputtered and grabbed his arm with water-wrinkled hands. Its strength waned not a moment later, falling limp. The sword rattled in Antony's hand, and he shook the discomfort off. His body was a tense coil, ready to release, but he couldn't tell if it was fear or excitement that drove him. A gut-wrenching sensation in his stomach made him keel over.

"Pull yourself together!" he ordered, forcing his wobbly feet that refused to obey him.

A pair of nocturnal eyes peered at him from the sea. He lifted his sword and torch, casting the yellow light across the mermaid's bluish skin. Her sneer displayed pointed teeth before she ducked under the surface. Antony drew a deep breath to regain his composure.

In a splash of commotion, the glinting scales of her tail lashed out in an arc, and with them, pointed projectiles whistled toward him. Sharp pain bloomed in his shoulder, and Antony fell back into the sand with a stunned cry. The thick spine from the mermaid's tail stuck through the top part of his shoulder while the other spines jutted in the sand beside him. The mermaid snarled and disappeared out to sea.

" What the hell happened?" Gavin exclaimed, taking Antony's good arm and helping him to his feet.

"It's not that bad," Antony lied through the pain, his face tight and flushed. "Shoot the mermaids if you see them. They can throw spines from their tails." He groaned with each step as the third engineer guided him further into the camp. Already, reflective discs peered at them from the waters, and Gavin fired off the plasma gun. The shot zipped into the water before them, and the mermaids scattered in violent thrashes.

"They're too scared to get any closer now." Gavin reloaded the gun swiftly.

Antony propped himself up into a sitting position and grabbed his bleeding shoulder, careful not to touch the spine. Pins and needles tingled through his fingers, and he had no strength to lift his arm. He ignored the pain, focusing on the situation at hand. "It doesn't seem that more of those crab monsters are coming. Keep the mermaids occupied and kill the crabs as swiftly as possible."

"Don't worry, cap. We know what we're doing." Gavin helped Antony to his feet and supported him as they went further into the camp. Antony observed the crew through a haze of swirling torchlight and murky shadows. A prickly feeling spread from his shoulder down to his elbow. Heat rose on his face, but Antony couldn't make sense of right from left. He swayed and fell back into the sand, gasping for air, his mind scrambling for clarity in the chaotic world around him. Voices became distant and muffled, and while he registered Gavin shouting at him, he couldn't make sense of it.

CHAPTER SEVENTEEN
DÉJÀ-NIGHTMARE

"Dragonheart!" Yerrik's urgent voice called to her.

Rosanne awoke with a scream. The bitter cold tore through her, causing violent trembles. Flinging her arms around herself, she desperately tried to resurrect heat into her shaking limbs. Her gaze darted around her, from the pooling seawater dripping off her clothes to the damp rocky walls, sending her chattering breaths back to her.

What in the name of Terra had happened? A giant hole seemed to have cleared the memories of where last night should have been. Nothing she could conjure in her mind explained how she ended up in a cave filled with prismatic glowing crystals. The trolls of the northern island weren't nearly as fancy.

She drew a shaky breath and assessed her surroundings further. She found herself in a cave thick with prismatic glowing crystals. Bluish light danced across the rocky ceiling, refracted through waves emerging from an underwater shaft filled with fluorescent corals. Though shivering, she stared slack-jawed and stunned into silence.

She struggled to her feet, her movements jerky. Sharp pains ran along her arms, and her torn shirtsleeves were pink with blood. Marked along the length of them ran red lines, as if a four-fingered creature had clawed her. The wounds appeared superficial but, like the cold, were another inconvenience souring her day. Besides the scratches and potential hypothermia, Rosanne couldn't find anything wrong.

A distant song permeated her mind, like a memory. She inhaled sharply and massaged the side of her head, staving the oncoming pain. "Mermaids," she muttered to herself, eyes gliding to the narrow pool leading into darkness. Blurry images flooded her mind, but all she could focus in her anger on was the ravings of a lunatic.

"That fucking useless piece of—" she began cursing out the former Captain Bernhart for allowing the camp to be overrun by monsters. This was the last time she would put her trust in that pirate, and it was already one time too many.

Her teeth chattered, throwing a clacking echo against the stony walls, bearing down on her in her isolation. Frost rime formed on her soaked shirt and pants, her fingers numb with cold. Where was everyone else? Would the creatures come back for her? Perhaps she just got lucky and woke up before that happened? Or was Yerrik's voice a sign that she was losing her mind?

With jerky movements, Rosanne made her way further into what she knew without a shadow of doubt was her worst nightmare.

A heavy clacking echoed along the stone walls, rhythmic and disconcerting. Rosanne's heart clenched in her chest, though she couldn't stop her cold trembling. She listened. The noise, drawing ever closer, emanated from a bend in a jagged hallway. Rosanne pressed herself to the ground behind a rocky outcrop by the far wall. She forced her breath through her mouth, forced her panic to take a fucking hike because this was neither the time nor the place!

A wide shadow with spindly legs wandered into the room, backlit by the crystals. The creature trotted at a steady pace towards the pool, paused, and then exhibited an erratic back-and-forth movement while letting out a frustrated guttural chitter.

Rosanne remained low but craned her head around and caught a glimpse of spidery, hard-shelled legs. The creature was massive, but the humanoid was smaller than her lieutenant. Could it bleed as well? They clacked with movements that appeared almost mechanical. A pair of broad-shelled arms plucked at the ground with hooked pincers as if searching. As she studied the creature, Rosanne realised there was more to it than she initially thought.

Perched on top of the flat oval arthropod body sat a human torso hidden beneath tatters of washed-out black cloth. Legs dangled in front of the large body where on a crab the eyes and mouth would usually be, the humanoid pelvis fused to the red-brown shell. A helmet of dead corals and shells adorned its head. The humanoid part craned its neck as it searched the room, and Rosanne spotted a thin slit for the eyes in the helmet. Reaching a pale arm around, it drew a bone spear from pulsating barnacles on its back, which hooked it in place. The obsidian tip glinted in the crystal light with serrated teeth. The sheer size of the creature made Rosanne tear up in fright, and she bit down on her lips to stop them from quivering. Sliding back out of view, Rosanne focused on her breathing, careful not to let even a single shaky breath betray her position. The creature let out a broken guttural cry, its exhalation steaming in the cool air, and stormed out of the chamber.

Rosanne remained trembling on the floor. Her eyes stung. Her chest hurt with each laborious breath, and her limbs were stiff with fright. Another minute passed, and even then, Rosanne's terror had barely calmed enough for her to move. Her shaking legs could barely support her when she finally mustered the courage to stand.

An ugly sense of déjà vu crept from the pit of her stomach; the horrors she lived through last spring came flooding back to her. She'd rather be in the company of trolls than this monstrosity.

Aros, you bastard. She let her displeasure for the man ground her instead.

Exiting the chamber, Rosanne found the path meandered down darkened hallways accompanied by the soft whistles of wind. Feeling the draught catch her frizzy and salt-laced hair, she followed the way toward what she could only hope was the exit.

An image flashed in her mind, darkness lit by a hail of plasmic bullets and a torrent of noise. A song cut through the cacophony of screaming men and zipping bullets, lulling her into a false sense of security. The details remained hazy, and a throbbing headache replaced the memory instead. Perhaps that was what Farand and the rest had described as a hulder attack. Then why the arthropod-sapiens? And Aros had spouted nonsense about mermaids ogling him from the waters. According to myth, mermaids could spellbind their victims in order to drown them. Perhaps they were in league with the crab-hybrids and had brought everyone here?

She paused, her heart sinking in her chest. It dawned on her that Aros had been right. Rosanne, in her bitterness, had trampled over him. She had no reason to trust him, but goddammit, she should have left more patrols to guard the camp!

This was her fault, and she damn well better pick up the pieces!

Rosanne decided she wasn't running away this time. These creatures were far more organised than trolls living in a hole preparing a feast. She couldn't count on everyone making it out themselves, and she didn't have time to muster a rescue party. She was on her own, but at least she was free for now.

The cave system was riddled with naturally formed passages and jagged outcrops, but there was no sign that anything lived there. No discarded crates, animal bones, livestock, or anything that might help Rosanne locate the others, just endless halls and glowing crystals she couldn't identify. The air was stale but curiously warm.

With a growling stomach and sleep deprivation setting in, misery overtook her. It was then she recalled Yerrik's voice calling to her in her dreams. Almost as a warning, he had awakened her again. Perhaps this was her punishment after her dalliance with the Forest Devil, and somehow, the Grey Veil connected her to him. She had been on edge since their arrival on this floating chunk of rock, but hearing his voice that first night shook her to the core. Perhaps this was his revenge. Or it could be the resulting hurt of having her heart broken because she was foolish enough to fall for the lies.

But he hadn't lied to her. Not even once.

Rosanne kicked the pebbles on the ground. They skidded ahead, leaving behind a *tak tak tak* echo that ended in a metallic clang among the grime. It was a plasma gun. Brushing it off, Rosanne looked it over in her hand. Water sloshed out of the nozzle, and the ammunition-light indicator was dead.

It was also then she noticed she had stopped shivering; the air was warm and welcoming. A red glow lit up the end of the hallway, and the low rumbling grew louder. Rosanne staggered when a wall of intense heat hit her, and her arms flew up to cover her face. A wide shaft cut through the relief before she saw between her fingers. Below nestled a pool of molten lava drifting on through a hidden river.

Breaking out in a sweat, Rosanne hurried to the side hall, continuing deeper into what she could only deem as the central mountain chain, hours from the shore. Tracing a hand over the scratches on her arm, Rosanne shuddered from the gap in her memory. Her hat was gone, but she wore most of her clothes, meaning something had alerted her in time to get dressed. Perhaps the camp fended off the danger, and Rosanne was the unlucky one, abducted to these halls surrounding a volcanic shaft.

Another few minutes passed before she caught the sound of unsettling clacking on the stone flooring. Edging around the bend, the careful captain craned her neck, staring into another room. A giant crab-like creature stomped past and let out short bursts of guttural shriek. Its shell was narrow and taller than the other Rosanne had seen, with longer limbs and less robust legs. Daddy Long Legs raised its spear towards something she couldn't see but lowered it after a moment of consideration. Was it a threat? When it turned its back to the entrance, Rosanne snuck closer, peering into the room.

A pile of plasma rifles, flintlocks, shoes, hats, sabres, and knives lay discarded next to the entrance. On both sides of the chamber, she spotted people were locked behind a wall of wooden bars, a crude form of prison with a simple opening secured by vines. The sentry was stomping about in the further reaches of the room, distracted by whatever homo-kaempferi found fascinating.

A pair of naked feet dangled in the front when it bent over and used its arms to study something it picked up from the ground, another rifle perhaps. Did they all have humanoid hosts perched on top of the shell like that, like a rider and its beast?

Half jogging, half sneaking, Rosanne made her way over to the pile of items, reaching for the one rifle with a blue indicator still active. The trapped crew jostled in their cage, some waving at her, others pointing at their captor. The crab began a slow turn, still riveted by a soaked flintlock. Kristoff shouted out, his voice cracking with nervosity as his actions drew the others into it to catch Long Leg's attention. The creature drew its head back in confusion and wandered over to the cage. The crew put on false smiles and began singing a shaky melody, resonating in the room and drowning out Rosanne's activities.

She would have laughed had she not been terrified. She fished out the plasma rifle by carefully rearranging the items over it like a sadistic game of Mikado. She took a knife for good measure. While the creature remained occupied, she tip-toed to the other cage and handed Carlos the knife. She snuck the rifle between the bars to Lyle while Carlos sawed at the hemp. The master gunner's eyes glinted with appreciation, and he scanned the weaponry, checking for damage. Rosanne returned to the stack and grabbed a sabre, her footfalls smothered by the ungodly singing across the room.

The creature kept its attention on the crew, who had now slung their arms over each other's shoulders and swayed to the drunken sea shanty.

"How many of them are there?" she whispered once she returned to the other cage.

Lyle leaned closer. "At least five, but we haven't seen the others in a while."

"Then we have to deal with this one quietly. Is everyone here?"

"Hard to say. We all woke up in the cages."

A panicked "Captain!" followed by a guttural shriek, made her spin around. A clawed pincer shot out for her. She sliced at the hard exoskeleton with a sabre, the metal averting the arm with a pathetic clang. Rosanne dodged to the side, narrowly missing the sharp-as-talons legs stomping after her. She stumbled from her clumsy leap.

Defence up! Her mind screamed, stretching out her shaking sword arm. Steady stance. She positioned her legs accordingly. The spindly monster lifted both pincer arms out to its sides and splayed its humanoid arms as if making itself big. Her jaw trembled so badly she bit her tongue, the pain bringing her a new focus that if she didn't stand tall, she would fall right here and now.

Long Legs reached for the black spear on its back.

"Get your asses moving!" Rosanne urged Carlos, who was slicing at the rope.

The creature snapped for her with curved pincers. The long arms were slow with their overarching movements but quick within striking distance. Rosanne ducked the first one and smacked the other away with the sabre. The hard shell against metal sent a shock through her arm, turning her wrist. The humanoid raised the spear and stabbed for her. Sidestepping, Rosanne let it come close as she took hold of the spear and stabbed forward with the sabre, slicing at the creature's torso.

"Shoot it, Lyle!" she hollered. A sizzling twang rang out in the cave. Rosanne flinched and dropped to the floor. Every sound tore through her skull like knives, and she squeezed her eyes shut, forcing breaths through gritted teeth. No! She couldn't break down now. Rosanne forced her attention to the monster swaying clumsily in front of her.

The masked humanoid dropped the spear and reached for its head as it went tumbling backwards. It tore off the sizzling coral mask and tossed it aside, letting out a wet and pained scream. With the white, shelled underside now exposed, Rosanne drove the sabre up to the handle between the cracks of the middle section of the exoskeleton. Screeching, the creature kicked out with its legs, its sharp pincers forcing her away from close combat. Rosanne released the sword, still stuck in its body.

Sprinting to the door, she tore at the hemp; it broke with ease after Carlos' sawing. The men poured out from the cell and dove for their gear. Carlos ran to the other cell and sawed at the vine that was locking the gate.

The creature flailed and turned, scrambling with howling determination. Its efforts were rendered moot by the sabre it couldn't reach, and two of its right legs fell limp beneath its weight. Struggling to keep balanced, it grasped the spear, aimed, and launched it into Carlos' shoulder. The man howled, and he dropped the knife. The spear jutted through the soft tissue of his shoulder, and he clutched the wooden bars to stay upright.

The men tore at the gate. The vine snapped under the barrage of movements, and the crew bore down on their equipment. One man tossed Rosanne another sabre. She leapt between the flailing legs and pinching claws, invigorated by the creature's vulnerability. With the circling mass of people, the beast turned and stabbed with reckless abandon, entangling its legs and collapsing. She stabbed the humanoid torso, driving the weapon through with frantic determination. The creature shrieked, reached for the sword, and brushed against her hand, enclosed around the sword hilt. Its hood fell back, and Rosanne gasped.

Where she had expected a normal face was instead a mass of gnarled barnacles and mutated scarred flesh. With gaunt grey cheeks and pale blue eyes, it stared at her with surprising intelligence and let out a high-pitched call, making her reel and cover her ears. The creature let out this call three times before its voice died in a broken gurgle.

Carlos' painful moans broke the quiet and frozen moment. Lyle en-circled an arm around him and propped him upright. Kristoff scanned the spear and assessed the damage, shaking his head. A shrill, singular cry echoed from somewhere inside the mountain.

"It called for backup," Rosanne said.

"We can't move him like this," Lyle argued, with Carlos slumped between him and Kristoff.

"Then break off the shaft! We barely held up against one; we're not prepared for more."

"Sorry, chap," Lyle excused and pulled off his leather belt, which he shoved into Carlos' mouth. His brown eyes widened in panic, and he feebly shook his head. "Hold him," the master gunner ordered, and two people ran to secure Carlos' squirming form. Blood squirted over the obsidian spearhead. Carlos' muffled screams drowned out the guttural chittering that was growing closer. Rosanne ground her teeth, trying to block out the noise as Lyle quickly removed the tip and slid the bloodied bone shaft free of the shoulder.

"We need to move! Follow the draft after the lava pit!" Rosanne ushered the men into the opposite hallway. Lyle and Kristoff held the half-conscious Carlos between them and raced after the others. Three hybrids stormed into the chamber just as Rosanne saw the last man out. Seeing their captives fleeing, they drew their spears and set after her.

Rosanne sped down the hallways, their angry howls echoing after her.

The walls stretched and squashed in front of her, closing in with the disharmony of clacking feet. She approached the lava shaft, slowed to avoid falling into the pit, and rounded towards the various hallways leading out of the room. A spear whistled past her ear, forcing her to the left, where the clatter of another spear glanced off her feet. She stumbled and crashed against the floor with a cry. Two creatures scuttled past into the tunnel through which the crew had escaped through. Rosanne groaned as she stood, ignoring aches and her scabbed knees, and headed in the other direction. The third creature set after her.

Her chest hurt so badly she wanted to hurl. The stifling air turned cold in the next bend. Her lungs burned. She heard them behind her but slowed before a fork in the tunnel. The draft caught her hair, and she followed it and ran until her legs turned wobbly. She didn't dare call out to anyone.

Another nightmare island, all because she wanted to understand why her father was here. Maybe the monsters had driven him off. Perhaps it was the nightmares and the dark pond where one's reflection didn't seem right. But this was all on her. She promised no riches, no glory, only adventure. And her crew, gold-eyed and high off their last success, dove headfirst into danger with her. Her reassurances had been a lie, a farce. She saw that now.

What a fucking idiot she was.

As she stumbled on through the hallways, light struck her like knives through her eyes. Rosanne shielded her face against the brilliant blue sky. It must be around noon. The forest was thick and imposing, but with the hybrids chasing her, she couldn't turn back. She bolted into the jungle, heading north.

Clouds rolled over the sky and soon showered Rosanne in the freezing rain. The jungle fell silent as the sun drowned in grey. The loud patter of water droplets against broad-leafed plants obscured even her own foot-falls, making Rosanne a shivering, hyper-vigilant mess on the lookout for a phantom hunting her. Seeing her father standing in the forest shook her in a way she hadn't thought possible. Why here, of all places? Was it a ghost? Or was it a creature able to change her perception to entrap her?

And then her thoughts slithered over to annoyance.

Why was she always running? Why couldn't she come in with guns blazing and swords reaping and emerge victorious for once? Had her quiet days smuggling across the Veil caught up with her as her age had, and she was no longer in any condition to sustain this lifestyle? Rosanne laughed at the irony. She should have used the money more wisely, but no. She wanted to fix her ship, not her life or her career. Now she could only hope Antony was at the beach waiting for her and was not trapped inside the mountain with no way out.

CHAPTER EIGHTEEN

KNIFE IN THE SAILS

The camp was sombre when Antony awoke a few hours later. Men sat around the fire, huddled under oilcloths or blankets, each clutching their choice of weapon. Their dark-ringed gazes shifted to him as he stirred.

"What happened?" he groaned in pain. Then he noticed his bandaged shoulder. "Well, that could have been worse. Damn, that hurts."

Creedy placed a gentle hand on him when Antony tried to sit. "The spines are poisonous, but you seem to have pulled through. You were out for a while."

Antony flexed his fingers; the tingling remained. "Did we drive them off?"

Creedy's slow nod and bloodshot eyes somehow didn't raise his hopes. "We killed six, but one hid in the shallows—a scout, I guess. It disappeared by the time we killed the last bastard. The sirens soon followed."

Antony's mind scrambled. What would Ros do in this situation? What would *he* do? He blanked, feeling the panic rise in his throat. He was a guest on the *Red Queen* and held no proper authority, but Rosanne had trusted him to take charge should the situation require it. What could he do? Creedy looked at him, the older man's face heavy with exhaustion. "What are our defences right now?" Antony asked.

"Fucked, that's what. We're missing nine people, including the captain, half the gun team, and Lyle himself." Creedy dug his head into his hands, rubbing the thinning hair; he let out a frustrated groan.

Antony struggled to his feet, shaky and lightheaded, but his momentary fear and drive kept him up. "We need to secure the camp or at least build a defence perimeter in case those beasts return," he said.

"What do you suggest, sir?" Creedy's attention wandered over the shambles of what was once the campsite. Not much remained of it, and even fewer men turned their attention to Antony, their worry now hopeful that he would take the reins. It was a look he recognised from after his men faced their first deadly encounter with pirates over Noval. The feeling was the same no matter where they went or what they experienced. The underlying fear of failure remained.

"We need axes and rope. We can rig traps along the forest edge. If the monsters return, we can fake a retreat and lure them into the traps," Antony declared.

Creedy mentally ran through his words before giving a nod. "You heard the man! Daylight's hours away, and we need to be prepared! No rest until we set those traps!" The people around them sighed but rose to their feet.

"If you're up for coordinating this, I'd be happy for your expertise," Creedy turned to Antony, his done-with-this-nonsense expression somehow easing Antony's concern about the ship's hierarchy. He'd gained at least enough respect from the volatile watch captain to do what was necessary for survival.

They spent the rest of the night chopping logs, drawing rope between trees, digging pits, and covering them alongside the forest edge. Only when dawn graced them with light did they finish and return to the broken remains of their camp. The weather was cloudy but holding, and they took shifts sleeping. Antony hadn't felt this worn and exhausted since his cadet days, but his growing worry for Rosanne kept him from sleeping. He would be here waiting should she return. He had to.

Squatting under a broad-leafed bush, Aros hugged the plasma rifle tight and shivered. Rain poured down from low-hanging clouds, unbroken by animal sounds or songbirds to disrupt the gloom. Soaked from his plunge into the ocean, Aros studied the dried brine-covered creases of his vest, watching the salt crumble from the fabric. The faint light breaking through the thick cloud formation told him he was south of the mountain range.

He was on the wrong side.

"I'm so fucked." He hugged his rifle even more tightly, whimpering pathetically. The battery had run out with his last warning shot, which he hoped had alerted the camp to danger. A score of mermaids had swum past him and his captor towards camp. In his panicking spasm as he fought for freedom, he spotted the cloaked, crab-like nightmares on the seafloor, armed with spears and determination like ghostly riders of a crustacean army.

Afraid to catch their attention, Aros clung to the mermaid as she whisked him away to his doom.

The waters darkened the deeper they went, and the sting of salt blurred his vision. His lungs screamed for air, and by the time he could draw his breath again, he was deposited in a cave. The mermaid hung from the pool's edge and winked at him. Though she had no words, she let out a distorted squawk. The vision Aros had of beautiful mythological women didn't align with her thinning brown hair, the severe lack of a nasal bridge, and her inky black eyes, which appeared as dark pools. Her ears were pointy, with fin-like formations resembling those of the Yellow Sea Dragonfish, and the scales covering her body stretched to mid-torso, stopping below her almost non-existent breasts. With each breath, slits appeared on her torso along the ribcage, presumably facilitating how she breathed underwater; it gave Aros the heebie-jeebies.

She beckoned to him, grinning with her sharp teeth. Aros did what any reasonable man would do: he ran. He didn't care where the tunnels led as long as it was away from the dodgy mermaid. Her disappointed cries reverberated within the walls, replaced by shrieks from what he presumed were crabby monsters in the hallways. Aros clapped his hands over his ears, weaving through the myriad passages and turning if the shouts drew too close until he reached the exit.

And now he was here, soaked, miserable, and alone. He scanned the forest for anything that might attack. The southern camp was at least three hours away by longboat. On this side of the mountain lay the northern camp, past thick jungle and alluring calls. Pounded by the incessant rain and trapped in a monster-infested forest, Aros fought against the hopelessness that begged him to sit down and feel sorry for himself. But no! He was a strong man who had already survived the Inquisition, albeit squealing like a pig at slaughter. He could do this! He would prove that red-headed demon wrong that he did, in fact, have a sense of loyalty, under contract or not. Besides, this island was not the place to set up shop. There were far too many monsters here, and the women were too fishy.

They say humour is the first trait to disappear when a person is faced with mortal danger. In Aros, it fueled his resolve and made life that much easier to deal with. Throwing inappropriate jokes when people expected grim realisation was his lifeblood, and he wasn't about to let some crabby, crawly monsters get the best of him.

Scanning the mountain, Aros plotted the best possible route to get to the other side. A relief between two adjacent peaks gave him a way through, but he wasn't sure if he could make it, even with proper shoes.

He would have gone back to the main camp for the simple reason that he didn't believe Rosanne would bother looking for him, but if she did and returned to find him safe and sound by the ship, she would tan him for various reasons.

The even pathway snaked between the mountain crevice as if someone had laid it out before him. Aros would rather have it obscured or, even better, unused because, in his experience, animals didn't pave trails like these, and the ones that did use it often, meaning monsters could traverse them. While he thought the path cut through the relief, further up, it snaked up the mountainside towards a flat-cut top. Perhaps it continued to the other side? Aros drew a laboured breath and hunched down on his knees. This far up in the atmosphere, the air was so thin and moist that he thought he was inhaling water. He supported himself with the rifle as a crutch and picked his way over the wobbly rocks. He always kept it close in case something attacked him. The weapon was sturdy and could crack skulls if needed.

The weather turned from a soft patter to a sloshing waterfall, coursing down the mountainside and forming muddy rivers. "Gimme a fucking break," he groaned when lightning struck the nearby mountaintop. The path split between the two peaks, and neither appeared to lead across to the other side. At the cusp of the hill squeezed between the mountains, the road turned into rockslides.

"Yeah, no." Aros shuddered and trekked up the side instead.

Another hour passed before Aros dragged his heavy body through the cloud layer and reached a plateau filled with green grasses and low-growing bushes. He collapsed on the soft ground, untouched by rain. A tickle in his throat prompted a sudden, violent sneeze. It echoed around him and down the valley, throwing the noise back at him mockingly. Aros listened for a petrified second, certain the entire island had heard him, and sent out an army marching for his capture. Only the whistles of the wind and the crackle of tumbling pebbles filled the air.

He spotted the path continuing over the lip on the other side of the plateau. A tired smile crossed his lips. At least he was getting somewhere. But then a bitter wind swept through the plateau and sent Aros' tunic billowing, making the man throw his arms around himself, teeth chattering.

It was fine. He decided he had rested enough and stood to leave.

"Aros," a voice whispered behind him. He screwed up his face in regretful terror, knowing he wouldn't like what he would see once he turned around. What unimaginable horror could it be this time? Harpies? Crabs? The ghost of his mother? But when he finally faced the whisperer, what awaited him was not a person but a squat cave opening. A short distance away, grey smoke puffed in clouds from a small crack in the mountain. That explained the phenomenon they thought was a monster activity: a stray volcanic chute. Aros relaxed his shoulders, feeling silly; he had let his paranoia claim his common sense. The wind whistled through the cave's darkened halls, and what sounded like voices beckoned him to it. It was faint but unmistakable, like the voice of Captain Drackenheart cursing him from across the Veil.

Nope.

Aros turned on his heels, and left. Further down the path, he spotted movement. The obscured form of a person trotted down the rocky slabs with twitchy movements and head-jerking turns. Aros rubbed his face, thinking he might be suffering from altitude sickness. It was hard to see in the thickening fog, but the person wore washed-out clothing and no headwear, their tangled long hair pulled in a low ponytail. No one from the *Red Queen* looked like that, Aros noted. If anything, they seemed disturbed. Considering he'd just escaped a lascivious mermaid and nature's circus exhibition, the scene would disturb anyone.

Aros dodged behind boulders and outcrops as he followed the person down the mountain towards the jungle. When they disappeared between the trees, Aros jogged to catch up. His foot caught in a crevice between the rocks, and he stumbled in a spectacular heap of flailing limbs as he rolled downhill, uttering muffled cries with each sharp edge digging into his side or scraping his hands.

When he reached the bottom, he spent a painful moment regaining his footing and had to check if his teeth were still in his mouth. He couldn't afford gold teeth, not with his pension or lack thereof. His pearly yellows were all still there, but his hands were scraped raw, oozing, and burning. At least he was at the bottom of the path, he told himself bitterly. Brushing off mud and gravel, Aros waddled after the person, his limbs stiff from the beating.

Rain poured the moment trees stretched over him at the lip of the jungle, like a cruel joke, as if he wasn't miserable enough before. Aros sneezed into his jacket, only letting a strained puff of air escape, which popped his ears. Despite the rain, animals bolted over the treetops. Birds in full screaming matches with each other strutted with umbrella-like head feathers. Aros paused at the crossing of a black centipede with orange mouth hooks and more legs than he had ever seen. He twitched into a dramatic shudder.

Fuck this island.

Aros spotted his target ahead. Up close, it appeared to be a middle-aged man, haggard, with dark, shifty eyes. His hands reached into the air around him as if grasping for something invisible. Aros kept low and out of sight, hoping he would encounter no more centipedes that would make him scream in terror.

"Yes, yes. I understand," the man said suddenly, turning his head to the side. "Oh, they're coming, are they? Better not be here, then. I don't want to become a tree. No, no." Shaking his head, he wagged a finger at an invisible entity.

Aros craned his neck, sticking out his ear to pick up what the rain obscured. He had no clue who or what the crazy old man was referring to or even why he was talking to himself. Judging by the washed-out and frayed clothes, the man had been here for years. Were there more people? Or was he talking to himself because of long-term isolation? A proper hermit, then.

Aros left his hiding spot and approached the man slowly from his periphery.

"Good afternoon," Aros greeted softly, his hands raised in a pacifying manner. The hermit let out a cry of terror and collapsed in a heap of his limbs, trembling on the ground.

"No man can be here! No, no, no, no!" he whimpered.

Aros winced. "Sorry, I didn't mean to scare you. Are you here alone?"

"Alone, alone, never alone!" The man said, cowering in the mud.

"You must have been here a while." Aros backed up as if giving the man more physical space would provide comfort.

He peered up at Aros with a gaunt look, flashing browned teeth. "Long time and time again. No people can be here. People are bad."

Aros didn't let the hermit's words deter him. "We're looking for something that's on this island. Maybe you know what it is? You can join us when we leave. Get off this island and away from all the monsters?" he tried, but the man shook his head, panicked at the thought.

"Monsters? No monsters live here. Man is bad."

Aros' eyebrows scrunched together. "Hey, it's okay. You're more than welcome to—"

"Never can leave! Must keep people away!" His shouts withered to mutters, urging Aros to step further back. The older man cackled and pounded his fist into the dirt, creating violent spatters of rainwater.

"Get out, get out! Out of my head, stupid man!"

"That's not very nice," Aros said, his patience spent, increasing his confusion. He left the man raving about his own business, feeling disturbed. Aros wondered if he should have tried harder to talk some sense into the hermit, but the truth was he didn't want to. Something was off, and he heeded his gut, feeling more than his fleeting compassion for a deranged human being. The thought made his fingers prickle, and he hurriedly massaged the discomfort away.

The man's cackles penetrated the jungle in waves of glee. He cried and raved into the high heavens until Aros was too far away to hear him. The hermit wouldn't be the first to fall victim to the Veil's antics. Aros increased his pace.

After another hour of heading north, Aros decided this had been the worst idea he'd ever had besides attacking a flying galleon fresh out of the Grey Veil.

Ever since Aros entered the jungle, he'd had an eerie sense of being watched, but whenever he searched his surroundings, he saw only the rain and birds sporting ridiculous feathers. They huddled together on a low branch, their feathers as black as night, holding their wings above their heads to create miniature umbrellas that Aros admitted looked adorable. The birds craned their necks at his approach and, with orange beaks, let out a low hissing noise that sounded like they were saying "Who" over and over, presumably to warn him not to get any closer. He let them be and wished he had wings he could use as an umbrella. He scratched his dreadful buzz cut, the hair finally regaining thickness after losing most of it because of stress.

God, he hated the rain. At least he didn't hear the captain's voice cursing him out of some creepy cave on top of the mountain. If whatever was hunting him wanted him to go in there, that was the wrong tactic.

"Aros!" an unfamiliar voice called. Rooted on the spot, Aros searched the trees. By a clearing, a dark brown-haired woman stood wearing a blue dress and a saccharine smile. Her eyes crinkled, and she let out a delightful laugh that hit him like waves of music.

"Where have you been?" she breathed and came running up to him with arms outstretched, embracing him. She drew him into a deep kiss.

Aros' thoughts blanked. He forgot all about his worries being lost in the wilderness, crawling with madmen and monsters, mermaids in heat and strange whispers. All he could focus on was the kiss, the warm and welcoming intimacy as if greeted by a lover. He drew her in and stroked her cheek with his hand. She seemed so familiar, but he couldn't remember from where. Her euphoric scent enticed him despite being soaked and stained with mud just as he was. She broke away from him with a deep sigh.

"What happened? How are you here?" she breathed.

Aros' mind was reduced to a puddle. "I—"

She suddenly turned her head to the side in alarm and, planting her hands on his chest, shoved him violently. He crashed flat against the ground, all the air knocked out of him. He thought he heard, "We'll meet up later," but he couldn't be sure, as the muddled voice sounded like two people speaking at the same time over the cacophony of activity. Aros lay sprawled on his back, feeling the waters seep deeper into his clothes, and the rain hit his face like a storm of disgruntled tears vying for revenge. He heard a deep chittering call in the distance, but Aros's addled mind couldn't process anything beyond that amazing kiss. Branches, vines, and bushes were torn aside by a barrage of movements ploughing through the jungle, leading away from him, but Aros saw nothing.

What in the ever-loving Terra happened?

Blinking, he ran his hand over his lips and studied his fingers. No lipstick marks remained, even when he could have sworn she wore some. And then there were those familiar voices he couldn't place, one so beautiful and calming he temporarily forgot about his miserable state of being, the other crude and cursing as if it wanted him buried alive.

Shaking off the excess mud and water, Aros trotted towards the beach, feeling like he was losing his mind.

CHAPTER NINETEEN
LEAVE US ALONE

A muted palette painted the jungle in depressing colours by the time Rosanne paused long enough to let out an unbridled, frustrated scream. Daylight was waning, and she was no closer to the beach camp. She kicked the nearest root of a banyan tree sticking out of the ground for no other reason than to expel her rage. How much more of this cursed forest was she going to suffer? She seethed in her misery, soaked from the rain and exhausted beyond belief. At least she had escaped the hybrids and released the captive crew. She hoped they made it back to camp, but Rosanne could only assume they were ahead of her, as she had little clue where she was.

She spotted the jagged mountain tops to her south and the central fuming plateau top to her south-east. What if the monsters spied her from up there? They were all doomed if tunnels cut through the entire mountain chain. Monsters could come at them from anywhere, and the crew could never fortify the camp at each new location. But for now, they had fought them off and won somewhat.

Her five-minute nervous breakdown wasn't doing her any good, and her surroundings weren't doing her mental state any favours. She needed to move.

The presence in the forest bore down on her as if every leaf and flower, singing bird, or howling monkey connected like a single giant entity. The Banyan tree, whose roots had offended her, stretched to the sky like a giant grey-cloaked creature with hundreds of tendrils snaking over the ground in search of prey. When Rosanne let her rage drizzle into acceptance that this was her life now, the whispers that followed her became clearer. Dozens of tiny voices chatted amongst themselves, some reaching out to her, but Rosanne couldn't pick out anything distinct.

"Oh, shut up!" she roared. Birds fled in a flurry of protests, and the jungle momentarily fell silent.

This is madness, she decided. Wet, cold, and stressed beyond belief, it was a miracle she hadn't fallen sick yet. Judging by the distance between her and the mountains, she estimated she had at least a few hours of trekking to the coastline. Her armed and drilled crew had left en masse. They would be fine. She was more worried about her safety, physical and otherwise.

Her breath froze in her throat as she turned and spotted a pale face staring emptily at her. It was him, the imposter who looked like her father!

Rain dripped from the brown, faded hat with the pristine blue feather. Rosanne reached for her own headwear, but the hat was back at camp somewhere, at least she hoped. The feather was already broken when the RDA gave it to her mother. Seeing it whole was like reliving a distant memory, but Rosanne couldn't recall ever seeing her father wear those clothes. He felt familiar, yet different. Most of all, he was dead.

"Who are you?" she demanded, her insides boiling. The man wearing her father's face didn't move, didn't reply, and didn't blink. He remained caught in a perpetual stare that unnerved her. The whispers grew around her, chittering and excited. Taunting.

"Whoever you are, leave me alone. I'm tired of your nonsense." Her firm voice trailed off as the man, or the mimic, didn't avert his attention.

They remained rooted to their places, Rosanne bearing her pensive stare down on him while he, as he did after the first time she spotted him, regarding her in an unblinking but curious fashion. The weathered lines on his face were those of her father, from the soft greys spattering his groomed beard to the sun-kissed crow's feet at the outer corner of his eyes. But her father had never borne such a cold expression, as if a monster had stolen his skin and worn it to confuse her.

The rain poured down even harder now, transforming the wet undergrowth into a mudscape. Her feet sank into the ground, distracting her from her father's mimic as she struggled to break free. From between the trees in her periphery, Rosanne caught movement. Sun-tanned hands and arms pushed leaves and bushes aside, revealing half a dozen blank-faced individuals wearing soaked tricorn hats and caps. All locked eyes with her as they came to stand right next to senior Captain Drackenheart like a motley crew in their various fashion statements. A young woman wearing a frilly turn-of-the-century dress covered with gaudy fabric roses regarded Rosanne with stiff lips. Smeared makeup ran down her pale cheeks, and her once elaborate hairstyle hung in sodden ribbons over bare shoulders.

Wrenching free of the mud, Rosanne turned to leave and slammed into a person whose hands grasped her by her wrists in a monstrous hold.

"Come with me, my little Dragonheart," he said, but his smile didn't reach his piercing eyes. She recoiled with a panicked cry, but she had no strength to match him. His face, contorted to that of confusion before transforming into anger at her defiance. He let out a hollow cry, deep and unearthly, like a ghost.

Freeing one hand, Rosanne reached for the dagger at her belt.

"If you don't come, you will become one with the jungle! Please, my daughter!" her father howled, but Rosanne's resolve did not falter.

"You're not my father!" She drove the dagger into his ribcage, silencing his outcry. The mimic hunched over, holding a hand to his wound, seeping with black blood. Rosanne stumbled back, staring into his shocked expression. His skin drooped strangely as if his body had turned to liquid. His clothes melted into each other, into his hair and skin, turning inky black that dripped onto the ground and disappeared in the mud with a splash.

"What the fuck?" Rosanne stared at the shoe prints, all traces of her attacker having sunk into the earth. She whirled around, expecting another fight, but the spectators had simply vanished.

Thick red liquid bubbled to the surface from the mud around her feet. Only then did she notice the trees surrounding her. The thick, dark, knotted acacia trunks bled scarlet sap like the trees around the area where she first encountered the mimic. Behind her stood a pond with a black surface, untouched by the rain.

The whispers intruded from every direction, almost as if invading her mind. Covering her ears, Rosanne fled.

Her sprint through the forest was a head-turning affair as she clutched the dagger in one hand, scanning the trees for activity. Only when she was sure no one was following did she slow down. Letting out a frustrated growl, she rubbed her arms to bring heat to her frozen limbs. How was the rain so cold in this hot-as-hell jungle?! Who were those people with her father's mimic, and how had they come here? What transport did they use?

Were they similar to Yerrik? Bitterness crept over her lips at the thought of that name, as it had done so often lately.

While the Forest Devil had appeared human, eloquent, kind, and even loving, she knew his nature depended on how people perceived him. This mimic had told her to leave, yet Jeffs had been spirited away, and Antony had been lured to the pond. Perhaps it was all connected. Perhaps she was losing her mind altogether.

Rosanne stared at the water droplets as they vigorously excavated the ground and formed small rivers running towards the coastline. Diverting her attention to the mountaintops, her train of thought gave her a pause. Was there something here the creature didn't want her to find? If the dream-invader wanted her dead in one place but gone from another, it signified secrets, and Rosanne loved secrets. The map was still the key to this place, and her pushing into the jungle had angered the mimics. Resolve overtook her despair. For the first time since they'd set sail, her fear had abated somewhat.

She saw the top of a hat moving through the vegetation. Ducking low, Rosanne peered through the leaves. An olive-skinned man with black hair, armed with a plasma rifle, wandered the space.

Antony!

She paused, struggling to believe he was there. Was this another one of the island's tricks? Another mimic?

"Antony!" she called for him in an attempt to assess the situation. When he turned to her, the biggest smile of relief spread across his face, and all of her worries melted away. They met in a deep kiss. Rosanne pressed herself into his embrace, unable to leave any space between them. Antony's hands tightened around her, hungrily leaning in.

His scent overwhelmed her, cradling her in a blanket of comfort and safety. She hadn't been this happy to see him since he had rescued the *Red Queen* outside the Veil, which now seemed like a lifetime ago.

Rosanne broke away from him, her breath erratic. Her knees wobbled, but she caught herself clutching to his shoulders. "What happened? How are you here?" she asked breathlessly.

"I—"

A wet shriek interrupted him. Stomping feet rushed through the forest like a raging bull. Rosanne spotted a hybrid rushing for them, its spear raised and ready to strike. She pushed Antony to the side.

"Split up! We'll meet back at the beach!" she called and ran in the opposite direction, leaving a trail of taunting hollers in her wake to draw the monster's attention. Antony was out of sight in seconds.

The creature charged after Rosanne with all its might and fury, but the captain, being smaller and more limber, navigated the jungle floor far more quickly than the broad-shelled body of the monster. Its spindly legs caught on roots and were thrown off balance at every step. Rosanne slowed her pace upon seeing it fall behind, her chest burning from the strain.

The thinning tree line told her she was closing in on the beach. The camp could be nearby! She upholstered the plasma pistol and set the charge to fire a single high-velocity bullet. Aiming upwards, she fired, and a shrill plasmic sizzle screamed through the sky. If anyone were within earshot, they would know she was coming with unbidden company.

Rosanne saw an opening in the trees, the dark waters of the shore welcoming her. She spotted familiar faces of her crew sprinting in tandem just past the treeline, pointing east and hollering something she didn't catch over the noise of the rain and the blood rushing through her ears. She changed her direction anyway and continued east. The creature followed, crashing into a smaller tree that snapped in half from impact. Its pointed limbs pierced anything in its path.

In her periphery, Rosanne spotted the shadows of people running alongside her from the beach, but then they shouted and beckoned her toward them.

"There had better be a point to this nonsense," she grumbled through exhausted breaths. Her legs ached, her mind a swirling mess of exhaustion, but she kept at it. She emerged on the beach at full speed. Norman caught her before she ran straight into the lake, and she collapsed from exhaustion. He lowered her gently onto the sand.

"Cut it!" she heard Creedy call from the forest's mouth, and Vincent hacked at a rope she hadn't noticed before with an axe, producing a satisfying snap. The hybrid creature threw itself at them with a piercing shriek. A spiked log swung from the treetops into an arch and smashed into the monster. The momentum drove the protruding sharpened branches into its main body and torso, and the log, supported by the ropes, snapped under the weight of the monstruous creature and crashed to the ground. The hybrid, tangled around the log, gurgled weakly and fell quiet.

Creedy kicked one of its legs and raised a thumb to the others. People erupted in cheers.

"Was that the only one?" Creedy called to Rosanne. She nodded, exhausted, to the point of remaining on the wet sand to catch her breath.

"Has anyone seen Antony?" she asked after a few painful moments of recovery. Men pointed down the beach, where other people jogged towards them. Spearheading the group was Antony, a smile as bright as the sun.

"Oh, thank the heavens. You're back!" he exclaimed, embracing her in a hug.

"You weren't followed by those things, were you?" Rosanne asked and then noticed his sling. Had he hurt himself after their separation? Antony's expression turned to confusion for a moment, but he shook his head.

"I'm alright. You were the only one missing. The others returned half a day ago."

"Damn. I must have taken a detour then." She laughed, confused for a moment but relieved to be back among the crew. "What happened?" She pointed to his wounded arm.

"A gift from our swimming friends. I need to exert as little strain as possible to let it heal. I prefer keeping two arms than just the one," he said, giving his arm the barest of flexes, the move evident in a painful hiss.

Rosanne nodded, but the sling didn't make sense. He had been fine when she saw him ten minutes earlier. She shook off the uncertainty. "I'm going to change into something dry, and you can update me on what the fuck happened last night. I'm far too cold and hungry."

"As you wish, dear."

Overturned crates and ripped tents met Rosanne when they returned to camp. Whatever was salvageable had been sorted or used as fuel. The battle had reduced their supplies to scraps, pilfered by much smaller, friendlier crabs and annoying birds. Rosanne peered through the tear in her tent and frowned but was otherwise glad it was still standing. She didn't have the energy for any major repairs, let alone a "there-I-fixed-it moment."

"Good thing I brought my sewing kit."

"You have one of those?" Antony asked, his surprise evident.

"Only for tents." She grinned and went inside. Rosanne changed into the clothes that had survived last night's brutal wake-up call. The cold seeped through her bones, and she let out a loud sneeze. Antony wrapped a blanket around her using his functional arm.

"Get Creedy and anyone else who can give proper accounts of last night."

Nodding, Antony left the tent, and a few minutes later, he returned with Creedy and Lyle. They sat down on the carpet after a brief greeting. Creedy handed her a cup of steaming coffee, which she accepted with shaky hands.

Shivering, Rosanne sipped the beverage, her teeth chattering miserably. The sensation grew worse by the minute now that she wasn't running for her life. "A-accounts of l-last night. Anyone?"

Creedy took point. "I think it was around two in the morning when someone shot a sound flare."

"Was Kavanaugh still on duty?" she inquired.

Creedy nodded. "He was gone when we came out. Instead, we saw these monsters in the ocean. They almost looked like the hulder we met before: flat-faced, ugly as sin, and scaly. They sang, too. Next thing we know, these giant crab-men came marching out of the ocean and attacked us. The mermaid song took a few, making them walk into the ocean. Crabsters grabbed others."

"Crabsters?" Lyle arched an eyebrow.

"Crab-men bastards," Creedy answered.

"I believe Gavin called them criders, like crab-riders? Though I prefer hybrids," Lyle continued.

"Anyway!" Creedy interrupted. "We were overrun by the bastard Crider-hybrids. People got snatched, and by some miracle, we fended off the rest. We didn't move from camp after they left, and we sure as hell didn't sleep."

"Sensible reaction," Rosanne agreed. "It's to my understanding that everyone who was under the mermaid song forgot what happened to them."

Antony followed up. "You were right next to me one moment and then gone. I saw you get dragged away by mermaids, along with a few others, without even fighting. We feared the worst."

Rosanne rubbed her face. So that's what happened. "Good thing they didn't kill us. They wanted us for something, but I doubt it was anything similar to the hulder, as you described, Creedy. When we escaped, the monsters tried to slaughter us all. Capture wasn't an option anymore. The bastard almost decapitated me. How many did you kill here?"

Though bobbing his head, Creedy didn't appear optimistic. "We got five, but they were tough as nails. We needed a full team to distract one while others attacked. Extra-captain-in-charge DiCroce here used military tactics to turn the tide."

Antony straightened at the mention of his name. "We rigged traps along the beach in case they attacked again. A safe point of retreat should they attack again by sea, and a nasty surprise should they attack from the jungle."

"Excellent strategy," Rosanne congratulated Antony, who only nodded. "Why bring us into the mountain, though? There must have been an underwater cave system if the mermaids dropped us off there."

"I'm not sure what unsettles me more: the hybrids, the mermaids, or that they worked together to attack the camp."

Rosanne chewed on Antony's words. Two water-based monstrosities and one land-based coming with the rain. The hybrids went out of their way to capture them alive, while the dream invader wanted them gone from this place but lured people in the south. It didn't add up.

Rosanne shook the confusing thoughts aside and focused on the positives. She looked at Antony, who fidgeted with his hands. "Is there more?" she asked him, and he snapped to attention.

Creedy and Lyle looked to Antony.

"It felt like a nightmare," he said low, but raised his head. "The mermaid's song was beautiful, enthralling, yet gentle—much like a cherished memory. However, when I concentrated on the melody, it was as though I could perceive the calling and the warning chimes interwoven between the notes."

"How did you anchor yourself?" Rosanne inquired.

Antony half-shrugged. "Can't claim that I did. The song drew me in, but the visions had inconsistencies that clashed with my memories." He glanced at the watch captain. "Mr. Creedy looked happy, pardon my frankness."

"Oy!" retorted the watch captain.

"Creedy was my saviour." Antony quickly followed up. "I wouldn't be here without his quick thinking."

Rosanne shot an incredulous look towards her usual volatile watch captain, who would never stick his neck out for anyone but himself and Dalia. People could change after all, she mused.

"It wasn't nearly as bad as the hulder song. It's the only reason it didn't take me this time, too." There, Creedy shrugged and looked elsewhere.

"I am pleased to hear there's a flaw to their methods," Rosanne said. "If we're all accounted for, I suggest we move further north and count our blessings."

"Kavanaugh still hasn't returned," Creedy said. Rosanne closed her eyes, sending a heartfelt thank you to the powers of the Veil for freeing her from the parasitical Aros Bernhart.

"Of course, he hasn't." She licked her lips and took a sip of her coffee, not betraying a hint of concern. A buzz of excitement from outside seized their attention. Freeing herself from the blanket, Rosanne left the tent in tandem with the men.

The rain had let up, but the sky remained cloudy. Aros shuffled along the beach, propping himself on a plasma rifle. Rosanne rescinded the divine gratitude and quietly cursed the Veil instead. The crew that met the former pirate patted him on the back and brought him coffee and a blanket. Rosanne came before him, arms crossed. His face was pale, and his uncontrollable shaking made it difficult to stand upright.

"C-Captain," he greeted through chattering teeth, practically gulping down the coffee.

"We need to talk." Her firm tone elicited a chorus of pained and amused chuckles from the bystanders.

Once inside the tent, Rosanne wrapped herself in the blanket and released a violent sneeze. "What on earth happened last night?" she demanded before Aros had even settled.

Rainwater dripped from him in fat droplets, but he shrugged it off and took a seat, regardless. "Mermaids, I swear. And not the pretty sort!"

She rolled her eyes. "I am asking why the camp was overrun. You were on duty! Did you nod off? Did you close your eyes and forget to wake up the next shift?" With each word, her voice escalated in agitation. Aros brushed her accusations aside with a nonchalant wave of a hand.

"I wish it was that simple, but the mermaids must have ensnared me before I was even conscious of dreaming."

"So, you fell asleep!"

"Not intentionally! The mermaid's song lulled me into this fluffy-as-royal-pillows dream that were out of this world. That ugly wretch had dragged me halfway to the ocean's depths before I snapped out of it. Do you know how utterly horrifying that was? I shot off the sound flare from underwater! You cannot deny the commitment in that." He rubbed his nose and went for a second cup of still-steaming coffee that someone had abandoned earlier. Despite being neck-deep in trouble for allowing the camp to be overrun by monsters, Aros remained nonchalantly confident about his actions.

The nerve of this cheeky bastard.

Rosanne shivered from the cold, yet her insides boiled with disappointment and an intense desire to punt him off the island.

The image of Aros squirming over the flames flashed through her mind again, making her nauseous that she had sought his painful demise in such a torturous manner while under Yerrik's magics.

She reeled in her fury, her rationality wrestling with her emotions, which trampled over her sense and judgement. The audacity of this damned man ... Rosanne quelled her thoughts before her mind, akin to a pressure cooker, exploded. "So, you're seeking commendation now for your valiant efforts?"

"I did my fucking job!" He rose.

"That's not what it sounds like to me!" Rosanne also stood, both of them staring each other down with matching glares. Once again, she wondered why she was so irate at Aros. How could an ex-pirate bring out her unbridled fury so?

An abrupt, violent sneeze tore through them both. Aros wiped his nose on the blanket. "I swear, lady. I warned the camp with a sound flare, and I fought off the witch who had taken me. Before I knew it, I was inside the mountain, and it was teeming with crabby guys."

Rosanne suppressed a smile and quickly composed herself. "Fine. How did you escape?"

"I ran, and I got hella lucky. Heard the monsters, got out of the mountain, and ended up on the wrong side of the island. I hiked through a pass to get back here."

"What about the jungle? Anything that followed you there? Any ... people?" Rosanne fished, hoping she wasn't the only one who met the mimics.

Aros paused and licked his lips. "No." He was lying.

"What happened?" Rosanne's voice was a soulless inquiry. She settled herself back on the carpet, huddling into the blanket during what should have been a formal meeting between employer and employee. Both were shivering, their noses reddened; Sniffles punctuated their conversation.

His scowl told her how reluctant he was to tell her anything, and considering how she had treated him in the past, she couldn't blame him. Everything about this place was bizarre, even more so than the last island they visited. Even Rosanne struggled to believe everything she witnessed. Likely, Aros felt the same.

"I thought I saw another person. She appeared human and even sounded like one."

"But?"

"I hadn't seen her before. I think. Not anyone who I recognised, yet she felt familiar, you know? That's it. And she was ... somewhat bold." He formed a prim, nervous smile.

Rosanne's hand swept across her face, wanting to lobotomise herself for even entertaining this absurdity. "You met a woman in the middle of the jungle who simply fell into your arms? This place may play mind games, but this tells me you are positively delusional."

Aros huffed an exasperated breath and theatrically placed a hand on his chest. "I would have you know that I am, indeed, quite the handsome man. Don't let my hair, or lack of it, deceive you. But you are too caught in your moral obligations to impress lover boy, so the fault lies with no one. However, that's beside the point." He coughed, regaining his composure. "The lady came to me and said my name as if she knew me. And yet, I could have sworn I heard your voice from somewhere close by. It's all foggy, as though I dreamt it all. The next thing I remember, she pushed me away before taking off."

"You couldn't have heard me because I was with—" Rosanne felt the colour drain from her face, her eyes widening. "Antony was here," she whispered.

Aros arched an eyebrow. "Yeah, he's been here. Who the hell did you see ... No, hold on, woah!" He sprang to his feet, the blanket slipping from his shoulders, as he lifted his hands defensively under Rosanne's deadly stare. "Listen, I did not know! She—you came onto me!"

"Get out!" She threw her empty tin cup at him. It hit the tent canvas next to his defensive pose and clattered to the ground.

"That was pretty great, by the way. We should do that again!" he chirped, exiting the tent post-haste, trailing a nervous laugh.

CHAPTER TWENTY

A. CREEDY

Pressed against the canvas of the captain's tent, Creedy and a slew of curious sailors members hinged on every word they could pick out through the thick fabric. From their heated argument, Isaac Kavanaugh was getting an earful, which was no surprise, as his negligence got the camp overrun by monsters. But the new hire's defiance caught Creedy off guard, for the captain rarely let anyone talk back at her. He knew they had shared history—not the romantic sort, but the "let's see who ends up killing each other first" variety, a past he both respected and understood. This whole damn island was a giant pain, and whatever mysterious forces that plagued them was done playing the good host. Perhaps it had gotten to the captain and Kavanaugh, too.

As the tin cup clattered against the canvas and Isaac emerged from the flap sporting a huge grin, confusion left them all momentarily stunned until they realised their error and resumed their tasks as though they hadn't just spent a good ten minutes eavesdropping on their conversation. Either Isaac didn't notice, or he didn't care, and he made his way back to his toppled tent to retrieve his blanket.

Creedy caught the tail end of the captain's frustrated growl through the flap and turned his attention to the grinning recruit. Whatever the captain was withholding, she'd better have a damn good reason. After her stunt with Nelson, along with the lieutenant, Creedy couldn't simply settle his grievances with an apology and promise of adventure. He wasn't that fickle. He wasn't the only one who shared this distrust; the others looked to him for answers. Whenever the captain and lieutenant had retreated to their private meetings, Creedy had been there to catch their whispers. Yet where he expected blackmail from the former captain of the *Blue Dragon*, instead stood a man desperate for escape. A pathetic, desperate man.

Kavanaugh deserved nothing short of half a length plank and a two thousand metre drop over the Baltansea, yet the captain had spared him. Did Isaac have leverage over her that Creedy didn't know about? Or had the forces of the Veil turned her icy heart to blood and granted him amnesty? Had Isaac truly turned away from his bloodthirsty pirating ways in favour of survival, much like half the crew members aboard the *Red Queen*?

Creedy eyed the recruit who chattered by the fire, wrapped in his blanket, his shoes propped up on sticks to dry. Denny popped by and gave him his flask, mixing the coffee with whatever brand of brandy he'd absconded from Hammond's pantry, no doubt. With a last pat on Isaac's back, Denny returned to his duties as if nothing was going on. Creedy couldn't recall seeing Denny that friendly with anyone outside of his small circle of Quinn and Vincent. Isaac sipped his coffee gratefully, a content smile spread on his lips. How could he be so calm after the screaming match with the captain and no reprimands to keep him busy like Creedy himself had suffered many times? Scratching his patchy stubble, Creedy approached Isaac near the fire.

"You doing alright there, mate?" he asked the shivering pirate.

"P-p-peachy," Isaac stammered, his words interrupted by a sneeze. He wrapped the blanket tight around him, and his pale face slowly returned with colour. Creedy settled opposite him, gaze piercing through the flames. He wasn't sure what to make of this man. Although the *Red Queen* had its share of ex-pirates, none had attacked them and lived to sail another day, let alone secure a position among said crew.

"What did you do to earn the captain's favour?" Creedy probed.

"I think I m-majorly pissed her off." Isaac let out a weak, faltering chuckle.

The watch captain's scrutinizing stare sharpened. "Yet, you faced no penalty."

"Perhaps I know her secret." Isaac flashed him a toothy grin. "Or maybe I'm the only thing standing between her and our ticket to freedom."

The man was so full of crap Creedy couldn't help but erupt in laughter. So much for his suspicions.

"You're off your rocks, you know that? Did the monsters hit you on the head or something?"

"Just keeping up my spirits." Isaac flicked his eyebrows in humor. "Terra knows this place doesn't have much hope left for the likes of us."

"Sure, mate. Stick to your coffee and blankie. We'll probably be leaving soon, and I ain't staying to nurse your sorry ass."

"Sure thing, boss." Isaac nodded.

Creedy watched the man in his periphery, noticing how the man's eyes searched around. Was he up to something even now? But then his face twisted oddly and let out a violent sneeze, which had the entire camp turn their heads towards him and snicker. Vincent approached him with a bowl of steaming soup. The ex-pirate captain thanked him with an expression of pure gratitude, uncaring for the carnage left from last night's attack.

Creedy scratched the back of his head, confused by Isaac's carefree reaction to everything. Yet he couldn't help but feel grateful he didn't have to intervene any further. Being the only watch captain in the scouting team and without a quartermaster, he bore the responsibility of the crew's wellbeing, a duty he'd rather leave to Dalia. Her knack for reading people was far superior to his own, where his temper would flare while she remained cool as an ocean breeze. But Creedy had lost the draw between them, his bad luck foiling his holiday extension yet again. Dalia always won. Cheating shrew.

The engineers emerged from their shared tent, exchanging swift words until their eyes landed on Creedy. Ida stabbed a pointy finger at him, which made him freeze and wonder if he'd unwittingly upset the little Novalian. Instead, she bounded towards him, a big grin on her face.

"What are you on about?" He asked pre-emptively and crossed his arms. Creedy sensed the familiar patterns, akin to a spouse confronted with the phrase "I've been thinking," which meant that he had his work cut out for him.

Ida glanced nervously to Gavin, then back to Creedy. "Do you remember the sphere we tested back at the first camp before we were ambushed by that dream-invader thing? You know, the reason why we had to flee in the first place?"

"You need me to climb another tree?"

Ida nodded, and Creedy immediately turned on his heel with a dismissive wave. "I got better things to do."

"We got time, and your help would be *invaluable*." Ida's doe-blue eyes implored the veteran sailor.

"Use a long stick," he suggested, sensing his resolve weakening, and quickly moved around the engineers to escape.

Gavin sidestepped in front of the taller sailor. "Sticks don't have fingers, and we are not skilled climbers," he retorted.

So, once again, Creedy found himself ascending the jungle's tallest tree. He teetered on its slender trunk, surveying the vast jungle that enveloped them. Mountains loomed to their south, and he spotted the shoreline and its sudden two thousand metres drop to the north. Clambering to the crooked branch, he held out the orb, watching it levitate autonomously. He lingered in anticipation, listening for any noise, expecting the little gadget to whirr with action.

Meanwhile on the ground, Ida and Gavin studied the display, with Lyle behind them, scouting for danger. A pit, bristling with spikes rested next to the team, obscured by twigs and leaves. If any monster came for them, they would fall to their sea-kebab death before the engineers had to run.

The tablet depicted a mostly unclouded forest canopy. However, a nebulous green haze meandered near the southern mountains, forming languid tendrils.

"Looks like normal rain," Gavin noted.

"I am aware," Ida remarked, adjusting the dial. The screen registered a slight change in hue of change, rendering the rainfall more pronounced.

"It's not the rain itself, but what's within it. Look there." She pointed to a thicker blob moving at the very edge of the screen, reaching out of the field with tendrils before retracting.

"What the hell? Rain doesn't do that. Could it be wind?"

Ida disagreed with a shake of her head. "I think it's the creature that lives here, the one that can influence our dreams."

Gavin's face took on a pallor that matched the screen. "And it's invisible?"

"To our eyes, yes."

"And again, I must point out the incredibly obvious problem that the thing on the screen is coming this way," he finished, casting worried looks at the camp.

Ida felt a raindrop in her hair and quickly scanned the darkening sky. She let out a frustrated growl. "I thought I had made enough adjustments to pick up on the weather changes too. This is useless!" Suddenly, the rain bore down like a waterfall and soaked them in seconds. "Creedy, we need to go!" she called to the watch captain clinging to the top of the tree.

He snatched the orb and used a rope to quicken his descent, rappelling down the tree in moments.

He thrust the orb into Ida's hands and coiled the rope over his shoulders.

"What if the dream invader is already here?" Gavin voiced concern.

"Hold the sphere. I have an idea." She activated it again and let it float in front of them. All four pinned their eyes on the screen. The vast shape weaved through the shadowy tree patches, heading directly for them.

"Run!" Ida snatched the sphere and bolted for the camp. Gavin followed, skirted by Lyle.

Creedy remained with a question mark on his face. Whatever the engineers witnessed had unnerved them, and Lyle hadn't raised any protests. Gazing into the forest, he saw only the rain. And then the whispers tickled his ears, like seducing entities sliding behind him.

He raced after the engineers.

Rosanne stared through the flap of her tent at the rain, a deep frown marred her face. "It's like it's following us." She grumbled and buttoned it closed. Antony sat on the carpet, engrossed in his thoughts.

"Hey." She placed a hand on his good shoulder, and the man jerked under her touch.

Antony rubbed his face, realising he had hurt her. "Sorry. It's been a long night."

Rosanne offered a sympathetic smile. "You don't seem like yourself." His fidgety state was so out of character from his usual confidence.

"I can't explain it, Ros. This place is maddening. It's toying with my mind to the point I can't make sense of what's real or what's a dream. I don't know how you do it."

"The monsters certainly don't help." She settled opposite him, taking his hand, but he didn't lift his gaze. "We'll get through this. We always do."

He responded with a weary frown. "This place has a presence that clings to you like a leech. It's a pull towards something I don't under-stand, and I can't seem to escape it."

Rosanne considered his words, hesitant with her inquiry. "Does it talk to you?"

"I don't know, Ros. But something is."

Before Rosanne could question him any further, Ida burst into the tent, drenched with a wild look in her eyes. "We need to leave! It's here!"

"The monsters?" Rosanne grabbed the plasma pistol.

"Worse. The dream invader! We have got a visual, or kind of."

Rosanne didn't have to be told twice. "Sound the alarm and let's get the hell out of here.."

Ida nodded and ran out to deliver the news.

Rosanne kicked into the ground, scattering sand over the floor canvas. "I thought we'd have more time. I am bloody sick of these monster ambushes, Antony. We need to bring the fight to them. If they want us gone, there must be a good reason."

Antony snapped out of his daze. "You think we're close to that place? On your father's map?"

"I'm sure of it. Weather be damned. We're heading north to whatever these creatures are guarding."

His face paled at the thought, and Rosanne almost regretted suggesting it. She had worn the very same expression after Nikor poisoned her, when her mind barely felt like her own. Perhaps Antony would have been safer at base camp. She should have brought the ship's artillery, brandishing the cannons as a deterrent instead of the free-for-the-taking she had turned them into. Given the creatures' eagerness to seize them, her motivation was partly spiteful.

Even though Antony was recovering from the attack, she reminded herself that he wasn't alone like she was. They would get through this.

The rain poured down, urging them to move swiftly. Antony huddled under an oil-cloth poncho. Ever since departing from the camp, the whispers constantly beckoned him. The rain seemed to infiltrate every crevice of his mental defences, the tent canvas and clothes a poor shield.

He hated feeling this useless. When mermaids lured Rosanne into the waters, he was powerless to stop her. She alone had saved herself from that horrid situation and he could have done nothing to improve that. While this might have been an everyday occurrence for her, Antony was treading water. He dealt with snotty nobles, poor mechanics, and incompetent pilots, not monsters!

For the rest, it appeared to be just another day. Was their valour rooted in their bond with the Grey Veil? Was it perhaps, despite his military training and leadership skills, did he remain ignorant of the true dangers of the seas?

The nightmares and illusions promised peace despite the nagging sense of danger in the back of Antony's mind. Could he trust these whispers?

It felt as though he was asleep, yet his eyes remained open. He sensed the people around him but felt trapped behind an invisible wall. A disassociation imprisoned him from the world around him, like his body wasn't his own.

He folded his arms around himself, the only thing he could do to bring himself comfort. It wasn't that Rosanne couldn't understand his distress; Facing pirates and plasma cannons over Noval's glaciers was a straightforward ordeal for him. But confronted by the dream invader, these horrendous beasts, and deceitful mermaids, Antony's defences began to falter. He couldn't muster the courage to tell Rosanne. She had enough on her plate. Carlos, nursing an injury similar to Antony's, seemed unshaken by the ordeal. Although they had been fortunate to escape with a shoulder wound, Antony's numbness lingered, hinting at

JOURNEY OF THE LOST AND DAMNED

the poison from the mermaid's spines. Perhaps he needed more time to heal. Or he was worsening by the hour.

The whispers grew stronger in his mind, invasive and beckoning. Antony pulled the hat low over his brow. Concentrating on the voices, they came like waves of distracted moments, discordant yet welcoming. They pulled him into the viridian fields of his parents' vineyard, and the laughter of his sisters as they raced against him to the end of the purple grapes. But Antony knew it was a long-forgotten memory, even if the illusion showed him his sisters as adults with babes in their arms and husbands at their sides. Antony posed with them and their parents for a family photograph to hang on the wall. It was a beautiful, quaint life he had longed for since childhood.

But it was all a lie, for the fire had claimed everything. The flames tugged at the memory like burning a photo to ashes, his smile a distorted black smear and eyes smouldering hollows.

You can have it all, you know, a voice said. The other voices agreed with it. Antony wanted to return to the farm and rebuild it from the ground up. Plant the grapes again, add a servant's quarter to annex the house so he could expand on it, and move his family and kids into the main house. The simple life he would never get as long as he travelled with Rosanne.

CHAPTER TWENTY-ONE

FARAND DUPLÀNTE

While the captain was off scouting the nine hills, Farand found himself mired in ship management. He almost wished he could be the one hunting for treasures and fighting monsters. The captain always seemed to have the best of times on these expeditions. But in all fairness, she also faced the gravest danger. Despite his envy, Farand understood that he was the right man for this responsibility. The truth of the matter was that he was bored out of his mind. Being stuck on the *Red Queen* did little to silence the voice of his inner workaholic, compelling him to conjure tasks where none existed. Having inspected the storage and ballast rooms twice, he sought solace in his tent by the beach, yearning for news of Rosanne's expedition or anything that could save him from this boredom.

From the corner of his eye, Farand watched as Higgs descended the *Red Queen's* ladder. The stout middle-aged man moved with a pronounced stiffness, groaning with each careful step until he stood beside Farand.

"Fixed the grav-ports, sir. Cleared out the crabs, and the air is breathable again. I say she's good for righting," Higgs said, easing himself down with an audible groan.

Farand closed his eyes and drew a deep breath of relief. "You're certain all the ports are operational?"

Digging out a grimy handkerchief from his worn vest, Higgs dabbed at his sweaty brow. "You doubt my mechanical skills, sir?" He laughed softly.

"Not in the slightest, Chief. I'd hate to watch the ship rise crooked, a difficult task with just the skeleton crew."

Higgs, with a grease-stained hand, gave Farand's shoulder a reassuring pat. "Wish my joints were as easy to fix. That blasted ladder will be the death of me."

"Then if it's all the same to you, let's get the *Queen* airborne again." Farand stared at the black spot left on his shirt, and with a stiff-lipped smile he nodded to Higgs as he clambered up the ladder with great difficulty.

The longer the ship was grounded, the more Farand feared an ambush by the forces of the Veil having snuck up on Rosanne and the scouting team. The sky was turning grey, and Farand knew that if there was any time to get the ship airborne, this was it. He rallied the skeleton crew to the *Red Queen's* bow for the righting operation and split them into two teams between him and Dalia. Higgs in engineering would activate the anti-gravity port, while the ground teams would ensure the ship rose level.

Farand inspected the ropes anchored to the deep-set palm trees around the beach, making sure they could act as pulleys. Judging by their exposed roots, he prayed they would suffice until the ship floated upright.

Dalia stood with her team on the starboard, rolling her shoulder after removing her sling but seemingly in high spirits. She gave the go signal, signifying her readiness. Using a rod, Farand tapped out a message on the ship's thruster panel in Morse Code, then retreated to his station by the ropes port side, watching for signs from the gravity ports.

The sand stirred like a wind only to curl around the hull, repelled by the anti-gravitational force of the ports. The ropes pulled the crew along as they wound around the trees, creaking under the mounting tension. Farand stood by the bow, observing the two teams embroiled in this massive tug-of-war.

"Watch Captain?" he called to Dalia.

"It's holding!" he heard her reply. "Ready to ease the tension!"

The *Red Queen* floated barely a hands-breadth above the trench. Several support beams fell free of the hull, thudding into the sand.

"Ease!" Farand's thunderous command rang across the beach. Dalia and the seven crew members at the ropes began a measured retreat towards the trees. They fought against the ship's insistent pull upwards with every stride. While the *Red Queen* didn't ascend significantly at first, the rope's tension escalated moment by moment as the anti-gravity ports increased in power.

A strangled snap resounded from the port side. Farand sprinted, trying to secure the flying rope before the ship lurched and jeopardised the remaining supports. Sand shifted and fell away from the roots of trees used as anchors, threatening to give in. The *Red Queen's* starboard angled sharply upwards, dragging a smaller palm from its hold while the others groaned under the strain. Farand dove for the rope, caught it, and dug his heels in the sand, leaning as far back as he could.

"Ease port! Anchor starboard!" he bellowed and fought the monstrous tension. The trees were not enough! Dalia, Swanson, and Olivier leaned against the pulleys before the trees were ripped from the ground while port side aimed to balance out the ship. But the rising starboard side yanked Dalia and the rest off their feet, sending them sprawling into the sand. The ropes snapped around the trees, and the ship groaned as it lurched sharply sideways.

"Release!" Farand bellowed, and the crew scattered, evading the lashing ropes that thrashed through the air with audible cracks. Farand's gaze darted upwards, half-expecting the *Red Queen* to keel over, her masts threatening to crash down.

With each moment, she tilted precariously. The remaining tree trunks wrenched their roots from the soil, causing eruptions of sand.

The *Red Queen* ascended in undulating moves, the mast bobbing back and forth like a pendulum.

In tense silence, they all waited for a long minute, visually gauging the ship's alignment by comparing the yawls and decks with the horizon. Breathing out a relieved sigh, Farand rested his hands on his thighs.

Dalia burst into cheerful applause, and around her, crew members exchanged congratulatory pats on the back or appreciative nods.

From above, Higgs's flushed face appeared over the main deck. "What in the blazing hells was that, Duplànte!? Trying to get this old man killed?"

Farand managed a shaky thumbs up, the energy rush preventing him from pacifying the chief engineer who had endured the chaotic lift-off. Higgs responded with a gruff snort, lowered the rope ladder, and vanished beneath the deck again–a gesture as close to forgiveness as Farand would receive.

Once they climbed aboard, Farand initiated a systems check at the helm. Given the crab invasion, there was no predicting the extent of damage or any certainty that they'd eradicated every last one. It baffled Farand how so many had even made it on board. The anchor's chain link provided no foothold, and most crabs that fell onto the ship as they sailed below the island met a crushing end. "Kill them before they lay eggs," was Rosanne's boorish order before she departed with the northern scouting party. Confronted with the task, Norman had suggested fire, while others favoured hammers or broomsticks. It was a moment in Farand's career you had to have been there to appreciate the effort he made keeping the ship afloat.

Now, with the ports mended and the crab menace handled (sans fire), the ship was ready to sail once more. Yet, this unexpected leisure had Farand practically twiddling his thumbs; after all, the notion of "personal life" was alien on the open sea. A renewed vigour spread through the crew after having addressed the primary issue concerning the ship. After solving the key problem, the faces of the skeleton crew faded to sheer boredom within an hour. While Dalia had relished her sunbathing opportunities at the beach in the preceding days, on an overcast day with the threat of rain, restlessness overcame even her.

Dark clouds gathered over the distant mountain peaks, accompanied by a low rumble.

The rain rolled over the forest, spreading out to the coastline as if originating from the mountains. If the rain was a precursor of the creature that attacked the scouting team, Farand knew they would be safer while airborne.

What sort of creature could it be? On the north island, they had a clear sense of what they were up against, based purely on observation.

However, out here, everything felt alien. The idea of an unseen adversary made Farand's insides flip. The hulder, despite their alluring songs, were as susceptible to mortal wounds as any being. An invisible foe might as well be the fear conjured by his mind.

Farand toggled the switches linking the sails to the thruster engine. Even with the sails securely stowed, they still channelled some energy to the engine. The lamp shone green. Farand picked up the intercom and pressed the side button. "Chief, what's the engine's status?"

"All green and golden here if you want to flee with your tail between your legs, sir." Higgs' gruff voice crackled the intercom, making Farand slap it against the palm of his hand to remove the interference.

"I might have to take you up on that offer. We have rain incoming. I'll order everyone back on the ship for now."

"Copy that, sir."

Farand rolled his neck and shoulders, glad to have the systems check out of the way. He could breathe easy once more. A raindrop splashed coldly against his cheek, and he opened his eyes to see the rain sweep over the beach in gentle showers. The people down there fled back to the ship, abandoning their tents and equipment as they couldn't be bothered.

Hwang stood on the forecastle deck, training his spyglass towards the forest. He lowered the instrument in a pause, wiped the rain out of his face, and then aimed it again. With a moment's hesitation, he dashed down the stairs, hurried across the main deck, and leapt up the quarterdeck where Farand stood with crossed arms, waiting for his report.

"Someone's at the forest's edge." Hwang thrust the spyglass into Farand's fumbling hands. Guided by Hwang's pointed finger, Farand directed the spyglass towards the misty jungle.

Through the lens, he spotted a white-faced man navigating the underbrush, making his way to the beach. Thinning hair clung to his pallid skin, and his faded blue clothes were sodden from the rain. Farand couldn't believe his eyes.

It was Jeffs!

The seaman trudged through the sand with heavy steps.

"Is he hurt?" Hwang asked, eager for the spyglass Farand had yet to lower.

"Let's get him aboard the ship," he ordered, and the two men met the stumbling man by the rope ladder, assisting him as he slowly climbed the steps. Jeffs collapsed onto the deck in a crumpled heap.

"By the stars, Jeffs! We feared the worst. Can you stand?" Farand exclaimed, seizing the man's hand to help him up. Jeffs' attention shifted wordlessly between Farand and Hwang and the forest and settled on them.

"Were you followed?" Hwang asked, noticing the man's split attention.

Jeffs responded with a lethargic shake of his head. "The dream showed me the way, and they followed." The slow drawl and hollowness in his voice gave Farand chills.

Exchanging a worried look with Farand, Hwang gently clasped Jeffs by the arm. "I'll get Hammond to prepare something warm for you, yes? Not easy being out in the jungle by yourself."

Farand remained by the railing, gazing at the shadowy forest as torrential rain thrashed the landscape with relentless fury. He thought of Jeffs' cryptic words and what they could possibly mean. Perhaps Jeffs wasn't in possession of his complete mind and was rambling nonsense unless he was led back by the rain and the elusive voices that reportedly accompanied it.

As sheets of rain enveloped them, Farand drew a deep breath and closed his eyes, allowing his other senses to take over. The aroma of the jungle, heady and primordial, blended seamlessly with the mist, and the rhythmic sound of raindrops striking the wooden decks and canvas pattered noisily around him. And then, he picked up the unmistakable buzz of whispers. They hovered at the fringes of his awareness, taunting him amid the windy gusts sweeping across the deck.

Farand's hand found its way to the grip of his plasma pistol, although he wasn't sure what good that would do him. Through the curtains of mist and rain, the elusive whispers beckoned him from the depths of the forest, suddenly impossibly clear in his mind. Watch Captain Dalia emerged from below deck, jogging to the quarterdeck while huddling under an oilcloth raincoat.

"We've checked the rigging and the gundeck, sir. Everything should be good to g—" Her words were abruptly halted by a sneeze. She wrapped her arms around herself, and caught his contemplative stare. "What's got your knickers in a twist?"

Among the green of the trees stood blank-faced individuals, their eyes peeled on the ship. They lingered at the precipice of the beach, standing there with indifference that their odd costumes were soaked through.

"They must have followed Jeffs," Farand remarked with a grim tone.

Dalia paled. "Jeffs is back? How? And who are those people?"

"Island settlers, perhaps?" Farand drew his shoulders into a shrug. "Look at their attire. I have never seen such outfits in my life."

Dalia borrowed Farand's spyglass, training it on the people. After examining it briefly, she shook her head. "My great-gran wore frills like that in her youth. Did they step out of a costume ball from the previous century? I know I would look at least a little bit miserable wearing that in this weather, so why do they seem so..."

"Uncaring, Watch Captain?" Farand offered.

Dalia nodded. "What do we do, sir?"

What would the captain do? Farand thought. The muscles in his face danced as he ground his teeth, turning the question over and over in his mind.

If the strangers had shown aggression, the situation might have been more straightforward. Instead, their unsettling expressions remained resolute, revealing no apparent motive. A murmur of unease spread among the skeleton crew amassing on the main deck, with some reaching for their firearms or blades. They seemed more ready to start a fight than prevent one, accentuated by disembodied voices.

Hwang hurried to join them on deck, using an oiled canvas to shield himself from the rain.

"What did Jeffs say?" Farand asked the able seaman, who shrugged.

"He didn't say a word. He looked around as if he didn't understand what he was seeing. The man's touched, sir." Hwang paused at the sight of the people down by the beach. "Friend of Jeffs, I presume? They must be who took him."

"We don't know if they did. If the captain says Jeffs wandered off by his own accord, I'm inclined to believe her."

"And now he's back with company," Dalia said.

"Company indeed," Farand echoed, tapping a hand impatiently at the railing as his mind raced for a plan, any plan similar to what Rosanne could conjure on a whim. A small smile stretched over his lips at the thought. "Let's improvise and find out who they are and what they want first."

Farand straightened with his hands on the railing and, drawing a deep breath, called out, "Hello there! Won't you come closer so we can talk?"

The group stood motionless and unblinking despite the downpour as if they hadn't registered his words.

Dalia sniffed, her eyes narrowing. "We can shoot them at this distance, can't we?"

Farand nodded, his expression unreadable. "Do not aggravate them, Watch Captain. We don't know if they're armed."

"Scared they'd steal the ship?"

"My concerns are more of the facts that they outnumber us two to one, and if their looks are anything to consider, they appear ready to draw blood. I'd like to avoid that."

Dalia nodded slowly. "Then, I ask for permission to go down to the beach, sir," Dalia asked, her fingers running over her plasma handgun.

"Granted, but do not fire, no matter what." Farand's voice betrayed no doubt, even though he knew he couldn't have stopped her if he'd wanted to. He was out of alternatives.

"Good luck," he called after her, his voice tinged with concern. She returned a resolute nod before making her way down the rope ladder.

Holding her pistol lightly, Dalia advanced towards the group, drawing their gaze. Whispers seemed to envelop her, yet none of the people before her seemed to speak—their lips sealed tightly. She had hoped to approach close enough for a civil conversation, but the voices gave her a pause.

Halting before the jungle's edge, she stood far enough to maintain a clear view of each individual but remained within a reasonable shooting distance despite her pained arm.

"You lot who took Jeffs?" she challenged. Without shifting their gaze, the crowd parted to reveal a lone man in the blue-grey sailor's cotton. He stopped just shy of the last tree, tilting his head.

"You should come with us too," the man said tonelessly, the brilliant blues of his eyes boring through her like a spectre. "The Dream will keep you safe."

Dalia furrowed her brows. "What's the Dream?"

The man remained silent.

Observing the crowd, she noted the lack of footwear—a peculiar choice, considering the jungle terrain. Their attire, with its frilly cravats and voluminous gowns, hinted at a bygone era. The rest remained eerily mute.

With a measured rise in posture, Dalia forced a semblance of a smile. "Why don't you show us some goodwill and come out of the forest, yeah? Let's get you warmed up and perhaps a decent meal. I've heard our cook is making a feast," she feigned.

The voices intensified, eerily close, as if they might lean in and speak directly into her ear. Dalia rapidly turned, trying to identify their source. Yet only sand, rain, and enveloping mist greeted her. Heart quickening, Dalia levelled the pistol before her, drawing the loading mechanism. "Whatever you're doing, stop it! If you don't come out of there, leave! You try anything funny, and I will shoot." Their gaze settled on the plasma pistol, regarding it as if it were a mere twig.

"Duplànte, sir! Permission to shoot!" she shouted, striving to be heard over the rain din. The pounding rain and those haunting whispers seemed to drown everything else out. But she caught his distinct approval, overriding her internal turmoil. All she needed was to act. She hesitated, her instincts cautioning against pulling the trigger. But there was an undeniable oddity to the scene. As still as statues, the figures lingered, and incoherent whispers clouded Dalia's thoughts. Their threat was palpable, yet its nature remained elusive.

Dalia squeezed the trigger. An electric *bzuow* rang as a luminescent blue projectile sped forward, striking the man in the blue cotton shirt. Though he recoiled, the expected grimace of pain was absent. Instead, an inky black substance seeped from his wound, staining his attire.

With trembling hands, Dalia lowered the weapon. No reproach came her way, neither for injuring one of them nor for her hasty decision to fire.

"Screw this." Dalia pivoted and dashed towards the ship. She scaled the ladder in mere moments, hastily drawing it up after her.

Lieutenant Duplànte came towards her with thundering steps.

"You disobeyed my orders, Watch Captain. They could have overpowered you in seconds! What were you thinking?" Farand bore down on her in a flash.

"I..." she stammered, clearly recalling having heard his approval. "I thought you gave your permission, sir. I swear I heard it!"

"They did nothing, you hear? Nothing!"

Dalia reached for the words, but they wouldn't come, and she lowered her gaze to the floor. She was certain she heard his call over the rain. Hadn't she?

Farand pinched the base of his nose and straightened. "It doesn't matter now. Next time they find us, they'll be hostile, and our chance for peace is squandered."

Dalia looked towards the gathering below. They hadn't crossed the beach, nor were they drawing any weapons.

"It's like they want us to come to them. Did they say anything?" he said.

Dalia pressed her lips into a taut line and shook her head. "Who knows what they are? I don't think it's safe to remain, sir." She didn't mention the cryptic words, primarily as their meaning eluded her. The people at the beach weren't in their right mind anyway. The man hadn't been in pain either.

"You think so, do you now, Watch captain?" Farand almost let his words build into a snarl, but the man drew a breath and calmed himself. "Secure the anchors. We leave this instant."

"Understood, sir," Dalia affirmed with a nod, swiftly turning to the skeleton crew and barked her orders. Cold blue eyes locked on the ship from the jungle, their unwavering gaze lingering on the *Red Queen* until they were out of sight.

CHAPTER TWENTY-TWO

A GAME OF SPHERES

Ida cursed every second they spent on this damn island. Although her dream-invader detection system worked as intended, it drained the power from their battery-driven plasma guns, leaving them defenceless. They couldn't shoot at an invisible enemy regardless of their firepower, rendering her efforts moot. And what was the point, knowing that the dream-invader travelled with the rain?

It rained. All. The. Time!

They were continuing their search for the Captain's map location. Ida had been briefed like all the others, but she knew better that this was more than an expedition for riches. The crew hadn't kept quiet about the potential lost treasures either.

Secret, my hindquarters, Ida thought.

Captain Drackenheart steered the longboats to a different beach within a secluded cove where they set up camp. They weren't getting anywhere at this rate, but at least they had distanced themselves from the mermaid shore and the creepy clacking horrors, or so Ida hoped. The overcast sky pursued them relentlessly.

She struggled to find any semblance of peace to sleep that night. Rain tapped persistently against the tent and turned the ground inside into a giant puddle. She drew the humid covers aside and stepped over Gavin, who was snoring on the camp bed, elevated by a mound of palm leaves to prevent it from submersion.

From her pack, she retrieved her goggles and magnifying set. After securing them to her head, she flipped a lens over one eye, the sphere suddenly huge before her. The incessant pattering against the canvas masked her tinkering, and Gavin remained undisturbed in his deep slumber. Nothing but catastrophic urgency could rouse him from his dreams.

She examined the adjustments Higgs had implemented into the sphere. This included trimming the cables, a task she had been too lazy to do herself, and swapping out the impure anti-gravity dust with a clean batch. Though tainted dust swiped from malfunctioning ports had sufficed until now, the readings should be more stable.

Ida flipped over a lens to further magnify the glass chamber containing the dust, working as the sphere's power source. She had based the design off the thruster engine's dynamo, but far less superior. Ordinarily, such technology would be unfathomable, but her tinkering during idle hours with the hazardous residual dust made it possible. When deactivated, the sphere remained stationary. However, once powered, the sphere's surface, combined with the anti-gravity force, exerted pressure on the power source's tiny pistons, which activated the laser they used to scan the area.

When she perfected the sphere, she would draw a patent and hopefully earn enough to open her own shop. That was the dream—if they survived whatever monstrosities this island threw at them.

Ida reassembled the sphere, securing it into position. Gavin roused with a confused groan from behind. "What are you doing?" He stared at her through sleep-swollen eyes. His hair, wild and featuring a prominent cowlick, made it hard for Ida to stifle a giggle.

"Sorry, I couldn't sleep, so I'm working on the sphere. See if I can fine tune it."

Gavin pushed himself up and rubbed his face. "Are you going to test it? It's pouring now, so might as well get stuck into it."

Ida let out a soft laugh. "You're sounding more and more like Higgs."

"Don't tell the old bastard. He might get chummy." Gavin shivered with exaggerated revulsion.

"I'm going to place it outside. Unless you volunteer?"

"I won't be throwing my head on the coals like that! Sticking my hand out will be enough." He crawled over to her and picked up the sphere, weighing it in his hand that couldn't even close halfway through it. "It's raining so hard I can't tell if there's any wind."

"I'll activate it then." Ida retrieved the tablet from her trunk, setting it on the table.

Gavin lobbed the sphere through the opening and watched it splash into a small puddle. "Will it be okay out there with the rain and all?"

Ida flipped the switch on the tablet. A soft green glow from the screen illuminated the tent's interior. "I've used plenty of grease and rubber. Shouldn't be a problem." Adjusting the tablet's dials, she calibrated the readings. Feeling the weight of Gavin's contemplative gaze, she looked up.

Gavin had a unique ability to concentrate tension to the point of creating its own gravitational force, pulling her from her comfort zone and prompting conversations she'd rather avoid.

"You've been working on that thing non-stop since we got here," he stated.

"It keeps me busy during downtime."

He ran his hand through his short-cropped hair. "I know you're a workaholic, but you've never been this bad. What's going on with you, Ida? Is it Nelson?"

Ida looked up. "No, Nelson's fine. He—he's back in Noval at his practice."

"And you're fine with him being there while you are all the way out here facing dream-vaders and physics-defying weather?" His tone edged with doubt, making it clear that her reassurances didn't convince him.

"I guess?" She set the tablet down and exhaled deeply. "It should be fine, right?" She turned sharply towards him. "All this relationship nonsense is so strange I can hardly make sense of it. I keep thinking about what this distance means for us and how it will affect our bond. I'm not comfortable being neither here nor in Noval!" Ida clenched her fists in exasperation, letting out a frustrated grunt. "I wish things were easy for once." Rubbing her face, her thought process quickly turned into that of contemplation. "You know what I mean?"

Gavin gave a thoughtful nod. "Sure do. Except I seem to lose what little wits I have when I have that feeling. And I ain't a very clever man to begin with."

"Truer words have I never heard from you." Ida teased, sticking out her tongue.

"Hey!" Gavin jabbed a finger into her side, making her squeal.

"I jest, I jest!" She waved him off, but their laughter disappeared as soon as it had come. "What about Kristoff? You two get along well."

Gavin drew his face into a frown. "We're just friends. He's been trying to out-drink me a few times, but other than that, I think he just likes to play around, and I'm not all that interested."

"You are making sense for once. What about, you know, last spring?" She hesitated to voice the matter that had strained their relationship. More so, Ida just wanted to know if they could still talk about everything, like before.

"That bit with you and Nelson? Nah, I'm over it," Gavin waved a hand airily. Ida's doubtful squint arrested him, prompting Gavin to raise his hands defensively. "Look, I'm as green to courtship as I would be as second engineer. It was a nice feeling, and now I guess I'll see where the horizon line stops."

"As in exploring your taste in people?"

"Something like that."

"Well, best steer clear of Kristoff, then."

They broke out in guilty laughter.

"Finally. I'm getting a reading of the camp. Look at the tents!" Ida pointed at the dark green square shapes on the screen, leaving a greasy print. "Higgs's tweaks certainly helped boost the signal," she began, adjusting the dial to broaden the map. "The range is terrible." Although displeased, she appreciated the improved clarity.

"Where are the watchmen?" Gavin asked, settling beside her. Ida's face screwed up in confusion.

"I'm not seeing any movement." She watched the static dance across the screen, and the scanner made its rounds, mapping out the dark green shapes of the camp's tents.

"There's someone there." Gavin gestured to a shifting dark shape on the display, moving with each scan's rotation. The dot navigated in between the tents, having just bypassed their own. Gavin peered outside, expecting a sentry. "Hello?" He tried and craned his neck out further, the quiet of the camp him instead. "The hell?" he looked back at the screen.

Ida noted his bewilderment. "Who was it?"

"No one, apparently. Or they were hiding."

Ida furrowed her brow in confusion, eyes locked on the screen. "I can't see the dream invader. A glitch, perhaps?"

"Could it be that we don't see it because it's surrounding us?"

"Don't say that! But you might have a point." Adjusting the tablet's dials again, Ida increased the reading scope. They paused momentarily for the image to sharpen. The darker blob engulfed the entire camp and neighbouring wood. "Damn. Whatever it is, it's already here." Ida bit her lips. The painful thudding in her chest relented, and through the rain, all she heard was the rush of blood pounding her ears. Blurred movements came and went in quiet waves on the screen. "You sure you didn't see anything out there?" 'Ida asked in a shaky breath.

Gavin silently nodded, his expression stiff. "Nothing but the rain and tents."

"That is strange." Ida reset the dials, turning back to the shorter range of the camp. The dark dot danced between the tents nearer the water, drifting away from theirs. "I'm going to see who it is," Ida announced and poked her head out. Gavin did the same. The sphere hovered a good metre and a half above the ground, silently reassuring them it was in good condition. The source of the detected movements was somewhere up ahead. Ida flashed the alchemical lamp through the flap, the harsh white glow flooding the camp, but they saw no one.

"Gavin?" Ida asked in a low, warning tone. He fetched the tablet, and they both stared at the moving dot, then looked out to the camp, seeing nothing but rivers and the rain misting the thick clouded sky. They hastily closed the flap and secured it from the inside, huddling on their beds.

"That must have been a fluke. No way there wasn't something there?" Ida asked.

"Crab, maybe?"

"Hilarious ..."

They fixed their eyes on the screen, tracking the black dot as it darted between their tent and the one next to it. Ida lifted her gaze towards the movements. They held their collective breaths as the dot halted in front of their tent. In her mind, Ida pictured it standing there, plotting, contemplating how best to scare the crap out of them. Whatever it had planned was working.

Gavin's sudden outcry made Ida scream in panic, nearly leaping through the canvas. In her alarm, she smacked him over the back of his head, uttering a frustrated grunt. "Are you out of your mind?"

"The sphere is moving!" Gavin declared sharply at the screen while rubbing the spot where Ida's firm slap had hit him. Ida seized the tablet and yanked Gavin by his sleeve, the two of them bolting through the tent flap. The rain bore over them, soaking into their clothes in seconds. Ida hunkered over the tablet to fend off the brunt of the rain. Beside her, Gavin held out the alchemical lamp next to her. The screen displayed the sphere darting southward across the sandy peninsula at an incredible speed.

They sprinted in pursuit. "There's no wind, Gavin!" Ida yelled over the thunder roar.

"Bastard's fast!" he growled. Rain lashed at them, forcing Ida to re-peatedly blink to see.

"It's already in the forest!" Gavin yanked Ida's arm just as she was about to dash into the jungle. Panting heavily, they paused at the forest's edge. Towering trees loomed overhead, their canopies plunging the area into deeper shadow. On the tablet, dense foliage disturbed the signal, making it impossible to trace the sphere's path. "How the hell is he moving past the traps?" Gavin looked ahead to the unsprung pit traps, still covered.

"He must have known where we placed them." Ida shivered, her clothes clinging to her like wet fur on a cat. "Then why make themselves known by taking the sphere? It doesn't add up! Forget it. Let's return to camp."

Realising they couldn't recover the sphere, they spun around. The emotionless stare of Antony stared right at them, barely an armlength away. Ida let out a startled scream, instinctively grabbing Gavin, who also jerked in alarm. Gavin let out a string of swear words between his chattering teeth.'

"Captain DiCroce. What are you doing here?" Ida asked. The man stared vacantly into the jungle. Taking deliberate steps, he pushed be-tween them, focused solely on the path ahead. Exchanging worried looks, both Ida and Gavin reached out, grasping Antony's arms.

"You mustn't go out there, sir! There's monsters! The dream-invader. Mermaids!" Ida pleaded, trying to restrain him.

"What she said. Damn, he's too strong!" As Gavin's feet dug into the sand, Captain DiCroce pulled them with terrifying ease. Antony turned his head to Ida, wrenched his arm free and, in the same breath, shoved her with such force that she tumbled into the sandy ground.

"Forgive me, sir!" Gavin said and clocked Antony on his jaw.

The man barely flinched and regarded Gavin with indifference before pushing past him. Attempting to hold Captain DiCroce back, Gavin was no match. Instead, the captain grabbed him by his shirt and landed a fierce punch straight to his face. Gavin crumpled to the ground with a cry, holding his bleeding nose. Ida rushed to his side just as Antony vanished into the dense greenery.

"We need to alert the camp. Come on, Gavin!" Ida dragged him to his feet, and they stumbled back to the camp.

Ida opened tent flaps, shouting for the others to awaken, but they remained still and unresponsive.

Bursting into the captain's tent, Ida shook Rosanne. The captain's expression was eerily serene, as if lost deep within a dream. Ida stumbled outside again, spotting Gavin outside of Lyle's tent. "I can't wake the captain."

"They're all dead asleep!" Gavin loaded the plasma rifle in hand.

"What the hell did that thing do?" Tears filled Ida's eyes, and she swallowed her strangled sobs. "I-I can't...!" Her hand flew to her chest, heaving for breath.

"Hey!" Gavin placed a hand on her shoulder. "They're alive, aren't they?"

"Yes, yes, they are." Ida choked out between her breaths. "It's the dream invader; I'm sure of it."

"Then what about DiCroce?"

"I don't know, Gavin. Maybe he's caught up in the same nightmare as Jeffs." Ida's voice broke, a sob stifled by the sudden sound of splashing footfalls approaching the tent. She ducked behind Gavin, who raised his rifle, aiming at the entrance.

The tent flap shifted, revealing an unknown young woman. Her black makeup, smudged and streaked by tears or rain, contrasted starkly with her piercing blue eyes. With a curious tilt of her head, she assessed the two engineers. The dampness had turned her once-styled hair into heavy, wet strands that draped her bare shoulders. Mud marred the hem of the flowing, azure dress, and here and there, tattered lace hung limply.

"Fuck off!" Gavin snapped, raising his plasma rifle. A reassuring hum emanated from the weapon, ready to fire. The young woman's vacant gaze shifted to the sleeping captain before she stepped further in, stretching to full height. Her slender figure seemed fragile as if the gust of wind might sweep her away yet she was taller than Gavin. Her gaunt eyes bore an eerie and haunted look. The ribbon in her hair drooped listlessly against her tangled blonde locks.

"Any closer, and I will shoot!" Gavin called, his voice holding an edge of panic. Ida noticed the slight quiver in his grip. Frantically, her eyes darted around the tent, finally landing on the captain's plasma pistol, half-hidden beneath the blanket Rosanne used as a pillow.

The woman in the ornate dress extended a ghostly hand towards the captain. Gavin's finger twitched and the plasma rifle responded. The plasmic bullet scorched the intricate lace of her bodice, leaving a smouldering hole in her pale skin. She reflexively covered the wound, and from beneath her fingers oozed a dark ink-like substance, creating shadowy streams down her attire. A pained gasp escaped her lips as she keeled over, her body contorting in an otherworldly manner. Her dress and skin took on a transparent shine. Face dropping, her blue eyes sunk into her skull. It seemed as though her very essence was melting away. In a heartbeat, she transformed into a pool of dark liquid, which was then absorbed by the earth below.

They shared an expression of mixed horror and bewilderment. Neither moved.

"What in Terra's name was that?" Ida whispered, her eyes wide, fearing that the woman would re-manifesting herself before them. "Was she ... mimicking a person?"

"That's the worst human interpretation if I ever saw one. Grab the gun," Gavin ordered, giving her shoulder a firm tap as he swiftly reloaded the rifle. Ida, with shaky hands, grasped the plasma pistol and disengaged the safety. "There could be more of them. If we're the only ones awake, we need to defend the camp." Gavin peeked out the tent flap, eyes small and sharp as he scanned the camp. "You ready?"

Ida shook her head.

The engineers charged out of the tent, weapons at the ready. A group of mimics advanced towards the camp while four others infiltrated the tents of the sleeping crew. They looked so ordinary, drenched to the bone, but their faces were as blank and lifeless as dolls.

"Shoot to kill, Ida. You can do it."

"After the hulder madness, this is nothing," Ida growled. She loaded the gun and, despite her shaking hands, took aim and fired at the nearest mimic. The imposter, dressed in a three-piece suit and adorned with a white wig under a black tricorne hat, crumbled and disintegrated like the previous one.

They weren't human, she told herself. They weren't human.

Gavin fired at the incoming group, hitting a grey-bearded seaman in navy attire. Yet, the figure didn't falter and continued its march.

"Focus on the mimics inside the tents. I'll deal with these!" Gavin ordered and advanced towards the flock of shuffling blank-faced creatures. Ida sprinted towards the bigger tents where she had spotted activity. She flung aside the tent flap. A young man turned sharply, his hand reaching menacingly for the sleeping Lyle. The mimic's brown eyes bore into her, small as pin dots. With trembling hands, Ida squeezed the trigger. The plasmic bullet whistled and illuminated the inside of the tent for a split second before burying itself in the intruder's skull. The boy fell to his back, his skin sagging and blackening, before turning to water like the others—a burnt hole decorated the tent canvas.

Lyle didn't stir.

Outside, Gavin fired shot after shot. With the four-second reload time, he retreated further and further into the camp, waiting for the plasma rifle to be ready. The group of mimics marched at an even pace with relentless abandon. They didn't rush, but their expressionless faces pushed him to the brink of panic. There were so many! With each step, his breathing grew more laboured, his chest all the tighter. Painfully aware of his mortality in the face of the unknown, Gavin resisted the urge to run. As he shot down another, a group of impostors paused en masse, heads turning to him as one. Gavin clutched the plasma rifle close to his chest, retaining a step. He licked his parched lips, reloaded the weapon, and aimed as they closed in.

They moved past Ida as she cautiously poked her head out. Swiftly, she pulled out her pistol, shooting a mimic in the back. The woman gasped, clawing at the bleeding wound before dissolving into liquid. Ida sprinted across to the other tents. Mimics emerged with sleep-heavy crew members, their eyes half closed and unresponsive to everything around them. Led by the arm, the mimics led Creedy and Lyle towards the jungle without a protest. Ida fired bullet after bullet, turning one of their kidnappers into dark puddles that the rain erased within seconds.

The freed crew remained motionless, soaked by the rain, as if they were unaware of their surroundings. Ida stopped before Lyle who stood swaying in the rain, the usual straight-backed master gunner oddly relaxed yet completely entranced by the power of the mimics. She waved a hand in front of his face but got no response. With his captor gone and the others pursuing Gavin, Ida went after the others being led into the forest.

She aimed, but the pistol's familiar hum fell silent. Its battery chamber ceased glowing, drained of energy. She caught sight of Creedy, led by a tall raven-haired man, both moving as though possessed. Summoning her courage, Ida reversed the pistol in her hand and struck the mimic at the back of his head. He stumbled, turned, his face an unflinching mask of emptiness. Ida, stood before him, a full head shorter, reminiscent of a rabbit facing a wolf. With a pronounced crack, she struck him again on the temple. The man collapsed, lifeless, to the ground. A watery film enveloped his clothes, rendering his skin dark and transparent. He began to meld with the earth, seeping in like rain. Ida's breath caught, and she bent slightly as if gathering her scattered courage.

The black pools in the eyes of the attacking hulder flashed in her mind, followed by the metallic conk of when she had hit one over the head with the thruster engine's dynamo. She had courage then; she had a fight in her.

Why was it so difficult now?

Ida shook off the memory and let out a frustrated cry, steeling herself. The distant flash of plasmic bullets pierced the camp in rapid succession. Gavin! She sprinted toward Lyle's tent, recalling a spare battery for the handgun.

She saw Gavin leading the mimics around the camp, picking them off. However, they had split, weaving between the tents, and now encircled him from all sides.

Ida plunged into the tent, grabbing the battery and forcefully ejecting the spent one. Struggling with the unfamiliar locking mechanism, Ida finally managed to click the battery into place. Bursting from the tent, she fired into the crowd. Roughly five of the entities zeroed in on her, accelerating with outstretched arms. Energised by her defiance, they lunged.

Ida's scream pierced the rain as she shot the one pinning her down, getting drenched in its inky substance. No time to regroup—other mimics were reaching for her weapon, their damp fingers scratching at her face and arms. She kept firing, her frantic shots echoing above her anguished cries.

When spent, Ida struck the pistol handle repeatedly. Around her, figures dropped, eerily still, yet not disintegrating—they were merely incapacitated. To her left, a woman dissolved into water, leaving Ida puzzled and alarmed.

A bearded man, appearing in his forties with deep hazel eyes, lunged at her. The feathered hat he wore caught her eye, a familiar garment donned daily by Captain Drackenheart. He wrenched the pistol from her hands and tossed it aside. Then he moved in and wrapped his hands around her neck.

"Ida!" Gavin swung the butt of the plasma rifle into the man's head with a deafening crack. The man crumpled, disappearing into the rain-soaked earth. Gasping and choking, Ida was blinded by her tears, the unyielding rain and a surge of terror. As she released a raw, heart-wrenching cry, Gavin pulled her up, enfolding her in a comfortable embrace.

"It's okay! We got them all," he assured. She buried her face in his chest, tears streaming.

"I want a raise, Gavin! After this is over, I want a fucking raise!"

Gavin let out a disbelieving laugh and held her tightly in his embrace.

"We need to return them to their tents. They're gonna freeze this way." He gestured towards the standing yet sleeping crew, swaying in the rain. Ida couldn't gather strength in her legs to stand, but with Gavin's assistance, she was quickly on her feet again.

Together, they herded the dazed crew back to their sleeping mats, wet as drowned rats but pliant.

"It's bizarre," Ida remarked. "They're asleep and unaware but still can walk. One can't do that unless they're sleepwalking." She prodded Creedy's arm gently. The sour-faced topman seemed oddly serene in contrast to his alert state.

"As long as those bastards don't come back, I'm not asking for miracles," Gavin said. He seized the topman by his arm and pulled him forward. "To bed with you, sir." To Gavin's surprise, the topman crawled into the tent, sprawling face-first onto his sleeping mat, plunging into deep unconsciousness.

Once everyone was sheltered, the pair stood outside, absorbing the events that had transpired. Ida inhaled sharply, her eyes finding Gavin's.

"You know the captain's hat?"

"The poor excuse of a fashion statement she's always wearing?" He blinked, as he couldn't understand how Ida thought of that after their ordeal.

"I saw a man with the same hat. The same type of feather, even."

Gavin frowned. "That's ... not impossible, but okay? I mean, it could be just another hat."

"The captain said she saw her father in the jungle."

"You have been eavesdropping again, haven't you?"

"Hell yeah, I was." Ida folded her arms.

A puzzled frown marred Gavin's features. "If the captain saw him at the other camp, and now he's here, miles away, that means that these things come back."

"And that they travel incredibly fast. I don't know why, but it seems familiar. Like the hulder clan."

"Please, don't go there." He let out a nervous laugh

Sticking up her chin and puffing out her chest, Ida smirked. "Are ye scurred, Gavin?" she teased with a mock accent and giggled when his frown urged her to drop the jesting. "Creatures of the Veil aside, what do we do about DiCroce? What do we say to the captain?"

Gavin paused as they entered their tent. "I don't know. He's gone. The captain deserves the truth."

"Then what about the sphere? Whatever took it was too fast to be human. Maybe it was trying to scare us?"

"It damn well worked, that's for sure," he muttered and massaged his trembling hands.

"What do we do the rest of the night?" She looked to him, drilling into his thoughtful frown.

"We stay awake," he said after a pause. "We find weapons, and we guard our people. It's what they would do for us. How many of those bastards did you get?"

Ida thought for a moment. "Eight or nine, I think."

"Hah! Eleven. I am a top engineer."

"That's unfair. You had a rifle. I only had a pistol!" Gavin's chuckled as he always did when he got a rise out of her, and Ida appreciated the gesture distracting her from the harrowing events that had happened moments prior. The torrential rain retreated to a soft drizzle, and the engineers brought their blankets and alchemical lamp to the central firepit, where they sat shoulder to shoulder, eyes trained on each side of the camp.

"Gavin," Ida began, wrapping the blanket tighter around her. She stared into the darkness, expecting pale faces in return. "As much as we jest about these things, it's still there... that fear that they might be back at any moment."

"Dealing with monsters is one thing," he mused, "but these things look like people. That's what makes it worse."

The rain whispered to them, promising them rest in the dream and happiness eternal if they joined them. And while uncertainty hung in the air about the return of the impostors, the foreboding allure of the night kept them vigilant, hands ever ready to grasp their weapons, until dawn painted the horizon in promising shades of orange.

CHAPTER TWENTY-THREE

ABANDONMENT

"We need to talk, Ros," Antony said as Rosanne entered the tent. She paused, holding a coffee in each hand.

"Sure." She set the mugs on the makeshift table and sat opposite him. Had something happened? The past ten minutes had seemed normal. She had slept well. He seemed to have, too, albeit he had been a bit quiet when greeting her. Now, he couldn't meet her gaze, his face sagged. Antony's look unsettled her, but she tried to shake it off, as she didn't want her emotions to get the better of her in case she jumped to conclusions.

He lifted his amber eyes from the floor, holding her with an expression she could only identify as guilt. "What do you want from me, Ros?" His tone was sharp as a whip, though without animosity. The confidence he usually carried was gone.

A lump rose in Rosanne's throat.

"What kind of question is that?" She tried to brush it off, but his hard look arrested her; it bore into her gaze, perhaps seeking validation. Confusion swirled within her. Where was this coming from?

"I want to be with you. Spend time with you and listen to your ails, your stories, your dreams. Maybe one day, we will be open for something more. We've talked of this." She smiled.

He wrung his hands and glanced towards the flap of the tent. "But why? We have no future together."

A cold, invisible hand grasped her throat. "Where is this coming from? Did I say something to upset you? Antony, talk to me." The questions spilled from her in a flood of panic.

His eyes clamped shut, and he stood. "Rosanne, we are like night and day."

"Only in our professions," she argued, growing agitated with his apparent increased apathy and withdrawing within himself. Her chest felt tight and heavy like the dream-invader had slithered into her mind and made her calm slip through her fingers like sand.

"And that is a problem. We can't fix everything by me turning blind to your past dealings."

"Once this is done, I might not even have to return to that life. This is my ticket out!"

"You are living an illusion!" he exploded. Rosanne retreated as if burnt, her eyes widening. Antony had never raised his voice like this before, but she relented in the face of his agitation.

"You said you could wait until after we are done here. You wanted proof that I was as invested in this relationship as you are."

"This whole place is wrong! I can't in good conscience ignore how you dive into the Grey Veil, knowing full and well the risks it carries!

How does any of this set your sail straight? I can't ..." his words trailed off as if searching for an excuse, his fire, his temper suddenly fizzled into nothing. "I am not strong enough to weather this storm with you, Ros." Antony lowered his head, and his fingers dug into her shoulders enough to make her grit her teeth. She wanted to cry out, tell him he was hurting her. But his words were a kick to her core, so unexpected and so painful she wanted to hurl. The skin on her face felt tight as cold dread surged through her.

Ever since their arrival on the island, she sensed a shift in him. He hadn't shared his fears or intimated to her just how much the haunting aura of the Grey Veil unsettled him.

She was in the dark.

Antony pushed her hands away with the gentleness of a feather. She raised her gaze to meet his, but Antony brushed the tent flap aside and walked out without a word.

In her stunned apathy, the scene unfolded obsessively in her mind, fixating on the nuances of Antony's words and facial expressions. She searched for that linchpin that made the dominoes fall, that word or tone which drove him away. The fault which was hers. Perhaps she had ignored the early warning signs, brushed them off in her search for answers.

Antony had always been honest with her. She had tried, right? She had been transparent with him from the beginning of this voyage. *This is wrong*, she told herself. It was too quick, too soon!

Emerging from the tent, Rosanne looked for Antony. In this god-awful rain, where could he have gone? She couldn't call out for him despite knowing the dangers. The invasive whispers, like raspy voices, clawed at the edges of her consciousness. She tried to shake them off and covered her ears.

"Captain?" Ida called from the fire pit. Adorned in oilcloth ponchos, she and Gavin had crafted an impromptu umbrella from ripped tent canvas. Ida held it over them.

"Are you alright, Captain? How do you feel?" The questions struck her as odd.

Rosanne blinked in confusion. "Did something happen?"

The engineers looked to each other in shared evident surprise.

"You don't remember?" ventured Gavin, his voice laced with disbelief.

Rosanne gave a slow shake of her head.

Ida cleared her throat. "Our camp was attacked last night. Creatures that can mimic people came with the rain and tried to take everyone into the jungle. We tried waking you, but you were all sleeping like the dead."

Words caught in Rosanne's mouth. How had she missed any of this?

"Captain ..." Ida began, wringing her hands. "Captain DiCroce went alone into the jungle."

"They got him?" Rosanne whispered, turning her panic-stricken eyes to the darkened woods.

Ida shook her head. "No, the mimics didn't touch him. He left by himself before the raid last night and even attacked us when we tried to stop him."

"He was different. As if possessed," Gavin interjected, his tone grim.

Their words threw Rosanne into more profound confusion. How could this be? She had only just spoken with Antony minutes earlier.

Did that mean his words were a product of this twisted dream? Did he let himself fall prey to the island and this mysterious entity? Rosanne's vision swam, and she gasped for breath.

Gavin supported her with two muscular arms and guided her back into the tent. Ida followed after. Rosanne rubbed her face, trying her best to steady her breathing. Calmness seemed a distant luxury.

Antony had been seduced by the whispers of the island, and the dream-invader had claimed him like it had claimed Jeffs. Rosanne, in her powerlessness, didn't know what to do. They all would have fallen prey to the mimics if it weren't for Gavin and Ida. She couldn't help Antony. He was gone. Rosanne drew a sharp breath, subduing the sob welling in her throat.

"We're leaving," she whispered.

"What about Captain DiCroce?" Ida looked to the jungle.

"The dream-invader took him," Rosanne choked out, her eyes fixed intently on the fire. Clamping her jaw shut, she suppressed the emotions surging through her and bit her lower lip raw.

"Then let's search for him in the jungle—"

"He's gone!" Rosanne near shouted, making Ida freeze and regard her with stiff expression. "Antony is ... he's just gone! We're too late to help him now. Unless the dream-invader wants to release him, we'll never find him."

"Captain ... how do you know?" Gavin asked.

Rosanne fought to her legs, knees weak from shock. "I just do. Now wake the camp. We're getting the hell out of here."

Ida and Gavin stared at each other, and Rosanne knew they could see through her false bravado. Yet, they nodded and did as told.

The crew scooped out buckets of water, trying to keep the longboats from capsizing as they journeyed west. Rosanne's hat did little to keep the rain from her face, but it masked her scowl and the tears threatening to spill the moment they were in the air. Creedy commandeered the second longboat. No one asked where Antony had disappeared to, but the Rosanne's unhinged, panicked order to evacuate the camp was all the explanation they needed. The tale came to light once they were airborne, and none scarce could believe Ida and Gavin had it not been for Rosanne's confirmation. The crew hadn't been conscious while the attack on the camp ensued, but they had been plagued with nightmares, like that first night. Rosanne's eyes glided over their weary expressions, which told all too clearly the realities of their situation. They were being hunted, and they all had almost perished.

How had Antony missed the peril in those whispers, telling him to abandon safety and reason? Rosanne gripped the leather-wrapped tiller as she guided the longboat around a bend along the beach. She scanned the coastline for that familiar sharp outcrop dotted with bare rock as depicted in the Thompson map, but so far, the island had been a beach-covered nightmare.

Ahead of them, flat woodlands with tall hills sat, covered in low-growing bushes and bare rock faces. The moss-covered sleek surfaces struck her as odd. Rosanne slowed the longboat and pointed. People peered out from under their oilcloths at what had caught her attention.

"Do those look human-made to you?" Rosanne asked. Lyle peered through his rifle scope at the smooth cut surfaces stacked over each other, now broken, crumbling or partially buried in soil.

A subtle headshake told her he didn't want to believe it even as he spoke. "Rather people than sophisticated creatures."

"Men from the stars." Gavin drew his hands in an invisible banner over his head to lighten the mood. The rest of the crew ignored his jests. Gavin shrank back, defeated.

The rain receded to a comfortable drizzle and the relentless whispers faded with it, as Rosanne neared the ruins. Steep drops on either side of the rocky hill would make an ambush impossible, making it a perfect place to set down. The crew spread around the ruins with eager chatter. Lyle's team stationed themselves around the hilltop to create a defensive perimeter, scouting the jungle for intruders. The oppressive gloom since Antony's disappearance was releasing its hold, but not by much. She shook the thought of Antony aside and tried to fight off the sting in her eyes as she focused on the work around them. She felt sick, ill in her core at the thought of what awaited him out there.

Should she have gone after him into the jungle where the mimics and monsters waited in ambush? Rosanne had been there, had met their insistent hold and will during the day. She dared not to think what they could do at night. She could only hope Antony was stronger than the mimics and braver than she was.

The temple offered a much-needed diversion in this time of need. Rosanne studied the crumbling design, so precise and clean cut compared to the wood-and-thatch houses in the North. Had people once lived inside the Grey Veil? What happened to them? Did the monsters claim them too?

She was tired of waiting, tired of being sitting ducks for the monsters. Now that they had the vantage point, she would see them coming before they could strike. She refused to leave without answers, no matter how much the monsters wanted them gone.

Rosanne stood on a ledge surveying the coastline and unfolded the map, taking in the crude copy of lead-drawn lines and distant isles. The area reminded her of nothing on the map, but for all she knew, this was one of the many secrets of the island. Let the monsters come. She consigned every last one to hell for their attacks on her and her crew.

She pivoted, assessing the aged stones, their smooth surfaces showing years of erosion and neglect. Not a single thing differentiated them from their surroundings besides that they formed a pattern as if once stacked on top of each other and then toppled.

Rosanne ran a hand over the surface, feeling the faint grooves of carvings lost to time.

Lyle crouched beside her, studying the broken pieces of a column.

"You think it was a temple? Like the ones found in south Cintecha after the colonisation?" she asked.

Lyle nodded. "The hill's pyramidical shape would suggest so. If we're lucky, the interior survived. But, Captain, look over there." He pointed west towards a set of hills. The soft arch in the landscape ran like a line between them, almost indistinguishable from the jungle as the ridge was covered in trees.

But if Rosanne squinted against the grey sky gloom, she could make out the symmetry of the dirt-covered hills. Was the ridge in between corridors or an elevated road that led from one structure to another, reclaimed by the jungle?

"Shame I didn't bring dynamite so we could crack open those tops more easily."

"You don't want to explore the structure as a whole?" Lyle asked.

Rosanne shook her head. "We're spread too thin. Better to concentrate on what we can see." She turned to the excited crew. "Listen up!

301

This might not be what we came for but we sure as hell are gonna make use of our time while we're here. Let's dig our way inside and see what we can find. Should the monsters return, we high tail out of here. Get to it!"

The crew grabbed shovels and other tools and began manoeuvring the slabs and columns. Excited despite the drenched misery they lived through, the crew set off in small teams to their assigned areas. Lyle's men kept watch while the rest dug their shovels at the edge of the fallen pillars.

Rosanne discovered a stair-like structure leading down the hill, with the remains buried under massive amounts of dirt and plant life. Thick roots snaked their way into cracks and crevices, breaking the stone apart.

She followed it in the general direction of where an entrance would likely be, but whatever pillars supported it had long since collapsed. She could envision the road cutting through the jungle in a straight line, but leading from where?

Even though this landscape wasn't a match for any depiction on Thompson's map, an inner conviction told her this was the key, or at the very least, a part of the bigger puzzle.

Rosanne paused, staring at the pile of collapsed columns. Doubt encroached like a creeping worm. What if it wasn't that island? They hadn't even found the Wandering Isles associated with Thompson's map, and yet she was certain this was the same one. There couldn't be that many others.

Could there?

Aros was ankle deep in mud and dirt, shovelling away. This temple was the first sign of anything other than complete disaster since they arrived, an irony he appreciated. The structure itself proved two things: one, someone had built it, meaning most likely people or sapient creatures; two, they deemed it important enough to raise a temple for whatever they prayed at. Temples always housed some form of treasure, be it precious stones, metals, or texts, and if Aros could pry it from the stone, he could sell it. Being here with no proper defensive perimeter besides architectural advances and Lyle's keen eyesight proved a third thing: Captain Drackenheart was clearly unravelling. She had been ever since lover boy disappeared, but it was still unclear what had happened. The crew's reaction to her orders had been interesting. Aros might not have been there long, but he recognised doubt when he saw it. People were scared and uncertain of their captain's state of mind; it was apparent in how they conversed among themselves in hushed tones instead of diving right into their given tasks.

"What do you think? Ruins or treasure?" Vincent asked, resting lazily on his shovel.

"Both?" Aros grinned with enthusiasm and tossed wet dirt into a pile.

Vincent shook his head. "There's probably monsters lurking."

"You always believe it's monsters," Aros noted.

"Eventually, I'm going to be right."

"And now the captain's neglecting our safety for her greed." Vincent nodded to Denny. "You should have had first watch on the beach, or we wouldn't have gone through this nonsense."

Aros' mouth twitched. "Oy! Don't blame me for that. Those mermaids knew their tunes and lulled me right into their trap. Plus, not many can hold their breaths and fire off a sound flare from fifty meters below the surface." He finished with a pretentious huff.

"Bullocks, I say." Denny snickered, shaking his head. But for all their teasing about Aros' botched night watch, none seemed too upset with him. Just another day in the Grey Veil, he presumed.

Aros kept his grumbling remarks to himself and stretched. "Piss break. Will be back soon."

The men waved him off, continuing their inane conversations with no interest in Aros.

He found seclusion by a fallen section on the side of the pyramid, which resembled shelving but also enough privacy to do one's business. Judging by the stench, he wasn't the first one here. Instead of doing said business, he dug through his vest's inner pocket and pulled out a folded piece of paper threatening to disintegrate in his hand. He studied the graphite copy of the Thompson map he had snatched from Rosanne's tent when she was occupied getting the camp organised. Given the disarray of their departure, she wouldn't miss this copy.

"Now, my dear Captain Drackenheart, what is it thee be hiding?" Aros muttered as he studied the map and drew from memory the coastline they had passed. He had spotted her studying this earlier, but Aros didn't find any similarities. No human-made (or troll-made) structures adorned the inky lines, and he couldn't know exactly what this mysterious Mr. Thompson had seen during his travels. Why focus on such a bland piece of land? And who was Thompson for the captain to place so much stock in the map's accuracy?

"No, 'X' marks the spot," he muttered and pursed his lips at the lines in case he missed notes or other helpful annotations. Nothing but unremarkable jungle and hill-covered landscape adorned the paper.

Sweat ran down his neck and over his chest from the midday heat. Thick fog rose from the forest in long ribbons.

Perhaps this temple was a distraction, a side trip Captain Dracken-heart deemed necessary as she probably had no clue what they were doing here. Looking to the sky, Aros was pleased to see they had plenty of daylight to burn before they had to move to a more secure location.

He met said grumpy-faced captain on his return. With her hat tipped low, her glare followed him as he passed. Aros replaced his immediate nervousness with a blank expression, or at least he tried until she arrested him with a question.

"What were you doing, Aros?" she demanded.

"I took a leak."

She shoved her hand inside his vest and withdrew the piece of paper he had studied minutes earlier. Aros mentally swore.

"Is that what this is? A gent's privy entertainment?"

"Are you spying on my most private moments too, Captain? Don't you have anything better to do?" he said and made to reach the paper, hoping to defuse the situation.

She unfolded the paper, her eyebrows pulling close together in a hard line. Her eyes turned a shade darker, her mouth twitched, and her nostrils flared. "You lying sack of shit."

Aros glanced around him, hoping they hadn't attracted too much attention. "I got curious, okay?" He raised one shoulder. "This whole trip is as mad as a cackling granny on shrooms, and I have my doubts, but not about you, but by that map's authenticity. Listen, I know we're all a bit strung from the last few days, but here's how I see it." Aros paused at her quiet contempt, teeth so firmly clenched together he thought she would pop a tooth if he didn't immediately shut his trap, which he did.

Rosanne took a tentative step closer to him, her lower stature somehow all the more menacing, like she could pronounce him dead with a single look.

Or a well-placed kick …

"This is precisely why I can't trust you or anything that you do," she forced out in a hushed tone. "What were you going to do, Aros? Huh? You think you can take over my operation like you tried on that island? You think anyone will follow your command after undermining mine?"

"That is not what's happening here!" he hissed. "You're off your rocks. I'm just looking out for myself. What is here, Cap? What are we so adamantly searching for that you would forego our safety? What is more important than our lives, than your lover boy's life?"

Rosanne's lips shut tight, but her jaw danced with movement. Aros had the sneaking suspicion he had stuck his head too far out looking for something he shouldn't have, and it wasn't treasure. The captain's expression told him if he said anything more, she would kick him off the temple headfirst. Instead, her expression softened, and a stiff smile replaced her anger. She waved the paper in front of him. "I'm confiscating this. Now get back to work, and I'll address your 'safety concerns.'"

Around them, people busied themselves with their chores, clearly having observed their spat. Had he hurt her?

A group of men tried to raise a column from a pile of rocks, pulling ropes and adding weight to the leverage jammed into the crevice. On three, the men pulled. The rock didn't budge at first, but after more pulling, it tumbled from the pile and came crashing towards Rosanne in a cacophony of splintering stone and shooting fragments. Rosanne stumbled away, landing on her back as the rock struck the ground in front of her. The cracking was followed by a rumble, and then Rosanne, who momentarily found a foothold, tumbled into the darkness as the floor collapsed beneath her.

CHAPTER TWENTY-FOUR

THE HERMIT

I n the dim morning light inside the cabin, Rosanne rested in a bed housing a familiar pine and birch scent. Shutters covered the second-floor window, and the air carried a faint hint of petrichor. Snug and warm beneath the covers, it was the first time she had dreamed of this place, with this level of detail after she left. Yet, the old log walls adorned with dried herbs and traces of heather brought a smile to her face.

"Rosanne, my love. You must wake up." Yerrik's voice soothed her.

She burrowed deeper into the covers.

"I don't want to," she murmured. She wasn't angry at this request, just savouring the peaceful moment.

"You are not safe." Yerrik settled beside her and stroked her cheek with the back of his hand. She never forgot how gentle his touch had been and how long it had lingered on her skin. Despair and a hint of helplessness clouded his green eyes, but she couldn't discern its cause.

She hadn't seen him since she left the northern island, not in her dreams or in her memories. His face had become a black hole she couldn't identify, but she remembered his voice, that low but gentle tone. Yerrik's eyes were the same as when she had flown off to save her crew's lives and livelihoods. His dark, tangled hair and the tattered sleeves of his cotton shirt, the gentle aroma of his tobacco blend filled her with melancholy. Why did she allow this dream to fill her with grief and joy, love and despair, when she was the one who had run away?

Yerrik leaned closer to her and brushed away a strand of hair from her brow.

"I'm sorry about Captain DiCroce. I know you liked him."

She screwed her eyebrows together. "How do you know about him?"

The light streaming through the shutters behind him threw his face in shadow. While Rosanne couldn't fully see his expression, Yerrik lowered his head and gave a cheerless smile. "Wherever you are now, Dragonheart, it isn't safe. You must leave."

Rosanne stirred in the bed and looked up at him. "How are you here?" she asked out of tender curiosity. She stretched out a hand to his cheek but hesitated at the last second.

"I'm always here, my love, in this very room. I've always been watching over you to keep you safe. But you need to wake up, or I won't be able to protect you for much longer. Your dreams are not your own anymore."

"My dreams?"

"If you die in your dreams, you'll never wake up."

A flash of blinding pain made Rosanne clench her eyes shut. She pawed for the sheets in the bed holding her captive, but her hands rasped over sharp rocky surfaces. She fought for air but inhaled a dusty compound which made her cough and sputter, each fit sending waves of cutting pain through her body.

"Yerrik!" she cried out, only to be met by the hollow echo of her own voice. She searched the gloom to find a single beam of light shining through a crack in the ceiling.

Rosanne lay on the floor, buried under a layer of rock and dirt. Sand and gravel fell away from her chest, and she gasped as she attempted to sit up. Burning spots radiated on her legs from the fall and the rocks which had rained down on her. She wiggled her toes, ankles, legs, fingers, and arms and concluded the pain was just that and not anything broken.

Something moist and hot ran down the side of her face, accompanied by a burning pain which prevented her from even touching it. Mixed with the dust, it left a caked clay-like texture on her skin that crackled when she grimaced. Her scraped hands and elbows stubbornly disobeyed her commands, but she could still flex her fingers. She heard muffled voices coming through the ceiling.

"Hello!" she called out in hope of the crew hearing her, but her voice came out as a croaked garble, and she coughed and hacked. With each movement sending sharp and dull pains through her, Rosanne stood. Everything in her body cracked as she slowly stretched. She let out a pained but satisfied sigh.

The raid on the camp, then Antony walking out of her life, and now this.

Screw this day in particular.

A soft rumble shook the room. Sand and pebbles rained from above, and Rosanne scurried to the wall in case of another cave-in. Until the vibrations died down, she leaned against a lower inner ceiling which circled the room on even-spaced columns. The inner structure seemed largely intact from what she could see in the dim light, save for the crumbling ceiling.

"Captain!" The muffled shout reached her, but she couldn't catch who it was. Ida perhaps, or Swanson. Both had a distinct pitch to their voices, but with tons of rock separating them, it was difficult to know who had called.

"Get me out of here!" Rosanne called hoarsely.

She caught chatter from above, and then came the message, "We need equipment to shift those boulders. We'll get the ship."

"That'll take hours!" she complained and was told to sit tight. "Hours." She huffed. "More like days."

She sat on the floor, groaning with each movement, and leaned against a column. She allowed herself in this rare instance of helplessness but safe, to think about the dream she had. When she closed her eyes, the cabin flooded her mind.

She touched her cheek where Yerrik's hand had stroked her. What mad obsession was this? Had she hit her head in the fall? Was part of her brain splattered on the ground? Rosanne scanned the spot where she had landed but found only rocks and a tiny puddle of black-crusted blood bathing in the thin beam of light overshadowed by clouds of falling dust.

She wasn't dead or brain damaged. Hopefully. Her memory of Yerrik had faded over the months, so why was he so clear to her now? Was she torturing herself with "what ifs"? Leaving him on the island had been the right choice. Rosanne couldn't believe anything else. So why did it still hurt?

In the weak light she considered the room anchored by a dozen pillars. Vines grew in every crack and crevice and the plants became alive with glowing creatures rubbing their feet or wings in a constant *bzzzrrr bz-zzrrr*.

A square opening in the floor led to the lower part of the structure, and Rosanne felt the urge to investigate further but was unsure about the building's stability and whether it had a proper light source. She looked around the room for a torch, cloth, oil ... a fire steel perhaps? No such luck. The contents in the copper braziers around the room were nothing more than ashes.

The crack in the ceiling might be large enough for a torch, though.

"Can someone send me a torch, please?" she called. An oily cloth-wrapped stick clattered to the floor, quickly followed by the clunk of the fire steel. She struck it against the torch, and the flame roared to life.

The centre of the room was adorned with a cracked pedestal, toppled to the side. She stroked a hand over the surface. A darkened stain marred the centre as if it had once housed an object of religious importance.

While the crew worked with shovels, trowels and ropes amid discordant orders, Rosanne paced the room, studying the walls, not wanting to think about Yerrik or the dream anymore.

Faded carvings decorated the surface with flecks of peeling paint. She couldn't find any letters from a language, but the pictographs told a story. The central piece on the far wall caught her attention: a flame-engulfed sphere soaring through the sky. A comet, she realised. Below, figures painted in vivid red stood with their arms uplifted, venerating the celestial spectacle. Next, the wall bore wavy lines, suggesting water. Amidst these lines tall and slender bipedal creatures with hollow eyes and long curved tails stretched their arms around the people. The pictograph lacked details pertinent to tell the story in full, but it reminded her of what Yerrik was. Depending on the person he was with, his shape altered to suit their perceptions of him, and she wasn't even sure if he had a shadow form, only what she had seen in her fever-induced dreams.

Rosanne knew more now than an hour ago, but the questions buzzed in her skull. How did the comet, these mysterious entities and the Grey Veil connect? What purpose did this creation serve?

The work quieted above, for whatever reason, but she picked up a shuffling of shoes against gravel on stone coming from somewhere close by. She jogged towards the staircase leading down and held out the torch. Perpetual darkness met her in the room below.

"Dammit," she muttered and went down. The chamber beneath had a low ceiling; fortunately for Rosanne, she was short enough for the ceiling to accommodate both her full height and the torch without issue. Farand would undoubtedly be happy to miss out on this part of the journey. The room was empty, an in-between storage perhaps, but was now bereft of everything besides tree roots burrowing through the walls.

"You cannot be here," a masculine but pitiful voice called from somewhere, his discordant words flitting around her.

Rosanne spun about with her torch leading but couldn't see anything beyond a certain radius. Such were the depths of the darkness in this temple, oppressing and invasive, as if the shadow was alive and longed to snuff out her torch. But the flames burned brighter still, and not even the softest draught disturbed it.

"W-why's that?" she asked and scanned for the owner of the voice.

"This is the temple he claimed, and you shouldn't be here. He's so angry he's screaming! Can't you hear him?" The desperation in his voice grew. Rosanne picked out the noise from the floor below her. Knowing he feared whoever this other person was more than she brought her some comfort, and Rosanne could gather what little remained of her fragile bravery. She had faced pirates. She faced Nikor. Every time a threat arose, she was reminded of that fucking island. This was nothing.

"That's a pity. We're just visiting. Any chance we can make an audience with the temple's owner?" She slipped through the doorway adorned with flaking, dotted paint. It led to a much smaller hallway with another staircase going further down into the structure.

"You've already met him," the ominous voice trailed off, followed by a soft cackle. Rosanne drew a quiet breath and pushed on.

"You say 'he.' I take it he doesn't look like giant crabs with human riders or mermaids. He's the one who invades dreams and lures my men to their deaths, am I right?"

The man didn't respond.

Rosanne licked her lips and tried again. "What about you then? How come you're here? Are there other people?"

"Gone all gone. Svartraug devoured them all." He paused to let out an unhinged cackle. "But me he spared. Me, he wanted alive." His grating voice faded into the soft rumble of the temple.

The name was unfamiliar to her, but she didn't let it sidetrack her. "You must be very special then?"

Silence. As Rosanne came upon another opening in the floor leading down, naked footprints marred the dust. A trail of screams reverberated down the hallway, making Rosanne fall to the floor in panic, listening for the fading wailing of a madman through quick, shallow breaths.

In the silence that followed, Rosanne got to thinking. *How does he navigate the temple without light? Where did he disappear to if the only way in was through the ceiling?*

Knowing she had a few hours to kill, she set after the man.

Rosanne meandered through a series of smaller rooms, heading deeper into the structure, following the stairs and dusty disturbed footprints. There was nothing inside the temple but the arranged polished stones and empty rooms. Indentations in the floor and along the walls told her they once could have been pools of water with aqueduct-like waterways, leading streams from one chamber to the next. From where or to, she didn't know. There wasn't much which told her of the temple's function.

Rosanne came to a long, dark hallway, the only way forward after passing a central dried-up pool surrounded by four pillars. The moaning wind batted at the torch's flame, uninviting as Rosanne considered the tall and narrow doorway. Mustering her courage, she slipped inside. The hallway appeared to be going on an upward slope, gradually lowering the ceiling.

A low rumbling from deep in the island's core obscured any lingering trace of the hermit's frenzied screams, but she was certain he had come this way. Dirt on the floor had been kicked aside or trampled by a bipedal with five toes, and not many of those, to her knowledge, weren't human.

She skulked, hunch-backed, up the corridor, pain coursing through her entire body. Rotten wood crumbled under her shoes as she stepped on the threshold. Whatever cover that had been used as a door had long since disappeared. A hallway of packed dirt lay beyond it. Rosanne stooped to squeeze through the tightest spots where the ceiling had collapsed, but with the light coming up ahead, she felt safe enough to abandon the torch. She pawed at the walls and grabbed for protruding roots as she slipped through a hole in the ground. Daylight blinded her as she stuck out her head, a curious sight, like seeing a mole peek out from its burrow.

Emerging outside, she found herself amidst bushes and low-growing plants. The familiar mountain range cut through the skies to the south. She stood on a hill above the jungle canopy, peering down at a colony of screaming howler monkeys.

Rosanne brushed off herself, leaving a cloud of dust which was carried off by the breeze. The hilltop was free of the violent showers now tormenting whatever poor bastards down by the beaches to her north in a misty haze. She spotted the square hill of the excavation site a good kilometre to her north. Why someone had bothered digging a tunnel from here was beyond her. She saw nothing of monumental value. No ruins to show this was an extension of the temple and its holy significance. More like holy shit-all.

The footprints had left deep impressions in the grass and soft dirt, and while it tempted Rosanne to follow the madman, perhaps she should let the rescue party know their time to shine had passed. For all she knew, the man from the temple was another mimic there to kidnap her.

She spotted an obscure outline of a hut erected between the trees and covered in wilted palm leaves. "Oh, hell no." She groaned, the familiar feeling of dread and curiosity flooding her mind with memories. While Rosanne knew she should somehow signal the rescue party, her curiosity overtook her logic. If the dream-invading creature spoke with the hermit, the svartraug as he had called it, perhaps he was close by. Rosanne was sick of being a target for monsters. Patting her belt, she found the plasma pistol remained in its holster, a knife on the other side.

With determination, Rosanne trudged through the damp forest. All around her, bizarre, feathered birds hopped around the trees or on the ground in elaborate and complex displays of dance and song. She halted, captivated by a black bird boasting a brilliant blue chest and antenna-like feathers sprouting from its head. The avian dance took place on a low-hanging perch. Undeterred by his audience, the bird shook its head back and forth, waving head feathers and seductively puffed out its chest in a flush of iridescent blue. Rosanne appreciated the bizarre display, applauding the odd-looking bird before continuing. Abandoning the dance show, she could make out a soft-treaded path. At the end of it stood a shabby hut suspended between a cluster of tree stumps to prevent it from seasonal flooding. Only one set of footprints led to a ladder by the entrance. Monsters that could turn into water didn't need shelter, did they?

Rosanne peered inside the doorless opening. The hut was made of simple materials from the forest, weaved bark for walls and flooring, and dried palm leaves for a triangular ceiling around a central pole. A pile of dried leaves made a poor excuse for a bed in one corner. An assortment of items ranging from coconut husks filled with pebbles and shells, a brown chewed-up pencil, a compass with a cracked lens, and other things littered the floor and broken shelving. A man with a scruffy mop of hair sat cross-legged on the floor in front of them and used his torn sleeve to rub a horse conch shell with the utmost care and respect. His fingers stroked over the glittering surface, his pallid face a vacant look.

"You've ventured too far," he said without turning to look at her. Rosanne straightened herself on the ladder, making her presence at least respectfully known.

"I assume that shell is precious to you?"

"To him!" The man growled, smacked his forehead twice, and took two deep breaths.

Rosanne lowered herself to the floor and sat cross-legged opposite him. "You don't seem like the others wandering the woods." As she said this, she didn't feel any less scared, given his violent outburst. Yet there was a human touch to his madness the mimics didn't have. Was he perhaps stranded here?

A look of confusion crossed his eyes and then grinned.

Rosanne didn't let it deter her. "Who is he, this svartraug?" she coaxed.

The man's grin flashed between elation and awe, then terror. "He is the night. He is twilight. He is the dream, and he is everywhere."

An image of her father's mimic in the woods flashed in her mind. If he could find her, the base camp wasn't safe. She hoped Farand had fled to find them, for Rosanne didn't know what she would do if she lost the ship again.

"What does it want with us?"

"He's calling for you like he called for me."

Rosanne struggled to gauge the man's mental state. His teeth had rotted away, and with his skin resembling a weathered canvas, he presented a stark image of shipwrecked madness. His hair was streaked with thick clusters of white, as if stress-induced, like how coal miners seemed aged compared to other people in their age groups.

"And what about the shell? It's quite beautiful," Rosanne observed, which prompted the man to clutch it even tighter.

"This is not for you!" He snarled.

She raised her hands in defence. "I'm not here for that. I'm only curious about it."

The man looked uncertain. He whipped his head to the side, searching, but Rosanne didn't hear anything besides the usual wildlife squalor.

"No. I don't want to."

Rosanne couldn't tell if he replied to her or to something else. "Answer me. Are you the one who called us to the pond? Who is this svartraug you speak of?" She got to her feet, ready to flee.

He shook his head. "Please. No more!" he cried and clutched the side of his head, his fear, at the turn of a dime, turned into giggles.

Rosanne's hesitation transformed into rage. She gripped a fistful of his shirt and shook him. "Did you take Antony? Dammit, focus and answer me!"

"He can't leave the rain, and I am too weak," The man said through gritted teeth, but didn't fight her.

In Rosanne's mind, it clicked. There was a limit to the svartraug's abilities and strength. Just like Ida confirmed, it was tied to the rain.

Rosanne leaned closer and asked in a low whisper, "Can you communicate with him? Are you talking with him right now?"

His gaze snapped to her, his pupils so small they were mere dots in an ocean of brown. He lifted an unsteady finger, blinking hard as if shaking off discomfort.

"He is the soul of this place. You must leave if you want to live," he said in a drawl.

"I have a personal errand to run, I'm afraid," Rosanne said, and was reminded of the map she kept in her breast pocket. The paper came away in the creases from excessive folding, but she chanced it anyway. With slow, clear movements, she unfolded the Thompson map and showed it to him. "Perhaps you can help me. Do you know where this is?"

With trembling hands, the man clutched the map, crumpling the paper between his fingers. "For they who are lost will be found by the dark, and those who are damned to be slaves of the dream." The hermit's eyes locked on the paper as if seeing a revelation.

"Do you know this place?" Rosanne tried and studied his reaction. His eyes darted across the lines of the coastline before, in a moment of paroxysm, he ripped the paper apart with violent abandon and tossed the pieces above him. "Nothing there! Nothing there!" he shouted before letting out another series of deranged cackling.

The paper pieces fluttered around her like sad confetti, and Rosanne applauded her past self for having copies made. The hermit's violent reaction confirmed her suspicion that there was something there. The svartraug? Or something else?

"Are you sure? If you tell me, I'll leave right now," she lied again.

The hermit pulled his face into a brown-toothed grin. "West! Far west. And south inside the mountains! You'll never see it. Only he knows how to get there."

"You sure? I got a ship that says I can travel anywhere. What is there? Something hidden?"

"The Dream," the hermit whispered before succumbing to another wave of pained moans. She retreated to give him space, his thrashing and whimpering growing by the second. "You must leave now!"

"Alright then. I guess we'll all go home." Rosanne saw no reason to argue with him further. At this point she would say anything to calm the man.

Spittle ran from his mouth, teeth clenched together so hard Rosanne feared another outburst. "Everyone will all be alright if you do. No more trees that weep the lifeblood of man. The forest will not grow today."

His words sent shivers down her back. Trees and lifeblood, like those with the red sap in the forest she had seen by ponds. "What are these trees?"

The man grabbed her by the shoulders and leaned close. Rosanne reached for her handgun but resisted pulling it out. His intense, dark eyes bore through her into her very soul. She felt queasy, straining every muscle in her body to not fight him.

"The trees see it all, and they suffer still! They weep for their kin, brethren who fall prey to the shadows and the waters. New shadows will arise, carrying the memory of man. But they are not men. More tricks to play. More lives to lead astray. People come and go, but the land prevails. Svartraug's dream is law."

Rosanne had heard enough, intending to stop his incessant ramblings.

"How about we help you return home? Or maybe you'd like to come with us on the ship? We can sail anywhere," she offered. The man shook his head back to the shell he had dropped and cradled it to his chest.

"No home! Mad Queen Mary will kill us all! Svartraug saved me, but he will not save anyone else. He will kill unless you go..." His voice trailed off as the reflective surface of the conch caught his attention, and he grew suddenly calm as if the soft-spiked item brought him comfort.

"We're going. You have my word." Through her torn lips, Rosanne offered a deceptive smile. She stood and took a few retreating steps. The hermit got to his feet as well, smiling. He then grabbed the side of his skull again.

"What is he saying?" Rosanne probed.

"He says you lie! You're not leaving. You will go to that place your father visited."

Rosanne's heart clenched in her chest. "How does he know that?"

"Your dreams reveal everything." He collapsed and gave a guttural sob while clutching his head. Rosanne took a tentative step towards the entrance, unsure how to approach the situation. The man wanted nothing to do with her or to return to civilisation, but this creature was far too invested in her hunt to her liking.

The heavy patter of rain drummed against the straw roof. The outside rumbled with the wet fanfare, and the jungle fell quiet at this rude interruption. The hermit ceased his twitchy behaviour, suddenly calm and blank-faced. His eyes whipped to hers, and Rosanne was overcome with an intense feeling of scrutiny. Icy hands grasped around her shoulders but there was nothing there. This abrupt change in demeanour made her reach for her pistol, still in its holster. She didn't want to attack him. It wasn't his fault he was trapped here with the monsters.

"He can't protect you anymore," he said with a guttural voice.

She drew the pistol, but the hermit was on her in an instant. Arms wide, he pushed her through the entrance of the hut, sending her crashing into the muddy ground with a splash and a cry. She struggled around to all four, fumbling in the waters for the glow of the plasma pistol. Another splash behind her tore her attention away from the weapon as a foot kicked violently into her side. She fell over, clutching her side. She kicked out her leg and connected with his knee, and the hermit fell over but didn't utter as much as a syllable. He rose to stand, but his knee buckled under him. He twitched his head around for the dropped plasma pistol nestled in the mud. Rosanne pushed him aside and scrambled for it, swiped it from the mud and pulled the reload mechanism. She heaved for her breath, but her eyes were fiery as she pointed the weapon.

"I will fucking end you if you get up." She coughed.

The hermit's blank expression told her nothing. She must have hurt his knee, but he showed no sign of it.

"I don't care what you do, but you leave me and my crew the hell alone, or I swear I will kill you."

His amusement turned into a wild, unhinged grin.

A series of discordant clicks sounded from nearby, making her insides coil with dread. Rosanne recognised them as the crab hybrids from the caves. "Do you control them too? Call them off." She flipped the switch on the side of the plasma gun, the positive hum barely audible through the rain. The grin widened on the hermit's face. Hybrids crashed through the foliage with shrill screams and spears raised, swarming the clearing on all sides like an army with relentless abandon. Rosanne moved before she could think and bolted into the forest.

The sound of their clacking exoskeleton and exasperated cries pursued her. A spear whistled past and lodged into the trunk next to her. She dodged to the side with a yelp and lost pace momentarily.

A hybrid crashed through the brush and stormed towards her, and Rosanne, in a moment of panic, slid into the mud and tumbled down. The creature pounced at her, pincer legs striking one after another. She fired the pistol, the bullet lodging into its barnacle-covered face. The creature howled and grabbed its melting mask. Rosanne scrambled past its legs and disappeared into the depths of the jungle.

CHAPTER TWENTY-FIVE

INSULT TO INJURY

C rossing the outer waters surrounding the island kept the *Red Queen* clear of the rain showers pouring over the jungle. The intruding voices had all but subsided in the drizzle.

At the ship's helm, Farand pondered the captain's well-being. Whatever entity occupied the island had clearly shaken Rosanne, fuelling her fervent quest to uncover the secrets within the Thompson map. She was adamant and strong-willed. And pissed.

He could get behind that.

Now he questioned if it was the right choice to leave base camp, if his choice was rooted in a rational state of mind or if he, like Rosanne, was driven by raw emotion. This land hadn't bared its mysticism and magics to him as the other island had, and he trusted Rosanne's words and worries. The people who approached them at the camp unnerved him, but were they the enemy? Their physical presence, not an assault, drove him to abandon camp. He didn't dare remain where those strange people lurked, even if they appeared passive. Crabs had been the least of their worries until they developed a taste for anti-gravity dust. Farand knew he would find the captain as long as he followed the coastline.

Off the island's outer lip to their north, inky clouds rolled in from the Grey Veil. Thunderous booms tore through them, thrown back by the mountains accentuating the storm's impressive rumble, which wasn't touching the island, as far as Farand could tell. The Grey Veil had many inexplicable weather phenomena. This was a nightmare meteorologists took to see their physician.

The storm headed west in slow waves, each cloud darker and more virulent than the last one. New forming clouds sparked with streaks of blue and purple lightning, showcasing a weather pattern Farand had neither encountered nor heard of before. The booms turned to thunder, whistling crackles cut through the air. The light unfolded like an umbrella around the clouds, there one second gone the next before the cycle repeated.

A wet, throaty growl resonated from within. Farand wiped rain off his brow and picked up the intercom. "Olivier, do you see anything in the storm?"

"Negative, brother. Storm looks local, maybe a kilometre wide," the youth said, his lisp obscured by the sudden crackling of the intercom. Farand gave it a couple of hard raps in the palm of his hand. The device fell quiet. He scanned the instrument panel, the compass spinning and the topographical map dancing with static that had been working moments earlier.

Wind tunnels of varying temperatures wove through the Grey Veil at different speeds, which they had learned through sudden temperature changes resulting in frostbite and blue lips. He would have asked Ida if her invention could scan the storm and provide any information.

A deep cetacean-like call, as if from a whale, tore through the storm, reverberating the waters below them with ripples of movement. Farand covered one ear in pained reflex, hugging the wheel so as not to lose his grip. It was the same call they had picked up below the island, close and invasive. Farand shook off the uncomfortable feeling.

The intercom crackled to life with incoherent, panicked muffles, followed by Olivier's high-pitched scream from the crow's nest. He stabbed a finger at the clouds.

At the storm's periphery, giant uniform tentacles curled over the lip of the island's ledge. They stretched several hundred meters, some bearing bony hooks and others unadorned, bare but curling. They bore into the waters, anchoring themselves as if to gain perch. From the blackened clouds and crackles of lightning emerged a massive transparent bulbous head, its tentacles converging below it. Cephalopod eyes spun inside its head, every organ laid bare under thick see-through skin. The creature appeared to be floating in the air, as if in water, its massive head upholding itself somehow. Hooked tentacles dragged the rest of its body closer to the flying ship in long terrifying strides.

Farand cocked his head back, mouth agape and paralysed at the incredible size of what he could only describe as a creature birthed between jellyfish and squid; his mind filled with legendary Novalian tales of the Kraken.

"Duplànte!" Dalia screamed from the main deck. "What do we do?"

Farand assessed the speed at which they were travelling, the direction, and the creature's incredible size and how fast it beelined for them. He had maybe less than ten seconds to act before tentacles ensnared them.

Farand spun the wheel, turning the bow towards land. Tentacles bore over them, throwing the *Red Queen* into shadow. They were going too fast for him to turn clear of the limbs in one move, lest he throw them all over and send the ship spinning. The tentacle chopped past the stern-castle by a hairbreadth and crashed into the waters below. A massive salt-water spray shot up beside them. Another tentacle curled up around the keel from below.

Hard-faced and grounding his teeth, Farand arrested his breath as the tentacle snaked around the *Red Queen*. He pulled the wheel towards him, sending the vessel on a sharp incline mid-turn. Dalia clambered to the main mast, clutching her safety harness in her hand; they couldn't afford a moment's delay. She just had to hold on.

Farand ground his teeth as he kept the *Red Queen* at a steep ascent and turned towards land. He could buy time if they crossed the mountain chain, and perhaps they could disappear into the jungle on the other side or hide below the island. The creature dragged itself over the waters, released its hooks, and floated in pursuit.

Farand's heart beat so hard in his chest he struggled to breathe, fought to keep his mind focused on the task at hand, and—*Sweet Terra, it's coming closer!*

The skeleton crew poured onto the deck, alert and ready.

"All hands to the cannons and aim for the eyes!" Farand hollered. Dalia abandoned the safety harness and ducked to the gundeck with Olivier on her heels. Farand gunned for the mountains as fast as the thruster engine allowed him. The instrument panel light bulbs glowed orange in warning, but he couldn't slow down for even a second. Yellowed hooks bore down on each side of them, splashing into the waters and sending giant fountain sprays all around them. The Kraken reached out, too slow with its massive tentacles as the ship slipped through its grasp, but then continued in a feat of impossible speed relative to its size, floated over them, casting shadows as it pulled itself in front of them and turned. It snapped its serrated beak at them.

Farand spun the wheel, turning the ship starboard. Seconds later, cannon shots boomed from the gun deck. Cannonballs bounced against the Kraken's bulbous head, its tough skin and gelatinous interior shielding it from the pellets of metal. The creature's eyes peeled, its focus entirely on them, and extended barbed tentacles in a slow, hungry reach.

A curious organ perched on the Kraken's zenith shaped like a tuning fork let out a warbling tone, reverberating the waters, cutting through the rain with massive force. The noise bore down on them with enough force to make Farand keel over with a pained howl. The assault lasted mere seconds, but Farand felt like he was about to throw up, his mind spinning, his ears ringing, and his knees weak.

With all his might, Farand wrenched the wheel down, the bowsprit pointing towards the waters. The thruster panel didn't have the angle required for this type of flying, and Farand could only watch helplessly as the tentacles swiped at them. A hook caught the crow's nest of the main mast, reducing it to splinters. The impact shook the ship, tossing its crew about and forcing them to clamber to safety. Farand clambered against the wheel. The crow's nest smashed against the main deck and came away in pieces.

Another wave of shots fired from the gun deck, discordant with the Kraken's hungry outcry. The shots connected with the hard beak in a series of clangs, and the monster snapped its mouth shut and retracted two of its arms, swiping at its mouth.

Farand used this momentary distraction to fly over it. Massive eyes followed them and reached out with a half-hearted swipe, which didn't even come close to changing the ship's course.

Farand broke out in hot flashes of sweat, and his vision swam before him. The mountains ahead became a blurry smear. *The atmos!* His mind cried. They were pushing their speed beyond their technology's limit. Only a little further, Farand told himself and shook his head. They were so close now! Behind them, the Kraken pushed itself off from the waters, floating towards them with outstretched tentacles.

Farand couldn't give up now, even as his heart fluttered in his chest and a sour, cold sensation invaded his limbs. Black spots danced across his vision, but he steeled his focus and clenched his thighs to keep his blood pumping.

The world swooned around him like an image-spinning inside a vignette. He drew laboured breaths, wobbling on his feet. He had to protect the ship and find the captain. She could save them from this monstrosity. She knew what to do. She could … save …

It was another few hours before the expedition team at the ruins cleared enough rubble for anyone to poke their heads through and peer inside. With the unstable ceiling, they placed Ida, the lightest person, in a harness. *How typical*, she grumbled as they lowered her enough to scan the room.

"Captain?" she called, but there was no answer or trace of Rosanne. Scant beams of daylight filtered through the opening, and Ida struggled to see even an outline of the room. "She's not here!" Ida called to the team above. The collapse had created a chute of rocky debris they didn't dare set foot on. Removing it had been a nightmarish game of stack, a slow and painstaking task involving many calloused hands and torn ropes.

"I think she's investigating the structure!" Ida groaned from the pressure of the harness around her chest. She pushed herself up from the rock and flipped around. "Bring me up!" She called and felt the tug as she bounced upwards. The rope snagged. She swung to the side and let out a cry as she crashed into the side of a crumbled column.

"Watch it!" A drizzle of pellets began as the larger rock formations crackled where sand and earth gave away.

Ida hung from the harness, covering her head from the rock barrage. When the noise subsided, she stared into a large opening and the pile of collapsed debris upon it. The room held the weight.

"Praise ancient architects and their sturdy buildings." She clutched the rope. "Lower me down!"

Ida carefully navigated the jagged descent into the room, her path illuminated by her hand-held alchemical light. Placing the canister on the ground, she swiftly freed herself from the harness and sent it up to the anxious crew.

Creedy came down next, the watch captain far more dexterous and skilled with such things. "Seen the captain?" he asked.

Ida shook her head. "I'm guessing she's investigating the other rooms, although with the cave-in, she might lay low somewhere. There are boot prints leading down those stairs." She waved the light towards the square cut opening in the floor where the dusty floor had been disturbed.

The light swished past red-painted markings on the wall that snagged her attention.

"Oy, Captain!" Creedy hollered at the top of his lungs down the hole, throwing Ida into a defensive ball on the floor.

"A warning next time!" she cried.

"Scaredy cat," the older man snickered.

Gavin came up behind her, having just freed himself from the harness. "Anything interesting?"

"Aside from Creedy's incredible lung capacity, we found pictograms of people. Maybe the ones who built this structure!" The two engineers marvelled over the artwork. "How old do you think it is?"

"I'm no archaeologist, but I think at least a few years older than Higgs." Gavin rubbed a finger against the flaking paint, which left a red smear with the sweat on his hands.

"Hilarious, short stuff," Creedy joined them after circling the room for anything of interest.

Swinging her lamp to the left, she followed the trail of painted people. A sudden grip on her arm made her halt—Gavin, his face drained of colour, pointed to a specific section of the wall.

"What is that?" Ida squinted at the black-painted, limber humanoids towering over the other people.

Gavin swallowed. "Could it be the creature the captain met on the other island? I'd rather eat Hammond's pickled herring than see that thing again. When it came aboard the boat..." Gavin wiped the sweat from his forehead. "Yeah, no thank you."

Doubt crossed her face and she pursed her lips. "This one's painted differently, though, and in a different context. It's probably another creature altogether."

Hunching slightly over, Creedy lifted Ida's lamp higher on the pictogram. "You kids familiar with svartraugr, or svartraug for those who can't master the Bunnsboroux dialect?"

Ida and Gavin looked at each other.

"I've heard stories but never seen it depicted anywhere. Even less in an abandoned temple in the middle of the jungle," Ida said.

Gavin fidgeted, his fingers brushing the pouch hanging from his belt. "I heard it was the spirit of a drowned man who haunts the shore."

Creedy shook his head. "That's the watered-down Queensland version. Svartraug are creatures that take the form of people who drown at sea. Where I'm from, it's said they can walk on land when it rains and lure you to rivers and lakes, even the sea. If one is close by it can invade your dreams and make you see things that aren't there. Other versions are that of an evil water spirit who can take on the shapes of its deceased victims. Nothing like luring people with images of their lost loved ones. Then there are others that live the high life in castles and protect their riches from grubby grave robbers." Creedy lifted the light closer to his face, throwing his temples in darkness as he drilled into Gavin with a piercing stare.

"That's demented," Gavin said, audibly swallowing. "They're just … stories." There was a quiver to his voice, one Ida hadn't heard since Gavin was a young teenager.

Creedy's expression was a calm ocean of weathered lines as his grey eyes glided over the painted figures. "Could be. Many years ago, near Bunnsboroux, a flood wiped out all the fishing villages. The entire coastline was washed away in a single night. No one could set foot there for years, but people came back nonetheless. They say they saw drowned men walk the shores. Can't say I've ever seen one myself, but there are traces of the stories painted in the caves on the coastline as a warning to never fish alone and always light a fire.

"How do you think it ended up here, of all places?" Ida asked.

"I don't think it ended up here as much as I think it might have come from here," Gavin said. "What if the svartraug themselves made those paintings? What if they can leave the Grey Veil and settle among normal people?"

Ida's eyes were thin as slits as to how exasperated this comment made her. "Your need for dramatics is fuelled by your fear of the supernatural, as always." Ida shook her head.

"How can you tell me I'm being dramatic when we don't know a lick about these things or what creatures live in the Grey Veil?"

"Because you usually are?"

A pause.

"Fair point, but I'm telling you, it's too coincidental."

"I think you just enjoy the attention," Creedy said.

Gavin blew his cheeks out in protest but quickly composed himself. "That is beside the point. My mum told similar stories of men coming with the rain and that light would keep them off. She was obsessed with them to the point she brought quartz crystals whenever we had to sleep on the road between towns. Said they would protect us."

A suppressed snort escaped Ida. "You sure she didn't just say that to keep you from sneaking out?"

Gavin's pursed his lips and bobbed his head. "That too. But the woman was paranoid and raved about it until she died. Besides, we never went outside when it rained. As a kid, I always thought I heard whispers from the rainforest. No one was allowed to go in there alone. We just called them spirits, but I suppose they could be similar to Creedy's svartraug."

Ida recalled a sliver of information she had picked up in her time with Gavin, and an amused grin spread on her lips.

"Is that why you carry around quartz in your pouch?" She held up the lamp in front of his face.

"No?" He turned away.

Ida bit her lip to prevent her laughter from escaping.

"Shall we look for the captain? She's waited a long time already." Creedy's sour tone penetrated the awkward denial Gavin feigned, and the youth nodded profusely to steer clear of Ida's smugness.

They followed the dusty footprints Rosanne had left behind. Gavin shone his light all around them, the columns, the walls. "You would think that a temple would be decorated. Besides the wall carvings and paintings, there's nothing here."

"Looks like aqueducts," Ida squatted next to the depression in the laid bricks running around the room. She uncorked her waterskin and poured a generous amount of water on it. It trickled into a hole by the end of the wall and disappeared out of sight.

Gavin raised an eyebrow. "What was that for?"

"Architectural science. I wanna see where it leads."

"You kids done yet?" Creedy said impatiently.

Ida waved him off. "I am just appreciating the hidden culture that exists on this island before it is all gone. Nothing lasts forever."

"A man can dream. This is all there is to it. I'm sick as hell of monsters, the Veil, the whole damn thing." Creedy spat.

"I bet the creatures are sick of us waltzing in here like we own the place, Creedy. It's a matter of perspective."

Gavin ignored them both. "This place is amazing. Can you imagine who built it?"

"Humans, preferably," Creedy said.

They came upon another empty room where Ida spotted a trickle of water meandering the room. "Hey, it's my water from earlier." She watched the trickle moisten the carved rocks until it ran dry. A stony overhang lined the ceiling above the pool, and the sconces for torches were placed far higher than necessary. "It almost looks like the temple once collected rainwater in these pools. What do you think they were for?"

"An elaborate bathhouse? Sacrificial blood pools?"

"You and your sacrificial altars." Ida chuckled. "Whatever it was for, it's not that anymore. Hey Gavin, stand with the lamp in the corner over there. Creedy take the other."

"Whatever for?" the topman questioned.

"Something I'm seeing."

When the men took their respective corners and pointed their lights at the same height as the sconces, the columns supporting the ceiling threw overlapping shadows in a pathway leading to the four pools and mid pool the room occupied.

"Creedy, remember what you said about the svartraug being afraid of the light?"

Creedy's face screwed up. "I see what you're getting at. The shadows form a pathway to that door over there."

Ida peered inside. The entrance was scarcely broad enough for her shoulders, yet it towered in height. "Meant for something tall and slender."

"Looks like we found Creedy's bathhouse." Gavin snickered.

"Oy!" The watch captain whacked Gavin on the back of his head.

Ida raised the light in Gavin's face. "You scared?"

"I was thinking of that creature we saw depicted on the wall upstairs and the fact that the captain isn't here. What if the creature took the captain?"

Ida let the light glide over the footprints in the dust. "Looks to me like she followed someone of her own accord, but not blindly. She backtracks over there, like she was searching around. Doesn't look like a possession to me."

"Do we follow?" Gavin asked as he rubbed the back of his head where Creedy had struck him.

"Ladies first," Creedy held out a suggesting hand and a mocking bow. Ida stuck out her chin and straightened her lamp in front of her. A loud rumble tore through the structure. The floor shook. Gavin dove for the nearest column and clambered on. Creedy pushed Ida away from a falling rock from the ceiling. She hit the floor and bounced back with a terrified cry. The floor sunk underneath her, and the blocks came apart one by one. Ida scrambled for the still-attached rocks but couldn't gain purchase. Roots revealed themselves among the falling rocks, and Ida grabbed one, which tore, then reached for another, which held fast. She screamed as the world collapsed around her. The root sagged and snapped, and Ida fell into the darkness.

CHAPTER TWENTY-SIX

SVARTRAUG

Antony knelt before a jagged black boulder, his palms raised in an ethereal gesture of prayer he couldn't recall beginning. He came to himself half-dressed, feet bare and bloodied, and with twigs and leaves stuck in his clothes as if he trudged through the jungle without thought or care.

The hot, damp air quickened his shallow breathing and accentuated that cold, dreaded realisation that he had been called by the dream-invading creature. Antony stared at his hands, feeling the betrayal within himself and how it isolated him from his sanity.

His conflicted thoughts clamoured with such violence he banged a fist into his chest to ground him. He didn't recognise himself, his actions, or even his thoughts. Why was he here?

Steadying himself, Antony stood. Dull, burning scrapes covered his knees and arms. A gash on his lip confused him even more. Had he gotten into a fight?

The last time he blacked out, he awoke by a pond in the jungle. This time, he was in a cave surrounded by luminous plants and a boulder so porous and brittle it appeared it would fall apart from the slightest touch. Yet its central placement spoke of reverence, and Antony almost forgot the predicament that he was in as he circled the rock to discern its purpose.

He searched his memories, the thin filaments of distant dreams fleeing his grasp. He found no images, only a sensation, a deep sadness as if he'd hurt someone. He couldn't remember who or why. Was this another trick?

Antony buried his face in his hands and roared into them. His voice resounded against the stony surfaces around him. Something stirred within a depression by the wall, pulling him out of his momentary misery. In the soft glow of alien plant life, he saw something long-limbed covered in a grimy substance of volcanic ash. A sharp-featured humanoid female lay curled up as if asleep. Her chest fell and rose in gentle waves. He approached the basin and, with curious tentative care, felt the thick substance between his fingers. It was unfamiliar and he couldn't make sense of its composition other than its colour.

Antony reached out a hand to wake the woman but stopped himself when he spotted an elongated growth on her lower back—a tail! He withdrew, suddenly aware of the chamber he was in. He scanned the room for other creatures, spotting a clay-covered face in the wall connected to the torso of a man. It seamlessly transitioned into a hard-shelled body with outstretched, spindly legs pressed flat against the wall. *Another hybrid*, he realized with dread. The more he looked, the more creatures he saw, all in different shapes and sizes, but all with the same humanoid part of them mixed with something horrifying.

Antony backed away, stemming his breaths as if any noise he might produce would wake the creatures from their slumber. They were all around him, and he was alone.

Branching out from the room were chambers upon chambers filled with slumbering creatures. The creature in the wall yawned, the arms pawing far too close to him. Antony recoiled and caught himself on the central boulder.

A sharp pain shot through his skull, arresting his movements. Images and colours in a muddled, oily artscape bombarded his mind. Distant whispers and far closer cackles reminded him he was prey caught in a trap. He could feel his body but only vaguely. The thoughts ran faster than his mind could comprehend. He searched for his body, felt for his hand connected with the stone and threw himself to the ground as his mind burned, face contorted from the pain. The headache remained, but the images subsided with his resting heart rate. What in the hells was that?

Creatures stirred around him. The female in the basin opened her eyes, connected with his and gleamed with predatory shock. Antony backed away, hurriedly searching the chambers for an exit. Arms reached out to him as the creatures roused one after the other. Their movements were lethargic, yet they seemed determined, heightening Antony's panic. His head spun from the intrusive images. He felt asleep when he was awake, trapped in a nightmare.

The woman swished her naked tail, the fuzzy tassel at its end splattering clay on the floor.

She tackled him, her powerful grip like talons digging into his shoulders and her eyes captivating, if not petrifying. Antony froze under her piercing gaze.

She opened her mouth and weaved a melody which tore into his mind. Antony let out a cry to counter it. She paused, but not from his defiance. She stared behind him, her hands on his shoulders trembling. Without breaking her stare, she scurried off Antony and crawled back to her pod, peering above the edge with fright.

He picked up a rhythmic heavy patter closing in behind him and scrambled to his feet. A dripping, black, broad body with squat legs and no visible joints for feet entered the chamber. Its almost neck-less head sat atop rounded shoulders, staring down at him with empty eye sockets. Antony's legs buckled under him, but even as he fell to the ground, his eyes remained locked on the creature. Its half-droopy ears rose and flattened behind its head as the creature licked a broad tongue around a toothless mouth.

The inky-black monster gripped Antony by his vest and dragged the shouting man into a side chamber. As they passed, creatures in their pods stirred but quickly fell back into rest, unbothered by the commotion. Antony pawed for hold, grasping at the side of a basin and tore open his hand on the porous rock. The creature tugged him free, and Antony turned, digging his fingers into the soft flesh of its arm, but found no purchase as they sank through.

A low, rumbling laughter escaped the monster's mouth as it threw Antony against the wall. Air and senses knocked out of him, he swayed, his head pounding from the shock. For a stunned moment, he watched as the creature tore into a pod, digging through the soft clay and extracting what he could only believe was a mermaid. It tossed her to the floor with a wet thud. Her eyes fluttered as she opened her mouth, gasping for breath, growing more agitated by the second. She twitched and thrashed her tail, searching for something, an escape perhaps.

Antony's vision faded in and out of clarity as he watched the mermaid claw herself across the floor in a wild panic. Her shrill screams echoed in the room as she desperately tried to flee the larger monster stalking after her. The creature lifted its massive foot and stomped her right on the spine—a crack tore through the room. The mermaid lay still with a vacant look in her eyes, arms limp out before her. The monster turned its attention to Antony. He wanted to move; he wanted to run, but his body did not obey his desperation.

His arms and legs were cold and numb, his shoulder a throbbing mess, and his heart all but skipped half the beats. Antony could only watch as the monster lifted him by his vest and into the pod, pushing him below the surface of black mud. The cold mud ran over his cheeks, over his gasping lips, and over his eyes. Antony thrashed against the heavy substance, but its cold grasp sucked him in and threw his world into darkness.

CHAPTER TWENTY-SEVEN

THOMPSON'S MAP

Rosanne's mad dash through the jungle brought with her torrents of destruction as the hybrids knocked aside anything in their way in pursuit. Their frustrated clacking calls at her back urged her on, but Rosanne wasn't sure she could keep this up much longer.

Her knees wobbled with each step, and she grasped a nearby tree trunk for support. Hearing discordant stomps from the bush closing in and nowhere to flee, she took refuge beneath the exposed root system of a tree. She pushed leaves and roots in front of her to cover her exit. The hole was barely large enough for her to sit with her knees bundled up against her chest, and the tight space intensified her breathlessness. She leaned against the dirt and focused on calming her breathing. The hybrid's clacking footfalls passed her hiding spot less than a stone's throw away. The humanoid issued *click-click-click* orders to its horrid friends. Through the thickness of the root system, Rosanne spotted it as it turned around, leading the monstrous shell it straddled around. Its body was a bizarre fusion of two beings borne out of a mad scientist's laboratory.

She studied them in her exhaustion. They differed, from the varying colours of their shells to where the body fused with the chiton. Some had almost their entire human body intact, feet dangling in the front and fused by the pelvis to the top shell. Others had mere remnants of a torso, arms and faces marred by barnacles and scars.

Another two hybrids joined, fanning across the area and searching the ground for clues. A third lumbered in. The human body was fused, chest-first to the shell, as if he was lying on his stomach, head hanging free at the front. Its contorted face clacked broken teeth in rhythmic commands. Rosanne was too exhausted to let fear drive her motivation to escape. These were not Nikor. These creatures could neither haunt her nightmares like that swamp monster nor infiltrate her mind. They were made of flesh and shells, tangible beings that could bleed and expire just like her. She knew the monsters' weakness, but the sheer size and number made her reconsider a fight.

All Rosanne had to do was stay hidden until the danger had passed. Her eyes fluttered closed as a great heaviness sank over her. She couldn't believe she could doze off while monsters searched for her. Her messy curls clung to her neck, and mud covered her traveller's vest, which had frayed at the shoulder. Would the monsters catch her in here? When was the last time she slept uninterrupted by nightmares?

Resonating booms in the distance shook the ground and startled Rosanne to attention. She blinked in panic, adrenaline surging through her body once again. The monsters were after her! But something was off. Sleep crusted the corners of her eyes as if she'd been out for hours. She was sure it had only lasted a moment, but the sun had glided closer to the horizon, throwing her burrow in orange hues.

The forest was a bustle of activity but nothing that seemed hostile. Except for the arm-long centipede crawling by Rosanne's feet, which induced from her a paroxysmic, uncontrollable scream. She lunged out of the hole, frantically patting herself. Her limbs twitched, and she searched the ground for the multi-legged terror, twitching as if it was still on her and hoping to shake it. The centipede scurried into a nearby bush.

Heaving for breath to calm her racing heart, the pain from her locked knees set in and subdued her panic to painful whimpers. She curled over with a slow-arched dramatic thud as she fought to stay balanced but resigned herself to a muddy fate, where she propped herself up on her elbows and felt sorry for herself.

Wherever the crab creatures were, they weren't around to take advantage of the demon of the sky's mud-stained and lock-kneed fall from grace. The pain gradually subsided, but defeat and shame remained.

Rosanne trudged to the nearest hill, seeking answers to how monumentally screwed she was. The crew must have searched for her when they didn't find her in the temple. Had she been the one to hear the shots earlier, she undoubtedly would have investigated it. On the flipside, trying to find her was a terrible idea. She should have stayed in the temple.

How did she always end up lost and alone or in terrible company? Why did she keep prodding the hornet's nest that was the Grey Veil when this was the result? Next time, she would remain on the ship, and Farand could play the explorer.

The uphill trek was a laborious affair where she got stuck in roots, tripped in mammal-dug holes, or snagged by anything sticking out from a tree.

Oh, how she longed for a hot bath and a glass of Cintechan '86 Smoked Oak and Anise whisky, her favourite pastime with Antony back in Valo. *Antony*. How could he desert them in the middle of their expedition? Was the dream-invader to blame? Or was Antony not the person she thought he was? She still couldn't understand it, the logic incomprehensible. This place had changed him. It had changed *her*! In a place of insanity, how could anyone expect to carry that burden? She looked at her own hands, clenching them into fists and opening them. Why hadn't he been stronger? Why wasn't she more understanding?

Maybe she was just upset because he had abandoned her when she needed him the most.

Flashes of Yerrik sitting by her bedside came to her. He had whispered soothing words when the nightmares from Nikor's poison tore through her. Yerrik wielded his magic to ease her discomfort, to give her precious moments of peace to recuperate. At the time, Rosanne thought it was brainwashing, but when she examined the memories of those dreams, she couldn't see the malice.

That is until she murdered Aros by burning him on a pyre.

Nausea washed over her, and her cheeks reddened with shame as she remembered how in the dream, she had sacrificed Aros for selfish reasons. With him out of the way, his crew was less likely to attempt a coup, but Rosanne knew that wasn't the true reason. It was her need to regain control in a world where she had none, a stupid moment of illusionary clarity when she was drowning in a bog of desperation and longed to feel sane and empowered, yearning for sanity and authority. But that wasn't quite it either.

Rage.

Pure rage over how her life had steered her decision that night. Every time she looked upon Aros' stupid face, it reminded her of that disastrous voyage, and she blamed him for it time and time again.

Yerrik, however, never blamed her for her poor choices. He offered solace when she couldn't find any, strengthened her fragile mentality broken by the event she was sure had killed Lyle. Rosanne had never felt as vulnerable as when Nikor dragged her and Lyle into the marsh. Over and over, the cold, dead hand of the drowned creature pulled her into the depths. Yerrik had given her everything she needed, and she squandered it on petty vengeance instead of moving on.

Her insides curled. She was a despicable person bereft of sympathy. Who could love a being with a cold heart like hers?

Soft whispers pulled at this thought, her self-doubt, agreeing with them. Rosanne rested on a bare rock, her chest heavy and her eyes raw and stinging.

The hill was taller than it led on from the ground, so besides a beautiful panoramic view, she was also graced with chest pain from the laborious hike.

As she studied the arching coastline, eyes settling on a rocky outcrop, an incredulous jolt tore through her. She stood, tracing the coastline with a shaky finger, when the realisation struck; she patted her vest and searched the inside of her pockets for the folded piece of paper, brown with mud water.

Rosanne compared the map to the arching coastline. In the distance, she spotted three floating islands that bumped into the ledge of the land. She inhaled sharply and whirled around, searching for what the map was leading her to.

The mountains rested to her south, but on the surrounding the hilltop there was absolutely nothing but thick jungle.

Her eyes stung, and distorted wet blobs reduced the forest into a mush of green. "I don't understand. It's here. It's right here. But there isn't ..."

She scanned for anything close to an artificial structure, another ship, or even a clearing in the jungle. How were the islands here when they could float off and circle the island? The timing was uncanny. Where was the logic to this hellscape?

"There's nothing here!" She tore into her hair, fingers scraping her scalp as if she could dig out the answers she sought. Where was the goal of her father's promise? Had she endured the Grey Veil, all the planning and the charting, losing crew, sanity, and even her love, for absolutely nothing but monsters and this accursed jungle?

What use had her journey been? Why would her father commission the map if there was nothing there? The isles must be the key! A strange, wrenched grin crossed her lips as she examined the map once again. She patted the map on the ground, smoothing out the violent creases, and searched the pencil marks with shaky hands.

It must be here! her mind screamed. *It couldn't have been all for nothing!* The temple was to her east. It should have been depicted on the map. If she could see it from the longboat, indeed anyone else could if they approached from the coastline. But there was nothing. No temple. No structures. No X marks the spot.

She collapsed to the ground, her voice a hoarse call. Birds took off in panic at her outburst.

"Your cries are like songs to the Veil," the hermit said to her. She didn't jolt or reach for her weapon, as it came as no surprise he found her with the ruckus she made. Every creature on this island always seemed to find them no matter how they travelled. She was done.

"Fuck off. No one asked you."

Her acidic reply prompted a chuckle from the hermit. He reeked of old sweat and grime, but her blocked nose spared her the worst of it. He moved in front of her and lowered himself to her level; his smile remained on his lips. "Your voice ... the Veil loves it. It resonates with it."

Rosanne's steel gaze shifted from the horizon to his excited gleam. "Whatever games you're playing at, I'm done. Leave me be."

"The heart is calling for you."

"The only thing calling for me is my insanity." She looked up. "This place is cursed, and you've been driven mad by its abnormality." Her spiteful grin didn't deter him in the least. If anything, he appeared happy to observe her contempt.

"It rarely happens, but on sunny days like this." The hermit drew in a deep, refreshing breath, closing his eyes to the golden rays kissing his weather-wrinkled skin. "I feel liberated. My head is quiet, and I can roam free of the svartraug's possession. I don't have to fight him for control."

Rosanne let out a hollow laugh. "So, what you're saying is that you gain reprieve on the whims of the weather?"

"Yes! You understand," The hermit agreed. The distant voice of Yerrik called in her mind, or she thought it did. A flash of their time together passed in a blur. The dreams where she heard his voice always happened when she was in immediate danger. The hermit's words made sense. And then it hit her.

"How did you find me this quickly? I reached the top no more than ten minutes ago."

The hermit trudged to the edge, pointed down the hill and beckoned her to follow. Without a question, she followed him to a hole in the ground and faint traces of a stone staircase.

"The tunnels run through the entire island. They did not build it for the shadow men but for us who serve them," he said. Rosanne's mind raced back to the peculiar murals and oddly shaped hallways in the temple. Some doors were high and thin, others barely high enough for her and the torch she had carried.

"There's more of you out there?"

"Not of me, no. This place was dead when I got here. There are helpers. You have seen them. Most don't have awareness like the svartraug and were born out of his will."

"Where does this lead?"

"To the heart!"

"And what is the heart? Why do I need to see it?"

"Because you can stop the svartraug's hold over the heart's dream. He will devour no more." He grinned before heading into a room.

This gave Rosanne pause. If the svartraug and the hermit occupied the same body, why would the hermit lead her to the heart? It seemed to oppose the svartraug's wishes for them to stay away. She thought of the map and the scale on which it was drawn. She could find the hill she perched on down in the far clusters of trees that dominated the surrounding region of that same area. Did he purposefully keep the location at the edge to throw people off?

"Fine then. Take me to the heart."

The hermit led them down a crumbling staircase. Rosanne was sick of traversing the island with no clue where she was going, and the narrow hallways didn't ease her discomfort. If the hermit was true to his words, this would hopefully give her some answers, in one form or another.

The hermit turned to her when she fell behind, and he waved to usher her forward.

They emerged into a tall, square cut room with four pillars and a central pool. "We can use this to travel. Best way to get around. Quick and easy. Faster than by boat." He cackled and stepped into the pool, which reached to his mid-waist. Rosanne arched an eyebrow.

"The pools are connected, you see. Come, I'll show you!" He waved her over.

Dark stone lined the bottom, obscuring its actual depth. In her periphery, Rosanne noticed small channels with rainwater trickling below the ceiling, cutting through central stone carved beams running into a pool held up by four pillars. Small sluice gates enabled the water's descent into the central pool. At the previous temple, she recalled the similar basins, albeit dried up and appearing to have no function.

Rosanne stared at the black, endless waters. It created an unsettling knot in her stomach, the same feeling she got when she stared into the pond in the forest.

Already grimed down from her jungle adventures, Rosanne forewent removing her disgusting clothes and stepped into the pool. The lukewarm water seeped into her shoes. With a wiggle of her toes, she braced herself for her shoes' sogginess. Better to get it over with.

The hermit reached out a hand. Rosanne checked her grimace before it could form and took his dirty and calloused hand.

"Now we go under the surface."

He seemed deranged, yet perhaps so was she for following his lead. Taking a deep breath, she felt the hermit drag her along underneath the surface. The floor disappeared under her feet, and a current caught hold of her. In surprise, her grip on the hermit's hand loosened, but he caught her with his free arm and pulled her up.

She broke the surface with a gasp, treading water to stay afloat. The room was dark, the pillars gone, the pool replaced with a cavernous lake.

The hermit swam for the bank, leaving a trail of echoing giggles in his wake.

With both feet planted on the floor, Rosanne stared at the lake she didn't recognise. The rocky surface amplified the soft rumble passing through at regular intervals as if the mountain breathed. The ceiling was aglow with crystalline shimmers—she thought of the crystals Farand and Nelson had mined on the northern island. Were they endemic to the Grey Veil? If anything, they were convenient.

"How did we get here?" She searched the room. The hermit clapped his hands.

"Svartraug powers are strong. Water is its home."

Rosanne stared at the blank surface which had allowed her to pass through from one pool to the next, as if by magic. She could come to terms with enchanting melodies conjured by mythical creatures, but this? It felt more akin to tales of high fantasy she was familiar with. She clearly felt a current in the pool after they submerged, yet it disappeared as quickly as it appeared. Perhaps the hermit had used a lever which opened the flow of water and propelled them here? The lake was deep, and, in her confusion, she had seen nothing but the rush of air bubbles.

Rosanne shook off the water as much as possible and drained her boots.

"This way! I'll show you the heart." The hermit rushed down the hallway. The half-collapsed entrance to the lake was a tight squeeze, and both she and the hermit struggled through.

"What is your name?" Rosanne asked, realising she hadn't bothered asking before. The hermit paused, his expression thoughtful.

"Name is lost. Name is useless here."

"Sorry to hear that."

"Svartraug takes it all. Fills your head and leaves you dead!" He chuckled.

"What happens when the creature takes you? Is he the one who invades our dreams?"

"Fill, fill, and fill. Beautiful lies, harsh truths, all mixed up and abstruse!"

Interesting word choices. "Do you know what he did to Antony and Jeffs?"

The hermit didn't slow but lowered his head. Rosanne was too focused to pursue the inquiry, knowing too little and too unsure to pressure him. Following the hermit might have been a mistake, but if the svartraug possessed the hermit as it had in the jungle, she couldn't see the signs. So far, the hermit was unhinged but cooperative.

He led them through a confusing array of tunnels. Rosanne struggled to breathe in the moist, hot air. They must be close to another volcanic source.

They came upon a wide chamber with several smaller rooms branching out from it. In the centre rested a black boulder on an elevated stone platform, its surface slick with an inky substance.

"The heart!" The hermit squealed and slapped a hand over his mouth, shushing himself through uncontrollable giggles. He blinked big, innocent eyes at her, like a fox with mange and missing teeth.

"What is it?" Rosanne questioned and looked at the boulder.

"A giver of life. Our Dream." The hermit said. The rumble was more prominent here as if there was a creature in the next room deep in slumber. But the stone was the least of Rosanne's interest, as subtle movements in her periphery snagged her attention. She struggled to see in the gloom of the cave, but there in the darkness, something was unmistakably alive. A sleeping presence in a basin, covered in the same grime coating the stone.

"What the hell is that?" she jerked back when she noticed a protruding arm twitch from the wall. Fingers curled in the air as if searching but with little zeal. She could trace it to a broad torso with emaciated ribs and a malformed bulbous head. The torso disappeared into the wall. The only indication of a lower body was the many spear-sharp extremities sticking out around it. A hybrid!

"This is our birthplace. Where we are formed in the dreams of the svartraug and awake to serve," the hermit laughed and did a twirl with his arms splayed wide. Rosanne patted the holster to find it empty. She must have lost it on the way here. The knife was still on the other side, but against any of these creatures, she might as well use it to slit her own throat.

"Why did you bring me here?" Rosanne faced the hermit. "What's so significant about this rock? What is the Dream?"

The hermit flashed a toothy grin. "The heart is our song. It is our guide, the giver of our lives. It shaped us all, and we live through it. But now," he paused to look around the chamber with a sense of calm-felt awe, "now it is mine."

Rosanne scrunched her eyebrows together. Again, with the songs and dreams. How was it all connected?

"Giver of life? The creatures are all born here, in this chamber?" She gestured to the sleeping female form in the basin.

The hermit swept an arm across the creatures in the room. "They're all pawns in the dream, but they make useful servants. Now, my dear Captain Drackenheart," the hermit turned to her, eyes ablaze with a hunger she couldn't place. She reached for her knife. "I think I'll save you for later."

Rosanne's insides went cold and arrested her breath. "You are the svartraug," she said through a sharp breath.

"You humans are so dull," he cackled and threw himself at her, tackling them both to the floor. Her head struck the coarse rocks, and stars exploded in her eyes. She threw out her hands and clawed for a hold on the hermit, just to get a sense of where he was and stop his mad barrage of uncoordinated fists and clawing fingers. She caught a chunk of his beard and yanked as hard as she could, sending the man toppling over past her with a cry. Rosanne rolled to her feet, readying herself for his attack.

"Stupid weak body!" he spat, shaking his head as he retreated a few steps. Rosanne rolled on all fours. Her vision was a blur. The hermit convulsed and writhed as if possessed. Black ooze ran from his ears, mouth, eyes and nose, pooling at his feet. From the inky darkness, a form pushed itself up from the floor, taking shape and solidifying. It rose high before her, nearly touching the ceiling. It resembled a massive mound of running clay, supported by stout legs and thick arms. Hollow eyes fixed on her from atop a rotund head. It twitched floppy ears that drooped to its shoulders from a round fat head. Rosanne didn't even consider the knife in her hand and bolted for the exit.

The svartraug gave a guttural howl, throwing the chambers in echoes. Rosanne staggered through the hallways in her dizziness and breathless desperation, supporting herself on the walls. She caught the thump-thumping of massive feet. Why was the room spinning? Her head throbbed with pain, and the world blinked in and out of focus. She passed several chambers filled with creatures in sleepy stasis. Her clacking footfalls on the floor stirred them to life. A mermaid grasped her arm from her basin, throwing Rosanne off balance. Rosanne jerked away, suddenly aware of all the faces looking at her as she ran past, all the distorted limbs she couldn't even guess what creature they represented, and the roaring call at her heels.

A massive wet hand grasped her shoulder and yanked her back. She fell flat on her back, the breath driven from her lungs. The svartraug's hand encircled her waist and lifted her off the ground with ease. Rosanne pounded against its runny arms, but the creature only lifted her higher and pressed her against the wall. The porous rock bit into her shoulder blades and so badly she howled. The svartraug leaned its weight against her, pressing Rosanne further into the stone; the stone suddenly soft and gave way. Like liquid, the rock crept over her kicking legs and writhing torso, crawling up her neck and face as the svartraug pushed her deeper into the wall.

She clawed at the monster's arms, but they melted under her assault and reformed quicker than she could find purchase. The svartraug released its grasp, stepped back, and grinned with a wide, lipless mouth. Rosanne pawed at the air as she was sucked into the wall. The muck crept over her mouth and nose, cold and intrusive. Tears spilled from her eyes, but she found no escape.

The last thing Rosanne saw was the clay-covered human face in the basin next to a broken mermaid body, the face of Antony.

CHAPTER TWENTY-EIGHT
FOUND IN THE DARK

I da was a whimpering puddle on the ashy floor, her sobs reverberating around her. She flinched at the pain from the bruised muscles and burning scrapes. Her trousers were ripped at the knees and torn at the hems. In the diminished light of the alchemical lamp, she made out that the wounds weren't as deep as the pain she felt whenever she moved or how badly she felt sorry for herself.

She remained on the ground, easing the stiffness in each limb one after another and determined that she suffered no serious injuries. She was sick of her bad luck and terrified.

No more cursed islands, she decided. She would go to Noval, set up shop, and maybe raise a few goats on a small farm by the coast. But first, she needed to escape.

Propped up on all fours, she fought to her feet like a drunken sailor after being tossed out of a tavern. Her head was a throbbing drum, and her shoulder was a thorny pain to move. But she was alive. No double vision plagued her, and her knees were steady after she adjusted to their aches.

Wherever she was now, it wasn't the temple.

The stifling air made her woozy. It was like trying to catch your breath underwater and felt far worse than the frequent rain showers. Ida was used to thin air from years of flying with sub-par atmos that couldn't keep the atmospheric pressure level, but this was a discomfort she couldn't shake.

The alchemical lamp lay buried beneath a thick layer of dust, its blue glow barely penetrating the particulates. Stumbling over debris, she brushed off the lamp, flooding the room with its harsh chemical light. She stared down into a corridor of jagged walls and a low ceiling.

"Fantastic, more caves," she grumbled. The halls seemed endless, their darkness deep and uninviting. The porous halls were rough to the touch and crumbled under her fingers.

One moment, she was standing on the lower levels of the Svartraug Temple (that's what she called it) with Gavin and Creedy; next, the floor caved in. Where did the earthquakes come from if they were on a floating island? After the scouting crew's epic escape from the legion of hybrids, whispers of molten rivers weaving through the mountains had reached her ears. Considering how hot it was, she must be close to one. It still made little sense, but she rolled with what she knew. When in the Grey Veil, and all that.

Ida searched the debris for Creedy and Gavin, knowing they could have been caught in the cave in just as she did. She shifted rocks but couldn't see the men anywhere.

"Gavin! Creedy!" she called, but all that met her was the oppressing silence. Above her, the hole was firmly plugged with debris at the top.

"Oh, balls," she muttered. If Gavin and Creedy weren't down here with her, and the way out was blocked, her sudden urge to cry like a small child threatened to expose her false bravery. Ida swallowed her self-pity. *You've faced worse*, she told herself. Ida's momentary need to escape fueled her determination, and she knew that if there was a way, she had the will to survive this place. Wherever *here* was.

After giving the alchemical lamp a shake, the rattle suggested to her it was a quarter full of pellets, which would last her maybe four hours if she was lucky. She lowered the wick; the light diminished by half, but she could still see enough to navigate the rocky ground.

Being in here made her miss the carved, illuminated, and adorned hulder caves. Every surface of this cave was sharp enough to cut her if she wasn't careful. Ida marked her path with stacks of rocks in easily spotted places in case she either got lost or Creedy and Gavin were also down here trying to find their way out.

Eventually, Ida paused, settling on slabs of obsidian, out of breath and too exhausted to continue. She knew she hadn't gone all that long, but the darkness around her, the constant soft rumble beneath her feet, and the hot, damp air only heightened her anxiety, which made breathing a chore. Volcanic ash turned her sweat-soaked shirt into black grime. Her blonde locks clung to her face and neck in itchy ribbons. She brushed them back in wet pats as disgust rose in her about her current hygienic state.

Ida missed Nelson's dorky grin. She longed for the ship; she felt disgusted by herself, and she hated being here. A workshop in Noval with access to baths daily was the life she aimed for, not this hellscape of monster-dodging, cave-exploring nonsense. She sniffed, her nose a runny mess. She should have sat this journey out and listened to Gavin's tales and ostentatious bravado, even if he lied through his teeth and blew things out of proportion without her there to correct him. He would have made the camp raid the siege of Otallo, facing an army of ten thousand with only twenty canons. She'd much prefer his lies to this, and she felt the press of tears once again. By the skies, how much did she have to cry?

A faint trail of whispers wormed into her ears, and Ida jumped to her feet.

"Hello?" She held out the lamp but winced when her ears were brutalised by the amplification of her own echo. How were the porous walls able to cast one? Why did nothing in the Grey Veil make sense? She wanted to turn around, but she had already explored alternate routes that were dead ends. Ida raised the wick in the lamp and threw the hallway into a bright glare. Something flitted from the shadow of a rocky outcrop and disappeared deeper into the cave system.

Ida wanted to pursue it, but the alarm bells in her mind checked her. The whisper returned, weaker but clear with a single word: *Come.*

This must be how the dream-invader lures people, by the whispers and the hypnotic pull of the creature's abilities. Except ...

Ida didn't feel any different. She was awake and alert, and they did not bombard her with illusions or promises. She always was too curious for her own good but there was no way but forwards. Swallowing the lump in her throat, Ida kept the light bright and brought out the small pocketknife from a compartment in her pants. With quick strides and constant vigilance, Ida followed the shadow that darted between the darkness of the cave. Could it be photophobic, similar to the anti-gravity-dust-eating crabs?

The whisper guided her, changing their tone at the fork of the road. The shadow stayed ahead of her, just out of reach of the lamplight. Why was this creature and the whisper so hellbent on guiding her anywhere besides to her inevitable death? Ida clutched the knife in her hand, a feeble defence that only served to alleviate her fragile mortality.

The heat subsided, and the air became more breathable. The lamp rattled in her hand as she felt cold. She entered a wide cavern with a low ceiling. A rounded rock-bricked pond stood in its centre. Crudely cut columns lined the walls, but there wasn't much else adorning the chamber as if it were incomplete. There was no other way in.

The whisper ceased, and Ida could finally hear her own thoughts again. She did a slow spin, scanning the room for anything that might jump out at her. Ida shone the torchlight over the pool and edged closer, her eyes locked on the pristine black surface. She waved the light over it, trying to glimpse the bottom, but nothing stood out to her.

Ida shook the alchemical light and listened to the rattle of pellets inside, the clunky hollowness apparent. Most of the fuel was gone. Hanging her head, Ida let out a quiet, pathetic sob and resisted the urge to shed twenty years and bawl her eyes out like a child, again.

Through the rumble of the mountain chambers, she caught a soft, wet splash. A dark shape peered at her from just above the surface, its eyes resembling inky marbles and skin that seemed covered in black slime. Her heart throbbed with a painful squeeze, her movements arrested by that alien creature's sudden appearance. A delayed, strangled scream escaped her throat, and in her panic, Ida tripped over her feet and crashed to the ground. The alchemical lamp rolled away; its light turned away from the pool. Seizing this opportunity, the shape stretched from the water, an elongated head balanced on delicate thin shoulders and a stretched torso with limber arms.

In her terror, she fumbled for the lamp, too scared to even open her eyes as she felt the creature bend over her. She twisted the knob, raising the wick to flood the room with the blue-white glare chemical light. The creature issued a thrumming shriek, throwing up thin arms to shield itself. It folded back on itself and into the pool with a violent splash. Ida panted, her heart slamming in her chest. Too terrified to divert her gaze, she raised the lamp, shaking like an aspen leaf.

In the pool, the creature squinted at her through the glaring light but didn't move. Ida locked her eyes with its dark hollows that had softened and now blinked at her.

"W-what do you want?" she asked between shaky breaths. The light in the lamp flickered, and Ida adjusted the wick in panic, drawing it down to conserve chemicals, but the light was now barely able to illuminate her surroundings. She kept it close to her as a barrier against the unknown presence in the water.

Undeterred by the now-weakened light, the creature lifted its elongated body out of the pool in a slow arch. It glistened from moisture, its skin loose and runny at first but then solidified into a black matte surface. It took long but cautious steps towards her with toeless feet, its eyes trained on the lamp. Ida kept her hand on the wick nob, but terror was written on her face.

Head bowed down, the creature cocked its head and blinked. Up close, Ida realised it didn't have a mouth or nose, just those perpetually dark and empty sockets that changed shape to indicate expression like eyebrows did for humans.

The dark shape stretched out a slender arm, its three-fingered hand forming a loose fist as it paused before Ida.

It wasn't going to maul her? Hesitant, she set the lamp on the floor and stretched out her hands with shaky receiving palms. She stared into its hollows, oval and relaxed. Were they indeed eyes or small bodies of water?

It opened its fist, and a cold metallic object dropped into her hands. The creature lumbered back to the pool and observed her with its head sticking just above the surface.

Ida looked at her palms and felt a familiar weight and shape of grooves. The stolen sphere! "It was you who took it? Why?"

The creature responded with a slow blink, like that of a cat. The sphere was wet but appeared undamaged. If only she had her tablet, maybe she could scan the cave for an exit, but the tablet was among her packed things topside.

"The temple," she muttered, furrowing her brow in thought. The creature bore an uncanny resemblance to the temple drawings. The people who made the paintings didn't skimp on the details. The svartraug didn't have any. Her discovery quickly turned her victory to dread. "You're a svartraug." She took a step back. Creedy was right! But why was it here, of all places? What did it want? The creature gracefully twirled in the pool.

Ida, surprised by its serene disposition, strained her eyes to watch from the safety of the light.

Emboldened by the creature's tranquillity, she settled on the pool's edge. "Did you send those people to our camp that night?" The svartraug slowly shook its head in response to her question.

"Then why lead me here? Why give this back?" The questions buzzed in her mind as the reasoning escaped her. If the svartraug didn't send the mimics, who did? And why did they look like people who had once lived? Seeing the captain's father among them was a shock and impossible. The man had been dead for fifteen years and hadn't aged a day.

After their run-in with the hulder at the other island, Ida was open to the possibility that the Grey Veil was more than just a meteorological and geographical anomaly. That the people on this island turned into puddles of black water when defeated was proof of such.

She didn't sense malevolence from the creature, but Creedy's stories made her think. Why would the svartraug lead her and Gavin away from the camp and then raid it? Were she and Gavin affected differently by the svartraug's power, or was there a simpler explanation behind it?

The creature stretched out a hand towards her, prompting her to take it.

"I don't want to drown, thank you." She scowled and cradled her light. The creature tilted its head and pointed a long finger to the ceiling.

"Above? You'll take me there?"

It nodded. As bizarre as the svartraug appeared with its absent mouth and unusually long limbs, Ida no longer feared it. The ominous presence in the rain didn't align with the creature before her. Was it a he, an it, or perhaps a she? A genderless god? She couldn't tell.

"If you do anything I don't like I'll shine so much light in your eyes you'll see the pearly gates of heaven," she said.

It arched its eye sockets and shook in a manner which made her think it was laughing, but no sound came from it.

Ida grabbed the alchemical lamp and strapped it to her belt, covering it partially with her tunic so her shadow fell over the svartraug. "This is insane even for me," Ida commented as she reached out her hand to the svartraug's three-fingered one, expecting it to be cold and slimy, but it felt like touching air, with only the hint of moisture from its skin.

The lamp would extinguish if she stepped into the water, but her curiosity at the creature's intentions overpowered her sense of fear. Besides, where else was she going to go? Ida stepped into the pool, and the svartraug ducked under the surface. Ida frowned, took a deep breath, and followed.

CHAPTER TWENTY-NINE

DESCENT INTO MADNESS

"There's your monster," Aros told Vincent as they stared toward the tentacled, bulbous colossus prowling to the far west. The other man scratched the back of his head, and his black, shoulder-length hair glistened with oil. Dandruff caught in his fingernails, his face screwed up between disgust and regret.

"I don't appreciate being right, but here we are." He flicked the white flakes.

Aros considered their situation as he leaned against his shovel. The temple ceiling had collapsed and sealed the way in. Something monstrous with a transparent head and hooked tentacles, colloquially named the Kraken from some ludicrous Novalian myth, caused the earthquake which tore through the island. Crew were missing, not only Captain Drackenheart and DiCroce but Creedy, Gavin, and Ida as well.

If Aros had half the wit he lost during his time with the Inquisition, this was the perfect time to hightail to the distant East. Unfortunately, he was a lowly deck hand stuck clearing rubble like the cog in the machine that he was, a link in the chain of men who passed rocks from the imploded temple ceiling.

People had talked about fleeing, but seeing as the monster appeared occupied, they decided on a second rescue mission instead. He had caught the sound of a distant shot from over the hills, but Lyle was focused on retrieving the people trapped in the temple. Aros was left with his theories like before. Nothing had changed.

Bastards. Biased bastards the lot of them, he thought sourly.

After sifting through the debris of the crumbled ceiling-turned-rubble for hours, the crew concluded the temple was sealed shut. The support beams, and stacks of rock had dominoed over each other in such a complicated manner that without the ship's crane, they couldn't remove anything without the entire roof collapsing and crushing everyone inside. Aros sat on a rock, sipped what little water remained in his waterskin, and dumped the rest over his itchy scalp.

A sudden plasmic shot followed by a cry rang out above him. Everyone turned their heads to the lip of the crater.

Aros clutched the knife in his hand. A string of *clack-clack-clack* preceded another scream. Everyone around him dropped whatever they were doing and reached for their hand pistols. An obsidian-pointed trident whistled through the air and hit the seaman next to Aros, pinning him brutally to the boulder. His blood-curdling cries scattered people to cover. Kristoff reached for the pinned man from behind his boulder, but another spear cut through the air and narrowly missed the boy.

Aros ducked behind a weathered column, flipping the knife in his hand and focused on the intruder hovering by the lip of the crater. Another damn hybrid, and it had spent its final spear!

"Cover each other and get out of this hole!" Aros barked. People scrambled up the crater with vigorous battle cries, charging the hybrid. A torrent of insecurity surged through him, but Aros's fear turned to resolve, which grew with the ferocity of the crew of the *Red Queen* as he charged alongside them.

The wet growls, followed by rhythmic clicking, scattered around the ruins. Aros picked his way up the slope, avoiding falling rocks and was the first to reach the top. Lyle's team formed a defensive ring around the hole, plasma rifles readied and charged bullets sizzled through the air.

What met Aros up top made him want to drop into the temple instead, and his legs froze despite his commands. A throng of hybrids climbed up the hillside, spears raised and pincer arms snapping. Plasmic bullets fizzled out against their tough exoskeletons, which warded off the worst of the searing heat, leaving only blackened spots.

Aros swallowed the lump in his throat and considered his knife as pressure rose in his chest.

Fuck.

A hybrid charged toward him and snapped out with its crusher claws, forcing him back towards the ledge.

Fuck fuck fuck!

Aros ducked the snapping pincers and dove below the hybrid's wide body. A surge of people flocked to Aros' side, each attacking a leg. The creature sprawled before swords sunk into its human torso. Damn, they worked fast this time!

Aros ducked behind the armed crew. "A handgun would be nice!" he called out to anyone. Lyle tossed him his offhand pistol. Aros fumbled it, dropped the pistol, dove for the clattering weapon, and caught it before the weapon bounced off the temple ruins.

Aros reloaded the pistol with a resounding, energetic whirr. Aros aimed for the fleshy torso of a nearby hybrid and squeezed the trigger. It kicked out with its legs, and the bullet pinged off it harmlessly.

A ghastly shriek pierced his ears and stopped the monster from attacking any further, and instead, it turned its attention towards the crew. A hard pinch on his back lifted Aros clear off the ground. He flailed and kicked out, but his resilient clothes didn't tear.

Curse you, high-quality Bunnsboroux vest.

Abernathy charged the hybrid with his sabre raised. Aros' captor kicked out with its hard-shelled leg, piercing through the man's stomach. He grunted a distorted cry and fell limp in seconds. Aros watched Abernathy's blue eyes gloss over, jaw slack and almost caught in a surprised expression. The monster shook him off with a shrug. Abernathy didn't stir.

The persistent sounds of Lyle's plasma rifle reached Aros, but his captor didn't pay them any mind as it proceeded down the hill.

"I can walk, you know!" Aros kicked out his feet as his last defiance against his captor but dangled like a piece of linen in the wind.

Aros peeked inside his pinched vest for the pistol he had tucked away. The blue light on the magazine glowed weakly, but he knew he could squeeze a couple of shots from it should the situation call for it. Technically, the situation called for it right now, but his curiosity arrested him, and he didn't see an opportunity for escape just yet, lest he wanted to end up like Abernathy. He'd keep his protests and the plasmic pistol hidden until he knew he had a clear shot at freedom and answers as to what the hell they wanted with him.

They trudged in silence through the misty gloom of the jungle. Gurgling wet breaths escaped his captor as if fluids filled its lungs. Aros hadn't seen the hybrids up close in daylight, but the humanoid part unnerved him more than the spindly crab portions. He caught glimpses of the humanoid fused to the exoskeleton; strange myriad burns, cuts, and barnacles dotted the grey skin. Aros wasn't religious or superstitious, but the horror of this creature's barnacle-covered face and pale eyes made him believe he was staring at the unholy resurrection of a drowned man. Countless people had lost their lives to the Grey Veil, so his imagination didn't feel all that wild.

The high-quality Bunnsboroux vest was tight around his chest, and breathing was uncomfortable, but Aros relented and spied for any landmarks and ideas of where the creature was taking him. The forest was alive with animal calls. Colourful birds flitted quick as recently-fired bullets, resting on a branch before taking off in a flurry of protests. Surprisingly, the wildlife paid no attention to the crab monstrosity that bonked against trees in tight places. It let out a wet chitter followed by pitched clacks. What it meant was anyone's guess. Maybe, "Honey, I'm home!"

Aros felt like a flea-infested child the way the pincers carried him out before itself, and he couldn't do anything but fold his arms and let fate roll its dice. The mountains stood before them, those everlasting spires separating north from the south. Icy wind blew from the snow-crested tops down to the valley. Aros shivered.

"Caves? Really? I think I can manage from here. Thank you, James."

The creature ignored Aros' flippant comment or didn't understand a lick of Angelsk. They proceeded into the darkened halls. Aros could only assume this was its lair, and considering how far west they were from his original escape point, the network inside the mountain must be vast.

Could he even escape a second time, or was his first escape successful because of a human-besotted mermaid who didn't engage in bondage?

Aros craned his head, spotting the gruesome deformation that was the creature's face, and thought he had better things to use his charms on. He had courted less attractive women before, but they were at least human. Well, more human.

This was his life now, being carried through an endless jungle of torture and despair to meet his maker inside some creepy mountains housing the craziest evolutionary unnatural selections Aros had ever had the displeasure of encountering.

They followed endless hallways in varying shapes and sizes. In some places, the ceiling hung high above them; other times, the monster had to squeeze through tight spaces, flailing and wiggling its body and limbs. The walls echoed with the footfalls, a series of endless clacks drilling into his skull, which he concluded was worse than waterboarding. This was as close to torture as one could get. They resonated with images in his mind of his summer house prison cell when the inquisitor came with a silk bundle and unrolled a series of polished metal instruments that clinked against each other. Aros wiped away the forming sweat on his forehead and drew a deep breath. He curled his fingers into loose fists and tucked them against his stomach, as if protecting himself from the memory that made his scarred digits ache.

The walls were lit with lights that brightened in pulses for each step the creature took. Waves of green and blue intermingled with each other. He was sure he spotted wiggling movement, like the glowworms they have down south. Aros thought he would be sick.

They passed caves with sulphuric smells that would give trolls a run for their apples. Other chambers held pools of bubbling lava, a perfect place to rid oneself of one's wedding band commitments. Jokes aside, it was unbearably hot. Sweat ran down his face in rivers and stung his eyes. Dry caves turned into saunas. They splashed through crossing rivers and came upon a chamber with a small mountain lake.

The crab monster dropped Aros in front of the dark waters that lay calm like an inky black mirror. The walls were vibrant with light and colours, pulsating, breathing. Aros didn't particularly like insects, but for now, he was grateful for the illumination of his otherwise dire situation.

The hybrid gave two distinct clicks with its mouth, diaphragm bouncing as he did, and the metallic sound echoed throughout the room.

The hybrid then exited the chamber, leaving Aros at the mercy of his reflection. The person in the water appeared calm and peaceful as if he somehow had regained the confidence he had lost. He touched his pale face with shaky fingers, his nails miraculously regrown in the waters. He reached out to touch the surface, which mimicked him with a predatory gleam.

"I wouldn't do that if I were you." The warning made him jump, and Aros whipped around to face this new threat. Except it wasn't a stranger. It was the hermit.

The man's calm and poised appearance didn't suit his haggard look. His wild, tangled hair, dry, greying beard, and the hard expression of a tropical island crime boss made the man seem a different person.

"Found your marbles?" Aros joked and clutched his bruised side. When the hermit stood in front of Aros, the very air changed around him. Aros couldn't see it, but a presence lingered about the hermit, dark and imposing. Lowering his gaze, Aros was unable to meet the unsettling expression of the madman whom he had met rambling in the forest just days prior. Something had changed.

The hermit pointed to the lake. "You saw something you wanted in there."

"I doubt it. It's not magical waters."

"Water isn't special, but the creature living here can fulfil your dreams. The Grey Veil provides."

"The Grey Veil is a cunt," Aros spat. Who the hell was this person? How did he seem so different only days earlier?

As he drew his hand through the water, the ripples bounced over the surface. "Many have searched the Grey Veil for riches and fame, others for powers."

"I don't need any of that."

"Then why did you reach out?"

"Because this entire place is insane!" Aros' voice echoed through the room and bounced back to him. He clasped his hands over his ears, but the amplified voice cut through him to where his knees buckled under his weight.

He fought for breath, fought for calm, fought for his pounding heart to slow.

The hermit bent down next to Aros. "You are tormented by the invisible bonds of your captors, by the wounds that have yet to heal and scar. The waters give you hope of becoming the person who you lost."

"Shut up. You don't know shit about me!" Aros said through gritted teeth.

The hermit cocked his head. "I was once like you, shipwrecked and stuck with a crew who jumped at whatever the Grey Veil threw at us. But not I. I became strong. I endured."

"You went batshit crazy." Aros fought to his feet.

The hermit's face morphed into a ludicrous laugh, his tone mocking. "You still can't take solid foods without thinking of those pouches with gravity minerals about to burst inside of your guts, can you? Still clutching your hands every time you see a sharp object like a knife or pliers able to pull out your nails?"

Aros clenched his jaw, his teeth grinding so hard they gnashed in his skull. All he recognised was the screaming voice in his head vying for control, telling him to fight.

"Shut the fuck up." He growled.

The hermit licked his lips and nodded. "You fight back. We don't want that. In fact, all we want is to be left alone."

"Shame on us for defending ourselves. Should have left Jeffs alone."

"Ah, but we're not the ones intruding. I have a proposition for you. Leave now, and all your friends will live."

Aros slid a hand over his incredulous smile. "You honestly think I have any power here? You think those people give a shit about me or what I have to say?"

Insecurity flashed across the hermit's face, but he dismissed it with a shrug. "I tried pitching the same deal to your captain, but she wasn't willing. You see, I'm not the only one here, but this is what I want. Leave the island and never come back."

The urgency in the hermit's tone piqued Aros' curiosity, and through it he could finally ignore the rushing of blood in his ears. "What's it to you? You're here alone with monsters and madness. Why not come back to the real world?"

"I have everything I want right here."

"The Grey Veil provides?" Aros echoed sarcastically.

"The svartraug provides."

Aros let out a burst of laughter. "Have you looked at yourself in the mirror?"

"Oh, the svartraug didn't do this. I did!" The hermit grinned as his lips drew into a toothy grin. "I was young and healthy with him occupying my body. I could travel to faraway lands and have women and riches as I desired. I indulged in my darkest desires with no one to stop me. I could even bring that bitch Queen Bloody Mary down on her knees! All the things I could never have in the real world are at my fingertips by the grace of he who devours dreams."

Aros mumbled the name. Why did it seem so familiar? "There hasn't been a Queen Mary for a very long time, old man. So, what changed? Why did you do that to yourself?"

The hermit huddled closer with twitching moves. "The svartraug is a hungry thing. It eats and eats until the mind is gone, and when there's only bones, it hunts for something new."

Aros' eyebrows scrunched together. "What is the svartraug? Truly?"

"A spirit of the Veil's Dream. It lives here in this very cave. It's grown tired of me, but I need it to survive. If it doesn't want me anymore, my dream ends." The hermit gave a sudden pained grin, which replaced his calm demeanour.

"So, nothing is gonna change then? Sorry, mate. I'll be leaving as you asked me. No issue with that." Aros stood and turned to leave.

"Your freedom isn't guaranteed," the hermit tried, desperation growing in his voice. "You will be interrogated again and again for information about the *Red Queen* and her journeys through the Veil. You'll be tortured like you were last summer. The question is: who will find you first, the inquisition or the people who released you from jail?"

Aros swallowed the lump in his throat. How did this bastard know so much about him?

"You want me to leave but threaten me with that knowledge? You're not very good at this, are you?"

"Oh, but I am thinking of something different!" He whipped his head around, finger pointed to his lips and shushed the calm waters. "Not now! Not..." When he turned back to Aros, that unsettling grin returned to his haggard face. "If you surrender to the svartraug, your friends can leave alive and well, guaranteed. If not they all disappear in the dream."

"What the hell are you on about, man? You are mad as crackers."

The water stirred with a single thump of ripples from the centre of the pool.

Aros stared at the newly forming ripples of something swimming closer to the edge. The hermit frowned. "Time's up. If you run, you might escape it."

"Escape what?" Aros's voice quivered.

The hermit whimpered, and his eyes filled with tears. His hands flew to his head with a scream. "I'm sorry! I just wanted to live a little longer. You don't need him!" He collapsed and writhed on the floor. Aros scurried towards the wall, away from the hermit and the bubbling waters.

A rounded, black, slimy head emerged from the ripples. Two hollow black eyes locked on Aros, and it twitched two angular droopy ears. It emerged with its massive bulk, stomping with sluggish steps over to the hermit. Aros pressed himself against the wall, hyperventilating. The svartraug glanced at him before absolving into runny liquid. It flowed around the hermit and entered his nose, eyes, and mouth as the hermit thrashed.

The caves swayed in a layered distortion Aros was familiar with from the Queen's dungeons. He covered his ears in panic, but he couldn't shut out the invasive screams.

As the cries continued, Aros grew increasingly unsure if he could move at all. The hermit gave a few spastic twitches and fell still. Aros watched his chest rise and fall, and then his body stirred as he pushed himself up chest first. His head lolled in front of him, hair dangling in knotted tangles. When he looked up at Aros, he wore a crooked grin.

"You look delicious." The hermit's distorted voice cut through him.

"I-I haven't bathed in two weeks. Trust me, I don't taste good," Aros' voice cracked. He inched around the svartraug-possessed human on the floor, who turned its head after him with the same stiff grin.

"He's so difficult to control. I need a new body to wear," it said.

"I'm already spoken for. But thank you for the offer." Aros edged away towards the crack in the wall, the only exit he could glean from the darkness.

The devouring svartraug cackled and stood. He came closer with twitchy movements, similar to how he was in the forest when Aros first met him.

"Are you sure? You can be free here. Free from everything."

"And be your puppet?' I'll take my chances with your serenading sushi."

"Man has wit and humour! This body has been no fun for many years. So hungry."

Whatever this creature was, it was a parasite feasting on the mind of whoever it possessed. Why was this invader of dreams different from the others in the jungle? Why were they blank-faced and mindless while this possessed a personality of its own?

"Wouldn't your friends get jealous?"

"Friends? Oh, you mean the other svartraug! My children are many. Many many. But they were born out of me, only a piece of me. They do as I say and nothing else."

"The crab men hybrids?" Aros stalled.

"Loyal creatures. They imprint on you in the dream." His head twitched to the side like a broken crane. "Listen, Captain Bernhart—"

"I am not that person anymore," Aros hissed.

"But you want to be!" The svartraug bellowed. "I have seen it! You desire it so desperately you sought out the dream, anxious for that shred of dignity and power you once possessed before that Drackenheart destroyed it all."

"That was my own doing!" he argued.

"Was it?" The silence hung between them, between Aros' panicked realisation and growing bitterness and the devourer's open-mouthed grin. "You can have your revenge. I can help you."

In Aros' mind, the seed had long since taken root. All the bickering matches between him and Rosanne, her dismissal of his every word came rushing back to him. The creature was right. If it hadn't been for her, he would still be raiding ships in the Baltansea, his crew would be alive and free, and Aros would have a home to return to. It was all gone ... because of Rosanne.

"How?" he asked, so low he hoped the creature hadn't heard him. It was a tether to something solid, a drive for change, a hope he hadn't felt in a long time.

The grin on the svartraug's face widened. "You can surrender the captain and her secrets to the crown. You've thought about the consequences of this already: the crown's monopoly of the World Trade

Association. Or you can have Rosanne on her knees before Gunny, spilling secrets of travelling through the Veil. But if you stay here, you can be king of the Veil. No one would look for you. No one would be able to pull as much as a hair from your head or instil that fear your captors did ever again."

Aros drew a deep breath and eased his stiff shoulders.

"You can't leave without a host body; how can you give me anything?"

"I can show you, but you must let me in."

Bad idea, Aros, the warning sirens sang in his mind.

The devourer stretched out his hand with the open palm side up, fingers coaxing. "I will give you a glimpse of my power. Then you'll understand."

Aros's hands shook, and he hitched his unsteady breath. Free of all his ails ... The life he had lost, back in his control ... Aros' desire to see it all again arrested his words. His eyes stung from salty tears welling up from the hope born out of this drive for revenge he didn't know he had. Was there a way? Like turning back the clock to when he prowled the northern Baltansea and ripped off rich merchant ships? Back to before he had been dumb enough to attack the *Red Queen* in the Grey Veil?

Images of his time with Rosanne on the island flooded his mind. He was the reason they had both been stranded there. He was the reason they got attacked by trolls. Aros was the reason half his crew died during the battle with the *Queen*. He had even mauled Rosanne twice!

He didn't want to be that person and all the problems and enemies it brought. She had every reason to hate his guts, and the ails she bore over him after sneaking aboard her ship were justified. But she hadn't abandoned him. She hadn't tossed him overboard like the broken man he had become.

Was his old life worthwhile? Did he cling to the romanticised idea that it empowered him when, in fact, it made him rotten to the core?

His jaw trembled, but he didn't let his bitterness spill. The pale hand was blurry in front of him, but Aros retracted his.

The devourer's grin morphed into a frown. "Suit yourself," he said and pounced.

CHAPTER THIRTY
THE GREY VEIL PROVIDES

R osanne drew on the tobacco pipe she had brought along for the journey. She rarely smoked, but when stress levels were this high, it was difficult to think about her survival options on this accursed island without losing her cool, and instead of growing frantic, she disappeared into the sweet fumes of tranquillity. At least for a short while.

The svartraug had set a trap, a devious one, and she fell right for it. Rosanne exhaled with a deep sigh and frown, watching the smoke twirl out of existence. Turning the pipe over, she tapped out the tobacco against the rock, emptying the charred leaves.

Her escape had been far from graceful, involving a lot of running and angry monsters eager to impale her with sharp utensils. Now, she was out in the wilderness, without her crew and ship, and with no food and water. When would she learn? Just her and a pack of tobacco and matches that somehow survived the magnitude of rain she had gone through since coming here.

Sharp rays of sunshine penetrated the partly clouded sky. With the growing heat, mist rose from the forest in wispy ribbons, amassing and drifting toward the edges of the island to join the surrounding clouds.

The weather had never looked this fine on such a dark day in Rosanne's life, mocking her state of dread and relentless doom. She did not know what to do, and instead of succumbing to the bitterness, her mind had reached a stage of inertia.

This was fine. There was little more the Grey Veil could take from her.

Farand was her only wild card, but how could she contact the man who was across the island, hidden behind an alcove by the beach? A box of dynamite might do the trick, but she had neither dynamite nor a volcano she could just—

Rosanne's attention travelled to the central fuming mountain, knowing there were pockets of lava hidden underneath billions of tons of rock. If she could find a major vein and somehow block it, she would never escape in time before the big bang blew her to bits or the horde of monsters chased her through the forest. She cast the suicidal thought aside.

Rosanne slid a hand through her tangled hair, her fingers snagging in the knots. Cursing, she yanked at it, sorely missing a bath and a comb. And Antony. She finished the pathetic attempt at calming herself by burying her face in her palms and letting out a muffled cry of anguish.

She wanted to scream but remembered the hermit had found her with terrifying ease during her last outcry.

It hit her then like a ton of rocks. The hermit could travel around the island with the power of the svartraug. Perhaps his hut had something that would help. That shell must be the key since he was so adamant about protecting it. If anything, she might use it to her advantage.

That was her plan, she decided. Find the hut, find the shell, and then force the hermit to take her to where she needed to go. Get Farand, retrieve her crew and then get the fuck off this island. Map be damned. Thompson be damned!

Rosanne made her way down the hill and toward the general direction of the hut she summoned from the vagueness that was her memory. Everything seemed fuzzy like a brooding migraine was about to hit her in the face with an iron skillet. She shook the feeling aside and focused on the half-beaten path. No people lurked nearby, mimics or otherwise. The wind rustled the canopy above her, and if Rosanne focused, she could hear the buzzing of insects. She could almost believe she was at peace and that no harm would come to her here.

Were her crew still searching for her at the temple? If she could find the hut, she could find the hill and maybe build a fire and signal them.

The hut with the sagging roof and bulging floor stood alone in the clearing. Rosanne crouched low behind a bush, watching and listening for any activity. The last she had seen of the hermit, he led her straight to the svartraug in the mountains. She had escaped once, and she would not be fooled again, not through force or love.

It was Yerrik's voice that had protected her. She could scarcely believe it. Why would he help her after she broke his heart in such a horrible manner? Not even she would have kept going after such treatment. If Antony leaving her wasn't the message she needed to understand, she unquestionably felt like a terrible person now. But Yerrik wasn't human, and leaving was the right thing to do, or at last, she told herself such over and over again.

Rosanne snuck up to the hut and peered inside. The hermit was elsewhere, perhaps parading somewhere being piggybacked by a nightmare parasite whispering sweet nothings in his ear. But he had left his precious shell sitting on the shelf.

Rosanne made sure no one was around before entering the hut and bee-lining for the shimmering shell. It was the most beautiful item among all the rubbish the hermit had accumulated. Old satchels, soggy journals, broken feathers, shells, and a mouldy blanket sat among an ocean of other useless things. Rosanne studied the conch shell in her hands. The spiralling layers reflected in a rainbow of colours and, at first glance, appeared to be a regular horse conch shell, albeit twice as large as her hand. If the hermit came for it in the temple, why leave it behind here, and what was it for other than mere ornamental purposes?

Was the svartraug connected to it somehow, and the hermit needed the shell to be possessed by the spirit? She put her ear to it like she had done to shells she picked up at the beach as a child. Instead of ocean waves, she heard whispers like those who had spoken to her in the rain.

Whatever magic the shell possessed, she wasn't sure she could even tap into it, but as long as it was in her custody, maybe she could use it as blackmail. After Nelson's stunt, she had no qualms with the method as long as it got her to safety. The difference in this case was that no one would get hurt. Much.

She brought the shell to her lips and whispered, "Shut up." A deep rumbling call resonated in the distance. Exiting the hut in a hurry, she dropped to the ground by a low bush. The noise faded into nothing.

"That is not yours!" the hermit cried out behind her, startling Rosanne to her feet. He threw himself at her, hands clawing for the shell. Rosanne wrestled with him for a clumsy second, and they toppled to the ground. Despite his appearance, he was fierce, and he clawed at her evading hand. The hermit coiled and launched himself after the shell in a paroxysm of fury and screams.

"Fine, take it!" She tossed it away from them. The hermit cried in horror and dove for the shell, caught it just before it splashed into a puddle, and poured over the grooves as if he feared she had damaged it.

Rosanne breathed hard, flabbergasted and overwhelmed by how her very simple plan had shattered in a heartbeat. The man was not just insane; he was too strong and too deranged to be reasoned with. His wild eyes locked with hers.

"Not for you. Not for you!" He snarled, listening into the shell several times over.

"What is it for?" Rosanne dusted off her breeches and vest.

"It's mine!"

"Fine, it's yours! But what does it do?!" Rosanne breathed hard and brushed her hair from her face. Their tussle in the mud had caked her locks once again. She would never get the mud out now. "I just want to know. I swear I was only looking at it," Rosanne lied. How often had she twisted the truth after coming to this island anyway? This was getting out of control.

"Cannot fool the svartraug!" he laughed and exposed his teeth to her like a wild beast.

Rosanne paused, reaching into her memories as if she had forgotten something. "Hold on. *You* are the svartraug? Not the madman who attacked me earlier?" The information ran through her mind as the pieces finally began to make sense.

The svartraug chuckled. Not his usual deranged cackling, but a calm and unsettling point of amusement. "You thought you got away from me? I never let anyone go."

"My father escaped," she countered and looked around for the svartraug's mythical creature entourage. So far, they appeared to be alone,

"Did he now?" The man grinned. Cold ran through Rosanne at the thought of her father's mimic. "I followed him in the Veil and sent him and his friends to the deep just like I'll end you. Where are your companions at, Captain? What about your precious ship? Your precious Farand Duplànte?"

Rosanne caught a lump in her throat. If the svartraug's reach made it to base camp, even for a moment, Farand would be wise to take off and head north in their direction. He could spot the temple team with ease on the hilltop. He would fly straight into the svartraug's trap!

Rosanne set off in a sprint to the nearest hilltop. Cackling followed her like oppressing echoes bouncing around her skull. The headache only increased with her heaving breaths, but she pushed through and picked her way up the hill. Treacherous roots caught her feet, and the steep climb left her breathless. Rosanne spotted the exposed top of the temple northeast. It was too far to see anyone working the grounds, but she knew they wouldn't leave unless forced to. Maybe they discovered the hallway too and followed her, but who knows how long ago that was! Rosanne had lost all concept of time as it somehow was midday, but she couldn't recall night falling. The sharp pounding in her head bloomed behind her temples.

She spotted a soft waft of smoke coming from the temple. Thank Terra, they were still there. The svartraug-possessed hermit stood next to her, invigorated as always, like the climb hadn't fazed him.

"You're not human, do you know that?" She rested with her hands on her thighs, too exhausted to try to flee.

The svartraug gave a sudden, unhinged belly laugh. She stood her ground as the creature composed himself once more. "I enjoy your company, Drackenheart. You're bold and exciting. Why not stay with your friends? No one has to be alone again. No one has to be hurt by their pasts."

"Gee, thanks. I'll pass and take my leave as soon as I can. Map be damned. This place isn't worth the trouble you've brought on me."

"The map to nowhere." The creature giggled. "Your father fooled you good." Rosanne's ears perked at the distinct crackle in the svartraug's voice, a tone which was all too keen to steer her to another conversation.

"There is something there. I just can't see it yet," she tried, refusing to let this go despite her earlier proclamations.

The svartraug let his eyes wander. "If you stay, I can give you everything you ever wanted."

"Do you even have that power?"

"It's within my grasp. The Dream guides us all, but on this island, you are at the mercy of *my* Dream."

Rosanne understood nothing. The man, the creature, was mad as a rabid dog, except he believed every word of his delusions. The other creatures she had met had no such concept. From what Farand explained, the hulder followed their queen and feared what Yerrik was, while Yerrik feared nothing. And the trolls ... were trolls. "How does a concept like that possess power?"

"How can I invade your mind as easily as I take a step?"

Rosanne raised a skeptical eyebrow at his twitchy gait. "You're not exactly giving me the impression that you're half as strong as you think you are."

"You don't even know what you're missing out. I can give you a taste of it before you accept. Or decline! You just have to let me in first." He held out its hand to her. The otherworldly feeling the madman gave her was that of disgust and cold. She couldn't help but feel like she had been through this before.

"I won't deceive you like Yerrik did," he whispered.

Rosanne's eyes widened and then turned into small slits of suspicion. "How do you know about him?"

"I can see it all!" The svartraug spread his arms wide. "You people are transparent to me. I wanna know more, see more, experience the world through your eyes! Your dreams and fears, courage and wonders are delicious food for my Dream!"

"Then what is the heart?"

"The heart is the spirit that created mountains and forests, streams and animals. It is the mother of us all."

"And you are its guardian?"

The svartraug threw its head back with a twitchy laughter. "The heart's Dream is mine!"

Rosanne took a step back. In her periphery, she spotted the red hull and golden sail of the *Red Queen* sailing in from the East. Base camp must have been attacked, the svartraug desperate to get rid of them one by one.

"If you say so. With that in mind, I'll respect your ownership of this place and take my leave." Rosanne's smirk of triumph turned to that of worry upon seeing the creature pull its human face into a crestfallen expression.

"What a shame," he murmured. Drawing the shell to his mouth, he whispered into it.

"What are you doing?" Rosanne asked, alarmed.

The man lowered the shell and turned to her, deathly calm. "The hermit fool wants you gone because you're a threat to him. But to me, you are food, food and entertainment. People rarely come anymore. Fifteen years since I was last visited by a man who wore that hat of yours."

His words were like a punch in her gut. "You met my father?"

"Long gone, but I remember everyone who visits. They're burned into my memory, trapped in the dream forever as a part of me. Their dreams are mine; their hopes and fears belong to me."

"You're fucking sick." Rosanne widened her stance, readying herself to attack. If she could get the shell back, she could at least derail the svartraug's focus. But the man stared towards the horizon with tranquillity, unbothered by her growing hostility. Rosanne ground her teeth. How dare this bastard underestimate her?

In response to the shell, a profound aquatic resonance sounded, trailed by rhythmic, resonant clicks which tore through her.

"What did you do?" her voice quivered as the implications became all too clear. Her hand hovered near her plasma pistol, ready to take this monster down.

His smile was almost burdened by a deep sadness as his eyes fixed on the horizon. "You came here chasing the ghost of your father, which is a moot effort. Will you stay if your love is gone? Or perhaps I can change your mind if your ship and your crew are gone as well?"

The animalistic rumble repeated, the same she had heard before they came to this island. From over the lip of the island appeared a massive transparent bulbous body, organs visible in the gelatinous mass. It was like a jellyfish and a squid in one, with floating tentacles accompanied by thread-like stingers. It let out a bellowing wail, which shook the earth and threw the shores into disarray. Rosanne clasped her hand over her ears and hunched over to best shield herself from the bombarding call tearing through her.

Her ears rang, and her insides coiled so painfully she thought she would hurl. "What the hell did you do?" she demanded. Whatever his affliction, the svartraug appeared unfazed by the noise.

"You and your secrets can never leave. I must protect the Grey Veil, protect the Dream!"

With its hooks, the Kraken tore into the ledge of the island, pulling itself over the lip with little effort, its massive body darkening the shore and the jungle with its shadow. Its bulbous head supported long tentacles that floated with its anti-gravity properties. Two enormous eyes spun around in different directions, taking in its surroundings.

With a single pounce, the Kraken glided towards the shore where the *Red Queen* sailed. Cannon-fire boomed from the ship, but the monster reached for it with enormous tentacles.

"Call it off!" Rosanne turned to the man in panic and drew her plasma pistol. The cannon-shots relented, and the ship dove out of the way of a swiping tentacle. "They have nothing to do with any of this! Let them go!"

But the hermit, or the svartraug, simply smiled. He turned to her, almost elated by her distress. "The Kraken is hungry too, but you have nothing to fear."

"Call it off, or I will fucking shoot!" The pistol trembled in her hand, the chamber loaded and ready. All she had to do was pull the trigger, yet her hand would not obey. She let out an unbridled scream, squeezing her finger over the trigger as hard as she could, but nothing happened. She couldn't fire it; her body couldn't obey her will. With a final nod, the svartraug turned and left, leaving Rosanne to the *Red Queen*'s harrowing confrontation.

The Kraken stretched out its tentacles, encircling the ship. The *Red Queen* evaded one, then another, but was ensnared by the third and came to a sudden halt. Distant screams reached her, and Rosanne could see the fervent activity on deck from the crew. Limbs curled around the ship, squeezing, the wood cracking and splintering. Rosanne watched in teary-eyed horror as the red wooden hull of the *Red Queen* caved in with a deafening crack and split in the middle.

Blood rushed through Rosanne's ears in violent pulses as she burst through the thick undergrowth of the jungle, tearing through vines blocking her path. Her breath came in choked hitches, but she hadn't noticed the pain in her burning lungs or how her legs wobbled as she picked her way towards the beach. The jungle was alive around her once more, but she couldn't stop for anything.

She didn't fear the Kraken getting her. The creature had floated over the waters and disappeared off the island as soon as it had broken the ship and discarded the vessel with disinterest.

She pushed aside the mental image of the *Queen* in its final flight before meeting its end and used this denial to fuel her determination. She had to look for survivors. The crew was her responsibility, and she had abandoned them for her selfish need for answers.

The desolate beach lay before her, waves gently lapping the shore. To the East, an enormous gouge in the sand had created tall sand banks like an artificial river running into the jungle. The ocean tore into the jungle edge with each rolling wave, carrying off loose soil from under thick-rooted trees. Her shoes sank deep into the sand when she crossed, struggling and panting from the strain.

The shoreline meandered in a bend out of view. Rosanne followed, chest tight, eyes locked on the path ahead. She came upon a battlefield of broken planks and ripped sails. A little further ahead lay the *Red Queen*, careened and half-buried in sand.

A crack ran through the middle of the forecastle, the figurehead buried in the sand and waves seeping into the snapped bowsprit. Deep furrows in the wood mimicked that of what Rosanne had seen on the *Retribution*, Ernest Blackwood's ship that had disappeared almost a year ago.

Rosanne traced a hand at the edge of the wood from where the tentacle had crushed against it. Her head felt light, the headache a screaming resonance in her brain of songs and whispers and clamouring voices. She fell to her knees and rested against the broken hull.

It was all gone.

Canvas fluttered in the breeze. Maybe if she could patch up the circuits like Creedy had done, if she could find him, then maybe they could salvage something from the ship and escape? She stood and wobbled towards the aft. The thruster panels were a wall of escaping electric violence. The tentacles had bent both panels inwards with terrifying ease and the ports were reduced to a mangled mess of metal. Exposed wiring and conductors crackled, and in their precarious state of function, they wouldn't hold up any length of time.

Higgs would know what to do. The engineers were the best she had ever met. Maybe they could ...

"Hello!" she called out. "Farand!" she tried again. Rosanne located the partially broken ladder on the hull and climbed aboard. The back half of the ship rested on the side, and Rosanne navigated with support from the rails and torn ratlines. No one was on deck. She wrestled with the door to her quarters and battered it free with a firm shoulder. Her room was split wide open. The entire back wall with the window was crushed inward, the collapsed floor gaping to the lower deck. What remained of the curtains fluttered in the wind. The scene reminded her of the *Retribution*, of how Nelson must have felt when he stepped into the room where his father had perished. A tight knot formed in her stomach, and she exited with haste.

She searched through the guest cabins on the sick bay and even climbed down the torn middle of the ship to the decks below. She called and called out to anyone who might still be there.

Turning her attention to the forecastle, she thought maybe the crew had hunkered up on the remains of the galley. The tables piled in a broken heap alongside the wall. Hammond's kitchen was an unrecognisable mess of flung pots, pans and smashed pickle jars. Among the wreckage of broken cannons, torn hammocks and planks on the gun deck was nothing but herself.

Rosanne exited the ship, took a few steps out to the warm sand, and collapsed.

Everyone was gone, just like the *Retribution,* just like her father and his crew. A soft patter of tears hit the sand by her hands, and her sight blurred beyond recognition.

"I was so careful. I had planned everything out and taken every precaution. Why the fuck did it go so wrong?" she shrieked through her sobs, the call scratching her throat and leaving her gasping. She curled in the sand, unable to sit up any longer as she let the pain wash over her.

CHAPTER THIRTY-ONE

UNSPOKEN WORDS

Minutes passed, maybe an hour or two. Rosanne didn't know. Spent from the tears shed and the screams curdling her insides, everything burned like a raging fever. With a gentle touch, she let her fingers glide around the socket of her swollen and tender eyes. She drifted between consciousness and memories like she was locked in a glass cage without the means to interact with the world around her. The sun was setting somewhere in the distance through the cloudy layers, magenta and Payne's grey. Was the sunset always this beautiful?

"Hello, Ros," a voice called to her. She sat up quickly to find herself staring at the familiar shape that was Antony. He gave her a rueful smile and sat down next to her. He was a week unshaven, with dark blues under his eyes, but still, the man who had gained her affection.

"Where were you?"

A look of confusion crossed his face, and he shook his head. "I ... can't remember. I was with you in our tent and in the next moment ..." He looked to the horizon. "I met the svartraug, the creature that devours dreams."

Her breath caught in her throat, but Antony didn't share her reaction. "You saw it? How did you escape?"

Antony splayed his hands out briefly before folding them again. "I'm sorry I wasn't there for you Ros. I ... I don't know why I left the camp."

The silence swept over them like a drizzle. Rosanne massaged the digits of her hands and sorted her thoughts in her mind before she spoke. "You said you weren't strong enough to weather this storm with me." She hadn't wanted it to sound like an attack, but bitterness welled up inside, and her emotions from losing the ship and the crew whose lives she was responsible for, overflowed.

"I did?" He looked despondent in his shame. "I should have told you about the voices, Ros. Should have told you a lot of things that," he searched for the word, waving his hand around, "This place has stolen everything that I am. Everything that I was. I saw you hold up so well while I wanted nothing but to run back home like a coward. And the nightmares!" He let out a hollow laugh which quickly disintegrated to a look of shame. "I can't even make sense of what's real and what's not anymore. My family's farm burned to ashes, and my siblings ... remembering broke my soul, Ros. And I never told you."

Rosanne's lips parted. A look of uncertainty shadowed her features. "I thought your family's farm was still thriving and your sister and brother were married with families. We were going to visit them after our trip here, remember?"

Antony's gaze flickered through waves of uncertainty, his brows furrowed. "But then the memories ..."

Gently, Rosanne laid a hand over his and squeezed. "It was a dream. Maybe the svartraug gave it to you for this exact purpose, to confuse you."

"What did you dream about?" he asked.

Rosanne shook her head. "Nothing that challenges my memories. Only echoes and images of what was going on around us. It's been a source of protection. That's how I found you by the pond that night. I can't explain it. It shouldn't even be possible, but everything here is insane! You leaving, I don't blame you. I truly can't lay that on you when we were tortured by this entity every day! What happened on the other island was nothing compared to this. I am sorry, Antony. I am so so sorry." Her voice broke as she burst into tears again, then subdued her sobs with a grimace. Antony pulled her close in a tight embrace.

"For better and for worse, Ros, you have shown me what man I am, and I am ashamed of my shortcomings. I think nothing less of you. You are by far the strongest person I know, in heart and in soul."

"I'm not." She sniffed. "I can't be. Not when I abandoned everything and let this happen. My crew, all the people I have spent years with, are gone. And it's my fault."

"It's the svartraug's fault, and you know it."

The last bit of sun disappeared behind the mast of the *Red Queen* as night settled in. The glint of a distant star rose on the horizon.

"Antony, how did you escape the svartraug?" Rosanne asked again. Her gaze lingered on his seemingly unharmed limb. "Your wound ..." she pointed to his functioning arm and shoulder, which he flexed.

He grimaced in pain, massaging the side of his head. "I was hurt. I was sure the svartraug captured me, but the next thing I knew I'm in the forest somewhere, and I heard cannon fire."

"No sign of people? Did the monsters come for you? What about the whispers?"

He shook his head. "No whispers. Though the weather has been clear."

Rosanne pushed herself away from Antony, a thoughtful expression lining her face. "When the weather has been clear, the monsters have attacked. When it rained, it was the svartraug and its mimics. Why is it leaving us alone now when we're at our most vulnerable?"

He stood with her as she scanned the beach.

"Come with me." She strode towards the broken ship.

"You have that look," he said, with a gleam in his eyes.

"What look?"

"The one you wear whenever you're about to figure something out."

Rosanne smiled, perhaps for the first time in days. "I shall try not to disappoint, then."

They climbed the ladder and headed for her quarters. Inside, she tore through drawers, opened chests and boxes and other concealed compartments.

"What are you looking for?"

"I'm not sure. When I was first here, I didn't question anything that I saw. I guess what I'm looking for are the things I can't see."

"Such as?"

Rosanne slammed her trunk shut after rummaging through her clothes. "The crew's belongings!" She exited the room in a hurry. Antony followed her down the rope to the second level. They hobbled against the awkward tilt of the ship. "Seek out any chest and container. The crew keeps their stash close to their hammocks."

Antony excavated a small trunk from the debris. "Here's one!" He opened it.

"What's in it?" Rosanne came up to him.

"There's nothing in it. Nothing at all."

"It's empty?"

They exchanged glances.

"Let's find other ones," she urged. They tore through all the trunks and chests they could to find, upending the gundeck.

"Why would the crew's belongings be missing?" Antony leaned against the wall to catch his breath after they had spent the better part of the hour looking for things that should be there.

"Makes little sense, does it?" Rosanne asked as she led the way to engineering. Admittedly, she had never been inside the engineers' private quarters since she hired them. She expected to find bunk beds and tables with strange inventions, at least by Ida's side. Higgs often downed brandy to ease his arthritis, but neither room had as much as a stitch in them. Only Ida's multi-focus goggles with their myriad lenses rested conspicuously in the middle of the worktable.

Rosanne took it in her hand, examining the well-worn leather. "Like your wound, a lot of things are missing. Or rather details," she trailed off and turned to him. "Antony, I don't think we're awake."

His eyes fixed on hers, but his silence spoke volumes. After a moment, he nodded. "We're still trapped by the svartraug. But how are we in the same dream?"

Rosanne shook her head. "I don't know, but something it said made me think. It remembers everyone it possesses, and we know it can imitate people. It creates nightmares to fool us, to weaken our mind, to lead us into its dream. The hermit told me that the svartraug's dream is law. That's how it feeds off us. What if it can't make memories out of things it has never seen, like the people it has never possessed?"

Nodding, Antony studied the strap in Rosanne's hand. "Then Jeffs' things would still be here. Yours and mine are. Where can we find his trunk?"

Rosanne chewed on her bottom lip in thought. "I ... don't know. The crew swap hammocks a lot, and I don't keep track. I know Farand's quarters, but I have never been much to rummage through my crew's things."

Antony pushed away from the wall and folded his arms. "Then what do we do?"

Running a hand through her curls, Rosanne drew a deep breath. "If the svartraug trapped us in its dream, it must have taken us somewhere it wouldn't be disturbed."

"The mountains, maybe?"

Rosanne tried to remember and grimaced. A mind-splitting migraine grew all the fussier and bombarded her skull with hazy memories. "The bastard's preventing us from remembering. There's something in the mountain, and it wants us there. Like the mimics in the forest tried to keep us away after we went west. That's where we need to go."

Antony placed a hand on her shoulder to prevent her from rushing out of the room. "Ros, before we do anything rash, you know how we wake up when we fall in a dream or become scared? What if we tried that first?"

Yerrik's words echoed in her mind, clear as day. She rejected the idea, saying, "We'll die if we do, Antony. I can't explain how I know; I just do. The mountain has many entrances. If we can find one, we might get to where the svartraug took us."

"But if this is a dream for us two, why bother with these theatrics?"

"I don't know. Maybe to distract us. Or ... entertainment!" Rosanne exclaimed. "I remember the svartraug saying it used us for food and entertainment." She paced the room, massaging her temples as the headache worsened the more she forced herself to remember. Rosanne paused as a certain pale-faced recruit entered her mind. "Aros spoke of a cave entrance on top of the mountain. On the flat top." She pointed through the broken window to the central mountain squeezed between jagged crests. "We have a way in!"

"We got a long climb ahead of us, then."

"Are you ready to face the monster?" Rosanne looked to Antony, a nervous smile painted on her lips.

"No, but I have to be."

They spent what little light remained of the day navigating the jungle to the foot of the mountain. Despite the ridiculous trek, they managed the distance in less than two hours, a journey that previously took half a day.

"If that isn't a sign this world is a dream, I don't know what is. It's like it's morphing to suit our needs." Rosanne navigated between her steps, sliding on the loose rocks, catching herself before she fell on her side.

"Why would the svartraug even design the dream that way? Any half-wit would realise this island makes little scientific sense besides the Grey Veil's usual circus." Antony said in a tone she hadn't heard him use, his patience clearly spent. "Or why don't we feel tired or hungry after realising this isn't the real world?"

"I am not looking a gift horse in the mouth. Antony, look." She pointed to where the rays of sun shone through the thinning clouds.

"A northern sunrise?" Rosanne let out an incredulous laugh. "The svar-traug doesn't know where east and west are? And it was day not that long ago!"

He raised a hand to calm her. "But if it can possess our memories, wouldn't it know?"

Her thoughtful expression gave him a pause. "Few if any have success-fully navigated the Veil before us. We're the only ones who know where north is, and if the island also spins, the svartraug would never know. But if, as you say, it possessed us, it should know. Something isn't adding up. Unless it, for some reason, hasn't taken us over completely."

Realisation dawned in his eyes. "This explains why the skies looked so strange. It feels like the more we believe this world is a dream, the more it falls apart." They stared to the purple and turquoise hues surrounding the sunrise, as if bathed in Aurora Borealis.

They discovered the path Aros had told her about and followed it through the nooks and crannies hugging the mountainside. This far up in the atmosphere, Rosanne should fight for breath with every step, but she felt fine. She didn't count her blessings just yet as they made the final ascent which placed them on the top of the mountain.

The rocky shelving dug into the mountain, but true to Aros' words, there was the entrance.

"Gentlemen first," Antony volunteered.

Rosanne looked around the grassy plateau, not spotting anything they could use to create light. "We don't have any torches."

"Maybe we can conjure some glowworms from our imagination?" He gave her a smile of the man she missed, one untouched by the Grey Veil.

"The sun rising in the north was an astronomical stretch, so I don't see why not?"

Poking their heads into the cave, the deep darkness was broken by a dim glow, outlining the floors and the ceiling. "The halls are lighting up," Rosanne marvelled at the moss-covered walls illuminated in green. She caught Antony with his hands cupped in front of him. "What are you doing?"

"Do we have Ida's alchemical lamp yet? Because that thing is a marvel." He cracked open an eye, and his face fell when he saw his empty hands. "Worth a shot."

Despite their dire situation, Rosanne let out a giggle.

They meandered through the many hallways, marking their paths and backtracking from dead-ends. In the absence of hunger or sleep, time withered like a distant memory. They didn't encounter a single monster.

Rosanne stared into the lava pool, the room scorching, but she shrugged off her discomfort, but aware that one misstep into the thick mass would obliterate her. She didn't want to find out what it did to her physical body if she died in a dream. Even if she didn't know for sure, she heeded Yerrik's warning. In his absence, Rosanne realised how dependent she had been on her wits after coming here, and she wasn't doing as well as she hoped. He had looked after her the best he could, by any means possible. As a creature of the Veil, she assumed this place connected them, like the svartraug being connected to every living creature on this island.

They came upon a cavern filled with light. In its centre stood a boulder perched on a natural volcanic altar formation.

Furrowing her brows, feeling the filaments of hazy memories solidify the more she took in the scene; a large room, volcanic ash and black mud. "The meteor. I remember now. The svartraug brought me here and shoved me into that strange mud all the creatures are born from."

"It's coming back to me. I woke up here, but then the svartraug..." Antony shook his head. Rosanne approached the boulder, listening to its pulsating melody like that of a heartbeat. She stretched out a hand, her fingers tingling with anticipation. No warning bells called in her mind, but she wasn't sure this was wise. She took a chance anyway and placed a hand on it. An assault of images flashed in her mind. In one moment, she was standing in the room; the next, she was floating in darkness dotted with distant stars and veils of white. Flailing, she tried to orient herself, coming to see a blue sphere shining from the reflection of a distant yellow light. Was this their planet and sun? When she turned, she spotted a blue flaming ball trailing a long tail hurtling past her. It shot towards the planet. Red flames burst off it as it penetrated the atmosphere, spreading in a spectacular umbrella of small fires crashing into the ocean. The large mass of the meteor disappeared into the blue depths, as quietly as its journey through space.

In one instance, Rosanne found herself above the impact site, a small crater at the bottom of the ragged sea floor. She grasped her throat, attempting to breathe, but soon realised the waters didn't sting her eyes or flow into her mouth and nose. Unexpectedly, air filled her lungs.

Looking down, she saw magma bubbling from the depths, rising and crusting as it stacked and built layers of rock and minerals. Surrounding it, a curious black mass stretched out from the centre,. It grew and grew at such rapid speed when Rosanne blinked, the impact site turned into what she recognised to be the bare island. Heavy mist flowed from the central mountain chain, spreading out. It snaked across the waters in long ribbons, elongating and thickening before rising high into the atmosphere. The Grey Veil. The meteor released its hold on her, and Rosanne gasped as she was back in the chamber with Antony.

"Are you alright?" Antony rushed to her side. "Didn't you hear me when I called for you?"

"I'm fine," she said, an incredulous smile replacing her confusion. "Antony, I think this is the birthplace of the fog. The meteor is the Grey Veil! The svartraug's ramblings made no sense, but seeing this now, it does." Rosanne was overwhelmed by the images still flashing through her mind. The bane of the northern hemisphere seas had a source, and she was standing right next to it. "You found it, Dad. You found the heart of the Veil and didn't even know."

"Ros." Antony's low warning voice alerted her to the distant clicks and cries echoing through the hallways. The creatures in the pods around them stirred. The hybrid in the wall nearest them yawned, barnacles dancing on his jaw. Another body in the nearest basin shifted and submerged itself. Rosanne and Antony stood back-to-back, observing the creatures with acute stillness. The shuffling and sleepy moans of complaints grew with the cries.

Antony sucked in his breath. "We need to see if our bodies are around somewhere."

With sweat running down her face, Rosanne nodded. They manoeuvred around the room with quick, light steps, studying all the different shapes they could see in the walls and pods. A mermaid sleepily reached out for her, Rosanne gently pushed her lethargic hand aside. The mermaid slumped as if bereft of all strength to follow through, returning to slumber.

Rosanne spotted a face almost seamlessly blending with the adjacent, recognising it as her own. She froze, staring at the perfect copy of herself—no, her actual body. It was eerie watching herself in a peaceful slumber undisturbed by the growing commotion around them.

She ran a hand over her grime-covered face. "Come on. Wake up!" Her expression remained unchanged. Behind her, the urgent clacks of the hybrids echoed out as they stormed into the meteor chamber. The smaller, with only a torso, arms, and a head, spotted Rosanne trying to wake herself from the dream, and launched its spear across the room. A sharp pain pierced her right below her ribcage.

Rosanne cried out, and her face in the wall contorted and screamed with her.

Antony rushed in from a side room and caught Rosanne before she collapsed to the floor. The wooden handle of the spear bit into her flesh, and hot flashes pulsated around the wound. Her voice morphed into an interrupted guttural cry. She saw his mouth move but could not hear what he said through the pounding in her ears. A twitchy shadow lurked in the background, closing in on them.

"B-behind you!" she finally choked out. Antony quickly released her, drew back, and dodged a hurtling spear. Without a moment's hesitation Antony jumped on the hybrid's vast body, yanking the spear right out of the humanoid's hands. Unable to turn and grab him at its shelled back, the creature lifted pincers and snapped for Antony, but the man redirected the spear and drove it into the creature's chest. With a howl, the creature thrashed, threw Antony off, and eventually collapsed on the floor in a heap of limbs. Antony raced to Rosanne and cradled her in his arms.

"More are coming. We need to wake you up." He moved to stand, but Rosanne grabbed his arm.

"Find ... find your body first!" she urged and moaned from the moving spear. Her head spun, and she struggled to make out anything around her.

"We need to get you out first."

"There's no time! They're coming." A fervent growl grew closer, by a flock of discordant cries, as if rallying. Antony took her hand, wetting his lips. His eyes locked with hers.

"None of this is your fault, Ros. I left the camp. I fell for the svartraug's lies."

"You don't know what will happen if they get you." Rosanne uttered, but Antony shushed her, a gentle smile replaced his distress.

"Let me go, Ros. Let go of your resentment and guilt. I was just as willing as a participant in this game of ours. We were comfort in an unyielding world, and we played dangerously with fire. I have no regrets, only that I wasn't stronger for you when you needed me the most." Even in those brutal, slow seconds, Antony's eyes softened as he regarded her with all the love that he had.

"I can't let you go! Not again..." Rosanne hitched a breath, but Antony stroked her cheek with a sad smile.

"You always were the strong one, Ros, and this pain isn't real. You can do it." He released her then, grabbing for the spear lodged in her abdomen.

Rosanne shook her head. "No! Don't!"

Antony yanked at the weapon, pulling it with a squelch. Rosanne's howl filled the chambers. A nearby creature stirred and let out pained moans as if resonating with her.

"It's not real!" Antony cupped her face. "It's not real, Ros." Rosanne felt faint from the intense pain, the deep burning and sharp throbs rushing through her, making her breath hitch and all the muscles in her body tense. Tears spilled from her eyes. A creature in the wall, another hybrid, snagged her attention, as its anatomy was malformed and skin lacked in places as if still being made. She locked on to this image, taking in the details of the protruding bare skeleton just to keep herself grounded when the pain raged, and her mind wanted to break down.

"I'll hold them off. Get yourself awake. Get out of here and don't look back," Antony's voice called to her through her muffled hearing. She watched him run out of the chamber, spear raised, shouting for the hybrids' attention. Her eyes blurred so much that her surroundings were wet blobs of movement. The creatures were waking up, arms flailing, and cries and moans and screeches filled the rooms. Rosanne breathed through the pain, breathed through the panic her body induced. Clutching her bleeding side, she crawled to her feet, whimpering, and supported herself on the wall where her body rested.

The pain wasn't real, but if she died here, she would never awaken. Through waves of dream-induced agony, Rosanne remembered the strange waters, the same waters where the svartraug lived. She felt separate from her reflection, disassociating from her physical self in favour of the reflection inviting her in. What if this was the opposite, that she had to reconnect with her body to get out of the dream?

Rosanne rested her forehead against her body's and closed her eyes. She breathed deep, her mind telling her that this was real when, in fact, it was not. She only thought it was real, but that her body, now that she could see it, touch it, knew that it wasn't real. Rosanne felt a kinship in the face she barely recognised. She knew this one, knew what awaited her on the island and who her enemies were. Rosanne fell forward, light as if floating, at rest with her battles. This was her struggle and no one else's, and finally, Rosanne felt she could accept it.

CHAPTER THIRTY-TWO

SQUID GAME

The last time Farand was this lightheaded was after military service cadet training when he was fifteen. His vision swam with shades of greens and blues, and he pawed the air for purchase. Finding the wheel, his knees wobbled as he stood. Bile burned at his throat, but he stubbornly kept it down. There was nothing he could do. Gradually, his sight cleared, and he could assess the situation he undoubtedly had gotten himself into.

The ship was anchored alongside the snow-crested mountains between the peak and the dense forest below, far higher than the atmos could handle. That explained the light-headedness and nausea. The monstrous Kraken lingered to the north, pacing the shoreline with gentle nudges of its tentacles while keeping its eyes glued on them. Farand didn't know why the beast didn't simply float over and devour them right there, but he didn't deny it gave him reprieve.

Farand had tried to push past the mountain chain by cutting through the island for a passage to the other side, but without the proper precautions, he would end up killing them all. They were stuck between the Kraken, the mountains, and the jungle.

Farand slumped by the wheel, already spent. He spotted Dalia and Hwang crawling up to the main deck from below. Dalia stopped every so often to catch her breath; her pale face was a sign Farand shouldn't push the crew any further in their attempt to escape.

"Sir," she greeted on all fours before collapsing on her side and rolling on her back, her pallid face slick and covered in sweat. "The failed atmos gave us all a bit of a shock. We should go lower."

"I apologise, Watch Captain. I couldn't find a passage through the mountains." He paused as his heart slammed in his chest, the uncomfortable thrumming in his body an unsettling feeling he wasn't used to. "It's not following us." He nodded towards the squid lumbering by the beach, waving angry tentacles. Dalia cracked open an eye and turned her head to the side.

"That's some good news. If we're lucky, the creatures in the forest won't realise we're here, but that might be a pipe dream."

Farand stood and leaned against the wheel to catch his breath. "I can take us above the canopy, but we need to stay vigilant."

Dalia gave a weak thumbs up before the arm collapsed to her side.

Farand grasped for the levers, leaning against the control panel as support. He pushed the levers and stepped on the pedals to glide the ship away from the mountain with a gentle push of the hull's thrusters. He lowered them towards the forest canopy, the massive ship gliding effortlessly in almost complete silence.

This close to the mountains, the forest stood on an elevation above the rest, the landscaping sloping towards the shore. Farand had little to go on, a mere hundred meters before the ship hovered above the treetops. The engine gave a loud sputter, and a resonating hum vibrated through the ship until it died into silence. Farand stepped on the pedals and pulled the wheel, but nothing happened.

He closed his eyes and, with a deep resounding sigh, muttered, "Merde." He turned his attention to the intercom, waiting for Higgs. They shouldn't have engine trouble after the upgrades they did, but you never knew. A minute passed, but nothing happened. Farand furrowed his brows.

The gentle mountain breeze suddenly disappeared, and the air filled his lungs. His ears popped and he rolled his jaw to even the pressure. The atmos was operational again. Farand allowed himself to lie down on the floor despite knowing another danger could sneak upon them. He was too exhausted to care. The forest below was alive with bird cries. *A good sign*, he told himself.

As the Master of Decks, Farand knew his first order of business was to ensure the crew's health and mental state, but his body wouldn't obey him. His muscles were like wildfire spreading down his limbs. It was a feeling unlike anything he had experienced before, showing him how close he had been to performing irreversible damage with his reckless-ness. He had been careful so far, but at that moment when the Kraken had attacked them, his critical thinking had almost been their doom.

He didn't know who to thank that the Kraken hadn't followed them.

Dalia was all but passed out, chest rising and falling in gentle waves. Farand laid his jacket over her before shuffling below deck.

The gundeck was reduced to piles of tossed benches and strewn can-nonballs. Hwang and Olivier leaned against the hull beside their can-nons. Olivier gave a lethargic wave.

"Get above deck. The air is better there," Farand said and helped Olivier to the stairs. The youth waved him off and crawled the remaining steps himself. Hwang refused Farand's help altogether and walked out on his own with the expert skill of a midnight drunkard.

Towards the front, the door to Doc's infirmary stood ajar. Farand peeked inside, spotting the ship's doctor slumped in the chair, legs elevated on the desk. Quinn lay on the sickbed. His face was pale, his lips cracked dry, and there was fervent movement beneath his eyelids.

"Doc," Farand greeted quietly.

"You bastard." Doc's moustache wiggled with his puckered lips. "You done near killed us all! We're not built to take air pressure changes this quickly, you wet sock!" The older man waved a finger with such force his head lolled. The small piece of hair on top of his head flopped to the side, exposing the fishnet base used to sew the strands in. Doc quickly flipped it back and combed the strands in place.

Farand drew an apologetic smile. "Forgive me, sir. It won't happen again." Despite having seniority in the ship's hierarchy, Farand never considered having such among the older crew regardless of position. Doc was an older gentleman, and there was only so much he could take, but Farand was glad to see him up and about, or at least somewhat. His lip certainly hadn't changed. Nor his temper.

"How's Quinn?"

Doc leaned back in his chair, energy spent. "Lad's in terrible shape, more so after your little stunt. His lungs are wrecked, and his breathing shallow. It's up to the good lord now."

The doc's words tugged at Farand's heart and left a lump in his throat. Farand hadn't needed to cross the mountains; if he had kept his attention on the Kraken, he would have realised it wasn't following them. Normally, his spotter kept an eye on attackers for him, but he hadn't had any as they were all busy firing the cannons. He had miscalculated, and Quinn was paying the price.

Farand ran a hand through his short-cropped curls damp from sweat and grime. "Please stay with him, Doc. I have to check on Higgs and Hammond."

"Those old men are going to chew your head off if you approach them now, mark my words. There's no bed for you here, lieutenant," Doc warned, but Farand simply nodded.

He continued down the stairs to the cargo deck. This deep in the ship, the atmosphere was protected from sudden fluctuation, but not for long. He found Higgs storming through the door, a wrench raised with his hand and a fiery glare beneath bushy eyebrows. Farand froze on the spot. Higgs wasn't usually this volatile. Was it a mimic?

"You son of a wallaby dingus! What the hell were you thinking?"

"Happy to see you too, Higgs," Farand's genuine relief was drowned out by the Chief Engineer's flaring temper.

"It'll take more than that to crack me! You, lad, just about got us all stranded on this godforsaken island. The strain on the engine fried my nose hairs!"

So, this wasn't about the failing atmos? Farand didn't ask. Higgs continued his tantrum with wide, gesticulating movements. "I suppose since you aren't the one usually driving—there are certain things you must never do, and *that* was one of them! Had you pushed on any longer, the whole back panel would only work in a scrapyard."

"I'm sorry, Higgs. I was careless."

"Damn straight you were, lad! The ship wasn't made for turns like that. Don't dare put us through something like that if you lose your head again." He lifted the wrench again before the tall bulk of a man, and

Farand, thin-lipped and respectful of the head-shorter chief engineer, nodded. "Now, where are we at? It's awfully noisy for being just us."

"What do you mean, sir?"

Higgs jabbed a finger into his ear and wiggled, then finished with a shake of his head. "I mean all the jibber jabber. I know my hearing isn't the best, so I know that it's loud. Can't make a word out of what they're saying, though."

Farand looked around the cargo hold, finding nothing but a couple of flies and Senior Petty Officer Ratcatcher chasing them.

Was this another one of the Veil's magic? Farand had been too busy with everyone's safety that he hadn't allowed himself to focus on anything else. He closed his eyes and listened. Soft voices like a breeze tickled at the edge of his ears, distant and tittering.

Farand lowered his voice. "Those aren't people, Higgs."

The engineer's bushy brows rose. "Damn spirit shenanigans."

"Even here?"

"It can reach us anywhere on this island. Damn annoying, that's what they are. Don't give them too much focus, sir. You might get lost in their calls and wander off. I'm going to maintain Sally while we're here. Don't move the ship. Don't even fire her up until I say so."

Farand nodded and left the older man to his work. He proceeded towards the stairs when he caught sight of a person whose back was turned, facing the wall of secured supplies. Farand didn't recognise him.

"Everything alright?" he asked. The person turned a pale face with wild eyes towards him. Farand paused as a chill ran through him. It was Jeffs, but the jovial man's usual expression was lacking and left Farand feeling like he was staring into a void.

With one hand on the rope securing the goods to the shelving, Jeffs gave it a sharp tug, and the knot came apart with ease. He then dragged out the crate, which he dropped. The crate smashed on the floorboards, spilling dried goods everywhere.

It wasn't his actions which had Farand frozen in his movement, but his eyes, those wild yet dead orbs, which bore through him.

"What the hell are you doing?" He reached for the seaman, who was pulling at a second crate. He shrugged off Farand's grasp, but the large man locked him by his arms and pulled him away. The crate crashed against the floor anyway and shattered. Dried biscuits tumbled out in piles.

Jeffs kicked out and clawed at Farand. Applying both brute strength and his bulk, Farand tossed Jeffs into one of the empty stalls for livestock, desperate for distance between them. The man crashed against the wall and paused as he gathered himself, but his expression remained unchanged. He then fixed his gaze on Farand, hunched over, and lunged. Farand backpedalled. Jeffs kicked out, making Farand retreat before he grabbed a crate lid, which he smashed into Farand's guarded side. The lieutenant staggered and caught himself on one of the stalls.

With a roar, he grabbed Jeffs by his curled fist and tugged, causing the man to overbalance and swing past him. In one fluid motion, Farand placed his other hand on the back of Jeff's head, then rammed his skull into the stall wall. Jeff's head exploded in a spray of inky black water.

Farand stared at his hand in horror as Jeffs' form collapsed, only to dissolve into the same black liquid, converging on the floor and seeping through the wood.

Farand blinked. The enveloping silence which followed stole the whispers, and he couldn't form a single thought with which to explain what had just happened. Then it dawned on him, the people at the beach staring vacantly up at him ... Jeffs was a mimic.

The wound on his hand bled a little, but Farand let it be.

The intruder had targeted their provisions. Without them, they would be forced to leave the ship to get food and water.

"Merde," he swore and thundered towards the kitchen pantry. He met Hammond on the way.

"I've been looking all over the blasted ship for you, sir! What the blazes is going on?. Our supplies are ruined!" The older man threw his hands out in frustration.

Farand tore open the pantry door. Overturned barrels of flour spread over the wet floor, and nets of potatoes had been ripped open and stomped to a starchy inedible mass. Garlic and onions lay crumpled and crushed, and whatever remained of Hammond and Hwang's kimchi mingled with the flour, leaving a spicy scent grabbing at their noses.

"We still have our water supplies, right?" Farand turned to Hammond, who looked alarmed.

"Didn't get that far."

Farand turned on his heel and descended to the ballast trapdoor in the floor. Tearing it open, he smashed the lid against the floor. Hammond handed him a lamp, and Farand skipped steps as he flew down the ladder. The arranged barrels of reserve water had all been tossed around, the lids opened or the barrels themselves cracked. Whatever water was stored here was now a puddle below the ballast.

Farand caught the outline of a person standing in the dark. He shone the light over the pale face of a woman in her twenties wearing a dishevelled, frilly ball gown and sparkling jewellery. Her wild look focused on the next barrel.

The woman blinked. Her dress greyed and blackened to a watery mass which ran through the rocky ballast and disappeared.

Farand roared and kicked an empty barrel. "They destroyed everything we needed to remain on the ship."

Above him, Hammond looked on, his face a grim mask. "Without water, we can't eat much of the dry stuff before people get sick."

"We must set sail, but the engine's damaged, and the nearest viable water with potential food sources is guarded by a giant squid."

Hammond opened his mouth, wearing the expression he did whenever he was about to make a joke or a clever comment, but he seemingly checked himself, and he clapped his mouth shut.

"We need to distract the Kraken," Farand muttered to himself.

"Sir, if I may. We're not in any danger yet. We have until tomorrow at least, before people go thirsty. Three days until the lines between friend and food gets fuzzy."

"A monster that size could wait for us forever if it wanted to. It is hellbent on getting us, but something is preventing it from coming here. Why?"

"It seems odd it attacked us out of nowhere, too."

"As if summoned here. Mr. Hammond, do you think a powerful spirit able to infiltrate a person's dreams can somehow call for a giant squid?"

"I only cook the squid, sir."

"Maybe we can distract it with fire," Farand muttered, completely unperturbed by the cook's quips.

A wry smile crossed Hammond's face. "The jungle is as wet as a—

"Do *not* finish that sentence, Mr. Hammond. But it gave me an idea." Farand tapped the lid of a red-painted barrel, the paint forming the letters O. I. L.

In the sole two-seater scouting boat, Olivier and Hwang sat crammed with two barrels of whale oil and excess gunpowder between them. The anti-gravity ports struggled against the additional weight, given how the transport over-arched with each subtle change made on their course.

Farand observed the boat weave between the massive trees until the canopy hid them from view. With their supplies turned to pigswill, the skeleton crew had spent the rest of the night scraping together whatever supplies they could find. The imposters had been thorough. Nothing remained save a few dates no one was hungry enough to eat and Kristoff's dry biscuit hoard. No one had had any water all day besides the occasional rainfall, and the mood among the crew quickly changed.

"Fingers crossed the Kraken doesn't understand what we're up to," Farand said as Watch Captain Dalia came skulking up to him. "What's wrong?" He straightened. Her sour demeanour was uncharacteristic.

"I'm hangry," she grumbled.

"Hammond's been salvaging what he can, but I wouldn't rely on it. If this goes according to plan, we can slip out and head west without the squid following us, and we'll be back to having food and water at your behest."

Dalia pursed her lips and nodded. "Respectfully, sir, was it a good idea to send Olivier on this mission?"

Farand chuckled. "I have never seen him more motivated than when he gets to set something on fire, and gunpowder and oil should keep him on his toes. Besides, Hwang is supervising. Hopefully, he doesn't take the entire island with him when the fuse blows." Their gazes glided over to the floating monstrosity. "There's no telling what will happen once the oil ignites, but if it draws the monster away, we can flee."

"I'm getting a sense of déjà vu to our last Paradise Island visit. Besides the hulder," Dalia noted. They turned their attention toward the rumbling call of the Kraken. It flailed tentacles in the air and beat into the shallows, sending massive sprays of saltwater into the air.

Farand rubbed his temples. "That thing hunting us makes no sense."

Dalia bobbed her head. "Like a giant ten-armed guard dog. How long do you reckon we need to get out of here?"

"Hard to say. Olivier and Hwang need to return first, and we know the Kraken is fast. Could be minutes."

Higgs came up on deck, covered in grease and scrapes, the sweat running through his shirt. "I've double and triple-checked Sally. She should be able to take a quick get-the-hell-out-of-here whenever our boys return."

Farand did a quick system's check before returning to the department heads, all three watched the forest with close interest. Minutes ticked by, then an hour.

In the distance, a sudden boom was followed by black smoke rising past the bend of the mountain, followed by a secondary explosion. Black plumes shot to the sky from the depths of the jungle, carried by the western blowing winds.

"I thought they only got oil?" Higgs questioned.

"So did I, Chief. Must have taken a stick of dynamite with them," Farand noted, not really mad at the sailors, but explosives weren't cheap, and someone had to pay for it.

The Kraken turned its head toward the smoke, stretching out long tentacles and grabbing a rocky outcrop to pull itself forward.

Farand knocked on the railing. "That's our cue."

"No sails?" Dalia asked.

"We run on reserves. Have a cannon or two ready in case the squid doesn't take the bait, and aim at the beak."

Dalia disappeared below deck while Farand stalked to the quarter-deck, and Higgs returned to the engine room to fire up Sally. The electric hum came alive within minutes, and Farand turned the ship westward.

The scouting boat came into view just as they were ready to move. Hwang and Olivier flew the little boat right to the main deck and set it down. They went to remove the cargo door, but Farand called for their attention. "Not time for that! Get below deck and ready the cannons." Farand spun the wheel.

The men did as they were told.

Farand kept the ship at a crawl in case the squid turned its eyes on them. They flew so low they almost touched the treetops, and Farand had a hard time concentrating on both the Kraken and the treetops, even with Olivier spying from the forecastle (the crow's nest was resting in the shallows somewhere). He didn't know how the captain did it. She made it seem so easy.

With the smoke plume a couple of kilometres east, the Kraken moved drew further away from, lingering just outside the forest's edge. Even at this distance, the thing was massive, but its attention remained firm on the smoke.

"It's working," Farand muttered to himself with a weak sense of relief.

They were patching one problem after another. With the ink-people forcing their hand like this, this was a small victory and just another hole in the boat he had to plug. Food would have to wait. It was water that was the problem. With the creature-infested ponds and rabid wildlife, their best chance was to rendezvous with the captain near a saltwater source and figure out from there how to solve their supply issue. Unless the dream invader had gotten to her too.

After driving for about a kilometre, the Kraken was a shrinking dot in the distance, and Farand chanced to speed up their escape. At a normal pace, the back panel would be a bright blue blaze of energy easily spotted a mile away, but their gracious head start comforted him. But, as with their luck, the weather took a turn for the worse and rain pattered against the decks. The relentless whispers bore into his skull in ever-increasing echoes. They overpowered him and made him deaf to his own voice and the world around him.

"Leave the ship!"

"You must flee."

"It's not safe there," the individual voices called to him in a discordant crescendo. Farand growled and pounded his fist into the instrument panel, creating a dent in the metal and a dull ache in his hand.

Farand could only hope Rosanne was better off wherever she was. But then he spotted one of the scouting team's longboats approaching from the west, and his heart sank.

CHAPTER THIRTY-THREE

THE METEOR

Rosanne's blood-curdling screams reached Aros somewhere within the tunnel system. The svartraug, a stomping mass of clay, was hot on his heels. Aros chanced a look behind him, and it opened its toothless maw and roared. Could he even find the captain in his current predicament? The ground here was smoother, the ceiling higher, giving him a chance to pick up speed. He rounded a bend, and the svartraug's roars grew distant. Aros veered into a side tunnel, spotted a hidden depression, and dove behind it. The massive bulk thundered past him moments later and only paused at a fork in the road, sniffing the air with a growl before continuing. It didn't appear to follow the sound of Rosanne's screams, which worked to Aros' advantage. He could sneak past.

Aros had his suspicions that something had gone wrong when the hybrids attacked following the temple collapse and the sudden appearance of the Kraken. Rosanne had sway with the crew, and the svartraug, or the hermit—Aros couldn't tell which was which anymore—had stated they offered her a way out. The fact that she was here meant that she had been baited just as he had been. He would recognise her distinct pitch anywhere, ever since the swamp when he had heard her desperately fighting against the marsh-ghoul. The crew would skin him alive if he returned without her.

Emerging from his hiding spot, Aros thought his heart was close to wrenching free of his rib cage. He followed the sound of Rosanne's torturous wails. The noise echoed deep within the mountain but distinct through the meandering hallways. It helped mask his movements. But if the Devourer was after him, what was happening to her?

Aros came upon a chamber with a central boulder. He didn't assess the room around him or pay any close attention to the slumbering creatures. They appeared dormant enough that he could rush through. He caught sight of Rosanne's screaming face, half buried inside the wall of the chamber. Her eyes were closed, and tears ran down her cheeks as if trapped in a terrible nightmare. "What the fuck?" Aros stared at her contorted expression, which twisted as if attempting to get loose, but she barely budged. He couldn't see her arms or even a leg, just her face.

He stepped up and patted her on the cheek. "Hey, Cap, wake up!" he hissed low, trying to silence the noise that was disturbing every creature in the chamber. She remained unresponsive to his calls. Aros dug his fingers into the somewhat soft mass of the wall, freeing the sides of her face. He clapped her cheeks again.

"Oi, lady! Rosanne!"

Her eyes flew open and morphed into panic as she struggled against the confinements of the wall. She let out a strangled scream.

Aros clapped his hand over her mouth. "Calm down! They'll hear you!"

She breathed through his hand, panic-stricken eyes turning into a spiteful glare. He released her once she had calmed sufficiently down to not curse him out. "What is happening?" she said through gritted teeth, restrained by the wall surrounding her.

"I don't know, but I'm getting you out of there. Hang tight."

"*Really*? Hang tight?"

He paused long enough to study her sour, pale-faced expression and let out an amused sputter. "Figure of speech, Cap."

Rosanne bit down on her lips, probably to withhold her reply as she waited for him to free her. He dug down to her shoulder, freeing larger chunks that were thick like clay.

The creatures in the chambers stirred. One barnacle-covered face yawned and lolled his head.

"This is taking too long," Rosanne remarked upon the increasing activity.

"I am going as fast as I can here, lady. Let me free your arm first." Aros tore into the soft mass around her shoulder, searching his way down her arm, which was locked in place. The clay crumbled under her struggles, and Rosanne pulled her arm free and immediately attacked the clay covering her torso with wild abandon.

"Breathing is... difficult." She choked out between strained grunts.

"Doesn't sound like it when you can still chew me out. We'll be out and about by dinner as long as the svartraug doesn't get any funny ideas."

She let out an exasperated sigh. "Always jokes with you."

Aros wiggled his nose and grinned. "My survival tactics haven't failed me yet. You're the one stuck in a wall in a creepy chamber filled with unborn monsters." Aros had not paid the creatures much attention but had noticed the dead mermaid with the mangled spine by Rosanne's feet. He didn't want to know.

She panted through the exertion of freeing her upper torso while Aros dug into the general area where her legs should be.

"What did the bastard do to you? How are you even here?" he finally asked.

Rosanne tore into the clay of her left arm. "I thought it was the hermit who brought me here, but those sons of bitches are tag-teaming who controls the human body. The svartraug offered to let me leave alive, but when it changed its mind and stuck me in the wall. I was trapped in this strange dream that was a mirror image of the island."

Aros blinked. "That is an awfully convoluted way to make sure you stay. Why would it do that?"

"It was a cruel joke, dismantled my life before my eyes. It broke the ship clean in half."

"By Terra." Aros paused and looked at her. "Are you okay?"

"I ... Maybe. It was just a dream. The svartraug lies. It's been lying from the start. All the dreams and nightmares ... it lures us away from what we know to be true and plants false realities into our heads. It doesn't want us to leave. It wants us as a food source." Rosanne paused, her eyes on the floor as if she had searched her memories.

"What?" Aros stood.

"Antony's here ..." her voice trailed off, and her breath hitched as she remembered. She turned her head around and searched the chamber. "That tub! He's in there!" she pointed. Aros abandoned his frantic digging and splurged his arms into the runny clay. He felt around the thick, cold mass, shivering, and felt pieces of fabric which he grabbed hold of. With a brutish tug, Aros pulled up the larger man. The sludge dripped off him in large chunks. Antony's head lolled lifelessly as Aros dragged him out of the basin and lay him on the floor, running a hand over his face to remove the substance. Rosanne let out a pained whimper at the sight of him. "Is he alive?" she prompted. "Please tell me he's alive," her voice disintegrated to a whisper. Aros placed a finger to Antony's neck, but he couldn't feel a pulse. Captain DiCroce was cold and unmoving, and not as much as a breath rose in his chest. A grimace twisted over Aros' face. He gave a slow shake of his head, finally turned to look at her. She gritted her teeth as tears spilled from her eyes.

"Grab my arms. I'll pull you out," he said after a moment's pause. Rosanne did as he told through many series of sniffs and deep breaths. He clasped his hands around her upper arms, and she onto his, and Aros leaned his weight backwards. The clay gave in, slowly but steadily.

They both fell to the floor with a gasp and groan. Rosanne rolled off him.

"Can you stand?" He stretched his hand out to her. She shook her head.

"My legs are stiff. Everything hurts. Everything..." Her eyes wandered to Antony's lifeless body. She looked away.

"We don't have time to stay any longer," Aros hissed, dodging a swiping claw coming from the nearby wall. "Bastards are waking up, and I wanna be gone from here before that time."

Rosanne cleared her throat and shook her head. "The meteor ... it's the heart of the Grey Veil." She pointed to the big rock.

"What do you mean?"

"The svartraug and all the creatures we've encountered are born here; the fog that the Veil is made out of emanates from this island." Her voice was distant as if she was retelling a story for the sake of distracting herself. But Aros heard the opportunity it presented them.

"If we destroy it? It'll all disappear?"

"Maybe."

They fell quiet at the distant roar of the svartraug. "No time to dally," Aros said and pulled Rosanne to her feet quicker than she could stabilise herself.

"What about Antony?" Rosanne glanced back at the body.

"I can only carry one of you, Cap." He threw her arm over his shoulder and supported her as they hobbled out of the chamber in all haste. Rosanne bit her lip as they exited into the cave system. Aros could tell she wanted to turn back, but time was a luxury they couldn't afford.

They halted at a fork in the road.

"Left or right?" he prompted. The call came closer, bouncing in from the left chamber.

"Right!" they both yelped. Rosanne leaned on him for support, but Aros noticed she was regaining the use of her legs. She hobbled along his quick pace, and although she wasn't half as heavy as he thought, the strain was killing him. The moment she was strong enough to support herself, she pushed away from him as if disgusted by his proximity.

"Thanks for the help back there," she muttered.

Despite the situation, he smirked. "Someone needs to drive the ship back to the colonies."

"So this *was* purely out of self-preservation?"

"Let's run with that."

Aros caught the Devourer rounding the bend behind them, and it paused to grin at them. The ground shook under its massive weight as it thundered after them.

"How do we kill it?" Aros shouted between his breaths.

"They don't like light, but that won't kill them." Rosanne huffed.

The air around them grew hot with dancing shimmers against the reddish glow at the end of the tunnel. Aros broke out in a sweat, his throat burned from the sweltering heat. Rosanne was falling behind. "Come on, Cap!" he urged.

But the Devourer came up behind her and with a single swipe of its powerful arm knocked her off her feet. Her panicked scream was drowned by his victorious roar. Aros turned to find the monster hovering over the captain, its arm raised in a tight fist. She rolled out of the way as it bore down on her, scrambling on all fours. Aros was by her side in an instant, pulled her to her feet, and pushed her ahead of him. They resumed their mad dash through the sweltering halls.

They came upon a larger room burning in warm oranges. A wide crack in the floor divided their path, the exit tunnel on the other side. The two captains skidded to a halt at the lava river some ways down in the crevice. Aros waved his hand over the opening, retracting it immediately as the rushing air scorched his hand.

He hissed and blew on his palm. "It's too hot to jump across."

Rosanne pointed to the reduced glow of the lava river. "The crevice is smaller by the wall. We can cross there."

The svartraug came howling into the room in a mad sprint. Its heavy bulk overbalanced it as it turned, and it leaned almost far enough to tip over. Catching its weight, the creature slowed, corrected itself, and set after them. Its glistening body lost its shine, and cracks of dried black clay lined its hand. With one hand shielding its face from the heat, it bore down on the two captains with the other.

Pressed up against the edge of the drop and the wall, Rosanne couldn't dodge the svartraug's massive hand when it was upon them, and it tossed her aside with terrifying ease. She hit the ground in a sideways roll to ease the fall. She coughed from the brutish treatment, struggling to get her stiff joints and knees to obey her.

Aros pulled the plasma pistol from his vest, but the svartraug was on him before he could charge the weapon. Thick fingers dug into his vest, and with a roar, the creature flung Aros across the room. The hot air bit at his feet that dangled just past the lip of the crevasse and he drew them to himself with a hiss. The svartraug lumbered over, stopping next to him and cocked his head.

"You will never leave," its hollow voice drummed through him, finished with an empty, droopy smile.

Rosanne stood frozen, clutching her side, staring as the svartraug lifted Aros high in front of it. Her mind cried for action, but there was nothing she could do against a massive creature like that. Her knife rested pathetically in her hand, but all she could use it for was to spare her the same fate as Antony.

With a huge soulless grin, the devourer opened its boneless maw impossibly wide. Aros cried out in panic, his foot sinking into the svartraug's torso as if pulled in. "Do something, Cap!"

Rosanne dove for the dropped plasma handgun nearby and fumbled with the charging mechanism. The weapon gave a low hum for what seemed like ages. The creature bore down on Aros, intending to devour him whole. The chamber glowed blue, ready to be fired.

"Hey!" Rosanne called out and aimed low. The blue ball of plasmic energy whistled across the room and seared into the creature's leg. The clay-like skin solidified and cracked, breaking under its weight. A pan-icked roar escaped the svartraug, losing its balance and tossing Aros aside in the process. its massive bulk toppled over, but the svartraug caught itself just in time. Hollow eyes turned to Aros, intending to complete the task. Rosanne charged, gave a desperate yell and slammed into the svartraug's side, sending it tumbling in a roll. The svartraug howled as it clawed at the lip of the crevice with both hands, its stubby fingers struggling to find hold and its weight too great. It fell into the molten river below with an audible glop, its terrified growls fading out.

"A little help here!" Aros yelled.

Rosanne dove for Aros, who dangled over the ledge. She pulled him to safety with a strained growl. He retracted his feet and collapsed into a heap of limbs. The exhausted captains took a breath as they sprawled out on the floor.

"Thanks for that," Aros gasped and wiped the sweat off his brow.

"I distinctly recalled your valiant efforts of something similar when we faced Nikor in the swamp."

"If I had lava, I would have saved you easily," he quipped.

Rosanne couldn't help but laugh, but then doubt crossed her features. "You think it's dead?"

Aros allowed himself the barest glance over the ledge, spotting nothing but the orange flow of the molten rock. "Lava gets the job done. People, monsters, auspicious artifacts ... If anything, I'm sure the bastard has at least lost its physical shape."

"Then there's a chance it's still alive." Rosanne bit her lip. "The svar-traug is a true master of lies and deceit. Who's to say we're not trapped in the dream still?"

Aros showcased his vest, torn at the seams. "In my dream, this thing is as strong as a thousand horses. The bastard ripped it at the shoulder where hybrids couldn't. What weak monsters."

Sound reasoning. And then she thought of Antony, poor sweet Antony lost in the dream. His body resided in the chamber of nightmares, now a part of the meteor. She let out a frustrated shriek, startling Aros. It took Antony away from her, but he had died to save her. He was the reason she escaped the dream. Rosanne caught herself and breathed through the bitterness. The svartraug was dead. She wasn't.

Aros remained silent but sat.

Rosanne paused when she noticed Aros waving his hat in front of his glistening face. "How are you here? You were at the camp with the others."

"For your information, we were attacked again, and the hybrids took me to the svartraug."

Her eyes narrowed. "Why you? Why not anyone else?"

"Hell if I know. The svartraug had a lot to say to me. The hermit too. I'm not sure which one was crazier. Their agendas were ... conflicting, to say the least. The hermit wanted us all gone. The Devourer, as he dubbed it, wanted us all to stay, but it needed a new host body, aka me."

"And use the rest of us as stuffing for the meteor or another tree in the forest," she concluded.

"There's more of those out there, although the svartraug said they weren't as powerful as him. Doesn't mean they're not dangerous."

Rosanne rubbed her face. "Let's see if we can get out first. I am so fucking tired of this place."

A shade of confusion crossed Aros' face. "You're turning tail without getting what you came for?"

"It was a pipe dream all along," Rosanne trailed off and hung her head, but then she remembered the svartraug's words. "No, you're right. There is something there. I found the place, but it's hidden well. The temple wasn't a part of those plans, or maybe it has something to do with the pools the creature uses."

"How so?"

"The svartraug, as a spiritual being, could travel between bodies of water. Don't ask me how, but it led me through one. There must be more to it."

Aros shook his head and blew an exasperated breath. "Without the svartraug, who knows what the other creatures will do when they're not controlled by that thing. Let's leave."

"Abandoning your thoughts of riches already?" Rosanne retorted and stood, dusting off her pants. At Aros' perplexed expression, she rolled her eyes. "You stealing the map made it clear that you had higher intentions from the start." Letting out a dignified huff, she felt her insides boil at her runaway thoughts and emotions. "You honestly thought you could sneak behind my back and pull a little scam on your own without anyone ratting you out for the piece of shit that you are? After everything I have done for you?"

Aros' perplexion turned into stone-cold neutrality and he crossed his arms. "Why are you being such a bitch? I know you just lost Captain DiCroce, but I've done nothing to aggravate you to this extent. All I did was pocket riches, which is tax evasion at best." He let out an incredulous breath. Rosanne fixed him a hard stare. When she didn't back down, Aros relented. "You know what, Cap? Have it your way. You come at me time and time again as if you have the moral high ground to single me out as the bad guy when your ship is full of ex-cons and pirates with rap sheets longer than the Kvenchester Canal!"

Rosanne's face contorted. "You have earned neither my respect nor the crew's, and you shouldn't even have been on my ship at all! *Of course*, I don't trust you, and of course, I don't take your advice or care for your excuses when you have done nothing but break whatever trust I've extended!"

"Are you fucking blind or just in denial? I have tried again and again and you've shot me down and blamed me for whatever misfortune befell us! Take the camp raid. You blamed me for that when I was the one who prevented it from getting any worse. *I* warned about the mermaids, *I* warned about the hermit, and you didn't even consider for one second that maybe, just maybe, there was *some* merit to my word!"

"You were ready to jump ship at any given moment!"

"I came back for *you*! Or did you forget that already? Fucking hell, woman. You have the emotional maturity of a seventeen-year-old at her coming-of-age ball. That or are you are so emotionally damaged from whatever fucked up life you led you can't take the good things around you at face value."

Balling her hands into fists, Rosanne's shoulders raised, and she grit her teeth. "As if you have the right to call me out! That shit you pulled in the jungle was out of kindness?"

Aros narrowed his eyes as he didn't immediately recognise what she was talking about. Then an amused smile stretched across his lips. "That's what this is about? That illusion-induced kiss which meant nothing?" He let out a hollow laugh. "Whatever you are going through, we're in much deeper shit than we've ever been in before, and this is not the time to berate me for something that was out of my control. Instead of owning up to the crap that went down, which was partially your fault, you push everything onto me to make me the scapegoat, and I'm *sick* of it!"

Rosanne didn't back down, standing stiff as a wound coil and trembling. "You're fucking corrupt and never do as you're told," she said, her voice dangerously low.

"Says who?" Aros rounded on her and raised his fist, unfurling a single finger. "I've done everything that you asked me." A second finger. "Everything you have thrown at me." A third. "Endured all the scorn and the distrust and kept my head low. And whenever we're in near proximity, you go off the rails and take your anger out on me!" He threw his hands in the air from defeat. "Is that why you hate my guts? Is it some central colonial need to ascertain the dominance memo I missed in my drafting? Or..." Aros folded his arms. "Is it that you hate me because I make you question every moment you thought was real with lover boy?" Aros knew he had stepped over the line, for he felt cold at the sight of Rosanne's expression. "I digress. It's not about Captain DiCroce. Are you still mad at me for mauling you at that other island?"

But she wasn't listening. She stared at the ground, her brows low and tight. "Antony has nothing to do with this."

Aros didn't back down. "Oh really? He followed you into the Veil like a lost puppy and he disappeared on his own accord. Yet I am the one to blame? How is that fair?"

"Don't talk to me about what's fair! I did my best to ensure the safety of the crew."

"The hell you did! You are so desperate to get answers that you threw all protocols aside. You have any idea what this island has done to us, or are you so stuck in your own pain you can't see when it's time to turn tail and leave?"

"I didn't ask you!"

Straightening, Aros' eyes were two pinpoints that drilled into hers. "You fucked up, Rosanne. You forewent all safety by the choices you made, and thanks to that, they picked us off. Did you ever stop to think how many have already died because of the monsters here? Jeffs wasn't the only one. Kristoff and Carlos were hurt in the raid, Quinn's halfway to hell already, and now maybe a dozen more are dead while you were gone."

Rosanne staggered, knees weak under her weight. Tears stung her eyes, and she desperately blinked them away, but they kept coming. And then the anger welled up inside of her, a deep darkness fueled by fire and rage which made her shake and heave for breath.

"Screw this. I'm done with your inability to deal with your own shit." Aros turned to leave, and at the sight of his back, Rosanne let out a blood-curdling scream. She launched herself at Aros, who, in a moment of confusion, turned. Rosanne punched him square in the jaw, grabbed his torn vest and punched him again, all the while screaming like mad. Aros threw up his arm, blocked the barrage of attacks, and tore at her fist enclosed on his vest. He yanked himself free of her, pushed and made her fall in a tangle of legs on the ground.

Aros rose, his hands in loose fists in front of him as he readied himself for Rosanne's next attack. And it came quickly. She barely looked around herself, dead set on Aros, and threw herself at him, punching and clawing for his face. Aros side-stepped and shouldered her away, but she got up again. Again and again. Rosanne kicked out and threw her fists, but she missed. Aros used his weight to bring her down and from behind and grabbed her wrists, which he clasped over her chest and held on tight. She screamed and coiled, throwing herself to the sides to break free.

"Stop it!" he called to her, over and over. Rosanne was a screaming mess fighting against him. She didn't register his words, only his arms tightly wrapped around her, both protecting himself from her attacks and from herself. They both fell to the ground, but Aros did not relent. Rosanne gasped for breath as tears streamed down her face, and she let out a hiccupping sob.

You fucked up, Ros. The crew's blood was on her hands, not the svartraug's. Aros was right. She had lost sight of what mattered and endangered everyone. She couldn't blame anyone but herself.

Aros said nothing for as long as she cried into his chest. She didn't care anymore. With all the things that had happened, losing Antony, her degrading self-esteem disguised as moving forward, it was all too much.

After a few minutes, Rosanne drew the breath that somehow stabilised her emotionally-spent spirit to assemble into something human again.

"Let go of me," she said with no zeal. Aros released his hold on her, and she rubbed her sore wrists. She could feel his attention on her, but maybe not the blame and spite he had launched just minutes earlier.

"You hit like a girl," he said.

Brushing the hair out of her face, Rosanne let out a humourless chuckle. "That's all you have to say?"

"You hit me way harder on our first meeting. I mean, you threw a mean-as-hell punch, but this was just pathetic." He flashed her a smirk which accentuated the swelling part below his cheek, making him wince.

"Whatever mood I'm in, you always got a punchable face," Rosanne retaliated with a smirk of her own. "You're right, though. I brought my problems into this mess when I should have walked away."

"And?" Aros prompted, and Rosanne knew he was fishing for an apology.

"And screw you."

Aros slapped his hands over his breast in feigned hurt, but quickly turned on his heel towards the exit, a smile plastered on his face. "I'll take what I can get. Let's leave, Cap. We're already cooked after staying in this place for too long."

"Captain?" a small voice called from across the crevice.

They both turned towards the opening of the chamber entrance, spotting a small pale face. "Ida?" they said in unison.

The blond second engineer beamed. "I can't believe it's you two! Listen, there's a way out this way!" she called from across the chasm and pointed back the tunnel behind her.

Rosanne leaned closer to Aros, lowering her voice to a whisper. "She could be a mimic."

"I for once agree on that. How do we know it's really her? The creatures can imitate people it possessed. Who's to say the mimics didn't catch her while we were away?" Aros looked to Rosanne who was deep in thought. Sweat ran down her forehead. Aros smiled.

"Hey, little lady!" he called out to her and received a frown from the second engineer.

"I told you not to call me that!" she barked.

"Could you come closer?"

"Why?" Ida's cracking voice drew out and she dipped her head between her shoulders like a gargoyle, deeply suspicious of his request.

Rosanne caught on to what Aros was doing. "Come into the room. I just wanna make sure you are you."

Ida pointed a finger at her chest in surprise, and whipped her head around to view back the way she came. Rosanne rested her hand loosely on the plasma pistol. The second engineer marched out of the tunnel and into the room, craning her neck as she studied the rock formations and the lava crevice before her. She fanned herself.

"How do I know *you* are not mimics?" Ida refuted, wiping her forehead.

Rosanne and Aros exchanged glances. From her boot, Rosanne fished out a small knife, the very same she had used to free herself and Aros from their bindings in the troll caves in the north. A trusty companion, indeed. She made a small cut into the side of her hand with a stream of curses. She valued her digits too much. Blood poured from the shallow wound and trickled down her arm, and she held it up. Ida squinted across the chasm and nodded. Rosanne handed the knife over to Aros, who poked into his arm and displayed the red blood to the suspicious engineer.

When she was satisfied, Ida pricked her ring finger with the tip of the knife she carried in her tool belt and smeared the blood on her hand, red as it could be. She shook her head at the still bleeding wounds to Rosanne and Aros, and he could swear he saw Ida mutter "idiots" under her breath.

Rosanne shot Aros a warning glance. "What happens in the Grey Veil stays in the Grey Veil." She drew a finger across her throat. "Or you're dead." Her voice didn't have that underlying rumble of a well-founded threat, so Aros simply lifted his hands in defense.

"Let's find you those answers," he said.

"Or maybe we'll find riches."

"Now we're talking!"

"Hey, Ida! We're jumping across!" Rosanne called. The two wayfaring captains did a short run up, skip and a hop and crossed the small gap of the crevice.

"By Terra, that's hot!" Rosanne patted the insides of her thighs.

Aros followed with a fair number of swearwords.

Ida shook whatever suspicion she had aside. "Listen, Captain. Before we continue, there's something you should know."

"You can update me as we go, Miss Simonsen." Rosanne waved her concern aside. Ida turned between Aros and Rosanne in panicked stutters.

"Yes, but there's something you need to know, preferably right now!" she burst out just as they rounded the blue glowing tunnel. Rosanne halted as she stood before a tall black shape with elongated arms and hollow eyes. It lifted its floppy ears, as if surprised.

"It's a svartraug!" Rosanne drew her pistol.

Ida launched herself at the weapon and wrestled with Rosanne. "He's friendly! He's our way out of here."

"How do you know that?" Rosanne tried to shake Ida off, but the engineer stubbornly held fast to the weapon.

"The temple!" She exclaimed. "It's a place of reverence, for him. He's a good svartraug. He helped me escape after part of the temple collapsed." Rosanne lowered her pistol and stared at the creature, who hadn't moved. It blinked slowly at her.

Raising her eyebrows, Rosanne looked at Ida. "There are friendly versions of these monsters?"

Ida frowned. "Please be respectful. It's a powerful spirit, and it means us no harm. The other one we called a Devourer, a corrupted svartraug that needs to feed on people to stay alive. Lucky for us, it's the only one."

"What keeps *this* one alive?" Aros asked.

"Water and darkness," she said matter-of-factually "It's not strong enough to manifest a physical presence like the Devourer. At the night of the raid, he made sure me and Gavin weren't drawn in by the Devourer's dream. It's the only reason we were able to fend off the attack."

"That is quite thoughtful." Rosanne holstered the plasma pistol, assessed the spirit for a second and bowed her head. "You have my thanks."

The svartraug blinked again and turned. Its long legs allowed it to take three times the stride of a human, and Rosanne would have struggled to keep up with it at normal pace. Aros trailed in the back, reserved, not saying a single word, but entertained the thought that the next thing they would see was Hammond's pigs fly.

They broke through the watery surface with a gasp and splash. Clutching the edge of the pool, Rosanne, Aros, and Ida pulled themselves to dry ground. The svartraug appeared behind them. Rosanne coughed and hacked from the surge of water. She wrung the hem of her shirt and wiped the strands of hair away from her face. They were inside the temple she recognized. The cave-in had bared the room to the open skies, and rain had flooded the pools; the small conduits brought water from above down to the lower levels. The shadowy spirit remained half submerged in the pool, with its hollow eyes semi-closed, as if pleased.

"Thank you for everything," Ida said to it. She rummaged through her pouch and brought out the metal sphere which she balanced at the pool's edge. "I have nothing from this land to give you, but I made this inspired by the Veil. It might not mean much to you, but to me it's the most valuable thing I have. I hope you can accept it."

The svartraug gave a slow blink. Rosanne, in a state of momentary panic, realised she should present a gift as well, but she had nothing of value on her. Her hat was out of the question and not here. "I uh ... hope you like firearms. This one helped destroy the Devourer." She placed the plasma gun next to the sphere. The svartraug cocked its head as it studied the blue light on the chamber and Rosanne took it as a sign that it accepted. They both looked to Aros, whose pale face turned to dismay. He rummaged through his pockets and brought out a single six-sided die which he placed with the others.

"Really? A die?" Rosanne arched an eyebrow.

"It's a weighted die. Don't judge me! The emotional value outweighs your gun, Captain." He gave a bitter smile. The svartraug's ears gave a curious flop. Reaching out a shadowy hand, it flipped the weighted die, which tumbled back to its sixth side.

"One thing, if I may ask you," Rosanne said to the svartraug. It perked up at this and floated closer to the edge. Rosanne pulled out the soggy paper that was the copy of the Thompson map and unfolded it. The graphite lines still held, but the paper was fast disintegrating. "Do you know anything about this place? What's there and why anyone might think it's important?"

The spirit rose so its head peered down at the paper. It then extended a single arm and morphed its four fingered fist into a thin single point.

It left an inky smear at the transition between the outlying rocks of the arching coastline and the sandy beach before retracting its hand.

Rosanne took the map and bowed again.

Ida waved. "It was very nice to meet you." She beamed.

The svartraug blinked in satisfaction as they turned and left.

CHAPTER THIRTY-FOUR

SECRETS OF THE MAP

What awaited Rosanne, Aros, and Ida on the surface of the temple was a horrific nightmare. The ceiling had collapsed in the middle, leaving a deep crevice littered with tools, rope and splatters of blood. They had exited through as small side passage that had opened during the second shock wave; Creedy and Gavin had already made their way topside.

Rosanne passed by the three bodies lined next to each other, covered with blood-stained blankets. The crew sat silently as they waited for Rosanne's orders. Her face was a grim frown. The hybrid invasion had left a deep scar on the remaining crew, and all were weary and spent. Three of the hybrids lay discarded off the side of the temple, caught in the treetops or crushed open against the ground. Rosanne crinkled her nose in disgust at the open-mouthed monstrosities, their almost translucent skin ashen and blue.

"How many injured?" she asked Lyle.

"Eight, and if Quinn is still holding up, that puts us at nine."

"Who are dead?" she asked after a pause, her eyes wandering to the cotton blankets.

"Swanson, Carlos, Abernathy."

Rosanne drew a deep breath. "Terra, have mercy on us all."

"What's the plan?" Lyle asked at length.

"We return to the ship. We still have supplies to last us in case anything prevents us returning home. Let's patch up our people the best we can and hightail out of here."

"Yes, Captain." Lyle signalled what remained of his men to hustle. Rosanne stayed on her rock, leaning on her thighs, all zeal lost to her sorrow. Swanson and Carlos had joined two years prior after the *Red Queen* made a trip to Cintecha. They were like brothers, thick as thieves and loyal to a fault. Now they were gone. Abernathy, she had picked up in Ottalo after his work permit expired. She never asked, not because she didn't care, but because the people she hired exchanged their loyalty for her silence.

Her silence now got them all killed. She should have returned to the ship. She shouldn't have pushed on after the raid. They were lucky then, but that's when it ran out.

Antony had paid the price for freeing her from the dream. She buried her face in her hands.

"Lady, I mean Captain." Aros stood before her. She breathed through the tightness in her chest. He fidgeted with his hands but waited. Rosanne looked at him then.

"Yes?"

"The sea monster you talked about, the Kraken, I think it's the same that was east to us before the raid."

"It's here?" Rosanne hadn't thought the Kraken was an actual creature, but it made sense since the svartraug couldn't create things to fill in the blanks. "How long ago?"

Aros turned to the master gunner, who wiggled his moustache, thinking. "Six hours or so. It disappeared out to the sea in an electric storm. It lingered for hours on the shoreline, as if hunting."

"Farand," Rosanne muttered. If the mimics attacked base camp, there was a high possibility Farand was on his way here with the ship, but if the Kraken was out and about, it could pose a problem. If Rosanne and the team circumvented the area where the Kraken was last seen, they might pass the ship altogether. "I don't want to risk any more lives as it is. Get all the scouts on duty and watch for the ship—"

A sudden commotion among the crew had Rosanne grab her hand pistol and fasten her eyes on the horizon. The soft orange-yellow glint of and aethersail caught her attention, followed by the *Red Queen's* crimson hull approaching. Rosanne knew in her heart they were going to be okay.

They had no supplies. No water. But with the Kraken elsewhere, they could put the boiler to use and scavenge the beach for fish and tropical fruits. Rosanne anchored the ship at the rocky outcrop, exactly where the svartraug had marked the map. A low cavernous opening rested in the cove, a perfect place away from the sandy beach. No mermaid or hybrids could reach them, unless the meteor had a monkey-crab hybrid she didn't know about that could fly. If the mimics decided they were worth the trouble, they would have to navigate treacherous terrain which could spell the end of them, lest they decided swimming was an easier option, in which case Lyle and his men would snipe them.

Rosanne knew her repeated efforts to ensure their safety was the definition of madness, but this time she was of sound mind and confident. She followed the svartraug's inky directions, hoping this was the X marks the spot and not another wild goose chase.

In her private chambers she excavated whatever things she would need to descend into the cave system, like supplies and extra clothes. She wasn't planning on staying long, but in case something went wrong and prevented her return, like when the temple ceiling collapsed, she could find solace in that she had tried. And she would at least be comfortable for a while.

Securing the leather straps on the rucksack, she glanced around the room and office that had been her home for fifteen years, wondering if this was the last time she would see it. With the sacrifices she had made, no one else would follow in her footsteps. Enough blood had been spilled for what seemed like a pointless endeavour. She had to finish this herself.

The door creaked open.

"You're not thinking of going down there alone, are you?" Farand came up to her as she slung the pack over her shoulder, his voice laced with scrutiny and disappointment.

Rosanne gave a rueful smile. "No one is to leave the ship while I'm down there. If I'm not back within three days, assume I'm dead and return home. You'll be in command, Farand." Her expression brightened, and she gave him a supportive pat on his shoulder.

Farand whirled after her. "Are your marbles at the bottom of the sea? What makes you so damn sure I'm going to let you leave by yourself? We've seen what's out there, and it's likely there's more!" His arms crossed over his chest, but his expression softened as her false chirpiness withered. The silence grew between them like a festering wound.

"I failed you all, Farand," she said finally. "I let people die because of my desperate need for answers. And now that I have them before me, I intend to go alone. I have done enough damage."

She could tell Farand couldn't argue against her logic despite wanting to. His mouth opened and closed, but his anxious eyes fell to the floor. She licked her lips and continued: "The crew trusts and looks up to you. You'll be a fine captain of the *Red Queen*. You always had more experience than me."

"Rosanne," His firm voice arrested her. Straightening, Farand squared his shoulders. She knew if she lingered any longer she would falter, but the gentle undertone to Farand's voice stopped her as efficiently as a locked door.

"I promised you I would always have your back. This doesn't change that. Whatever happened, happened. There's no redemption in getting yourself killed. Antony didn't die so you could throw your life away."

She crushed her lips together into a tight line, but Farand continued, "We're a great team. Always have been, always will, and I'll be damned if you don't return because I let rank dictate our friendship."

Rosanne smiled. "As if I could ever stop you once you set your mind on something." She waved him over, and they both exited to the quarterdeck.

What crew wasn't bound to the sick bay milled about on the main deck and forecastle. Their faces wore a mixture of weariness and exhaustion. They turned their bloodshot eyes towards the duo coming upon the rails of the quarterdeck. Rosanne let the rucksack slide off her shoulder and dropped it on the floor.

"Friends," she began. The crew shuffled closer, quiet and observing. "I have let you down. This journey wasn't the discovery of riches like we thought it was, but of nightmares. Countless men and women have tried before us, and they've all failed and perished. Those of us who remain will not die here on this island. Not today, not tomorrow. You will all see safe shores again. This I can promise you." Rosanne paused and licked her lips. She took in the disappointed looks in their faces, including Dalia with her arms crossed, and shook her head. "We have lost too many; Jeffs, Swanson, Carlos, Abernathy, and DiCroce with far too many more wounded. You are the people who stand against the creatures of the Veil and the cutthroat world that awaits our return." Their faces faltered. Rosanne swept her eyes across a few of them, Norman changed his stance from one nervous foot to the other. Dalia and Creedy, side by side as always, looked ready to pounce at whatever was thrown their way. Hammond's grim nod never failed to cheer her up, and Gavin fidgeted with a pouch hanging from his belt. Ida's weary gaze fell to the floor. "We have sailed through hell and back again countless times. We can weather this storm just like those times, because this is our turf, this fucked up world that we live in is ours and no monster is going to take that away from us!" A round of low agreements spread amongst the crowd, lifting heavy heads and fallen gazes. "I can't promise to be there when the tides turn and we see the sky, but I'll be damned if I let you down again."

Taking a deep breath, she continued. "I have one last mission ahead of me, and I don't know what will happen. Should anything befall me, Farand can take you home, or whatever path that isn't laden with mythological fuckalls and death. You can prosper again."

Slowly nodding faces and soft eyes spread through the crew, but even with the impact of Rosanne's words, there's only so much a group of dispirited people can hope for after suffering the ails they've been through. Patting the railing, Rosanne straightened and looked at Farand, who nodded.

"Let's get going then." She scooped up the ruck-sack and strode towards Creedy, who waited in the longboat by the main deck, ready to drop them off. She paused upon seeing Aros leaning against the railing, staring into the distance.

"What are you up to?" she asked with no subtle hint of suspicion.

"Oh nothing." He slid a hand over the lip of the boat. "Just thought you might need a hand going down into whatever hellhole you're visiting."

"Out of the question."

"Based on what?"

She tossed the sack into the boat. "Enough people have been hurt."

"Aww. Are you worried about me, Cap?" He cocked his head in a grin.

"Not in a million years." She pointed at him with a frown.

"Numbers mean something here, and I believe I am decent collateral should anything happen."

"You're awfully ready to throw your life away."

"I simply believe we can increase our chances of survival and profit if you allow me to accompany you. For all we know there could be treasure down there, and I'm honouring my baser instincts by following adventure wherever it might lead me. The honest way, this time."

"Can't believe I'm saying this," she muttered. "Fine."

Aros tossed his prepared sack in and jumped aboard and nestled on the middle seat. He patted the seat in front of him and wiggled his eyebrows.

Rosanne suppressed a smile. "Try anything stupid and I *will* use you as collateral."

Farand lumbered aboard, tipping the longboat on the side with his weight. They wobbled to stability once he was seated.

"You gentlemen ready for whatever is lurking below the island?" Rosanne asked.

The two men nodded gruff and determined faces.

Creedy drove them down to the rocky patches in front of the massive cave opening. It was impossible to spot from land, but if you approached from the sea it was easy to discern. Rocky walkways snaked alongside the inner walls as if chiselled. They weren't scarce for space, but Farand had to watch his step, edging sideways.

They lit the chemicals in their lamps, flooding the passageway with light and peered inside.

"It just keeps going," Rosanne said, sidestepping to let Aros pass.

"Is it just me or is this waterway unusually deep?" Aros shone the light over the dark waters, and the bottom was beyond sight. Shadows flitted past, and he hastily retreated by the wall. They followed the path into a narrowing in the road which meandered and circled down. Aros paused, frowned, and whirled on Rosanne.

"Ladies first." He stretched out his arm. Rolling her eyes, Rosanne took point.

The crude spiralling staircase felt endless. Rosanne could only see a few steps ahead on the tightly coiled steps.

"Think the devourer made this?" Farand's voice carried down in fading echoes.

"That fat bastard? He could barely fit a leg in here and it's too short for the lanky guy," Aros replied.

The temple came to Rosanne's mind. "I still can't believe there were two different spirits occupying the same island. Both Higgs and Creedy had their own versions of the creature from their homelands, but they overlap too much to be coincidental. They aren't inherently malevolent, but one became the devourer of dreams after people came here."

"The temple built for the lanky guy only shows that someone cared enough. The other, not so much. Maybe that led to a conflict of interest." Aros shuddered.

Farand leaned closer to lower his voice to Rosanne. "Why would it show you the entrance to this place instead of just taking you there?"

Shrugging, it was all Rosanne could do. "Maybe it was gratitude. I think the svartraug was trapped by the Devourer. It could possess and control people after all, while the other could only take shape in dank and dark places. With the lava river inside the mountain, I imagine finding a way out would be difficult without evaporating."

"It was so hot!" Aros let out a groan. "I aged ten years in that heat. But our lanky boy looked happy inside the temple once the waterworks got running. Best renovating we could have done for it."

Rosanne paused at the widening in the stairway and wall of darkness ahead. "Do you hear that?" she whispered and turned to the side. A soft gust of air permeated the room followed by a rumble, but not deep enough to shake the walls.

"Is that something breathing?" Farand twisted a knob on the lamp to extend the wick and flooded the area around him in a bubble of harsh, white-blue chemical light. The floor was black volcanic ash mixed with moisture from the air. Thick sludge ran down the walls on either side of the entrance and disappeared in slow running rivers further into the room.

Touching the floor with a finger, Rosanne rubbed the substance between her fingers. "It looks like the same stuff that was in the meteor chamber. But there's more of it here. A lot more."

Moisture dripped from a distant ceiling in noisy *plat-plat-plat* into small pools of water. The deep rumble of something shuffling against the floor permeated the room. Rosanne, Farand and Aros hunkered by the entrance and lowered their lights. They held their collective breaths. The scraping like scales on gravel fell back to the repeating soft breaths.

Gathering her courage, Rosanne stepped out once again, keeping her footfalls soft and her light to her front as she looked to her left where the breathing was louder. The blue illumination fell across a rounded, scaly form reaching high above them, expanding and contracting along with its breaths. Rosanne shone the light over the creature, but its sheer size was too grand to be viewed in one go. It was covered in the same material as in the meteor chamber, but exposed, rainbow-coloured scales shimmered where the moisture dripped from the ceiling.

Farand came up next to her and continued along the shape. Not wanting to be left behind, Aros jogged as quietly as he could after the lieutenant.

"This thing's alive?" He came upon a triangular shaped head with a long snout, two massive nostrils set wide apart and two scaly eyelids fluttered with movement. Air blew out through the nose like a hurricane, sending Aros' hat billowing.

"A sea serpent," Rosanne whispered. "Like in the meteor chamber; this is where they are made and remain sleeping until they're called upon."

"How do *you* know that?" Farand inquired.

Rosanne, normally reserved to secrecy when confronted with the impossible, had to restrain herself from withholding this from him. She knew what she saw, and Farand was a trusted friend. "There was a moment when I touched the meteor. It flooded my mind with images, like memories. I could see it when it crashed in the ocean, the rising lava and geological formation of the anti-gravity minerals created by that process, and how the fog was created at this place to shield the islands. This clay-like substance comes from the meteor, and gives birth to these creatures. It is like a memory of somewhere far away, on a distant world, where these creatures perhaps existed. I can't say what they are, but they are living and breathing just like us, and they're connected to the Veil and the meteor. The Devourer said that the meteor has a dream of its own and awoke the kraken to protect the veil from the outside world."

"It's doing a banger job so far," Aros muttered.

Farand stroked his chin. "If something that large gets outside of the Veil, there's no telling what it would do. Maybe the kraken isn't the only one out there."

Rosanne drew a thoughtful breath. She considered the serpent's elongated snout, massive pointed teeth peering past scaly lips as it shifted its head. "Remember the old stories in Noval of a great sea serpent, a monster long enough to bind the world? Maybe this inspired those tales."

"Meaning, people either came here before us or these creatures once roamed free. I'm not sure what bothers me more." Farand gave a subtle shake of his head, as if ridding himself of the unpleasant thought.

"There's more over here. Come along." Aros nodded towards the darkness. Elongated pods hung from gelatinous tubes in the ceiling.

The light penetrated the dim, transparent surface with ease, outlining a squishy shape inside.

"Mini-krakens. Fantastic." Aros let out a tinny, pathetic whimper.

Rosanne raised her light. "There's so many of them. Why would the meteor make this many monsters if it was only protecting itself?" The creature inside wiggled its tendrils then settled down. "Could the Devourer have done this?"

Farand rested a hand on Rosanne's shoulder. "Perhaps your father didn't mark the map because of these."

"You mean in case someone was foolish enough to wake them and unleash hell on Terra?"

"You mean the exact thing we're doing right now? Poking the hornet's nest and all?" Aros quipped.

Rosanne considered Aros' sarcasm-laced observation. "You want to leave now that we're here? The chamber keeps going. We should at least assess what we're up against." All three stared into the darkness. Aros adjusted his hat and shook his vest before picking up the lamp again.

"Ready when you are, Cap and 'tenant."

"That's *lieutenant* for you, Mr. Kavanaugh," Farand corrected.

They trudged in silence, their footfalls drowned out by the incessant *drip drip drip* and the rumbling breaths of the beasts. Further in was quieter, but Rosanne didn't take that as a good sign.

Their echoing footsteps came back to them quicker and louder. Rosanne chanced to extend the wick and the light fell across a wide set of stairs ascending into the darkness. She looked to Farand who took point. The stone was squarely cut and smooth in places from water erosion. Jet black columns of obsidian stood erect on each side of a wide archway. Farand waved the others up.

"It's another svartraug temple," Rosanne breathed, recognising the pyramid structure. While damaged by water, the structure bore remarkable similarity to the other temple, the top decorated with a square slanted ceiling. Two idols rested on each side of the doorway, squat and rounded hunched creatures with obsidian eyes.

"I think this is the temple of the Devourer," Rosanne concluded.

"That bastard had his own place? Talk about greedy when he muscled in on the lanky guy's temple." Aros said as he went further inside, coming to a rest by the far wall.

"Greed knows no bounds, as I'm sure you're familiar with," Rosanne's almost humorous reply summoned a snicker from Farand. When he shone the light across it, he spotted indentations in the stone. Placing his light by the side of a column, the light skipped across the surface, leaving only the grooves bathed in black.

Rosanne came up to Farand and studied them. The rounded svartraug held a shining object in its hand in the shape of a shell.

"It's the shell that summoned the Kraken."

"You didn't happen to see where it went, did you?" Farand asked. Rosanne shook her head.

"No, but I suspect it's out of reach from human hands."

"Hey cap, look. This svartraug is eating people."

Sure enough, Rosanne spotted the smaller rounded mass of the malevolent spirit reaching stubby arms towards a flock of fleeing crudely-chiselled people, the creature growing larger on the next image, and then tall and hulking the next.

"It ate its followers?"

"And possessed others to make them do or say anything."

Aros nodded. "Longevity, fake power, and all you could ever dream of, literally. The Devourer could grant it all. And then it wanted more."

Rosanne placed a hand on the pedestal with the shimmering mica laid over the stone, similar shine to that of the shell. The room was a mirror image of the water temple, even the central pedestal and the copper braziers. But what she thought was the waterways guided thick rivers of sludge deeper into the structure. Rosanne located the way down to the lower levels and followed the stairs. As she suspected, the rooms were the same as the other temple with its central pool and waterways, except black sludge filled the pool instead. A bubble of air welled to the surface with an audible *glop*.

The whispers spoke to her then, permeating her senses and flooding her thoughts.

"Captain?" Farand's massive hand leaned laid on her shoulder, and Rosanne snapped out of her daze.

She whirled on him, eyes wide. "The Devourer isn't dead. It knows we're here."

Farand's eyebrows scrunched together and peered around her to the pool.

"Guys! We need to leave," Aros called from above, startling them both, and stuck his head down so they could see him. "The whispers are getting loud. I say we hightail it outta here."

"For once, I agree with Mr. Kavanaugh," Farand murmured.

"What has this world come to?" Rosanne shook her head.

They exited the temple in rapid succession and trudged hard-faced through the cave. Searching with the harsh alchemical lamps, Aros huffed his breath. "Krakens, leviathans, svartraugs, as if this place couldn't get any more horrid. What the fuck do we even do with this information? What good does any of this do?"

"What would *you* like to do, Captain?" Farand asked. This wasn't even a formal question posed by her lieutenant. This told her that he, too, was as perplexed and lost as she.

She gave a soft humourless laugh. "Nothing short of a giant plasma cannon would do them much hurt. We wouldn't have the firepower to fight off a threat of this magnitude. Who knows what drives them, what they eat or what attracts them? Hell, we don't even know if they're able to leave the Grey Veil. For all we know no one has seen the Kraken outside of the fog, yet fables of svartraugs and hulder somehow made it."

Farand grunted. "So, we do nothing and hope the monsters never awaken because of human trespassers."

"If the Queen's United Colonies get their hands on our routes, the Veil will be just another way for her to exploit the trade discrepancies. She could muster armies weeks earlier than anyone could retaliate, and who knows what a fleet of that scale would awaken if the meteor feels threatened by it."

"Her campaign against Cintecha lasted a decade, thanks to the Veil. Without it slowing her down, she could go further, if not faster."

"Sounds like it's settled then. Let sleeping serpents lie," Farand said.

The whispers in Rosanne's mind had grown beyond intrusive until the sudden silence of their absence gave her a pause.

"There's something there." She looked around in alarm.

Aros increased the wick in his lamp. Light flooded the space around them, followed by a row of pale faces with wild, pin-sized pupils. Rosanne and Aros retreated to Farand's side, drawing their pistols.

Their eyes flitted between them.

"They're too many," Aros assessed. Rosanne recognised some the mimics from her second encounter, her father's copy among them. She frowned and slid a finger over the trigger and pointed the barrel at him.

"Everyone knows where the exit is?" Farand prompted with a recharging click on his pistol. Aros grunted his reply.

The mimics converged on them in unison, pouncing and lunging with outstretched arms and blank faces. Three shots fired almost simultaneously, hitting three different mimics with plasmic bullets searing through their skulls. Losing their integrity, they disintegrated into puddles of water. A woman grabbed Aros by his arm, moving to seize his weapon, but Aros smacked the butt of the pistol into her face. She staggered but held a firm grip. He kicked her instead, and she fell to the floor, dragging with her. He wrestled himself free and fired a shot through her eye. She exploded to liquid with a soundless cry.

Farand smashed fist through the watery skull of the sailor-clothed creature with ease. Rosanne spun around Farand's back, reloaded the plasma pistol, and fired at another hostile circling around them to attack from behind.

"They're surrounding us!" she cried out and sidestepped a lunging mimic, using its momentum to push it into one of its brethren. They crashed to the floor.

A sudden metallic cry rumbled from one of the slumbering creatures. The mimics froze on the spot, turning their heads as one in the noise's direction. Something massive stirred. A thin watery film spread over their skin and clothes, enveloping them, and then they exploded in a spray of water and disappeared in the porous stone floor. Farand, Aros and Rosanne looked away or covered their face, spitting at the sudden burst of liquid.

A deafening roar shook them to their knees.

"Get to the exit!" Rosanne called through the noise, ears ringing, head pounding, legs unwilling, but she pushed through the piercing cacophony assaulting her senses. Something massive slithered over the stone floor, the scraping of scales against rock growing louder with each passing second. Aros' lamp passed over the leviathan's elongated snout, its jaw open with rows of massive teeth and its orange eyes studying them with a predatory gleam. A forked tongue sniffed the air, its head unmoving as its body coiled underneath its body. The leviathan stretched as tall as a two-storey building.

Rosanne dared not move. Farand barely drew a breath, eyes speeled on the creature. Aros picked up a decent sized rock and tossed it into the darkness. The serpent turned its head. "Time to go, Cap!" Aros sprinted past Rosanne and Farand, who quickly shook off the paralysing spell rooting them in place.

The leviathan roared after them, swishing its tail around as it coiled its body in pursuit.

"Where's the exit?!" Rosanne called over the noise.

"Someplace up ahead, but I can't see—" The leviathan's massive tail smashed against the cave wall, sending a deep crashing tearing through the chamber. Rosanne caught its glinting scales from Aros' alchemical light, hurtling towards her. Rosanne dove for a depression in the floor, immediately assaulted by the lose clay weighing her down, the tail swept over the floor and passed just above her head. She struggled against the sludgy mass clogging her nose and mouth.

"Farand!" she cried for the big man. Rosanne caught Aros' terror-filled screams turned insults thrown the leviathan's way as a means of distraction. She clawed onto the lip of the pool, bogged down by the clay.

Farand was upon her in seconds and dragging her out by her arms. His lamp shattered against the stone floor, a sudden blaze which illuminated the rainbow scales of the leviathan's face and its slithering body. It hissed against the flames and tasted the air with a forked tongue. The light burnt through in an instant.

They plunged into darkness, catching only the barest sign of Aros' fervent movement in the distance. Rosanne and Farand fumbled in the dark, stepping on loose rocks and uneven ground which sent them sprawling or wobbling. "We need light!" Rosanne called to Farand over the ear shattering shrieks of the leviathan.

"Kavanaugh, we need to go! Get your ass over here!" Farand's voice carried through the roar. Aros' light waved back and forth as he set into a fervent sprint towards them. Farand caught the man just as he was about to crash into them both. Aros buckled over, wheezing, but Farand dragged him up with a firm yank.

"Move! Farand barked while Rosanne snatched the alchemical light from Aros' hand.

The group half jogged half limped in the direction of the entrance. The sea serpent shrieked at them, its breath hot and foul on their faces even at the distance. They couldn't see it but felt the vibrations in the rock as it slithered towards them.

The tail swept over the floor again, its tip crashing into the trio. White light flashed in Rosanne's eyes and paralysing shock swept through her body. She scraped against the floor, gasping for breath and comprehension over what had just happened. A sharp pain shot through her arm and side.

"F-Farand," she tried to call out, but her hoarse voice caught in her throat.

The sea serpent hovered over the discarded light still shining on the floor, almost curious as it regarded the burning chemical in its loneliness. Turning its head, it searched the room with its tongue whirring in and out of its mouth. Picking up a scent, it slithered out of sight.

Rosanne tried to move, tried to seize the opportunity of the serpent's absence, but her legs weren't listening to her commands. Panic and cold shock tore through her, rendering her immobile. She wanted to call out to anyone, but everything seized, and only her whimpers escaped.

Through the blurriness of her tears, blue light dampened to a barely discernible glow. It moved around in wide arches, sometimes unveiled for the barest moment only to disappear again. It flashed before her eyes.

"Thank Terra, Cap," Aros whispered as he bent down before her. "Are you alright?"

"C-can't m-move," her voice trembled. Farand was by their side in an instant.

"We got you, Rosanne. I'll carry you out."

Sharp jabs of pain tore through her when Farand scooped her into his arms. She let out a blood curdling scream, followed by the serpent's excited cry.

"I'll lead, you follow" Aros said, and they started running. Every step Farand took sent burning waves through her. She barely registered the movements around them, tentacles reaching above the light to swipe at them, or the mixing roars and shrieks of the cave denizens.

Rosanne couldn't focus on anything anymore, not the breaths of Farand or his steps against the stone, Aros' panicked commands each time the ground shook or when rocks and pebbles rained down above them. Her mind slipped away from this reality, lost in the darkness of her mind where the whispers turned to cries.

CHAPTER THIRTY-FIVE

LITTLE TALKS

E arly morning light filtered in through the stained glass panels of Rosanne's quarters aboard the *Red Queen*. With a groan, she lifted a hand to shield her face from the rays.

Sharp jabs tore through her arm, and she lowered the limb with a pained whimper. Her left arm was wrapped in a sling, and bruises lined her ribcage on both sides. She tucked in her shirt, grimacing from the strain. Sitting upright was agony, and Rosanne eased back into the soft pillow, abandoning all thought of leaving the bed.

A bell rested on her nightstand that hadn't been there before. She reached for it with her free hand and with great effort, shook the living pin out of it. Dalia popped her head in, a broad smile replacing her worry seeing Rosanne awake, and came inside.

"Good to see you among the world of the living, Captain."

"How long was I out?" Rosanne croaked. She coughed and tried to clear her throat from the wet slag caught in it. Dalia was by her side in an instant and poured her a tin cup of water.

"A day or so. Duplànte and Kavanaugh made it out with only bruises, but you got a broken arm from whatever forces you awoke."

Rosanne inhaled sharply as she forced herself to sit again. "Did any-thing make it out?"

"What do you mean?" Dalia's response had Rosanne snap her mouth shut and bring her mind up to speed.

"Mimics ambushed us in the caves," she redirected, although it was part of the truth.

Dalia's look of concern transformed into elation. "Lucky for you, they didn't. Not without giving you hell first, though." She pointed at Rosanne's injuries. "Broken arm, bruised ribs, concussion probably. Doc says it's bedrest for the next few weeks."

"Weeks," Rosanne moaned. "Listen, call for Farand and Isaac, and get them in here."

Dalia arched an eyebrow. "Why Kavanaugh?"

"Just do it for me, please."

Dalia nodded and exited the room. Farand and Aros came in a few minutes later.

"No one ask me how I'm feeling," Rosanne said with a deep warning under her tone, and then pulled her lips into a weak smile.

"It seems it falls upon me to captain this boat until we return to the colonies," Farand pulled up the stool next to the bed. The little furniture was so tiny underneath his bulk that Rosanne secretly hoped it would snap and give her a laugh to distract her from the aches in her body.

"What happened after I passed out?" Rosanne asked.

Aros leaned against her desk, crossing his arms. "As soon as we left the caves the monsters settled down. Gone back to sleep by the looks of it."

She relaxed her shoulders. "That's good at least. I hear the crew doesn't know what had happened." Rosanne studied the men. Farand had ban-dages on his arms, bruised knuckles, and scrapes, while Aros sported a shiner that would make the moon blush. She tried not to smile. "What did you tell them, Farand?"

"I said the caves were crawling with mimics and they ambushed us. Hopefully that will deter anyone from being too nosy about it."

"Let's keep it that way. We wouldn't want to draw any ambitious whalers into the Veil."

She attempted to shift her position, but Farand moved in and supported her while propping the pillow behind her. She eased into it with a pained sigh and then waved Aros over, who wrinkled his nose but came next to the bed.

"Listen gentlemen, we had the chance to destroy the Grey Veil, yet here we are, bruised, alive, and the monsters asleep. The meteor, its power, and what it showed me was a precarious world so alien it changed the way I see the Veil; It is alive and thinking. Can you believe it? A sentient thing disguised as a world of fog and monsters, which protects its existence from the likes of us." She let out a wet cough. "It was never the threat that I thought it was or the nuisance keeping us from living peacefully. The Veil always minded its own business. We are the intruders."

Farand grunted his agreement. "Knowing we could destroy it was ... eye opening to me. While I can't fully understand how any of this is possible, your reasoning is sound and I trust your judgment."

Rosanne's eyes flashed to Aros, the man who knew the full scope of her failures. He looked away. Licking her lips, Rosanne shook her head. "I was a fool, Farand. I acted rashly and put lives at risk. This wasn't anything like the other island. I could have avoided so much if I had just ... listened."

Farand's gaze glided towards Aros but he didn't pursue his thought past a simple nod. At least not now. "Regarding the Veil, it comes down to money and monopoly. With the Veil gone, there would be no stopping the Queen. What would we gain from destroying the Veil to achieve but aid our greatest enemy? I prefer the world as it is, known and at the precipice of conflict."

Rosanne scowled, but her expression quickly softened. "I suppose you're right, Farand. In the end, it was for our benefit. Not because of some twisted compassion for the creatures, but because it gives us a ward against the Queen's tyranny. And we never realised it was there. I already dread the paperwork waiting for us at home." She gave a small laugh.

Farand nodded. "I can live with that choice, regardless of how many souls the Veil has claimed in the past. And I say that with a great deal of reservation for your personal loss." Turning his gaze to the window, she wondered if he recalled his fight with the hulder she had only heard in bits and pieces. It weighed on him even now, and like her, his choices had impacted his moral decisions, making him hesitant. Perhaps now they could both put their shame behind them.

Aros straightened, drawing their attention. "That settles it then. We bury our secrets here. We leave nothing that can lead anyone back to this place."

Rosanne and Farand exchanged sombre looks. She nodded. "The world is better off with the Grey Veil as a constant reminder that we're not invulnerable and that we cannot bend nature to our will even if we have a way to end it. We have what we need to survive. We don't need to bloody these waters and lands with our hands, not like we did with the hulder people." Eyes on the floor, Farand's jaw danced. "This land my father explored was the heart of the Grey Veil itself. All its mysteries and magic converged at this point like a site of the religious worship of creatures we thought of as monsters. We should let it be a story and nothing more."

Rosanne let her eyes glide from Farand to Aros. "This knowledge must never leave this room. Never be foolish enough to entrust it with anyone else. Not the crew, not your best friend, not a loved one or in drunken stupor. Our lives are already in danger enough as it is." Her eyes remained on Aros, whose grim expression matched her own. He massaged his fingers where the nail beds were barely visible, still sore she imagined. Rosanne didn't feel like she needed to say anything more on the matter.

"A word, Farand. Alone."

The urgency of her voice prompted Aros to leave without a word and he closed the door behind him.

Rosanne let herself take a few breaths in preparation. She licked her lips and stared at the bedsheets spotted with grime.

Farand beat her to it. "You're trusting him to keep quiet?"

Rosanne had to laugh at how high Farand's quizzical eyebrows had shot up. "Aros and I have set our differences aside. He's still a backstabbing bastard, but I think we're good for now."

Narrowing his gaze, Farand pursed his lips. "I'll be keeping an eye on that one,"

"You always were suspicious of our shady employees."

"It lies with the word 'shady.'"

With her chuckling quickly turned into a sputtering cough, Rosanne leaned her head against the pillow to focus on her breathing. Thoughts swam in gentle ribbons, drawing her into a world of calm, and then *Him*.

"Ever since we came to this island, I've heard his voice," she said.

Confusion crossed Farand's face.

"Yerrik, the man we held at gunpoint and told to get off the ship," she explained. "His voice was in my dreams when I fell asleep at night, warning me of the svartraug dangers and that if we die in the dream we never wake up again. He knew all along, Farand, and I ignored it." Rosanne fell quiet, deep in her memories.

Farand leaned back on his stool as if not quite sure what to do with himself.

"I tried to push him out of my mind all summer, tried to forget his sweet words and moments shared in confidence." Rosanne realised this was the first time she had talked about Yerrik to anyone. "I fell in love, Farand," her voice cracked.

His eyebrows nearly touched, and he scrutinised her dejected expression and fidgeting hands.

He opened his mouth to speak, but Rosanne cut him off before he could. "Nothing flippant, please." Farand raised his hands, giving her the opportunity to continue. "After the troll attack, I was stuck with Aros. The bastard really tried to kill me more than once just so he could survive. Lyle found us, and we made for the meeting point when a monster living in the bog attacked us. It looked like a living corpse, a creature that still haunts me. It dragged Lyle into the bog, and I went after him. Aros was about to put us both out of our miseries when we were saved by something... inhuman. Saved by that man you saw on this ship." She licked her dry lips. Farand wordlessly leaned on his elbows. A tightness spread over her chest and the sting in her eyes relented.

Her thoughts and words felt alien and heavy, but she relented. "Yerrik cared for me when I was suffering from the toxins that the swamp-creature uses on its prey. He eased my troubles and soothed my ails. He made me feel alive and cared for like no other before him. Not even Antony. He could have left us to die. But no. He sent Lyle to the hulder, saving his life, cared for mine. And I, in that moment of vulnerability, fell for him." She wiped the tears falling down her cheeks and drew a quick strained breath.

"I wanted to bring him with us to Noval, but he wasn't human, Farand. And in my lovestruck idiocy, I forgot that." Rosanne's voice wavered and she let out a broken incredulous laugh. "He looked and acted human, but he most assuredly was not. I left him there because I cared for him, but feared what the outside world would do to him. And ever since we came to this damned place, I have been reminded of him every day. The shadows in my dreams, the reflection in the water, and the Devourer that told me the Veil had touched me. Feels like the Veil cursed me instead."

The lieutenant's expression softened as he looked at Rosanne with an empathetic gentleness he rarely gave. Rosanne withheld her sobs, drying the tears with hopeless abandon and hardening her face as if that would somehow save her pride. He took her hand in his, and for a moment her mind calmed. She met his soft brown eyes.

"You haven't let anyone care for you since your father was alive," Farand said, slow at first, but so gently Rosanne let out a strangled sob and hitched her breath. "I don't blame you for falling for this man, not because my limited knowledge of him, but because I believe you saw what you needed in him. You're not cursed, Rosanne. You're suffering from the broken heart you left behind on that island and have been diving headfirst into this journey to keep your wits about you."

She drew a few breaths to catch herself enough to form a sentence. "Then why do I keep seeing him? Hearing him? That isn't normal,

Farand! It's like he's here and I feel like I'm going insane." She pressed her trembling lips shut, but like her tears, and her emotions spilled from her with each breath. Farand squeezed her hand.

"I'm not sure it makes you cursed. You connected with this ... person. You bonded with him and him with you. If he is a creature of the Veil, as you say, perhaps the connection spans further than physical presence. The svartraug living here can coax us despite not being physically present, the meteor, as you said, was connected to all the living things in the Grey Veil. What if Yerrik is as well?"

"What the hell does that make me, then?"

"Rosanne, whatever you believe his intentions were, you are suffering from guilt and self-inflicted pain. You want him to be the monster so you can abandon all feelings you have for him. I saw how you looked at him, I saw the pain in his eyes when we forced him off the ship. There was no animosity in him. If anything, he loved and cared for you equally, if not more."

Rosanne snorted a laugh. "Listen to you being all sappy."

"I'm serious."

"I know you are. I just hate not knowing what to say. When Antony left I ... it was Yerrik all over again. Only I was the one abandoned. When we returned to Noval, after that island, I wanted Antony to be more real, more genuine than Yerrik. And perhaps I used him as a crutch to seem normal, to feel normal. But he's gone now, Farand. I failed him and I failed myself."

Farand paused, and Rosanne knew he didn't have the power to wash her faults away like an artist painting something new on an old canvas. He instead gave her hand another gentle squeeze. "We know far more now than we did before."

"Do we? I don't even know what to do with myself. I feel so lost. I don't feel like I can guide anyone home when I can't even leave that island behind!"

"Whatever you decide, I will be with you all the way. Monsters or another botched Georgetown run."

Rosanne gave a pained laugh and clutched her side.

Farand continued undeterred. "I do believe love transcends forms and space. I don't know what sort of future that would look like or even if it is the right choice, but you would be a fool to abandon that ship before it's even sunk. It's not over just because the masts are broken and the provisions are gone."

"Are you taking a stab at my piloting skills, Mr. Duplànte?" Rosanne teased.

"I would never." Farand overplayed a dramatic toss of his head and a rumbling laugh escaped his lips.

"We should inform the crew that Antony died because of the svartraug, along with Jeffs, and that we couldn't recover their bodies because of the monsters."

"Is that the truth?"

She gave a sombre nod. "For once, it is. I wouldn't have made it out alive if it weren't for Antony. He died for me, and it's my fault he was even here." Rosanne clutched her chest, fighting for calm and control, but found none. "Will it always hurt this much? What did you do when Mina died?"

Farand's hand glided to the wedding band hanging on a chain around his neck. He twirled the gold between his fingers, his eyes shrouded in memory.

"I was lost. So very lost. One night I had drunk myself stupid and stumbled to the rooftops of Kvenchester to end it. But then I heard a voice. It sounded like Mina, but I knew I was hammered and out of my mind. Yet, when I looked to the stars I swear I could see her gazing down at me with that warm smile of hers." A chuckle escaped his lips and with a shake of his head, he said "It could also have been the alcohol and Jerry leaves, but at that point I didn't feel lonely anymore. The day after, you rolled into the academy and I got to beat the snot out of you for being the little upstart that you were."

Rosanne burst into laughter. "I was so angry at you for humiliating me."

"You made an impression from the moment anyone laid eyes on you. Only female cadet in that class, but then you got to work to show the boys who was the boss."

"And it was all uphill from there."

"And here we are. Years later, weather-hardened and frequent flyers of the Grey Veil."

"Impressive resume." Rosanne flashed him a grin. Farand patted her uninjured hand before he stood.

"I'll make preparations to return to the colonies. You should spend your time recovering and *only* recovering." Farand's stern warning arrested her thoughts of filling out the paperwork she would have to deliver once they returned.

Left to her thoughts, Rosanne drank the silence which enveloped her. The soft creaking of the timber in the ship permeated the room, but in a way that was non-intrusive and comforting, as natural as breathing.

Yet guilt slithered into her moment of peace, of her duty to the crew and her ability to lead them having faltered and failed in such a horrible manner. Farand's words rang clear in her mind but they weren't loud enough to chase those dark thoughts away, and while he hadn't offered his undying gratitude or reassurance that all was well, he had acknowledged her shortcomings, as she had his in their last voyage. She had been tested and failed and people had died for it.

Rosanne fought off the increasing sting in her eyes and the shame reddening her cheeks. She kicked the covers off and stood, whimpering from beaten muscles and her sore arm. In the window she spotted the dark tunnel leading to the leviathan chambers, undisturbed, as if the sea serpent had never awoken.

Even if she trusted herself and Farand, maybe even Aros, to keep the secrets of the Veil, it was on borrowed time. People had made it here before, her father among them, only to meet his end at the svartraug's whim. Perhaps the world would be better off if they all perished here, but her crew had no part to play in this as they remained ignorant.

Would Yerrik grieve her if she was gone? Did his abilities reach across the Veil to shield her from the Devourer's dream? It made her feel guilty, like she used him as she used Antony when she didn't know how to be content with herself. But Antony, like Yerrik, had thought she was worth it and had sacrificed for her. Antony had died for her.

What would she tell his family?

Rosanne listened to the activity outside, the thumping of shoes against the wood on her ceiling, the idle chatter by the helm, and the distant intelligible shouts.

No, she decided. She would carry the burden so they don't have to. But for now, she had to figure out what to do ... after she recovered her mobility. She winced and crawled back to bed.

CHAPTER THIRTY-SIX

LOVE OF THE SEA

On the gundeck, past the third port cannon, hung Aros' sleeping hammock and a small chest tied to the beam next to it. He flipped the rusted metal flap, opened the chest with a squeal, and stared down at the belongings he accumulated on his voyage: his old pair of piloting boots, which were comfortable in the cobblestone streets of the city but terrible for hiking, spare cotton shirts and breeches, and gloves and a cap for cold days, but little else than meaningless trinkets he thought he could use at the market for trade. He changed out of his sweat-stained shirt and breeches. The last few weeks had done wonders for his physique, he thought. He was still pale as sin but at least he couldn't count his ribs as a pastime anymore.

He missed and longed for his private quarters on the *Blue Dragon*, even if it had been a cramped space with just a bed and nightstand. Pulling a new shirt over his head, he halted, whispers tickling his senses. The deck was abandoned save for him, and no rain fell outside.

Was there a mimic aboard? He had heard talk of the mimic's sabotage just earlier. He reached for his only weapon, the modest dagger inside his vest, when he noticed a lump under his folded breeches in the chest.

The whispers permeated his mind as if seeking entrance to his innermost thoughts. Aros gritted his teeth through the noise and flung the clothes aside.

The rainbow shine of a horse conch glimmered back at him. He hadn't seen it before, but he immediately knew what it was. Aros's fingers trembled as he brushed them against the smooth surface. The whispers arrested to silence as if satisfied.

This is impossible, his mind screamed. Rosanne said the shell had disappeared. How was it here among his things?

"A word, Mr. Kavanaugh?" The captain's firm but rounded question had Aros slam his trunk shut.

He plastered a stiff smile on his face and twirled around. "What's up, Cap?"

Her uneven expression scanned him from top to toe. Her arm rested in a sling, and her hair was hidden underneath that faded brown hat with the broken feather she would wear until Kingdom Come. She usually carried an air of ceremony borderlining on arrogance, but now her posture was hunched, and it wasn't the broken arm's fault.

"What will you do once we return to the colonies?" she asked. Her tone was relaxed, and her expression lacked her classic "begone from mine eyes" look. The question caught him off guard.

Aros shrugged. "The only thing awaiting me there are blood-thirsty inquisitors and gangs. If we stop by Ovrack, I can hail a ride east to where the Queen hasn't invaded yet. Might buy me a few years before her goons bother looking for me there."

A look of confusion crossed her features. "You have the perfect information to buy your freedom, and you're throwing it away?"

"I am aware." Aros chuckled despite himself. "This is far bigger than me. The Devourer, albeit a lying sack of shit, had some truth to his tales. Like, what if I sold you out to the Queen? The Veil would be gone, the monopoly on the trade, would flourish, and no one would be safe from her armies. If I sold you out to Gunny, he would keep the secrets for himself. He's a land thug, and land thugs and pirates don't mingle well in the same room. You would all be gone, and I quite enjoy our banter even if we don't always see eye-to-eye and you had me thrown into jail."

Rosanne nodded with gratification from the memory of their aerial battle no doubt. He continued, disquieted by the last thing the svartraug told him. "The Devourer offered to make me its new host." They stared at each other for a few contemplative moments. Aros drew a quick breath. "It looked promising, oh so very promising. My dreams fulfilled and life at peace. Nothing could stop me."

"You do know that was a pipe dream, a literal dream."

He let out a humorless chuckle. "With the life I've led, that didn't seem so bad. But nah. I always take the easy way out. Didn't feel like it now." He tried not to look at his chest of belongings, reminded of what rested between his breeches and tunic. Should he tell her about the shell? "Either way. Perhaps there's a mad scientist out there who can change faces." He gave her a crooked-tooth grin.

"Oh, I don't know about that. I'm thinking of extending your contractual obligations to the *Red Queen*."

"Pardon?"

"You know too much, Aros Bernhart," she replied, a hint of deviousness in her voice. "I am not letting you roam free to spill our secrets to the next man or beast who comes knocking."

"What about the crew?"

"What about them? Should I fire everyone with a crooked past? Most wouldn't be able to own a rowboat with the rap-sheets they trail."

"That's uh ... a fair point."

Rosanne straightened. "Without going all mushy here, which we both know doesn't suit me ..."

Aros gave a quick nod.

She extended her left hand and locked eyes with him. "Thank you for your services, and I hope you will remain among the crew." Aros clasped her small hand firmly, which he shook awkwardly.

"I'd be happy to, Cap."

"Again, this extension is out of convenience. I'm still going to watch your every move." She squinted, but the action was made as a jest.

Aros gave an exaggerated nod.

She made to leave.

"Hey, Captain," Aros called.

Rosanne turned and gave him a tired look, but no real feeling was behind her eyes.

"This crew, this ship ..." he gestured around them. "You got a good thing going."

She offered a smile. "Ah, before I go, one more thing."

Sweat formed under his shirt as guilt weighed on Aros every second he spent in Rosanne's company. If she lingered any longer, the whispers would kick up again and expose the shell hidden among his belongings.

"Since I'll be drawing up a new contract, are your papers...?"

"Legit," he replied.

"Morals?"

"Corrupt as the Bunnsborough jailers but loyal to survival."

She chuckled and waved as she disappeared up the stairs. Aros let out his breath. A warm, fuzzy feeling flowed through him like he'd received a bear hug, and he knew that at least for a while, he would be okay. She didn't throw him to the wolves but would keep him in a den of dragons, where the dragon wasn't trying to eat him.

Aros opened his trunk and stared at the conch shell as it whispered words he couldn't understand but whose meaning he could discern. Even outside of the Veil, the shell had an alluring power that drew him in and prompted him to speak his commands to it. Whoever holds the shell holds the power of the Kraken, a power no one should possess. That's what the voices told him. He could use that power to ensure his everlasting safety. Perhaps even gain the riches and comforts he'd sought his entire life!

Aros snatched up the shell as it flooded his mind with blurry images of whatever he fancied one second to the next. They kept growing ever clearer in his mind. He concealed the shell beneath a shirt and carried the bundle with him to the forecastle. He leaned against the rail, looking out to the expansive sky and endless ocean. The whispers amplified to pounding drums in his mind, coercing him to call for its power. With no one around, Aros unveiled the shell, caressing its sleek surface and admiring its intricate patterns while holding it over the railing. The whispers increased as if panicked at his intentions.

Taking a deep, resolute breath, he let it go. The shell descended silently through the clouds and was gone in an instant, along with its accursed whispers. Freed of the possessive call of the Veil, a burden lifted from his shoulder. Maybe this way, no one would ever find the shell, and that would be the end of it. Aros wanted to regret his decision but, strangely, found himself absolved of any residing guilt. He looked at his mangled fingernails, which for the first time since he boarded the *Red Queen*, had ceased to ache.

CHAPTER THIRTY-SEVEN

CALL OF THE SHELL

"To the *Red Queen*!" Dalia cheered and banged her cup against the raised ales and wines around the table, drawing merry laughter, hoary gurgles, and spilled drinks.

The port tavern at St. Emmanuel bustled with activity in the later hours of the night. According to the watch captains, the modest port spire housed the best drinking accommodation in town, whose arms were slung around one another's shoulders as they sang an off-tune shanty that induced more laughter around the table.

Farand sat at the end, chatting with Hwang, heads bowed. Conspiratorial shifts of their eyes were followed by expressions of mirth. Kristoff and Gavin engaged in a game of dice, spectated by Norman. Olivier crossed his fingers as he placed a wager on Kristoff's loss, and pale-faced Quinn, who had recovered enough to leave the sick bay, sat next to Denny.

Aros rubbed the two copper coins between his fingers, betting on Gavin's wager of the dice totalling no more than ten. Olivier exchanged glances with him, a grin spread across white teeth, and he raised three coins against his two.

"I'll wipe the floor with your smile," Olivier challenged.

"Bring it on, chuckles."

Gavin swiped the dice into an empty cup and, giving it a firm shake, rattled the wooden pieces inside and turned the cup on the table with a clang. People slapped their coins noisily next to the men, calling their bets on either Gavin or Kristoff. Norman drummed his hands on the table, raising the expectations and drawing the attention of most of the table, who craned their necks to get a better view.

Gavin lifted the cup, the dice showing two, five, three, and six. A collective groan resounded.

Aros tapped the table, leaning back. "That's enough losses for me. I'm getting another round."

Olivier grinned, patting Aros on the back. "I like the jingle of your coins in my pocket."

"Yeah, yeah," Aros waved him off and stumbled off the bench, squeezing between people and making his way over to the bar. He lifted a finger to the woman tapping kegs, three cups in one hand while deftly working the taps with the other. She raised one skeptical eyebrow at his droopy, drunken stare.

"You don't seem steady on your feet, mate. How 'bout you take a breath of air outside?" There was no indication that it was a suggestion.

"The night's still young, love," he excused, but the woman folded her arms and gave a sharp nod towards the door. He glanced over to the table where the landmen were again throwing bets and money. A smile crept over his lips as he realised he wasn't so alone anymore, but like with everything, things take time. Besides, he was feeling tired and didn't want to impose too much. Aros nodded his compliance and swayed towards the door.

The fresh sea air glided across his face with a cool and gentle touch, and he exhaled at the pleasant feeling against his burning cheeks. The sky was dark, with a ribbon of stars growing brighter by the hour. Shuffling his feet over the alchemical-lit streets on the disk, Aros made his way toward the stairs leading to the ground level as the central elevator was closed for the night. He leaned against railings and stumbled on steps with a nervous laugh but kept his eyes peeled on the road ahead. He weaved through alleyways of residential buildings underneath the first level and headed like a confused insect for the docks, periodically drawn to the streetlights.

Down here, low burning gas lamps lined the timber of the quays running alongside the city's bay. He passed darkened sailing ships, blue-coats patrolling the area as part of dock security. Aros spotted the *Red Queen* bobbing in the water up ahead, lit by only a few lamps. He couldn't remember who remained on the ship, but he was more interested in finding his hammock and sleeping before his morning shift north towards Noval. They were first heading to Bunnsboroux, and then onward to the home city of the *Red Queen* in Valo. He hoped it wasn't snowing yet, as he was far too underdressed to stave off the northern cold. Now that they were done with the Grey Veil, hopefully for good (as far as that stretched in terms of exploration, adventure, and foolhardy chances), it was back to shipping goods and earning their wages like ordinary people.

His mind buzzed with images of deep fjords and snow-crested mountains. It would be a nice change of scenery for once, and he wouldn't have to dodge the law in every city he visited, protected by his real identity and his contract to the *Red Queen*.

The world had turned upside down since his promotion in Cintecha, from deckhand in the inland routes to raiding the Baltansea and captaining his own ship. Then he lost the ship, his crew, and his fingernails while entertaining Her Majesty's inquisition in the Bunnsboroux dungeons as his summer retreat. After everything he left behind, Aros hadn't imagined in his wildest dreams he would see *her* again, imaginatively or otherwise. The mermaid's song had awoken the memory of her, the scent of her, and her playful smile, which made his heart leap with joy. A year ago, he had hope. What did he have now?

"I hope you're happy, Isabella!" he shouted towards the open sea, stumbling as he attempted to keep a straight course. "I made captain, and that wasn't good enough! You had to run off with Mr. Naval Officer Jerkbag to his fancy coastal estate."

Aros paused by the gentle waves and sat down on the edge of the dock. "At least you're not struggling anymore." He let the words disintegrate under the weight of his drunken stupor, and his eyes clouded over with memory. Leaning his head back, he inhaled the salty air. He had definitely had too much to drink when something as simple as the sea could make him grin like an idiot. He let out a laugh.

A splash below caught his attention, and Aros blinked against the gloom of the black waters. A pair of eyes stared back at him through a veil of wet hair. He raised a hand in greeting.

"Evening," he said, leaning unsteadily to the side and jerking back to a straight position.

Emerging halfway from the surface, a woman with a flattened nasal ridge gazed at him with a relaxed expression. Blue scales of a veiled tail glinted, refracting the light from a nearby lamp, flashing just below the surface.

This is new, Aros thought, focusing on the details of this very amusing daydream. Or was it a nightdream?

She cocked her head, studying him. Aros had to stop himself from leaning too far before plunging into the sea. A whisper grazed his ears, like the soft touch of a finger caressing him. The mermaid hadn't spoken, her lips untouched by movement. She raised a hand then, revealing a large shell.

Aros' breath arrested in his throat. Bile rose from his abdomen, and his vision swam. The whispers grew loud and intrusive, calling to him, almost screaming.

"Where the fuck did you find that?" he choked out, but the mermaid, blinking with her black-eyed innocence, tossed the shell to him effortlessly. His hand fumbled but caught it. The whispers died instantly.

He looked at the horse conch, hands trembling so badly he almost dropped it.

"How do you have this? I left this behind in the Veil!"

The mermaid opened her mouth, and her hoarse, wheezing voice penetrated the air. "The dream is calling for you."

She disappeared below the surface, trailing ribbons of glinting fins. The shell felt so real in his hands, smooth with a blank surface reflecting his drunken stupor back at him. He had wished for power so badly, and he still did. So much that he dreamt of the shell he had tossed into the ocean and the whispering voices along with it. Would the dream return to him if he longed for power again?

Aros stood on wobbly feet and returned to his hammock aboard the *Red Queen*.

⭑⟡⭑

A shot rang out through the skyport, permeating the buzz of the tavern. Farand lowered his drink and looked toward the window. People were gathering outside, drawing attention to blue-coats patrolling the disk. Frowning, he set the cup down and stood.

"That's our cue, people. We're going back to the ship," he called to the merry crew, who were far too embroiled in their own conversations to have noticed the commotion. Immediately, their chatter turned to groans.

They stumbled out of the tavern in a pile of hysterical laughter. Farand scanned their surroundings, searching for the source of the firing. By the foot of the bridge crossing the conveyor belts were three blue-coats, two hunched over a man who lay face down on the cobblestone.

"Apologies, ladies and gentlemen. The bridge is temporarily closed while we're investigating," A blue-coat said.

"Did someone die? By the hells! Look at the blood!" Norman pointed, leaning against Gavin and Kristoff as the two men hauled him between them. Farand considered the large man on the ground and the puddle of blood still running between the crevices. A headache swirled around his skull from the wine he mixed with the local brew, clearly the wrong choice. Alcohol certainly played a part in his rising paranoia and choice to evacuate the crew back to the ship. If someone got shot on the portspire, it was time to leave. Hopefully, Aros was back on the ship with the rest, and not being dragged off by the inquisition.

While Rosanne ... Farand ran a thumb over the wedding band hanging around his neck and prayed he would never need a memento to remember her by. He wished all the luck in the world she would find her way back to the ship in due time.

EPILOGUE

M ist pearled on the sailboat's lacquered surface as it sliced through grey skies with ease. Not a breath of wind disturbed the wisps, save for the gentle hum and blue flame of the small thruster engine installed at the stern. The sailboat's single mast stood straight and bare, its sails squared and lifeless amidst the perpetual fog of the Grey Veil.

The built-in compass on the instrument panel veered to the side, indicative that she had arrived at the rock belt surrounding the northern island. Rosanne eased the engine to a soft glide with the push of a lever. The subtle hiss of the bowsprit mini-thrusters issued as the boat slowed down.

In the gloom, hulking shapes drifted along an invisible field. She guided the sailboat before the rocks, ranging from pebbles to single-story houses. Her arrival was swifter than expected, having homed in on the magnetic field inside the fog almost immediately upon entering the Grey Veil.

Her compass jerked towards a giant boulder as the rock floated along the belt and then jumped to the other side as another boulder the size of a small building drifted closer.

Echoes of colliding debris crackled in the air, yet the delicate balance of the floating rock belt remained undisturbed and harmonious.

Rosanne dug into her fur-lined vest and withdrew a pocket watch, struggling to press the button to release the lid due to her quivering fingers. Her chattering exhale heavily fogged the glass, which she wiped away with a gloved hand. The handle ticked past twelve, but no less than ten seconds later did it make a jump to five minutes. A jolt of elation surged through her, and a grin plastered on her mouth.

Her theory had been correct: during her first visit to the rock belt, Rosanne had no clue about its shape or size. The intervals between the magnetic pulses were identical to her last entry point in the belt, meaning the rock belt revolved around the island inside in a spherical orbit, or close to it.

Clicking the pocket watch shut, Rosanne turned the crank on the single mast. The reinforced steel-plated parts broke into three segments that folded in on themselves. The rigging, as expected, piled to the floor of the boat, and she tucked it to the sides lest she trip on the ropes. Next, she toggled a switch on the instrument panel, disconnecting the wheel from the engine. By the stern, a lever released the tiller from a locked state, engaging thrusters with more manoeuvrability, perfect for slow-flying in packed skyports or in this case, a floating debris field.

Twisting the tiller, Rosanne commanded the sailboat in a slow glide. She eased or increased speed depending on the need as she moved between spinning boulders, using another lever controlling the small hull thrusters to the left of the seat. Her inner voice thanked Farand for the sailboat and reminded herself she had made no guarantees she would return the vessel whole, considering where she was going. He remained in charge of the *Red Queen* ever since their ordeal at the meteor island, which had rendered her bedridden for weeks. It had only been a fortnight since she had regained mobility and the use of her arm. Farand's attempt at stopping her had failed as always, but Rosanne enjoyed the sentiment and told him this was a trip she needed to take by herself. He had given her a stiff-lipped nod and offered help in any way that he could. She borrowed his boat out of Gernera after getting a lift from the northern colonies.

Massaging her wrist, Rosanne almost regretted leaving the ship and crew behind. Her arm remained stiff and weak, accentuated by the prolonged sailing she pushed herself through it. Returning to this island alone was a madwoman's quest, born out of the insanity which followed from the Grey Veil like a curse. But she knew what she had to do, or this accursed fog would rob her of everything she had left.

Free of the laborious task of moving boulders around or waiting for larger ones to pass Rosanne cut through the belt in less than an hour, with barely a scratch on the boat's hull. She consulted the compass again. The needle flicked madly between the rocks behind her and a signal originating somewhere ahead. Without wasting time, she pursued the second signal ahead and kept the mast folded. The last thing she needed was to crash into a flying whale, potentially leaving her stranded in the Grey Veil. Again. The sky brightened with golden hues of a morning sun, and the thinning wisps of the fog receded with the climbing temperatures. In the distance, she spotted a thin strip of land.

Her heartbeat quickened with a series of painful thumps, and she drew deep breaths. If seeing the island could disturb her this much, Rosanne didn't know what would happen once she set a foot on it. With a twist of the tiller, she cranked up the thruster engine, the hum blasting behind her as she sped for the shore.

White-painted cliffs and rock formations jutted from the sea like spears. Grass covered the rocky outcrops and towards the forest in vast fields of green, flowing like ocean waves in the wind. The contrast made this place almost seem inviting, with lush vegetation erasing the brown and yellowed fields she, Aros, and Lyle had snuck through last spring to avoid trolls.

The thruster engine light on the instrument panel flashed red. Rosanne raised the mast and unfurled the sail, and the gleaming hexagonal photo-sensitive receptors caught the sunlight with dazzling shimmers. The hum slithered from the fringes of the conducting cloth towards the mast in hundreds of electrical currents.

Rosanne cruised southward alongside the shore in a gentle arc, scanning for familiar territory and potential danger. The tall grass hid any creature smaller than a deer, and the wind swaying the fields obscured any movement she might pick up on. Some twenty minutes later, she sailed over the ship graveyard tucked away in a bay. The broken decks and crooked masts covered in bird faeces remained unchanged, and she continued south. The floating boulder with the wreckage of the *Blue Dragon*, was nowhere to be seen. Had it drifted off somewhere? Ignoring the intruding memories of her last visit, Rosanne kept her focus and eyes sharp until she spotted the low, rocky mound by the black volcanic cliffs. The sparse vegetation clumped together in patches of dirt. Fog crept over the small pools where fish floated through large schools, snapping at flying insects buzzing in the grass. The area remained mostly the same since their spring visit.

She descended from the sailboat near the mound, the terrain too frail for mooring. Rosanne dropped the anchor unceremoniously to the ground, untethered, but the gentle breeze lacked the force to carry the boat away. Struggling down to the rope ladder, the heavy pack on her back offsetting her balance. The elongated stack of rocks rested there as a glaring contrast to its sparse surroundings. Mustering her courage, Rosanne approached it.

"Hello, Iban. It's been a while." Her bravery withered as she stood in front of the grave of Iban Vasilyev, Kristoff's late brother and her former landman. "I brought you a gift." From her pack she excavated a bottle of Quindecimus whisky, about to lay it on top of the rocks when her attention snagged on a glassy surface glinting through a layer of dirt. With a gloved hand, she dusted off the grime.

"Farand, you sneaky thief." She laughed, spotting her favourite whisky already resting on Iban's grave. "I'll open this one too, then, so you can enjoy both," she added, and removed the wax seal from the second bottle. Rosanne popped the cork with a satisfying fhump. Usually a prude when it came to quality whisky, this time she drank from the bottle. The smokey oak aftertaste tingled her throat. She corked the bottle and placed it next to the other. "I hope you enjoy the whisky and that the monsters leave you alone. I probably won't be able to come back after today, but if I'm ever in the area, I'll bring you something from Katshov," she said. Rosanne was thankful nothing had disturbed the grave in the months she had been away. Had it not been for that damn electrical storm that stranded them all, Iban would still be alive. A small voice in the back of her mind blamed her for his death but she knew she was powerless in the face of mother nature.

A wry smile crossed her lips, and without another word she climbed into the sailboat and sped towards the inland. The wide expanse of fields turned into smooth mountains and valleys of crooked birch forests. Rosanne kept herself south of a particular mountain she recognised from when Nikor had attacked them. She wondered if the bog monster was still alive, stalking the murky depths and feasting on whatever creature fell in.

The valley expanded on each side into a vast birch forest. Small flocks of birds scattered at the approaching hum of the sailboat. Rosanne quickly furled the sail, not wanting to draw too much attention to herself. The small aether sail reflected so much light it could be spotted from miles away, which was attention she didn't need as she had heard, and met, creatures that wouldn't hesitate to kill if they found her. She kept her distance from the canopies, hoping nothing would suddenly fly out and pierce her.

Rosanne spotted the overgrown turf roof of Yerrik's log cabin. She had dreaded this moment for days, but now that she was on familiar ground, her heart squeezed painfully While contemplating whether she should land in front of the building or moor down in a clearing somewhere, she knew she was stalling for time. A small voice in her head told her to hightail back to the colonies and never return, but she brushed it aside.

Be brave, she told herself.

Rosanne lowered the boat by the yellowing oak and secured the mooring line around its trunk. The surrounding area appeared wild and untouched. Next to the cabin, the snapped laundry line fluttered in the breeze. Closed window shutters transformed the once-welcoming, cozy home into an uninviting abandoned cabin. Her insides coiled. Had something happened to Yerrik?

Rosanne waded through the tall grass, water droplets clinging to her trousers and soaking her in quick strides. Her shoes clacked on the porch, making her wince. Softening her footfalls, she knew this action was to appease her nervousness.

Rosanne stared at the old wood panels of the door while her mind raced. Yerrik might not want to see her. What if he resented her so much he wouldn't talk with her. What if he had found someone new? Her face prickled, muscles tightening over her cheeks as she fought for calm. The voice of doubt and jealousy ate at her mind like an intruder, but there were no svartraug tormenting her here, only her regrets and insecurities. She swallowed the discomfort and momentary shame. She rapped a gloved hand against the door and waited. Distracted by her trembling hands, Rosanne laced them in front of her and then at the back, but ultimately straightened instead, stiff and unnatural, like a soldier off to war.

No sudden footfalls pattered over the floorboards.

"Yerrik?" she tried. Silence. She turned the handle. The door gave a stuttering creak as she pushed it open. The draft flowing through the doorway whirled up filaments of dust. She studied the overfilled hearth, and spilled ash. Blackened footprints trailed across the floor and a soup bowl rested on the kitchen counter. Rosanne made a wry face at the blue fuzzy contents. The washroom door stood ajar. Anxiety rose in her throat as she pushed the door open. The old hinges creaked. Assorted garments lay discarded in the corner, but besides a bucket and cloth, the room was otherwise uninteresting.

"Yerrik?" she called out, louder this time. "It's D-Dragonheart." How sour her nickname tasted in her mouth, when Yerrik's voice uttered it like liquid gold. He always sounded sincere. Even when he had protected her in her dreams, had his sincerity shone through the foggy darkness as a constant presence. He had reached out to her when she was in trouble.

After the Devourer's demise, there had not even been a whisper from neither mimic nor monsters. Not Even Yerrik. Where had he gone?

In the room upstairs, the worn cotton sheets lay rumpled in a heap. A thin film of dust rested on the bed instead. Rosanne sat on the bedside, staring at the bare log wall. Guilt arrested her thoughts in the silence. Had she driven him to leave his home because of her betrayal? Rosanne couldn't imagine staying when haunted by such painful memories. He was not here. Burying her face in her hands, her eyes stung. Why did she have to cry so much? It was ridiculous, she told herself.

Rosanne drew a deep, shaky breath. "Yerrik, where are you?" she whispered, but the silence, dust, and flies were her only company. A sob escaped her lips. Her shoulders trembled, and even now she tensed to calm the torrent of emotions, biting down the swelling pain in her chest.

"Don't cry, Dragonheart." Yerrik spoke in a soft voice. With a start, she stood. Dust whirled from the bed, creating a pillar of particles as they passed through a beam of light from the shutters. The room was otherwise empty. She swore he had been next to her, like that of her dreams. Was this another creature-induced illusion, or had she finally lost her sanity to the Grey Veil?

Rosanne focused on the sounds, fighting through the pressure in her chest and the hot sting in her eyes. She noticed his presence teetering on the edge of her perception, like a ghost. It wasn't the svartraug's call, the illusions designed to entrap victims by mimicking people and lure them to their deaths. No sweet lies eased her worries, as she had been on edge since arriving on this island. And yet, the sense of reassurance which washed over her didn't appear to please her or tell her what she wanted to hear. It just was.

491

Pinching her arm, the pain told her she in control of herself, accompanied by the call that was Yerrik. But what if it wasn't? Doubt seized her, for it could be something different? *No*, she thought. She had come too far to turn back now. She had to find him.

Swallowing the lump in her throat, Rosanne followed the pull tugging at her senses. She exited the cabin and circled around to the unkempt backyard. The feeling pointed the mountains, yet she swore she was closer to her destination than that. The path cut through the forest, which she followed. She pawed through the grass, soaked to her thighs in dew and shivering, but relented until the path lead down into a ravine. Its bare stony walls were a sharp contrast to the soft arched mountains, as if the ground had opened its maw and forgotten to close it.

Rosanne trotted alongside the ravine until she reached a cave opening.

Why did it have to be caves? She knew better to take it at face value: dark, uninviting, probably riddled with monsters or sentient rocks. Perhaps this was just another path to get to Yerrik? She was sure it was his voice, his power, that guided her. The Devourer was gone and couldn't influence her anymore. No spellbinding songs weaved into her mind and distorted her memories, as far as she was aware of. The pull was stronger now, familiar, pacifying even. Like that of the meteor.

It could be a unique creature altogether.

Glancing around to make sure no monster would jump from the cliff's edge, Rosanne entered the maw. Through the waning light, Rosanne struggled to see further than a few metres. No luminescent algae or convenient insects of the glowing sort lit the path before her. Yet, every step felt sure and firm, as if the dark was a minor inconvenience. Was this a temporary gift from the supernatural creature that led her?

At the end of the jagged stone hallway, the ground opened to a vertical drop. Rosanne peered into the darkness accompanied by a soft swoosh of air, like a giant creature sucking its breath. It reminded her of the path to the Leviathan chamber, without the stairs or lamps, or Farand and Aros. Grimacing, she knew she wasn't mad enough to jump off with no climbing gear.

But sure enough, all doubts washed out of her. Rosanne didn't know what madness possessed her to trust whatever magics was calling to her, but Yerrik was gone, she had suffered near-death experiences to last her ten lifetimes, and she wanted to—no, *had* to find him. If some unknown creature held Yerrik prisoner, she needed to help him. She owed him that much, and she would be damned if she didn't get to say what she came here for.

When logic came to her a few seconds later, she felt silly. This was a massive hole with who knew what at the bottom. Best-case scenario, she would be a red smear on the bottom of the shaft, with no one knowing where to find her or able to retrieve her body. Next worst scenario would be stuck with broken bones, no climbing gear and no rescue. She would starve to death or die of dehydration. Then why was she tempted to plunge into the unknown?

Only a single thought gave her some semblance of reassurance: the sentient meteor had bared itself to her, pleaded for its life to the one person who remained protected from the devourer's invasive powers. Was the meteor calling to her using Yerrik? Did its power extend this far north? Perhaps the shared consciousness of the Grey Veil, with its spawn now free of the Devourer's possession, was her guide. The alternative terrified her. No creature would make her leap without reassurance of what awaited her at the bottom.

This was madness.

Straightening, Rosanne sucked in her breath and jumped. Unbridled panic rushed through her as she plunged into the darkness with an ear-shattering howl. She spun in the air, the wind like ice on her cheeks. The pull of gravity caught resistance. Not air, she realised, as her fall slowed as did her terror seize, replaced by confusion.

The tunnel shaft lit up around her in hues of yellow and green. Another powder-blue light emitted from further down. Was this more magic, or another illusion? Rosanne spun in gentle revolutions, waving her arms to stabilise her descent.

"I always thought it was the floor that would catch you if you fell," she muttered, grateful for this bizarre phenomenon. The very air itself was aglow with tiny pearls of yellow light, like that of pellets having a luminescent chemical reaction with the air. The surrounding walls broadened, with crisscrossing stalactites and stalagmites which merged into massive pillars in a weaved complex pattern.

Rosanne floated between pillars covered in clusters of blue crystals. Extending a hand, she grasped a column and stilled in the air, unhindered by the gravity. If anti-gravity dust filled the air, she would have noticed the effects by now; intense burning pain in her lungs as her tissue dissolved into fragments, blood coughing fits, her eyes red with burst veins while her insides liquidated. The air felt clean, crisp, and non-lethal.

Clinging to the crystals, Rosanne scanned the chamber. The otherworldly pull was stronger here, as if saying, "come find me."

Rosanne turned her attention deeper into the cave system and aimed at the nearby column and leapt. She soared through the air in a gentle arch and stretched out a leg for the landing. She bounced on the rocky surface, propelled into the air again. Sucking her breath, the world spun, crystals emerging and disappearing, columns appearing near and far. With panicked flails, she sought purchase and found none until she slammed back-first into another column. Its rough surface scraped into her flesh. She let out a gasp, fought through the sudden pain, and grasped a cluster of crystals. With an iron grip, she remained floating, breathing through the burning discomfort on her shoulder. Her vest had taken the brunt of the abuse, but she knew she suffered fabric burns under the cotton tunic. Wincing, Rosanne searched the winding cave formations up ahead. A blue-white light pulsated from one of them. Taking aim again, she leapt between the columns, shooting for the split in the room where side passages led to other chambers.

Scraping a gloved hand along the surface of the tunnel, she slowed her glide. Fragments chipped off, either trailing her or whirling away. With a swift kick, she redirected her direction with ease, and grew more confident with each leap as she traversed this strange world. She half expected to see the walls littered with bodies of the island's inhabitants, new creatures of hulder and trolls, maybe even more like Yerrik, whatever shape they took. Crystals, the lack of gravity, and the lights filled the tunnels instead.

A cloud of darkness waited at the tunnel. She caught hold of a cluster of quartz lining the walls. The momentum turned her around, her feet dangling towards the smoky forms dancing around a ball of blue and yellow light.

As her eyes scanned its undefined shape dancing in the space of a brightly lit room, a sense of relief washed over her. The familiar sensation reached out to her. "Yerrik?" Her voice was barely above a whisper. The syllables rang out from her, as if magnified by the surrounding crystals. The writhing smoke ceased its dance. Rosanne braced her feet against the wall, and readied to launch herself back the way she came. The vapour converged in ribbons to a single cloudy shape, floating in lazy motions away from the light. It stopped a short distance from her.

Whatever terror which should have passed through her at the sight of such an ominous presence, Rosanne wasn't feeling it. Instead, she searched it with curious eyes, anticipation even. "Yerrik, is that you?" she breathed. The smoke grew into a shape a little bigger than herself, with four limbs and a head that vaguely represented a human. Head tilted to the side, she swore it looked into her eyes. It stretched out a wispy hand, hovering over the palm next to her, brushing against her hair. Rosanne's breath arrested in her throat, her thoughts uneasy yet hopeful.

"Dragonheart?" it said, its voice low and unearthly, as though filtered through something lacking a physical body.

"What happened?" she uttered, desperate to know if she had done this to him. Would he even tell her? The humanoid shadow, Yerrik, turned away, studying the wispy form of his hand. Rosanne kept hers close together, as she wanted nothing else but to reach out and touch him.

"I had to protect you from the svartraug, Dragonheart. When I couldn't find you in the dream anymore, I thought it had taken you."

She could imagine his rueful smile and his forlorn look, but not an ounce of skin or muscle gave any emotional indication save for his movements. She reached for his hand, which he accepted. It was like touching a cloud, though one with a vague sense of shape and resistance but no substance. No warmth either.

"It had ..." she said. "I realised it was an illusion and managed to escape. If it weren't for you, the svartraug would have taken me before I understood what I was up against." She gave his hand a squeeze.

His hesitant nod made her insides turn as he seemed to merely acknowledge her gratitude. How desperate she must have looked to him now. She felt pathetic. What was she even doing here? But she pushed the doubts aside. "You have no idea how much you grounded me in that wretched place." Rosanne drew a sharp breath, her gaze travelling over his inhuman form. "I'm ... I'm so sorry. What I did to you was horrible! I—"

Yerrik silenced her with a hand, sending her into emotional turmoil until he directed it to her cheek again, "I understand you did what you thought was right for you, Dragonheart, and why you cut me with your lies and left me behind." His voice remained light and understanding, and she could almost imagine the gentleness in his expression hidden somewhere behind this strange form. "I shouldn't have expected you to accept my ways after such a short time and I so wished we had more time. But you were pressed for it, deprived of hope, when faced with the choice of leaving. I do not fault you that."

"But you were right!" she burst out, the blurry shape of Yerrik obscuring by the second as tears spilled forth. Not those damn tears again!

She grasped his arms, the other-worldly sensation reaffirming that he wasn't human. Yet she cared for this creature who mimicked the expected perception of the people who saw him. What did she expect from him now? "Instead of cowering behind my fear, I should have just told you I couldn't see my life any differently. And you ... you were great. Everything you did was what I had always wanted and needed, and I ..." She didn't meet his gaze, afraid of the scorn and disappointment he might harbour, and instead focused on the blue lights at the bottom of the tunnel. "I threw you away like you meant nothing," she said at length.

Yerrik encircled his arms around her waist. The sudden intimacy made her flinch, but she knew it wasn't because of discomfort. She feared having him close, physically and mentally. With how much she shook, she would drift off if he let go. A laugh bubbled up at how she could distract herself in a situation such as this. She shook off the thought, bringing herself back to Yerrik.

"My crew, us stranded and the blackmail having over us ... I hid behind them." Her lips trembled, and her insides seemed ready to burst. "I am cold and defensive. I hurt you because of my immaturity, my fear of ... of ... connecting, like I always have." Why did everything have to be so difficult?

"Dragonheart." Yerrik's soft voice pulled her from the torrents of uncertainty. "It's not your fault you had no room to grow, no room in your heart, regardless of the circumstances. When faced with ..." he paused as he searched for the right words. An imaginary weight lay on her chest, constricting her, choking her. "It was a battle you never had to face before."

She knew why he said it, understood the depths of his knowledge of her. He saw her pain before she did, like the meteor had read her. Those were words that had frightened her. Yet she felt selfish, the guilt overwhelming that even after the hell he protected her from and in being reduced to a smoke creature, he still thought of her.

He stroked her cheek. She mustered the courage she needed to say her piece. "I wanted more, Yerrik. That warmth, your words. I craved them so badly that I was ready to abandon everyone for it. But the price," she drew a breath and shook her head, "I used my responsibilities as a captain as an excuse. I was afraid of what it would mean to have another person in my life ... another person I could lose." The shadow dissipated from the shape of him, revealing pale skin with dark hair reaching to his shoulders. Brilliant green eyes sparkled back at her. She could see him clearly now, as if being with him chased her doubt away but also reinforced her perception of him. Farand's words echoed in her mind: *"You want him to be the monster so you can abandon all feelings you have for him."* Even now, she couldn't envision him as a monster. She had expected him to appear hideous in one form or another. Instead, she saw smoke that had turned into a man she knew. Was this Yerrik's power on display before her?

Yerrik glided a thumb over the tears falling down her cheek while his other arm pulled her closer, secure but gentle.

"As much as it hurt, you were right to leave me behind." He gave a mournful smile. "I am not human, Dragonheart, nor will I ever be. People may believe I'm a man, but it won't change that I am born of the star."

Her brows furrowed. "The star? You mean the piece of the meteor that crashed here?"

His smile widened, and he inclined his head toward the blue light. "This is the desired shape the star took. It created this network of tunnels and lights. I came here to regain my strength. Who knew waging a war with a corrupted spirit could be that hard?" He skirted how the battle had weakened him. He was being considerate again.

Rosanne didn't reply, letting her gaze wander to the crystals and the dots of light flickering around like buzzing insects. This entire chamber was alive and one entity? The boulder was one thing. That it could change shape while connecting all creatures in the Grey Veil, was another. How far did the meteor's abilities reach?

Yerrik caught her confusion and worry, sucking in his breath, and drew her attention. "Do you understand now how I read your emotions? The star gifted me that ability. We're all different but united in its Dream. With the Devourer gone, the star allowed you to be a part of it. That is how you found me."

"You're glossing over that in protecting me you weakened yourself. You put yourself at great risk for someone like *me*." Rosanne tried to pull away, but Yerrik gripped her by her shoulders, using barely any strength. The movement rocked them both, and they drifted a little way from the crystals.

"The choice was mine, Dragonheart, as was you to come here. You have grown so much since I last saw you. You showed immense bravery facing what you feared the most." His hands slid from her shoulders to around her back in a tight embrace. Rosanne stiffened, curling her fingers as she was unsure what to do. She wanted to break free of her prison and invite him. Everything in her mind screamed not to. She leaned into him, resting her face in the crook of his neck. Her arms followed, going around his waist. She didn't question how he had manifested clothes from the shadow, another humorous comment her mind created to ease the discomfort. She ignored it. Rosanne let the emotions wash away any lingering logic, uncaring of the lack of gravity or that Yerrik was a creature of the Veil.

"Why me?" Her voice broke from that single question, and she drew back from him. "Even when you helped me the first time, what I discovered about myself made me sick." Those damn tears came again with a vengeance, as did the tense bite of her self-loathing doubt. "I wanted to burn a man alive, Yerrik! That isn't natural!" She waited in quiet anticipation for his scorn while she planted a grievous stare into his eyes. She felt nauseous as the guilt of her actions and thoughts surfaced. Inside, she was falling apart, as all she wanted was his forgiveness, and knew she didn't deserve his kindness.

No, Rosanne thought. She had isolated herself for long enough and pushed people away for the last time. The past should stay buried in the past. This trip wasn't merely to seek closure, but that she wanted to move past the pain of loss that her father had instilled in her. She wanted to be happy.

Yerrik's breath was sharp, making her insides coil as all bravery fled like a deer from a pack of wolves. But she breathed through it and met his gaze. Was it pity that she saw? Sympathy born out of understanding? Or perhaps was it pride? Her mind scrambled. Yerrik chuckled and brushed a strand of hair away strand from her fretful face.

"Remember, Dragonheart, sometimes thoughts and feelings have no deeper meaning than the time it takes for them to surface. They just are. While you can't control your emotions, you can control their outcome, like how you didn't leave a man for dead despite wanting to do so," he added at length with a bob of his head, a joking gesture she had picked up from him during her first visit.

She gave a sheepish laugh. "You saw that."

"The meteor lay bare everyone who touches the Veil." He wiggled his eyebrows.

"Did you also see," she licked her lips, "what happened with Antony?" She regretted the question as soon as it left her mouth.

His smile faded and he gave her a sympathetic nod. "He faced the dream's corruption, knowing it would be the end of him. He understood why you couldn't commit to him but was no less loyal to you."

"I never told him about you." That was the crux that would be her undoing, she convinced herself. Losing Antony ... This entire trip seemed like a kick to his memory now.

Yerrik took her by the chin, drawing her attention to him. "He understood, Dragonheart. You lost someone you cared for, and you chose to move past it. You're not besmirching his memory by being here. Your guilt is. It was his choice to make sure you escaped the dream."

His words eased her doubts. Had he always been this eloquent with his words? Then again, he read her like an expert librarian. Rosanne feared the thoughts she didn't want him to see or whatever it was he envisioned when he looked at her. *No, stop it!* she told the intruding thoughts and straightened as she gathered her courage.

"The meteor has no sense of privacy. The audacity of it!" She laughed then and wiped her cheeks. She felt naked in his eyes; how he could see her far better than she could herself.

"What ..." Rosanne tried, averting her eyes despite being locked in place. "What happens if you try to leave the Grey Veil?"

Yerrik suppressed a smirk. "That I do not know."

A hopeful smile tugged on her lips, and as she ran her hands along his arms, creating a little distance between them so she could view him, a sense of calm washed over her. "Could we start over again?"

"Always, Dragonheart." He drew closer, and for once, she wasn't burdened by the incessant voices and fear which told her she would only get hurt if she let anyone close. He stopped just short of her face. Hazel eyes locked with green.

"I'll never stand in your way, Rosanne. No matter what it is. I will be there for you ... if you let me. Right in front of you."

His words flowed through her with such ease her heart leapt with excitement. Rosanne leaned into the emotion and kissed Yerrik, letting all her regret and fear wash away in his embrace. The star's blue light pulsated in dramatic flashes in the centre of the chamber. Rosanne and Yerrik broke away from each other with a start, the moment lost to the distraction. Yerrik held her gently by the waist while Rosanne's alarmed expression flickered between him and the star.

"What's going on?" she asked.

"Not sure," he began, but his brows creased. "Are you sure?" he directed at the star, which gave a blinding white flash, flooding the room once more. Rosanne shielded her eyes.

"Come." Yerrik drew away, drifting towards the star, his hand pulling her along.

"What does it want?" Her trembling voice gave away her unease, but Yerrik flashed her a grin.

"It wants to welcome you."

"I thought it already ..." Her words trailed off as they reached just outside the ball of flashing light, its surface obscured like fog. Calm and elation filled her, transforming her pain and worries to dust. Yerrik turned to her.

"Do you trust me, Dragonheart?" A smile crossed his lips, eyes aglow with excitement. Rosanne nodded, and before she could question the situation further, he pulled her forward.

The white light weaved around them in a welcoming embrace and the sensation Rosanne had felt when she first connected with the meteor washed over her with such intensity she burst out laughing, tears spilling from her eyes in overwhelming waves. She knew then that everything would be alright.

She could finally leave behind all her hurts and bitter memories, and she would be safe with Yerrik by her side.

ACKNOWLEDGMENTS

When I wrote the first book years ago, I had no idea it would end up with a second volume, and that lies with the people who asked all of the questions I couldn't answer in the first book.

I thank my stalwart champion agent, Tina, who pulled me from the depths when the book was the worst thing in existence. To everyone at Rising Action Publishing Collective who made my stories see the light of day.

To Chris, who again provided so much inspiration and will never know the full extent of it.

And lastly but not least, my cat, Drizzt, who helped me maintain a daily schedule and kept my lap warm during cold winters.

ABOUT THE AUTHOR

Norwegian-born and resident Lilian Horn brings life to Scandinavian folklore through her debut Perils of Sea and Sky. With a degree as a biomedical laboratory scientist, hobby painter, and game enthusiast, she lives in the arctic city of Tromsø with her introverted and demanding cat. Journey of the Lost and Damned is her second novel, the sequel to *Perils of Sea and Sky*.